Carson Valley

PANTHEON BOOKS
NEW YORK

Carson Valley

A NOVEL

BILL BARICH

Library of Congress Cataloging-in-Publication Data

Barich, Bill.
Carson valley / Bill Barich.
p.   cm.
ISBN 0-679-44210-3
I. Title.
PS3552.A6163N4   1997
813'.54—dc20   96-29260
                                CIP

Random House Web Address: http://www.randomhouse.com/

Book design by Fearn Cutler
Title page illustration © 1997 by Dan Brown

Printed in the United States of America
First Edition
2 4 6 8 9 7 5 3 1

To Bob McCord

Carson Valley, an agricultural area about eighty miles north of San Francisco and inland from the Pacific Ocean, in Sonoma County. The valley is protected by the Coast Range mountains and offers an ideal microclimate for growing wine grapes, although it is smaller and not as well-known as neighboring Dry Creek and Alexander Valleys, with only fourteen bonded wineries. It is named in honor of James Carson, a pioneer settler from St. Louis, who came west in search of sea otter pelts in 1838 and ultimately received a land grant of six leagues from the Mexican government. There is a town of the same name (population 5,867 as of the 1990 census) notable for its library, a fine example of Beaux Arts classicism. The town has lost some of its rural character of late as Santa Rosa, the nearest city (which see), has continued to expand. Not to be confused with Carson Valley in Alpine County, in the Sierra Nevada.

—Burkhardt's Guide to Historical California

Carson Valley

1

Victor Torelli, an old man of almost eighty, bitter in some ways but not in others, rocked forward in his desk chair and fiddled with the remote control device for his VCR. Behind a double-locked door in a cluttered office in the town of Carson Valley, he was watching a porn video on a big Sony monitor this crisp winter morning, squinting through cigar smoke at a pair of sweaty young actors whose energetic performance filled him with wonder. Nothing in his own experience had prepared him for the carnival of miracles he was witnessing on-screen. He was absorbed, transported. It did not seem possible to him that men and women could be so skilled at sex, so robust and acrobatic. Seated close to the action, his lips unconsciously parted, he felt a pang of regret over all the opportunities for pleasure he had passed up on his long march from cradle to grave.

The end of things was much on Torelli's mind these days. His dear wife Claire was in failing health, weak and tired and frequently bedridden. He had accepted the fact that she might be dying, but he was older than her and felt cheated not to be the first to go. He could not abide the thought of losing her really. They were bound together, fiber to fiber, through forty-two years of marriage. Often he brooded about the injustice of it for hours, looking glumly out a window and studying the flight of birds from tree to tree. He had a keen eye for nature, for its subtle turnings. He was a farmer by trade, although not by inclination, the owner of one hundred supremely productive vineyard acres that his ancestors from Tuscany, early immigrants to California, had acquired through stealth, cunning, and outright theft in the 1890s. Wine grapes had made the family rich and powerful, but Torelli had never enjoyed the punishing solitude of the fields so, decades ago, he had rented his office in town as a cure for his loneliness, doing the farm's accounting and selling some insurance on the side. The office served him as a refuge now.

An unexpected knock on the door, light and tentative, startled the old man and interrupted his intense scrutiny of the tape. He didn't have a clue who the caller could be. His cronies liked to drop in on him for bourbon, gossip, and a game of cribbage, but they never showed up before noon. He panicked for a minute when it occurred to him that someone might actually be seeking his professional services. He had no real clients anymore. His Allstate signs and stationery he had junked at the county dump, and the number of his business phone was long gone from the directory. The very idea that a person should work hard throughout life seemed ridiculous to him now. The world, Torelli had come to believe, needed nothing at all from human beings. It was meant to delight, but human beings were incapable of lasting joy. They couldn't tolerate their own unimportance on earth, so they were purposeful and dutiful and made their existence a misery. People, he thought, admitted the truth too late.

Grumbling and cussing, he rose deliberately from his desk, the sheer bulk of him listing a bit, and undid the two locks with his gnarled fingers. Before him stood Antonio Lopez, a field hand from his farm, who was gripping the brim of a baseball cap and staring dismally at the floor. Lopez had the doomed look of a messenger about to deliver some news that could not in any way be construed as welcome.

Torelli invited him in. "Antonio," he said, with a polite nod.

"Sorry to disturb you, *señor.*" Lopez remained on the brink of the inner sanctum. His manner was very formal and apologetic. "But we got some trouble at the home place. He has disappeared again."

"Who? Atwater?"

"Atwater, yes. He's been gone for four days now."

"You don't think he'll come back this time?"

Lopez shrugged and pinched his cap brim more tightly. "Maybe it could happen."

"Why did he take off?"

"He got some papers in the mail. Legal papers from the courts. His trailer looks empty. No stereo and no TV. The only thing left in there is his dogs."

All at once, Torelli became aware of some loud orgasmic moaning and realized that he had neglected to turn off the X-rated tape. Such errors were common to him, a function of his age, but he no longer worried about them. Instead, he was amused.

"You ever watched one of these dirty movies, Antonio?" he asked, throwing an arm around the smaller man's shoulders and drawing him toward the screen.

Lopez stood firm, his feet planted as though to resist an undertow. "I seen one once."

"You don't have to be ashamed of it." Torelli was further amused by Lopez's squirming. "It's not a mortal sin, you know. You afraid you'll have to go to confession?"

"I'm not afraid of that."

"This is the first one I ever watched myself. Usually I go in for westerns. You like westerns?"

"Sure. Everybody likes westerns."

"Everybody but the Indians." The old man tilted his head to examine a huge set of genitals that were on view in a close-up shot. "Is that fellow's dick really so big, or is it the camera angle that does it?"

"Could be it's a camera angle trick," Lopez allowed. An expression of relief came over his face when the old man killed the video. "Ever since *Star Wars*, they have all kinds of special effects in movies."

"So," Torelli inquired, his eyes twinkling and merry, "you figure it's a dick from outer space?"

Lopez looked puzzled. "I'm just saying about special effects."

"Well, maybe you're right. Come and sit down, will you, Antonio?"

Torelli hobbled back to his chair, favoring an arthritic knee, and gestured for his visitor to sit opposite him. This Lopez did. He was a handsome, copper-skinned man in his mid-twenties with long black hair gathered into a sleek ponytail and held fast with a rubber band. A dramatic six-inch scar ran down the left side of his throat, the souvenir of an adolescent knife fight in his native Guadalajara. He had crossed the border illegally just after his sixteenth birthday to join a distant cousin in Carson Valley where, by luck, he had been hired to pick grapes on the Torelli farm. He had worked the harvest with care and speed, never complaining, and the old man had taken a liking to him and kept him on. Now Lopez had a green card and a permanent job with a small but steady hourly wage. He was very grateful for both and did not get into fights anymore. To honor his good luck, he went to church every Sunday and mailed a check for twenty dollars to his mother down in Mexico at the end of each month.

Lopez sat quietly and waited for whatever came next. He seemed comfortable in the absence of words and unperturbed by the strong odor of the old man's ropey Toscano.

"Goddam that Atwater," Torelli muttered at last, shoving his remote control device to the floor. He sounded more frustrated than angry. "You give a man a chance, and nine times out of ten he'll let you down. Piss on him, I say. You know how hard it's going to be to find somebody to replace him?"

"Very hard?"

"You're goddam right. How many dogs are out there in that trailer?"

"Three, Victor. Two grown-ups and a puppy."

"You want any of them?"

"I got no room at my house."

"All right," the old man said, sighing. "Come on, Antonio. Let's go deal with it. *Vamos.*"

Again Torelli got up with difficulty. He opened a tall metal cabinet and took out a Winchester 30.06 and a fresh box of shells. He had been an avid hunter in his youth, stalking both deer and elk in the Sierra Nevada, but he didn't hunt anymore and used the rifle strictly for target practice at an abandoned quarry outside town. He and Lopez left the office together and stepped into the clear morning light. Though Torelli was big in the belly, his stomach spilling over the fancy silver buckle of a hand-tooled leather belt, he still cut an impressive figure, erect in posture and walking in a haughty and defiant way that exaggerated the broad span of his shoulders and chest. He had the commanding presence of a great building, one that was gradually collapsing from within, ruined by the stresses of time. He wore faded jeans that were loose in the waist, scuffed work boots, and a simple flannel shirt from JCPenney. He went hatless in every kind of weather to show off his single vanity, a full head of wavy white hair.

Torelli's pickup, a Ford V-8, was parked at a curb on the town square, where a few benches were arrayed around an urn-shaped fountain and some ornamental palm trees offered shelter to noisy grackles. Lopez settled in next to him, leaving behind his own battered and rusted Toyota hatchback, its manifold dents a record of minor collisions gone unreported to the police. The farm lay fourteen miles to the northeast, in true Carson Valley, where the land was zoned for agricultural use only and could not be subdivided into parcels any smaller than twenty acres, sparing it from the rampant real estate development that was going on all around it.

Torelli drove with alacrity, an elbow thrust out the window. He followed the roads that he had traveled since childhood and marveled again at how much the town had changed in recent months. On Taylor Street, he passed the old Jolly Donuts shop and saw that it had been magically transformed, almost overnight, into something called Patisserie Parisienne, a bakery and cafe that flew a tricolor from its newly installed flagpole. Henderson's Haberdashery next door had burned down in a freak electrical fire less than a month ago, and Wine Country Woman, a fancy clothing boutique that catered to tourists, had already risen from its ashes. The bowling alley down the block had closed for lack of bowlers. A sun-bleached FOR SALE sign rested in the window of Ed's Sporting Goods, next to a placard of rusty fishing lures, while La Perla Roja, the last rowdy Mexican *cantina* around, was empty of customers and would probably remain that way until the harvest was in full swing and the seasonal army of pickers that descended on the valley had some money in their pockets to blow.

There was a time when Torelli had railed against such gentrifying, but that, too, seemed ridiculous to him now. It was obvious to all but the self-deluded, he thought, that ceaseless change was at the core of life, and he was doing his best to survive in the midst of it. He had lately been banished from his beloved old home on the farm, in fact, by the demands of Claire's illness. She needed better access to her doctors and the hospital in town, so he had leased a two-bedroom tract house for them on Quail Court, in a newer subdivision. The house was an ugly brown monstrosity that stank of chemical fibers and shoddy construction and induced a terror in the old man. He felt as if he were serving out a sentence, being disciplined for staying alive so long. Never before had he slept in a bedroom apart from Claire, although in truth he did not sleep much. Instead, he lay awake every miserable night and listened helplessly to her cries of pain on the other side of a wafer-thin wall. It hurt her just to shift her weight on a mattress.

Torelli couldn't bear to think about it. He closed his eyes against the terror and let his mind drift. Images from the video he'd been watching filtered unbidden into his head and triggered a string of sensual memories, and soon he was chuckling to himself as he reminisced about his very first girlfriend, who was blessed with the most perfect breasts he would ever see or touch or lick, although he didn't know it then, of course, and was still innocent enough to believe that he would be awarded such bounty on a regular basis.

"How would you like to hear a story, Antonio?" he asked cordially.

Lopez sat up to demonstrate his interest. "If you like to tell it, Victor, I like to hear it."

"It's about how I lost my virginity. You know what that is, don't you?"

"Sure, I do."

"Well, when I was a junior in high school I dated a girl named Lucy Carpenter," the old man began, his lips curling into a smile. "She had a reputation as a hot one, but she wouldn't take off her pants for me no matter what I did. She kept saying that I had to get some protection. I was slow on the uptake back then and didn't understand what in the world she meant, so one night when we were necking in our barn, she wrote the word *Trojans* on a matchbook and told me to bring it to the pharmacy in town. I caught on pretty quick after that, but there was still a hitch. The pharmacist was a deacon at our church, you see." He paused to check on his audience. "They have condoms in Mexico, don't they?"

"Not too many," Lopez told him. "The priests are against it."

Torelli's smile widened. He was enjoying his memories, the salt and spice of them, the warp and weave. "Anyway, the day finally came when I worked up enough courage to go into the pharmacy. I was shaking in my goddam boots! I picked up every pill bottle on the shelves and pretended to read all the labels, and when I went up to the counter at last—the Trojans were in a drawer behind it—I took one look at that deacon, lost my nerve, and asked him what was the best medicine he had for a case of the runs."

"Did you get to do it with the girl anyway?"

"Praise the Lord, Antonio, yes, I did! The very next morning, I borrowed a car from one of my brothers, drove all the way to Santa Rosa, and stopped at a drugstore where nobody I knew had ever been. I was still shaking in my boots, but I got what I needed."

"Did you love Lucy Carpenter?"

"That's a funny question," Torelli said, pondering it, his brow furrowed. "I guess I did, all right. But it wasn't a big love."

"More like a small one?"

"That's it. More like a small one."

"How did it feel with that thing on?"

"I didn't have much to compare it to," the old man answered, with a laugh. "But at least it served the purpose. Lucy didn't get herself knocked up. How's that little girl of yours, by the way?"

Lopez glowed with a sudden burst of pride. "She's really fine, Victor. She's almost ten months old, and already she can walk pretty good. You want to see a picture of her?" Without waiting for a reply, he pulled a snapshot from a wallet that also held some tapped-out lottery tickets and a religious medallion pinned to the imitation leather. Dolores Lopez was posed in a frilly white baptismal gown and was beaming angelically at the camera.

"She's a beauty," the old man said, whistling between his teeth. "She looks just like you, doesn't she?"

Lopez nodded. "And she's smart, too. She could grow up to be somebody special, maybe." He put the photo back inside its plastic envelope. "Probably we might have some more children real soon."

"Well, I goddam commend you on that!" Torelli rewarded his grinning passenger with a high-spirited clap on the thigh. "You people do things the right way. A Mexican is not afraid to be natural. Us white people, we get all tangled up in our brains." He was cogitating, making connections. "Did I tell you my daughter's coming out here to help with her mother?"

"That's good, Victor. Where's she going to stay?"

"Out at the farm. There's no room for her at the house in town."

"I like Anna," said Lopez, with genuine fondness. "She's a nice woman."

"Sure, she's nice, but she has some crazy ideas." Torelli, too, spoke with affection and good humor. He loved his daughter, although she had put him through many trials. "When I talked to her on the phone the other night, she was carrying on about her biological clock. 'My biological clock is ticking.' What person in their right mind talks like that?"

Lopez seemed to find this very funny. "I never seen any biological clock," he joked. "We don't have any bio-logical clocks in Jalisco. What's that clock supposed to look like?"

"How the hell should I know?" Torelli growled at him. "It's her way of saying she wants to try and have a baby again. Why can't she just say it that way? 'I want to have a baby.' 'Course, she's divorced now, so it's going to be a little tougher for her."

"That's what Atwater was. Divorced. It could be they said in the mail they were going to put him in jail or something."

"Piss on Arthur Atwater," the old man reiterated with disgust as he turned onto Carson Valley Road, the main arterial into vineyard country, where the value of the wine grape had been raised to its highest power. "Everybody's divorced, except for me and Claire and you and Elena. Nobody sticks to the bargain anymore."

"Me and Elena, we're not exactly married," Lopez said quietly.

Torelli scarcely heard him. "The thing with Anna is, she's never had her feet on the ground. She graduated from Berkeley summa cum laude, she had a whole bright future ahead of her, and what does she do but insist on marrying that asshole lawyer from Palo Alto! She goes off to New York with him, she gets pregnant, she loses the baby, then she can't get pregnant anymore, and Bud-fucking-Wright deserts her for another woman. That's ten years of Anna's life in a nutshell. At least she's got a good head for business. She and that partner of hers have made a success of their bookstore. You know what my other kid is doing?"

"Roger?"

"Yes, Roger. He's a forty-year-old soupmaker at a vegetarian restaurant up in Mendocino County."

They were journeying through the heart of the valley now, through a landscape framed by rolling hills and dominated by acre upon acre of neatly staked and planted fields. Only a few dull brown remnant leaves were still clinging to the grapevines, and the rootstock itself looked black and stunted and utterly worthless in this dormant month of January. Crews of pruners were at work in some vineyards, moving determinedly among the rows and using hand shears or lopping shears to thin the twisted snarl of brittle and hardened canes and allow for new growth in the spring. The winter grass was an emerald green and held the last of the morning's moisture, damp and dewy in spite of the sunshine. They went by ramshackle farmhouses and a couple of grand estates and saw Hereford cattle grazing in pastures and some saddle horses cantering about in a fenced paddock. A peppery scent of bay laurel was in the air, and they could see, looking west, the timbered tips of the Coast Range through a strip of cirrus clouds.

"Sparrow hawk," Torelli said, dipping his head to point out a kestrel perched on a telephone wire. The hawk took swooping flight as if at his directive, hovered above a patch of weeds with its wings beating frantically, and plunged at a terrifying speed toward some oblivious creature down below.

"Poor little mouse," Lopez said.

"He'll never know what hit him."

Torelli puffed contentedly on his cigar, taking note of the parcels of land that he was passing. Here, at 13711 Carson Valley Road, the Petersons had once resided, operating a tiny but profitable dairy and producing three children who were famous among their peers for being able to burp at will. Over there, in a wet gulley lined with towering redwoods, lived the Vescios, a foul-mouthed bunch notorious for raising hogs in a fuming backyard pen and carrying around a squealing piglet swaddled in a baby blanket whenever they made the circuit of holiday parties and barbecues. Up on a far ridge, in dense chapparal, Torelli had once cornered and shot a sick coyote with his boyhood pal, Thomas Atwater, who later ran some sheep on the same property and could now be counted among the ever-increasing dead, his brief obituary having appeared in a recent edition of the weekly *Valley Herald*, where it had shocked Torelli and brought tears to his eyes.

Old Tom Atwater, now there was a man, Torelli thought with admiration. Old Tom weighed more than three hundred pounds and had a nose that covered half his face, but he could cast a flyline accurately without a rod, using just one bare hand. His friends had mourned openly when he'd sold off his holdings and retired to a ranchette on the fringes of Sacramento to be closer to the blue ribbon trout streams that he loved. Never again would he be seen in Carson Valley, but a grandson of his had turned up not long ago. That was the redoubtable Arthur, who came looking for work as a vineyard manager and canvassed his grandfather's pals until fate had dispatched him to a logical employer, Victor Torelli. The old man needed someone to act as a caretaker and see to his grapes while he was stuck in town with Claire, and Arthur certainly had the experience to fit the bill, plus he was willing to live in a ratty bunkhouse trailer on the farm and settle for a nominal salary against the promise of a sizable bonus if he brought in a bumper crop. There was no reason to check his references. An Atwater could be trusted implicitly, Torelli had been foolish enough to believe, never bothering to ask why Arthur couldn't find a job in the Napa Valley, where he'd grown up and surely had plenty of contacts.

"You ever get the feeling you're always cleaning up somebody else's mess?" he asked Lopez.

"No, *señor.*"

"I didn't think so." Torelli gestured toward the unstoppable parade of vines. "To be honest with you, Antonio, I'm tempted to sell the whole goddam operation. We very nearly lost money again last year." For a few seconds, he was overwhelmed by all the variables and combustibles involved in nurturing wine grapes and wondered why on earth he still took any pains with it at all. He had no heir to whom he could pass on the torch. His son had never showed the slightest interest in farming, and Anna—well, Anna was a woman first off and also headstrong and independent, full of her own ideas, and besides she had never heeded a single piece of advice he'd given her. The old man was forced to admit that his family was a total loss when it came to vineyard matters.

Torelli's concentration was broken by the sound of Lopez clearing his throat.

"One thing about Arthur?" Lopez said, in a quavery, ingratiating way. "He's a good worker. He tries really hard."

"Yes, I'll grant you that," the old man said distractedly. "But he wasn't here for a month before he went off on his first toot."

"Maybe he shouldn't be fired. Some people deserve a second chance."

"I already gave him that."

"Could be he needs a third one?"

"There aren't any of those, Antonio."

The road into the farm was a ribbon of pocked and rutted dirt. Lopez jumped out of the truck to unlatch a gate, then jumped back in. A creek to his right was running high and muddy from a recent storm. It was known as Wappo Creek, after an Indian tribe that had once camped along its banks, and in a wet year it rose to the very margins of the road and sometimes swamped it. As a child, Torelli had actually rowed down it once in a skiff. Now, he shifted into first gear and proceeded through a mixed woodland of alders, madrones, and California buckeyes. Blue and live oaks grew among them and were hung with a feathery green webbing of Spanish moss. Threaded among the oaks, too, were wild grapevines that climbed everywhere in ivylike profusion, their little berries eagerly pecked at by finches and scrub jays.

The trees soon drew back, gave way. Ahead the land was all in vineyard cultivation and offered a vision of space, light, and amplitude. The same hills that flanked the valley on all sides dropped here at a gentle incline to the Russian River, a stream that grew wider and deeper as it flowed on through town and from there out to the coast, where it emptied into the ocean. The steepest ground on the property was planted to Cabernet Sauvignon and Zinfandel, drought-resistant red varietals that could tolerate flinty soil, while the more gravelly and porous soil near the river was planted to Chardonnay. A broad meadow rich in alluvial loam bordered Wappo Creek, but it flooded

even in dry winters and was impractical for wine grapes. A few ancient fruit trees, sturdy survivors of an old orchard, still stood in the
meadow and always yielded enough pears, peaches, and plums for
Claire to put up an annual supply of jams and jellies.

The eccentric house that Torelli's forebears had hammered together by intuition rather than by plan occupied the highest rise on
the farm. No architect would have approved of its design. It was
a three-story, wood-frame place with weather-beaten white clapboards
that rested on a foundation of rough-dressed ashlar. The porch
wrapped around its front had turned columns and a balustrade and
afforded a lovely view of the valley downriver to where the Russian
swirled into an oxbow. The dark oak floors inside were worn, spotted,
and rarely level, and the wallpaper was peeling away in tattered furls,
but the big country kitchen was bright and inviting. There were bay
windows in an old-fashioned parlor that looked out on the fields and a
pond where coots and mallards were usually splashing. Each upstairs
bedroom had its own peculiar history compounded of the secrets of
its many past residents, and it was the sum of those intimacies that
had made the house so precious to Torelli and his wife.

A circular drive ran from the dirt road to the front door. The old
man parked his truck, set the brake, and paused for a moment to
admire a huge Douglas fir spiraling into the sky.

"You see this tree, Antonio?" he asked, patting the trunk. "I grew
it from a seedling I brought back from Yosemite when I was a boy in
short pants."

Lopez seemed fascinated. He patted the trunk, too, and tested the
bark with his fingertips. "It's a good tree," he said finally.

"Thank you."

They entered a foyer lined with rubber boots, some of them caked
with vineyard mud. The house was cold, and it felt damp and smelled
of mold. Nobody had cleaned it for months. Torelli made a melancholy tour of the rooms downstairs, postponing the task ahead of
him. Although he did not list thievery among Arthur Atwater's vices,
he was still pleased to find that nothing had been stolen. He stopped
to browse among a gallery of family photos that Claire had arranged
on one wall as precisely as in a museum. There were his great-
grandparents on their wedding day in the Tuscan city of Montalcino.
There were his children at different ages, progressing toward adult-

hood through billowy rings of time. There were his brothers and his only sister, all dead and buried now, gone for an eternity, and he, the youngest of the five, left behind and forced to carry on. He shuddered at the losses.

In the kitchen, Torelli boiled some water for instant coffee and warmed his hands on the mug. He sat at a table and watched Lopez, who was patient again and waiting for his next set of marching orders. The old man remembered the first Mexican he had ever hired, a Tijuanan called Eduardo Sereno, and saw the faces of all those who had come after that, fifty or sixty field hands down the years—he couldn't be certain of the total, he kept no such records— an infinite procession of workers, at any rate, whose labors had made his success as a grower possible. Some men had been as close to him as blood relatives, borrowing cash for emergencies and inviting him to christenings and funerals, while others had vanished from the farm after a single morning of picking. There was seldom any explanation either way. Torelli's only rule of thumb was to try and treat a man fairly. It was all he knew to do. So little could be saved or preserved or protected in the end, he thought. So little could be controlled.

"You been doing any pruning since Atwater disappeared?" he asked Lopez.

"We worked yesterday. But the guys, they didn't show up today."

"Chew out their asses, then. You're the temporary boss, okay?"

"Okay."

"Are you using that same crew of fellows from last year?"

"It's almost the same," Lopez said. "Ernesto Morales, though, he's becoming a problem for us. He's too slow. The others slow down for him. They don't want to hurt his feelings."

"You sure are a sensitive lot."

"We're all from the same *pueblo*."

"I knew there had to be a reason." Torelli struggled to his feet and hitched up his jeans. He snatched a dusty bottle from a shelf and poured two shots of the homemade grappa his father had taught him to brew. "Dutch courage," he said, downing his in a quick swallow. "Come on, Antonio. Let's go see about those dogs. I hate like hell to do it."

"Maybe you can call somebody to take them away," Lopez proposed. "Somebody from the county?"

"No, I've tried that before with strays," Torelli said. "It's all just government bullshit. They stow them in a kennel somewhere, nobody adopts them, and they get put to sleep anyhow. They're better off this way."

Torelli fetched the Winchester from his truck and walked with Lopez to Atwater's trailer. It was fifty yards from the main house, a single-wide set beneath the spreading limbs of a huge live oak in which some Bullock's orioles, feathered in brilliant orange and black, were preparing to nest. He could hear the dogs before he could see them. They were yipping and howling in distress, a pair of Golden Retrievers and their pup. He was sure that they hadn't been fed for a couple of days, at least.

"Is it locked up?" he asked Lopez.

"Yes, Victor."

He selected a master key from the keyring in his pocket. The dogs reacted to the jangling sound by wailing more loudly. They panted and dug at the carpeting with their paws. When Torelli had the door open a few inches, the bitch stuck her nose into the gap. Her teeth were bared, and the old man had to nudge her back inside with the rifle stock, breathing heavily, his heart pounding.

"Her name's Rosie," Lopez told him.

"Get back in there, Rosie." Torelli opened the door a bit more and gingerly petted her head. She did not snap at him as he feared she might. Instead, she began a pitiful whimpering. "Who's the other one?"

"Prince."

"All right, Prince, just settle down now," the old man said, but the dog rushed at him anyway, leaping up and landing so hard against his chest that he almost toppled over. He reeled backward and banged into a wall, swinging the rifle stock before him to keep the animal at bay. The pup, very small and furry, cowered under an armchair in a far corner of the room. Prince soon quit his wild gamboling and started whimpering, too, and Torelli ransacked the kitchen until he located a can of food and put it out on plates.

The trailer was in absolute squalor. The dogs had been drinking out of the toilet, and the bathroom floor was splattered with water and smeared with paw prints. Dog shit was heaped everywhere in mounds. The old man was surprised to discover that Atwater had not moved out all his belongings. His furniture, including his stereo and his TV, was pushed into the bedroom at the rear of the trailer, along with several cartons of books. Torelli searched for a leash in drawers and closets, but he couldn't find one and had to make do with a clothesline still in its original packaging. He ripped off the cellophane and instructed Lopez to tie the line to Rosie's collar. The big dogs were both calmer now, more trusting.

"Take her down to the river, Antonio," Torelli said.

Lopez made a mooching sound with his lips, and Rosie ran to him with her tail wagging. He bent to rub the dog's forehead with his knuckles and led her out the door. The vineyard behind the trailer was fenced against deer, so they took a path at the edge of it downhill through some willows and cottonwoods to a sandy bank. The river, too, was high and muddy, the color of coffee blended with cream. All manner of flotsam was scattered about on the shore, here a hubcap and there a pair of socks that had caught in the bushes when the water was last at flood stage.

Torelli had trouble getting down to the river. He had to lean on his rifle like a cane and use it for support, the stock pressed to the ground. Twice he almost slipped and fell, and he cursed his age and his bum knee and shook a fist at the heavens. He was thoroughly winded, his chest heaving, when he reached the spot where Lopez and Rosie were playing, and he sat on a rock to rest and collect himself.

"We'll just wait for a minute," the old man said.

It was a beautiful day. That was the thing Torelli would remember most vividly forever after. He would remember the bright blue sky and the last few gold leaves of the cottonwoods falling all around him. He asked Lopez to tie Rosie to a tree trunk with as little slack in the clothesline as possible. The dog sensed immediately that something was wrong and strained against her tether, standing up on her hindlegs and batting her paws in the air. Her tongue flapped about, and she slobbered and started whimpering again. A stream of urine escaped from her bladder and hissed in the sand. Torelli tried not to think about it. He tried not to think that he was about to shoot an innocent animal because some pitiful human being had let it down, but it did him no good. In a blind and obliterative fury, he shouldered the Winchester and took aim.

2

The cottonwoods along the river were stripped bare by the time Anna Torelli finally left for Carson Valley toward the end of January, her emotions in conflict and her bags packed for an open-ended stay. She was in her midthirties, tall and long-legged, with auburn hair that fell to her shoulders and a rich olive complexion inherited from her Tuscan ancestors. There was a simple brightness about her that some people took for confidence and others for innocence. Her eyes were her mother's, very green and striking, but it was her father that she resembled most, being just as stubborn and defiantly proud. Headstrong, obsessive, impulsive, too smart for her own goddam good—the old man had called Anna all those things and more during the battles between them that had begun almost with her birth.

A snowstorm over the Rockies slowed down her flight to San Francisco. The trip took almost seven hours, but Anna flowed into the space of it with something like gratitude. She looked forward to being away from Manhattan for a while. Her life in the city had recently gone stale on her, and she was bored and restless, hungry for some change. Then, too, she was in the throes of breaking up with a man who was her first serious lover and companion since her divorce, and she felt glad to be spared the inevitable fallout from their affair, the accusations and wounded sentiments, the tears and rage—an entire catalog of sophisticated romantic despair that was, Anna believed, a hallmark of the century. Why was the air in America so filled with longing? She asked herself that sometimes. Longing seemed to blow about like pollen; it was as pervasive as the flu. She had suffered through an awful case of it herself once and had ended up paying a heavy price for her illusions.

She became anxious as the plane started its descent. She had not visited the farm since the cancer had been diagnosed and worried about her ability to cope. No longer could she indulge in a child's view of her parents as immortals—she would be tested on this trip, and she felt extremely vulnerable. She had never lost anyone close to her, either, and dreaded the possibility that her mother might be dying. Her sense of family loyalty was unusually powerful and complex and stemmed from an ornately branching tangle of obligations that was another aspect of her ancestry. Claire Torelli had always been her staunchest ally in every struggle, offering a boundless and forgiving love; so Anna, who loved her just as fiercely in return, had arranged to remain in the valley for as long as she was needed, thanks to a sympathetic friend and business partner, Jane Weiss, who had volunteered to cover for her at the bookstore they owned and take care of her apartment. She and Jane were as intimate as sisters and often traded favors back and forth.

Her father was waiting for her at the airport gate, Victor Torelli in the flesh, an unlit cigar clamped between his teeth and his face contorted and wary. Anna was shocked by how befuddled he seemed as he stood blinking forlornly in the bright lights of the terminal. He had aged terribly in the past few months and looked so fragile and agitated that she berated herself for not coming out to help him much sooner. His jittery fingers flew about and scratched at his cheek and his neck and burrowed blindly in his trousers, and she was so upset by the tic that she had to turn away.

The old man embraced her warmly, gathering her in, laying claim. She felt the raspy stubble on his cheek and smelled the tobacco worn into his clothes. "You look good, Anna," he said, holding her at arm's length to appraise her. She had dressed for the country in jeans and a leather jacket. "You got a new boyfriend or something?"

"Nope, no boyfriend at all." It was uncanny, she thought. He had managed to insult her in under a minute.

On the freeway traveling north, he was better, more relaxed and in his element again behind the wheel. The truck was an extension of his personality, she realized, its seats torn and frayed and the dashboard littered with matchbooks, crumpled receipts, and scraps of paper scrawled with cryptic notes. Anna took the opportunity to study him in profile as he drove. His grand head gave him a curious nobility, something Roman and imperial, and his hair was snowy in what moonlight there was. She understood that her own reality had always been a secondary fact to him, less important than the fact that he had fathered her, and though she had often resented him for it in the past, she was overcome at the moment by a profound affection that soared beyond all such barriers and consumed her heart.

She watched him puff away on his Toscano while he served up an ornery recitation of rainfall statistics and perennial grudges, deliberately avoiding any talk about his wife because of the pain it would cause him.

"How's Mother doing?" she asked him presently, unable to resist any longer.

His lips tightened. "Claire had a rough time today," he told her, his expression somber. "That's how it is. She goes up and down. But she's happy you're here, Anna."

"Am I staying out at the farm?"

"Yes, ma'am. We just have the two bedrooms in town. I got the house fixed up real nice for you."

"I'll be lonely out there by myself."

"The pruners will keep you company. There should be four or five boys working on the Chardonnay tomorrow."

"Who's on the crew this year?"

"Antonio Lopez is the only one I know. I don't give a good goddam what goes on in that vineyard anymore. I'm tired of pissing money down a well."

The refrain was legendary. "Haven't I heard that before?" Anna asked him, teasing.

"Could be. Anybody as old as I am is bound to repeat himself every now and then."

Yet he talked on. The field hands were not as trustworthy as they used to be, he said, and it was a hassle to hire even a few honest fellows. Half the men in vineyard work had no notion what the hell they were supposed to be doing, they got drunk and ran off on you, they were responsible for annoyance and misery, they left their dogs in your care, they were always begging for another chance, and when you came right down to it, he continued, the soil itself seemed to have lost some of its richness and vigor and felt thin and grainy if you sifted it through your fingers—and so on and so forth until it dawned on Anna that he might actually be asking her for some assistance in his devious, roundabout way.

"Maybe I should go over the account books while I'm here," she proposed cautiously. "You might have missed a thing or two."

She expected a thunderclap and a parting of the clouds, but all he said was, "Maybe so."

It was past ten o'clock when they turned onto Carson Valley Road. The roar of freeway traffic dropped away, and Anna sat up, alert to the sudden stillness all around them. Lowering her window a crack, she heard frogs croaking in puddles and ditches and breathed in the pungent menthol scent of some eucalyptus trees planted along the road as a windbreak. She could remember riding by this very prop- erty in her school bus, cowed into obedience by the no-nonsense driver, a beefy woman who combed back her hair in a greasy ducktail and handed out jellybeans to well-behaved passengers every Friday. The next farm up belonged to Charlie Grimes, her father's best friend. A famous prankster, Grimes had entertained the neighbor- hood kids with his dimestore magic tricks, teaching Anna the proper method for hiding a whoopee cushion and fooling her with a plastic King Tut that kept jumping out of his little magnetic coffin.

"What's Charlie Grimes been up to?" she asked.

The old man chuckled. "He got it into his head that he's an artist. He painted a mural on his barn to attract the tourists to his winery."

"Did it work?"

"I wouldn't go that far. He stole the whole goddam setup from Walt Disney."

Within minutes, they were headed down the familiar dirt road to the home place and soon pulled into the circular drive. The only light in all the pitch-black night was a lone bulb that cast a hazy halo on the porch of the house. Anna got out of the truck and shivered in the cool, unruffled air. Her father hobbled up the stairs with her suitcases and opened the front door onto an interior so slovenly and wrecked that the farm might well have been taken for abandoned. Thick layers of dust covered every surface, mice had chewed through the kitchen pantry and left a trail of tiny turds across the counters, and the fridge was crowded with bowls of leftover food that had solidified or decomposed beyond recognition. The unrivaled chaos suggested a fall from grace to Anna, and the blame, she thought, was obviously the old man's.

He knew it, too. "Whatever you do," he warned her, his fingers jittery again, "don't you dare mention this to your mother. I've been meaning to clean up, but I get so goddam busy."

She was about to say, *But you never cleaned house in your life!* Instead, she bit her tongue. For the first time ever, she pitied him.

As if to absolve himself, he proved to her that he had indeed done a few things to make the place more habitable. He showed her some cans of soup on a shelf, tomato and chicken noodle. There were supplies of coffee, milk, soda, and bread. She had grape jelly, butter, and sugar. He switched on the heat for her and fussed with the oak logs that he'd stacked on a pile of kindling in the parlor fireplace. He had laid out clean sheets and a patchwork quilt in her old bedroom upstairs, too, but Anna still couldn't bring herself to bestow the praise on him that he seemed to think he deserved.

He gave her the keys to the family's fancy car, a boatlike Taurus for church outings, and drew her a map with an arrow aimed at Quail Court. "Come in the afternoon tomorrow," he instructed her. "That's a good time of day for your mother. She should have some energy then." He added a phone number below the map. "The furnace has been acting up on me. If it cuts out, call my vineyard manager."

She looked out at the bunkhouse trailer. It was completely dark. "He's asleep."

"Well, wake up the son of a bitch."

Then Anna was alone in the enormity of the house, rattling around in it just as she feared she would. She had almost nodded off during the ride up from the airport, but she was wired now, speeding past any jet lag. She talked to herself as she roamed from room to room downstairs, still in awe of the incredible mess, and when she spotted a bottle of homemade grappa in the kitchen, she poured herself a generous glass to calm her nerves. The first sip burned going down, but the second was much smoother, and the third was really very nice. She lit the kindling in the fireplace and pushed a couch up close to the hearth, feeling a rosy glow all through her. The fire gave her a wonderful sensation of being protected and brought back a memory of the time in her early teens when she and her brother Roger had put together a lean-to by the river from some cast-off barn siding, where they smoked a few purloined cigarettes, threw a jack-knife at the trees, and concocted a never-to-be-executed Huck Finn plan to build a raft and drift downstream to meet their glorious destiny.

There was a snapshot of Roger in her mother's picture gallery on the opposite wall. He was costumed as a Beatle on a long-ago Halloween, with a mop dyed black on his head—more like dreadlocks, Anna thought, than any style that the lads from Liverpool had ever sported. Roger was the Torelli clan's free spirit, dedicated to having fun and thoroughly useless in any crisis, and she had always envied him enormously. While she sat chained to her desk and her homework during their school years, he was allowed to chase around with the Mexican kids in the fields, playing soccer or tag. Perfect Anna, he called her pointedly whenever the folks held her up to him as an example, and she supposed that she had deserved it—National Honor Society, captain of her volleyball team, editor of the school paper, Most Likely to Succeed, she was snobbish about her triumphs and desperate to escape from the rural confines of Carson Valley just as soon as she possibly could.

She had gone about that escape in a calculated way, in fact. Her first step was to get into Berkeley, and the second was convincing her parents to send her to Europe the summer before her junior year. Along with Jenny di Grazia, a girlfriend from the valley, she had spent a month touring France, Germany, and Italy. Another photo on the wall showed them posed together at a café in Montalcino, with a bottle of Brunello in front of them. Who had taken the shot? Ah, yes, it all came back to her—Guido, a skinny Renaissance faun, who wanted to practice his English on them. Guido had ringlets of hair and wore tight bell-bottoms in fluorescent green. He had invited them to zoom around Piazza Cavour on the back of his motor scooter, but only Jenny had risked a ride. Montalcino was dank and medieval, a walled Etruscan stronghold not far from Siena. The Torellis had reportedly originated there, but Anna, nosing around in a graveyard, could find only a single weathered headstone that suggested a link. The name Tomasso Torelli meant nothing to her father, though, when she told him about it on a postcard.

Cathedrals, frescoes, a midnight stroll along the Thames, the atmospheric Turners at the Tate; the radiant Madonnas at the Uffizi; liters of pilsner and bock in a Munich beer garden; the Tuileries, Monet, Van Gogh, Rimbaud—the incessant, seductive scheming of Europe's huge complement of Guidos, Francos, and Helmuts, all of them hot to practice their corruptly faulty English on American girls and all of them rebuffed by Anna—she couldn't vouch for Jenny, who had a habit of disappearing mysteriously from their various hostels and pensions—that journey had transformed her. It marked the precise moment in time when her longing was at its most acute, when she was most intolerant of her family and anything remotely connected to farming. She returned to college in the autumn feeling advanced and cosmopolitan and began dating Bud Wright, who had access to the big world she wished to be a part of. No photos of Bud were on display anymore, Anna noticed. Her mother must have packed him away, editing him out of her gallery like those corrupt cardinals who'd been banished from the Vatican museum and stored in a drafty cellar somewhere.

Poor Bud Wright. He had impeccable breeding, a BMW convertible, his own apartment, and nothing much in common, really, with Anna Torelli. She could see now that she had chosen him simply because he fit the fairy-tale stereotype she was pursuing, although she certainly didn't understand it at the time. Bud came from a wealthy family in Palo Alto, the scion of stockbrokers, surgeons, and attorneys. His future was already clearly written, but Anna lacked the experience to read it. Handsome, intelligent, conversant enough with the arts to negotiate a university cocktail party, and possessed of a seven handicap at golf, he switched his major from history to prelaw as a senior and started down the path that had been prepared for him in his infancy. Anna knew no better than to be thrilled for him, and when he proposed to her before graduation she accepted on the spot against her father's volubly expressed wishes and moved with him to Manhattan, where he entered law school at Columbia and they began what she imagined would be their perfect life together.

She poured out another splash of grappa. Could she ever have been so naive? The answer, sadly, was yes. Without any encouragement from Bud, she had turned herself into a dutiful young wife committed to forwarding her husband's career. She shopped for silver and china, decorated their place à la mode, signed up for some tennis lessons, subscribed to *Vogue,* and even clipped gourmet recipes from the *Times* magazine section and pasted them in a notebook. When Bud joined a powerful corporate firm, she hosted elaborate formal dinner parties for his influential associates, slick and oily men whose very presence at her table made her want to throw up. The only elements missing from her carefully constructed fantasy were the three perfect children she hoped to have, but she and Bud had no luck in that department, going through a miscarriage and an ectopic pregnancy early on. Anna never managed to conceive again, despite their heroic efforts; and for a full ten years she had carried on in the role she had assigned herself until the whole rusty load of continuity came crashing down.

The collapse of the marriage was a terrible embarrassment for her. She had never failed at anything before, had never made a fool of herself in public. People assured her that she was fortunate not to have any kids, but Anna wasn't so certain. At times, she still felt a yawning emptiness in her that she could barely tolerate, although the sensation never lasted long. More often she cherished the new life she had built for herself, valuing her freedom and independence. That was the source of her recent head-butting with Sam McNally, the first man since her divorce to hold her interest for more than a couple of weeks. But Sam had started pressing her for some kind of relationship, with rules and boundaries, and she had decided, however reluctantly, to stop seeing him for a while. She told herself that she didn't love him enough, but in truth she mistrusted the very concept of romantic love and believed it was merely a useful fiction human beings had invented to explain their inexplicable attachments.

She slept on the couch that night, bundled in the quilt from upstairs, and woke to a morning of hard frost. The fire had guttered out, and the house was freezing cold. Anna bumped up the thermostat, but the furnace had quit on her just as her prophet of a father had predicted. Why hadn't he repaired it, then? That was an easy one—because repairs cost money. Furious with the old man, she phoned the number he had given her and left a message on an answering machine. The vineyard manager was probably already at work in the fields, she thought, as she stood by a window and took in the landscape, remembering how beautiful the valley could be in winter. It looked as though the lightest possible snow had fallen to turn the ground everywhere a silvery white, and the river was like a blue-black ribbon of ink pulsing along the western edge of the farm. Five Mexicans were pruning in a block of Chardonnay near the creek, Antonio Lopez among them, and they resembled figures in a Brueghel painting, deep in concentration and oblivious of the crows and ravens sailing about them in graceful arcs.

In the ruined kitchen, Anna made herself a pot of coffee. She browsed in a hall closet, discovered an old navy peacoat, and put it on for some added warmth. Her father had neglected to lay in any extra firewood, naturally, so she was reduced to burning some yellowed copies of the *Valley Herald* rolled into logs. She stayed close to the hearth until she heard a stagey clomping of boots on the porch, followed by a dramatic fit of coughing. The local farmers liked to announce themselves that way instead of ringing the doorbell, so Anna rose from the couch and opened the front door on a lean, wiry, oddly elegant man, whose posture had a trace of the military in it. His close-cropped hair was flecked with gray, and he wore a down vest over a red flannel shirt. There was a searching wildness in his eyes, but at the same time he held himself rigidly in check, as if his every word and action were being tallied somewhere and maybe even judged.

"I'm Arthur Atwater," he said politely. His breath came in clouds. "I got your message."

Anna gripped the hand that he offered. His fingers were icy and blistered, scored with nicks and abrasions. "Won't you come in?"

Atwater didn't budge. He appeared to be wrestling with a knotty problem, studying it from every angle before he made a move. "One of my dogs is with me," he said, finally. "Can I bring her in, too? She'd keep to the foyer."

"Of course. This house has seen generations of pets."

He whistled and yelled, "Here, Rosie," and a golden retriever bounded to his side. Anna knelt to stroke her luxuriant fur. "Isn't she a pretty girl?"

"Yes, she is," Atwater agreed.

She gave him a sarcastic look. "Rosie's lucky to be alive, I understand."

"It takes a cruel man to shoot a dog," Atwater told her, glancing away.

"Have you ever tried?"

He ignored her. "Could you show me to the furnace, please?"

They descended into the basement behind the beam of a flashlight that Anna held. A wooden rack against one wall was stocked with bottles of wine that the Torellis had been given by their neighbors. Each bottle was neatly labeled by hand—Pepper Harris Merlot 1994, Fred Vescio Zinfandel 1990, Charlie Grimes Premium White. A robust odor bubbled up from a dilapidated grape press and some ancient oak barrels stained with the lees of vintages past. The furnace, a forced-air model, was a relic from the 1940s. Atwater removed a panel at the base of it and jiggled a thermal coil. "I smell gas," he said, squatting down. "Did you check the pilot light?"

"I wouldn't know where to begin."

Anna braced herself for a clever retort, but he paid her no mind and stretched out on the concrete floor, stomach down, to conduct a search. The task could not be called complicated, but Atwater addressed it with the intensity of an astrophysicist confronted by a perplexing equation. She admired the look of him in jeans and had a fleeting recollection of the many high school boys in Levi's who had pursued her in her prime, boys she had disdained because they were already rooted in the valley and could never take her anywhere. More missed opportunities, experiences swept away by the wind.

"Here it is," he said. Atwater sounded pleased with himself. "Have you got a match?"

She fetched him a box of kitchen matches. He flicked one against a thumbnail, and there was a little explosion of sulfur. He stuck an arm into the furnace, touched the match to a gas jet, and drew back quickly when it erupted in a burst of blue flame. Whisking the dirt from his shirt, he raced up the stairs ahead of her and adjusted the thermostat. Anna heard a muffled pop of ignition, and soon warm air was pouring through the floor vents. She stood over one with her head thrown back like a sunbather. "That feels so good," she said, hugging herself. "Thank you, Mr. Atwater."

"You should be okay now." He was making ready to go. "I'll have Antonio bring in a load of firewood later."

"Can I offer you a cup of coffee?" His company was a welcome distraction.

"I prefer tea."

"Tea it is, then. I won't be keeping you from your work?"

"They'll get along fine without me," he said. "Antonio can prune circles around me, if you want to know the truth. Nobody listens to a vine better than he does."

"You don't really believe that mumbo jumbo, do you?" Anna asked him. An old valley superstition had it that the grapevines talked to attentive and solicitous pruners and gave them helpful suggestions.

Atwater regarded her soberly, as if under oath. "Yes, I do."

Rummaging through the ravaged cupboards, she saw that her stash of tea was limited. The mice had demolished the Earl Grey and the Irish Breakfast, so Atwater was consigned to a bag of Morning Thunder. Anna sat across from him at the table and inspected him more closely. He was about forty, she guessed, and more than a little battle-scarred, his face creased heavily from working outdoors. His graying hair was misleading, though. Every other aspect of him seemed youthful and vigorous. She thought that he might be the most tightly wound man she had ever met.

"How long have you been living out here now?" she asked, aware that a silence was gathering around him once more.

"Since November."

"It must be satisfying work. Growing grapes, I mean. The physical side of it, anyway."

"It can be. But I expect you already know that."

She shook her head. "They didn't let girls into the vineyard on this farm. Not when I was a kid. My father practically stood guard. He could be a tyrant about it."

"Victor's been real good to me," Atwater said stoutly, his voice rising. "I won't let him down again."

His passionate declaration startled Anna. "He didn't tell me exactly what happened between you two. Why don't you fill me in?"

"I'd rather not."

"Come on, don't be shy," she insisted, smiling at him over the rim of her cup to encourage him. "I can keep a secret."

Atwater sighed and waved a hand distractedly. "Well, I got some bad news in the mail, and I went a little crazy."

"That isn't much of a story."

"I'm not trying to sell it to the movies, am I?"

"No, really, Mr. Atwater." She saw something dark and difficult in him then, a side of himself he didn't want to reveal, and it intrigued her all the more. "I deserve to be told. Honestly, I do."

He stared at her hard, his eyes bright with mockery. "All right," he said evenly, knitting together his blistered fingers as he leaned toward her, as if in challenge. "The story is that when I got the bad news, I ran away. I stopped at every bar I could find and bought some cocaine and did so many other stupid things I can't even remember them all. Nobody was taking care of the vineyard while I was gone, either. Most growers would have canned my ass, but your father didn't. He saved my dogs and gave me another chance when I came back. It's my third. That's two more than anybody ought to have. Third chances, they don't grow on trees, do they?"

"Anything else?"

"Yeah." Atwater permitted himself a toothy grin. "Victor said he couldn't see the point in punishing somebody who was already doing such a good job of it on his own."

Anna decided that he wasn't trying to be funny. She was not at all sure that he had it in him to be funny. "I know something about running away," she told him, drawing her legs up under her. "I ran away from here as soon as I could. I married the very first man who asked me."

He seemed uncomfortable with her confession, even moved by it. "That's awfully sad," he said, brooding over his tea.

"I suppose it is. There are sadder things, though. And we get over them, don't we?"

"Some do and some don't." He whisked more dirt from his shirt. "But maybe it's for the best. Maybe you're back for good now."

"I don't think so," Anna said. "I'm just here for my mother's sake. I *am* ready for a change, though. I'd like to explore San Francisco on this trip."

"Cities make me squirrely." Atwater looked at the floor. "Too many people."

"You know what's been bothering me this morning?" Anna went on, ignoring his comment. "I can't identify a single tree or plant on this farm. It was just a beautiful blur to me when I was growing up." She watched some chattery little birds flutter around a shrub outside. "Can you tell the birds apart, Mr. Atwater?"

"Arthur," he corrected her firmly. "Yes, I can. Those are vireos."

"I should learn something about wine grapes while I'm here." She had never before given much thought to the fact that the farm would belong to her and Roger someday. "If I have any questions, could I ask you about them?"

"Yes, you could." Atwater pushed aside his empty cup and rose abruptly from the table. "But I should be going now. This is a small valley, and people talk."

"What do they talk about?" Anna asked coyly, entertained by his stiff and armored stance.

"They talk about how much time a man spends with a woman when she's home alone." Without another word, he went striding into the foyer, where Rosie was napping under a bench, and bent to whisper in her ear. Rosie stuck out her front paws, arched her back, and yawned, and together they walked off into the vineyard.

Noon came with a shower of sun that burned off the last traces of frost. The light fell on a rickety barn where Charlie Grimes had painted his folksy mural of Dumbo and Goofy stomping on purple grapes as big as cannonballs, on the field hands hanging around outside Roy's Market, the only general store in vineyard country proper, and on the imposing hillside estate that the Poplingers, a wealthy Bay Area couple, had lately constructed for their weekend retreat. Anna passed all those landmarks on her drive to town in the Taurus and passed, too, her father's truck parked by the Bullshot Saloon just off the square. She pictured him inside with the cigar smoke curling around his head and the ache in his heart ever expanding, and she felt tired now, tired and apprehensive. Her long night was catching up with her, and she hoped that she could summon the energy and strength to deal with what lay ahead.

How could it be that croissants, pâté, coffee beans from Madagascar, and lingerie from Victoria's Secret were now available in the shops of Carson Valley? Anna could hardly keep up with the pace of change. She stopped at Safeway for some groceries to take back to the farm and at the post office for some stamps before continuing on to Quail Court, a typical subdivision of starter homes. The house where her mother lay waiting was a dull brown box nearly identical to the houses next to it in a horseshoe cul-de-sac. How miserable it must be for a sick old woman to live out her days in a neighborhood so devoted to expectancy, Anna thought. She was angry with her father for not renting something better. He must have been pretending that the arrangement was temporary, but wasn't everything on earth, every human pact, temporary in the end?

Claire Torelli was in a bedroom at the back of the house, all alone, a blanket pulled up to her chin and her withered arms draped over it. She had lost at least fifty pounds during her first round of chemotherapy, and her face had a skeletal look. She appeared to be dozing, yet her eyes were half-open and seemed to have grown larger, more fluid and expressive. Her hair, pure white and so thin that her scalp showed through it in reddish patches, boiled up around her head in unruly strands and created an otherworldly impression. She could have been floating among the galaxies, on her way to a destination far beyond her daughter's reach.

From the depths of her being, Anna felt the tears well up. She fought against them, but they came anyway, along with another surge of anger toward her father for preparing her so poorly. She had depended on him to keep her informed about her mother's condition, but he had let her down. He had hidden the ugly details from her. There would be no remission and no cure—Anna knew it in an instant. As gently as she could, she lowered herself to a bedside chair and reached for the bony fingers on the blanket, imagining herself as a kind of ballast that would keep her poor mother from vanishing into the clouds. So soon, she thought. Too soon.

"Anna?" Claire asked hoarsely. "Is that you, dear?"

She bent to kiss a sunken cheek and felt the skin like parchment on her lips. "Yes, it is."

"I must look horrible to you. It's a shock, isn't it? The way I look?"

"You look fine, Mother."

Claire offered a weak smile. "You were never much of a liar, Anna. Oh, I feel so guilty about dragging you to California!"

"I want to be here. It was my choice."

"Well, then." Her mother faltered for a second, then plunged on. "It's a relief to me, really. Your father gets so depressed. He can't stand to see me in pain."

"Does he leave you alone very often?"

"Hardly ever. But he has to get out of the house to clear his head. Have you got everything you need at the farm?"

"Everything. It's perfect."

"With Victor on the job? I rather doubt it, dear."

There was a TV on top of a bureau, tuned to a talk show with the volume down low. Anna stared dumbly at the screen while she collected herself. The worst of it was over for her now, but she understood that something in her had been altered forever. A sense of the broadness of existence, a certain quickening in the presence of possibility, a promise of deliverance in the air—all were gone in a few brief seconds. Overwhelmed, she masked her distress by acting cheerful and upbeat, chatting with her mother about her work, her life, and even her brief errands in town, as though such things could truly be counted as adventures.

"You'll never guess who I bumped into at Safeway," she said, nervously babbling. "Betty Chambers from my high school class. We're going to have lunch next week. Do you remember her?"

"I believe I do. Wasn't she a cheerleader?"

"Yes, she was. But then she married an accountant, and now she's an ex-cheerleader with five kids."

"Goodness! Some women don't know when to quit," Claire said. "How about you, Anna? What happened to that nice man you were seeing in New York?"

"He stayed nice, Mother. Plus he started talking about marriage."

"Couldn't you just live with him for a while and try him out?"

Anna blinked. Could this be the same woman who had once scolded her for kissing a boy good night? "That would be living in sin, I believe."

"Sin doesn't seem to matter very much anymore, dear." Claire fluffed the pillows behind her head. "Did your father tell you that Roger has a new girlfriend? He's very happy with her."

"Roger is always happy, Mother. Roger was born happy."

"Don't be unkind, Anna."

"Is he still working at the same restaurant?"

Claire nodded with effort. "He makes the soup," she said, laughing, and the laugh became a racking cough. "It's a mystery to me how my children turned out the way they did."

When the news came on at five, Anna left her mother and dragged herself into the kitchen to fix a simple supper. She found some spaghetti, a jar of marinara sauce, and enough lettuce for a salad. While she was filling a big pot with water to cook the pasta, Victor Torelli rolled into the house, his wanderings apparently completed for the day. He greeted her with a grunt and a wheeze of whiskey and tossed a video on the table, the John Ford version of *Stagecoach*, but he didn't speak for a minute or two. Anna could feel him watching her. She swore that she could feel him thinking.

"How's your mother?" the old man asked at last.

"She's taking a nap."

He asked next, "What's for supper?"

"Spaghetti."

"Excellent." He stood up clumsily and brought down a cribbage board and a deck of cards from a shelf. "How about a game, Anna? Nickel a point, same as ever."

"I'm in the middle of making dinner here, Dad." She was exasperated with him. He was always the intruder, always invading her space.

"Just one little game while the water boils."

Anna lacked the will to argue and sank into a chair. Her father cackled wickedly at her, shuffled the deck, and dealt out the cards. He had taught her to play cribbage on a camping trip to the Sierra Nevada when she was about ten, and she still had a vivid memory of those craggy mountain peaks, the resinous pine trees, and the perfect disc of a moon mirrored on a stream. They had hung their Coleman lantern on the limb of a tree and used a boulder for their table, and though she had trouble mastering the game, he never let up on her or gave her a break. If she failed to count all her points, he claimed the ones that she had missed and pegged them on his side of the board. He would do that even now, she knew. She thought that she must love him and hate him in equal measure.

"Fifteen-two, fifteen-four, and a pair is six," he said, as he moved his peg. "You shouldn't have tossed me that ace, lady."

"Don't be so cocky."

"Did those pruners get started early this morning?" the old man asked her.

"They were already working when I got up. The furnace broke down, by the way." Anna gave him a chance to reply, but he remained silent, refusing the bait. "Your vineyard manager fixed it for me. He's a strange character, isn't he?"

"He comes by it honest enough." Torelli peeked at his cards. "His grandfather used to run some sheep in the valley. Old Tom Atwater, he had a face like a goddam beagle."

"How charming."

"He still got all the girls."

They were rounding the corner toward home, and Anna saw how her father's fingers trembled with excitement as he reached for his peg. The trembling was hard for her to watch, another sign of his advancing age and all the terrors that accompanied it—yet she also felt her own blood beating faster. She wanted to win as badly as he did, in fact, and when he counted too quickly in his eagerness and missed a run of spades on his next turn, she was overjoyed to finally possess the edge she had always craved. She was ready to pounce on him and take the points for her own, even to gloat over his error and exact her pound of flesh—but something stopped her at the last instant, and she let him go on and peg out. It was a moment of triumph for her, really, although she didn't know it at the time, a moment she would reflect back on years later and see as a bridge that she had unwittingly crossed to begin the other half of her life.

3

Pruning continued at the Torelli farm, on into February. Days drifted into days that were the same yet always different, defined by subtle judgments, each man deeply attentive as he adapted his individual rhythm to the rhythm of the crew. This was a good time of year in Carson Valley, steady with work. The pruners lived in the work as they might have in a piece of music, adjusting to its tonal variations, its arpeggios and minor chords. The big winter storms washed them out some mornings, and they would all pile into a car, turn on the heater, and listen to the radio while they waited for the rain to let up, but there were other mornings when the sun at dawn was fiery on the horizon and the air was crisp and clear. The men were immensely grateful then because they knew that by noon they would be stripped to their shirtsleeves and basking in weather as mild and warm as almost any in Mexico.

On such a morning, Arthur Atwater sat on a dry patch of ground eating a tuna sandwich. He often took his lunch break before noon, having started in the vineyard at first light. Stretched out beside him was Antonio Lopez, who was already down to his last layer of clothing, a pair of old jeans and a treasured black T-shirt from the Hard Rock Cafe. He lay flat on his back with one knee raised and a leg crossed over it, chomping on an apple. The others on the crew were resting under a bay laurel some distance away. One man was singing a song in lilting Spanish, his voice rising and falling as it rode the sweeping tides of his emotions.

When Atwater had finished his sandwich, he began a troubled examination of his right hand. He held it in front of him and regarded it with disgust. It could have been an alien thing grafted onto him for no known purpose. "Watch this," he said to Lopez. He extended his fingers as far as he could, but they curled right back at him, drawn into a claw. "I'm going to be a total cripple before long."

"That's ugly, man. You should see a doctor about it."

"I did see a doctor. He told me to quit pruning."

"How can you do that when it's your job?"

"That's the same thing I asked him. He still charged me seventy-five dollars." Atwater nodded disconsolately at the hand shears on the ground. "Plus I paid fifty bucks for those Felcos brand new. They're supposed to be the best around. The Swiss make them."

"Do they have grapes over there?"

"Good question! I don't know how the hell you put up with it, Antonio. You could probably do two hundred fifty vines a day and not even feel it, couldn't you?"

"Probably I could. But I'm a lot younger than you." Lopez bit into his apple, and the crunching sound was loud. "This is really tasty, Arthur. You want a bite?"

"No, thanks. I got some chocolate cupcakes." Atwater tore open a Hostess package, split a cupcake in half, and sucked out the creme center. A scrub jay, its blue feathers shiny in the brilliant light, hopped up to him, and he tossed it a few crumbs. "Here you go, you aggressive little bastard," he said, as the jay hopped closer. "I'll bet he's never done an honest day's work in his life."

"He doesn't have to," Lopez told him. "He's a bird."

"You've got a point there."

"Birds are lucky. They have it easy compared to us."

"No rent to pay," Atwater said dreamily. "No car insurance. No income tax. No alimony."

"No nothing, man. Everything in the world is free to them."

They were quiet for a while, their faces lifted to the sun. They could hear some crows cawing down by the creek, chasing one another around, black specks against the sky, and also the pruner who was singing, his voice louder now as he poured out his agitated heart and let it flow into lyrics that were drenched in gloom, in dust and bitter tears. Each sound stood out in the big silence of the vineyard.

"Doesn't Morales know any happy songs?" Atwater asked. "All that son of a bitch ever does is whine!"

Lopez laughed. He was still flat on his back, still enjoying the sun. "This *is* a happy song, only it's a little bit sad, too," he explained. "A man falls in love with a beautiful woman, and they get married, but a horse runs over her, and she dies."

"Tramples her, you mean."

"Yeah. The horse tramples her."

"That's a happy one, all right," Atwater told him curtly.

"You know what your problem is, Arthur?" Lopez sat up to offer instruction. "You don't like anything romantic. How can you live the way you do, all by yourself in that trailer? It's not natural, *amigo*. How long now since you and your wife split up?"

"Three years. But the divorce just became final. I showed you those papers from the court."

"You showed them to me," Lopez said in a withering way, nailing shut his case, "and look what you went and did."

Atwater remembered quite well what he had done. His flight from the farm was etched into that chamber of his brain where he stored similarly retrograde experiences, those embarrassing incidents that were the psychological equivalent of shooting himself in the foot. He remembered shoving all his furniture into his bedroom to hide it from imaginary thieves, deserting his dogs, flopping from bar to bar as he traveled north, conversing with a wide variety of crackpots, dead-beats, and philosophers, picking up a nineteen-year-old student nurse who was hitchhiking to Portland, and subsequently waking up with her at the Buckin' Bronc Motel in Redding, California, his wallet empty and no idea in his head about how such a travesty had come to be.

"Something about those papers must have set me off," he said, amused by his own foolishness. "The 'final' part, I guess."

"You have to find yourself a girlfriend," Lopez told him sternly. "I mean it, Arthur. You're not being normal. At least you should have somebody to be fucking, even if you don't love her."

"Love is the last thing I need," Atwater muttered, although he wasn't sure he meant it.

"No, it isn't, man! You're just being lazy about it. I think you're scared of it, really. It's like when a person gets hit by a car, and it makes them afraid of the traffic forever. The person doesn't even dare to cross a street anymore."

Atwater was impressed by the logic. "You're a regular Oprah Winfrey, aren't you? Why don't you open your own therapy shop?"

Lopez stood up and paced the vineyard row, his hands locked behind his back as he carried on his lecture. "Okay, Arthur," he said. "Let me put it to you a different way. What if you die, and nobody cares about you? Don't you ever worry about that?"

"Give me a break, Antonio. This is ridiculous."

"Hey, I'm offering you some help here! Believe me, you're going to die someday. It's going to happen."

"Jesus!" Atwater shouted at him. "You think that comes as a surprise to me?"

"All right, then," Lopez said calmly. "You know what, Arthur? Here's what to do. Take a good look at yourself tonight. Go right up to the mirror and don't be scared. Look at your hair, for example. It's already got a lot of gray in it."

"But I'm not dead yet."

"That's what I'm saying to you, man. Time is on your side. Find yourself a girl you like and go after her before it's too late."

"I've never been much for wining and dining," Atwater confessed, with a fervor that denied the fact that he was stating the obvious. "I hate all that moony bullshit."

Lopez stared at him in awe. "You expect to get something for nothing? You expect a girl to spread her legs for you because you were, like, *nice* to her?"

"Listen, Antonio, there's a basic problem here. I don't meet a whole lot of women while I'm out pruning. They don't tend to be wandering around with a pair of Felco shears in their back pockets."

"Let's start again from the beginning." Lopez was visibly frustrated. "This is like dealing with a baby, you know? Say to me real plain what kind of girl it is you want."

Atwater thought it over. "Victor's daughter isn't bad," he said, grinning broadly at the notion. "She doesn't show you much, but she's a looker. If I had a someone like her, I'll bet my whole life would change."

"Don't even joke about it, man!" Lopez cried. "Anna's way above you. She's Victor's daughter, and he's your boss! Come on now and say for real what type of girl you like. You like big tits or what?"

"How in the hell can I have a special type when I don't ever meet anybody?"

"What about parties? Don't you have any invitations to parties or anything?"

Atwater laughed and got a little squinty-eyed. "Sure, I do. I'm invited to a Valentine's Day fund-raiser for Carson Valley Elementary at the grange hall next week."

"You should go!" Lopez paused to savor an enjoyable barb he was about to deliver. "Maybe it isn't the pruning that's making your fingers so crooked, *amigo*. Maybe it's something else you're doing to yourself at night in secret." He motioned with his hand, up and down. "Something you're pulling on?"

"I don't have the energy for that."

Lopez swept a bug from his cheek. "If you see someone at that party who attracts you, go right up to her. Don't hesitate, man! My Elena, when I met her outside our 7-Eleven that night, a ton of guys were coming on to her. But she went home with me."

"That's because you're so handsome and smart."

"No, Arthur. It's because I had the most desire for her."

Atwater knew where Lopez lived, in an unincorporated area of Santa Rosa. It was a neighborhood of small rental houses occupied primarily by Hispanic families. Tracts were beginning to surround it as the city grew.

"I saw where they're putting in a new subdivision over by you," he said. "They've got billboards up along the freeway and everything."

"Yeah, it's getting too cramped over there," Lopez said, with distaste. "Before it was much better. Maybe we might move if we can save up some money. I should ask Victor for a raise."

"You know what he'll say, don't you?"

"Sure. He'll say 'no.' That's why I never asked him yet."

"Well, they'll turn the whole county into a suburb sooner or later."

Atwater studied the orderly curve of vineyard rows arching from east to west and admired the symmetry. "They'd do it in Carson Valley if they could. God bless the grapes, I say."

"God bless the grapes," echoed Lopez.

Atwater ate the last of his cupcake and walked away, a signal to his crew that it was time to start in again. He worked with them for a while each day just to keep them from shirking. He liked the contemplative aspect of pruning, in fact, and how it freed his mind to ponder other things, but his ruined hand truly couldn't tolerate the repeated clutching motions anymore. The first cuts he made that afternoon were sheer torture, but gradually the stiffness in his fingers disappeared and the pain was not so bad. He pruned next to Ernesto Morales, who seemed always to be lagging behind the others, and corrected his mistakes, gently and with respect. If he spoke one harsh word, he knew that Morales would throw down his shears and be gone, his pride insulted, and tremors would ripple through the crew and upset an essential harmony and balance.

"This way, Ernesto," Atwater said, demonstrating a cut. "Okay?"

Morales had a droopy bandit's mustache and murky, lifeless eyes the color of gravy. "Okay," he replied dully.

Atwater quit at dusk and left Lopez to dismiss the crew. Down the hill toward his trailer he went, filthy and fatigued and whistling for his dogs. They ran to greet him, and he played with them in the fading light, Rosie and Prince and the still unnamed pup, who had a habit of rolling around, panting, and begging to have her belly rubbed. "You're a sexy number, you are," he said, as he knelt to oblige her. The trailer had a plywood deck on two sides of it covered with worn all-weather Astroturf that gave off a sort of duff, and he sat in a lawn chair out there to take off his boots, propping his stockinged feet against a redwood railing that was falling apart. He watched in wonder as bats sailed out from their spectral community somewhere under his aluminum roof, little winged Draculas emerging from their hidden caves and tunnels. There were dozens of them, gleeful and intrepid as they looped about in goofy cartwheels to celebrate their nightly release. What a thing it is to be so free, Atwater thought jealously.

He padded inside, filled a pot with hot tap water, and soaked his right hand in it for about five minutes. The aching, crippled sensation slowly went away. He could smell the faintest trace of urine rising from the shag carpeting, a lingering reminder of the mess that he'd had to deal with when he returned from his run to Redding, miserable and chastened. He did not dwell on the memory. He fed the dogs, put some canned chili on the stove to simmer, and repaired to his lawn chair again to make some notes in his vineyard log, a record he kept of daily events. Frogs in the pond, in the creek and in the shallows of the river, cranked up their coarse serenade. It was conducted to a score that Atwater could almost decipher by now, and it increased in volume as the sky grew dark.

> FRIDAY, FEB. 3RD. Cold early, then good sunshine to 3:30 p.m., high temperature of 62 degrees. Hillside ground drying out. We pruned in a block of Cab, old vines. Morales still too slow, no more than 150 vines for the day. Replace him?

His writing done, he began his evening routine, a drill he had devised to get himself through the empty hours until bed. He could perform its rituals blindfolded—start a fire in the wood-burning stove, turn on the TV news, have dinner, and drink Spicy V8 or Diet Coke instead of beer because one beer on a boring night led inevitably to another. Sort through the mail—this evening, it brought him a telephone bill and a chance to own a gold Visa card without paying an annual fee—do the dishes, poke the fire, fruitlessly consult the *TV Guide* for something else to watch, eat a bowl of ice cream, stretch out on the couch, and find a book to read. He had been an avid reader for as long as he could recall, with a special interest in detective novels and stories of espionage. His grandfather, Tom Atwater, used to joke that it was all the reading he did that had caused his brain to be so scrambled.

Tonight he dug into a mystery set on the Italian Riviera, where dazzlingly rich people were being murdered at an alarming rate. The book was fairly entertaining, but he was so tired that he nodded off before nine o'clock. He threw a big chunk of oak on the fire and brushed his teeth, staring at himself in the bathroom mirror as Lopez had ordered him to do and registering what he already knew. His hair was indeed going gray. He studied his face from different angles and decided that he wasn't too homely, just frayed around the edges— nothing that two weeks on the beach in Viareggio wouldn't cure. He supposed that he might even be judged borderline good-looking under certain loose circumstances. In high school, he'd been a star half-miler on the track team, and there was still an appealing litheness about him that made him confident he would never go to fat as most Atwaters did in middle age, including Old Tom, whose stomach had bulged as though he'd swallowed a basketball.

Then he was alone in bed and suffering once more from a familiar hollowness deep in his soul. He felt this way almost every night, haunted by the loss of his marriage and able to remember only its positive aspects now. It seemed to him that he had spent his entire life searching for love in one form or another, and yet when he had finally found it in the person of his wife, he hadn't valued it enough. He had turned away from it and made it go sour. He still had bitter regrets and believed that he was scarred now and would never be granted an- other opportunity. He wasn't honestly certain he wanted one, either, because of the problems that love could bring. His efforts to find a girlfriend since he'd settled in the rural wasteland of the valley had been discouraging, too. The few women who had caught his eye were married or attached or not interested in his tentative advances—he was absolutely pitiful when it came to dating, still nervous and awk- ward even at his mature age, and wished that he could live in a world where a man just grabbed up the object of his lust in some mutual and wordless biological rite and started fucking—while those who did take to him soon proved to be seriously flawed, desperate for a hus- band or, in one outstanding case, even crazier than he was.

It had always been like that for him. The transitions were never easy. As a child growing up in Napa, he didn't mesh smoothly with so- called normal life, and his parents couldn't handle him at all. That was one of the reasons he had sought refuge in his grandfather's ex- pansive presence. Old Tom was three times as eccentric as his pal Victor Torelli, Atwater thought agreeably, and he had accommodated his grandson's need for a safe harbor by introducing him to vineyard work. The boy had flourished in the fields, at least when he was left to his own devices and not subjected to the supervision of any promi- nent authority figure. Atwater knew himself to be a first-rate defier of teachers, cops, bureaucrats, and anyone else inclined to be a bully or to wield power like a club, and his run-ins with such types had been legion, landing him constantly in after-school detention and once in jail for pushing an asshole highway patrolman who had given him an unwarranted ticket, and also earning him the promise of purgatory from his minister after he had dropped out of his confirmation class at the local Presbyterian church. He required all his fingers and a few of his toes to count up all the jobs that his explosive temper had cost him over the years.

Ah, Atwater, he told himself, you make it so difficult! Still, in spite of his multiple flaws, he had managed to patch together a kind of life for himself in Carson Valley. It was nothing special, of course, but he could not be considered altogether a lout. He played poker once a week with some other grape growers, he fished the river for steelhead, the big sea-run rainbow trout, he swapped lies with the few anglers who continued to frequent Ed's nearly defunct sporting goods store— Ed had absconded, in fact, and his mother was running the place while she tried to sell it and had lately begun stocking cute fly fishing apparel, much to Atwater's chagrin—and he had a few good friends over in Napa that he visited on occasion. He was neither happy nor unhappy, just mostly on an even keel except for his nightly bout of melancholy, and in the vineyard, where he labored as hard as anybody, he flourished in response to the land and its quietly urgent demands.

MONDAY, FEB. 6TH. Heavy rain, six inches by evening. No work. Shit.

TUESDAY, FEB. 7TH. Morning showers, tapering off. 7.2 inches since Monday. Finished the hillside Zin in the afternoon, just Antonio and me.

WEDNESDAY, FEB. 8TH. Fog all day. Whole crew pruning riverside Chardonnay. Good day, no mistakes. River muddy and high. Saw a mallard riding down it on a log, looked like a damn admiral.

THURSDAY, FEB. 9TH. Fog all day. Pruned more Chardonnay. Morales went to town at lunchtime and didn't come back. Fingers real sore tonight from the damp.

FRIDAY, FEB. 10TH. Drizzly a.m., then sunny by 2 p.m. Pruned
more Chardonnay. Morales all apologies. Claims he had a
toothache. What a pain in the butt he is!

That evening, a miracle occurred. Atwater allowed himself to
break with his routine. He did not build a fire, turn on the TV news,
or even look at his mail. Instead, with Lopez's prodding still fresh in
his mind, he showered, shaved, and put on his dress Levi's, a clean
shirt, and some shiny cowboy boots, preparing for the fund-raiser.
His mood was unusually upbeat. What did he have to lose? "I ain't
a gonna hesitate no more," he sang to himself as he drove off in his
old Jeep. "No more, no more, no more." Carson Valley Grange Hall
was midway to town, at the end of a gravel road not far from Roy's
Market. The building, clapboard and painted the amber color of
stoplights, dated from 1927. A sign placed by the local historical society listed the five benefactors who had been instrumental in getting it
built. Their purpose, said the sign, was "to provide a congenial space
for the social, educational, and recreational welfare of all those who
inhabit our beautiful valley."

Atwater paid ten dollars for a ticket at the door and ran smack
into a wall of throbbing energy. The dancers inside were generating
it, lively couples in all shapes and sizes done up in denim and lace,
each improvising a version of the Texas two-step while a country and
western band, fiddler to the fore, performed a rousing rendition of a
Bob Wills tune. Sweat dribbled down the fiddler's nose, it gathered in
soppy half-moons beneath his arms and fell in droplets on his fevered
bow. The floor was old and plank, and the pounding feet of the
dancers richocheted off it and echoed through the hall. The men and
women who weren't dancing shouted encouragement, helped themselves to pie and cake in heaping slabs, or took part in a rousing bingo
game that was improbably underway in a far corner. Atwater was
amused to see some little boys doing their duty by chasing after some
little girls and trying to pull their hair. Hearts cut from cardboard and
construction paper served as decoration, stapled to the walls and even
dangling by strings from the ceiling, all aflutter.

He spied several men grouped around a stand-up bar, Victor
Torelli among them, bantering and fulminating and rattling dice cups

for drinks. He hoped to slip by his boss without being noticed so that he could circulate and cruise for women, but Torelli was too quick for him, lofty in his whims and not to be resisted.

"What'll you have, Arthur?" the old man said genially, seizing his prey by the arm and dragging him over. "Name your poison."

"Club soda, please," Atwater told the bartender, a pimply teen sporting a 4-H pin.

"Do you want a cherry in that?" the bartender asked him.

"No, of course not, he doesn't want a goddam cherry," ranted Charlie Grimes, who was red-faced and tottering a bit. "You know what rhymes with cherry, son? *Fairy*."

"Charlie's all upset," said another man, a fellow Atwater recognized but could not immediately place. "Reality has caught up with him at last."

"You've met Wade Saunders before, haven't you, Arthur?" Torelli offered a courtly introduction. "He's with Consolidated Vintners. They're trying to buy my grapes again."

Saunders had wooly sideburns and a balding head. He was thin and rangy and worked a toothpick around in his mouth. "If this old coot wasn't so stubborn," he said, nodding at Torelli, "he'd have signed up with us years ago. It would have saved him a lot of trouble, and he'd have a lot more security, too."

"Security!" Grimes yelled, although he hadn't really been included in the conversation. "I'll tell you a few things about security, my friend."

"We're all ears, Charlie," said Pepper Harris, who had twenty acres planted to Merlot up on Pine Ridge.

Grimes ignored the comment. "What security is, is having a shit-load of high-paid lawyers like this here Walt Disney." He yanked an official-looking document from a shirt pocket and fumblingly unfolded it. It was smudged with dirty fingerprints, but Atwater could still make out the Disney Corporation letterhead at the top. "Cease and desist, my ass. They're ordering me to paint over my mural. They think they own the rights to Dumbo forever and ever."

"I wonder where they got that idea," said Dick Rhodes, a dry and witty man who ran the Grange Association.

"Screw you, Dick, and screw the horse you rode in on. I won't stand for this." Grimes hitched up his trousers for effect. "I'm going to Hollywood and talk to Walt Disney man-to-man."

"He's dead, Charlie," Rhodes apprised him.

"Well, I'll talk to his son, then!" Grimes snatched back the letter, blew his nose in it, threw it on the floor, and ground it under a heel. "This isn't over yet," he added, as he stomped off.

Saunders grinned indulgently. "Poor old Charlie Grimes."

"For your information," Torelli said, "poor old Charlie is worth a couple of million dollars on his land alone." He pushed a dice cup across the bar. "Shake 'em up, Wade, and we'll see who buys the next round."

While the dice were tumbling, Atwater listened to Saunders pick up the thread of his sales pitch, breezy with enthusiasm. Consolidated Vintners was a giant in California, Saunders said, second only to the vast empire of Ernest and Julio Gallo in the size and scope of its operations. Its corporate headquarters were in Sacramento, but the company purchased grapes from every viticultural region of the state, crushed them at many different wineries, and marketed the wines it produced under a number of labels—primarily jug wines, fortified wines, and brandies, although the grapes from Carson Valley, being of the highest quality, ordinarily went into the finest varietals that Consolidated bottled.

"To be honest with you, Victor," Saunders went on, leaning against the bar, "it doesn't make any sense to me why you bother with the pissant wineries around here. Those boutiques, they're so goddam small, they're always short of cash. Tell me the truth now. Have they ever paid you on time?"

"Not that I can remember."

"That's what I figured," said Saunders. "Pair of aces."

"But I've been doing business with some of those people for thirty years," Torelli told him, tilting back his leather cup to look at his dice. "Three aces."

"Well, loyalty can be damaging, can't it? Those boys might produce some classy wines, and they sure can create a fancy-assed label or two. The only problem is, you're never certain if they'll still be there in the morning." Saunders shifted his toothpick to the other side of his mouth. "Our industry has an awful rate of attrition, and you know it, Victor. Consolidated's been around since 1954. Our checks don't bounce."

"I'll vouch for that," said Dick Rhodes. "They've always paid me right on time."

"A contract with us is as good as gold." Saunders pressed his advantage. "I mean that for real. Take a Consolidated contract to your banker, and he'll let you borrow against it if you're in a tight spot. You can use it for collateral on a loan."

"That's so," Atwater agreed. "A grower I worked for up in Lake County did that once."

Saunders studied his dice. "Four of a kind," he said. "I'll put it to you once more, Victor. Consolidated stands for security. It stands for integrity. The minute you sign your name on the dotted line, a field agent from our farm advisory department will visit your vineyard and share with you the latest scientific research to improve your quality and yield. Come harvest time, you just haul your grapes over to our winery on Black Oak Road. If you meet the standards we've specified by contract, you'll get the best price in Carson Valley, bar none. And we'll pay you in under thirty days."

"Four aces," Torelli lit a cigar. He eyed Saunders narrowly. "How come all this sounds too good to be true, Wade?"

"Because you've been living in the past! Maybe you'll finally get it through your thick head that it might be worthwhile to join the Consolidated team. Five aces."

"What if our grapes don't meet your standards?" Atwater asked. "I've heard that happens sometimes."

Saunders lowered his voice, as if to impart a sad bit of news. "Well, I'm not going to bullshit you fellows, Arthur. Ninety-five times out of a hundred our contract growers leave Black Oak Road satisfied. More than satisfied—they're goddam ecstatic! But life isn't perfect. You know that, and I know that."

"I know that!" shouted Charlie Grimes, who'd returned. "Of course, I know that! What a stupid thing to say!"

Saunders gave Grimes an evil look. "Sometimes it does happen that a grower brings in a substandard load," he continued smoothly. "Maybe the grapes are a little too sweet, or maybe the color's a little off. Maybe there's a touch of bunch rot. What we do in a case like that is to downgrade him. He goes from A grade to B grade, and we drop our price. It's only fair because those grapes are going into our fortified wines and our cheapest brandies. Now if the grower doesn't like the price, if he can do better somewhere else"—Saunders smiled and threw his arms wide—"we release him from his contract."

"You're lying, Wade," Torelli said.

Saunders appeared to be flabbergasted. He sputtered, and blood rushed to his ears and turned them crimson. "Why, you have no cause to—"

"I'm calling you, goddam it. You're not holding any five aces."

The salesman's relief was enormous. He showed his dice, and they all bent their heads and counted. There were only four aces. "Well, as the chicken put it to the butcher," Saunders said, his raw color receding, "I guess you got me by the neck!"

Torelli was enjoying his victory. "Let's see some of your money on the bar, then."

"It's my round, sure enough." Saunders pushed a twenty toward the bartender. "But honestly, Victor, what about it? Do we have a deal here?"

"I don't make deals over drinks." The old man sounded irritated. "Big corporations, I don't much trust them. Don't take it personally, Wade, but they'll stick it to you faster than a two-bit whore."

"If we were out to fuck over our farmers—pardon the expression —they wouldn't have let me in the door tonight," Saunders reminded him. "Think about that for a minute."

Torelli glanced at Atwater. "What's your opinion, Arthur?" he asked.

Atwater considered the situation. "You'd lose some freedom, for sure, but the security might be nice. It would certainly be nice for you to get paid on time. No offense, Victor, but you're not all that attached to the vineyard anymore."

"There you go!" Saunders exclaimed. He patted Atwater on the back as he might have a favorite student. "You got it there in a nutshell!"

The old man seemed not to have heard. Instead, he raised his glass to salute one of the circling dancers. "My daughter," he bragged proudly to the assembled company. "Isn't she pretty?"

Atwater had not spoken to Anna Torelli since he'd fixed her furnace, except to say a quick hello when they passed each other on the dirt road. She was in town almost all day and did not come back to the farm until late at night, often after he was asleep. He had never seen her in a dress, had never seen her legs or how she carried herself in public, with a stunning confidence. She simply sparkled.

"Go on and dance with her," Torelli whispered to him, giving him a little shove.

"She's already dancing with Jack Farrell," Atwater protested. He looked enviously at Farrell, a paunchy Casanova with curly brown hair and a gold neckchain, who worked for Carson Valley Chamber of Commerce and had earned a reputation as a ladies' man by bedding most of the available women around and some of the unavailable ones, too.

"I don't want that lardass anywhere near her!" The old man was hissing, practically beside himself. "You know where he goes for a haircut? To the beauty parlor! They give him a goddam permanent. Cut in on him right now!"

"No way," Atwater said, rebelling against the injunction. "It's silly."

"Goddam it, Arthur! You *owe* me. Just do it!"

With a woeful resignation, Atwater crossed awkwardly onto the dance floor. He squeezed past the McClaren sisters, who always danced together, and past a couple who were ignoring the fiddle music entirely to do an interpretative tango that involved some manic and disorderly movements, locating Farrell in the crowd and tapping him on the shoulder.

"Excuse me, Jack," he said in a mumble, wishing he could be anywhere else. "May I cut in on you?"

Farrell glared at him, as if he'd told a particularly inane joke. "Be serious, Arthur."

"I *am* serious. I'd like to cut in."

"How gallant, Mr. Atwater." Anna took leave of her partner and glided into his arms. He quivered when her breasts brushed against his chest, and felt an immediate and agonizing hunger for her that he did his best to conceal. "I'm very sorry, Mr. Farrell, but rules are rules."

Atwater followed her lead. He was clumsy and constricted. His jeans hugged his legs, and his cowboy boots slipped and slid over the waxed planks. Anna's cheeks were rosy from the heat, and he could smell some wine on her breath and deduced from it and from her frisky manner that she was probably a little smashed.

"I'm having fun tonight," she told him as they danced to a slow number that made conversation possible. "I didn't expect to, but Betty Chambers said I would if I came along with her and Lloyd, and Betty Chambers was right. So from now on I plan to do whatever Betty Chambers tells me to do. Isn't that a progressive attitude?"

"Very progressive."

"It may sound strange to you, but this is the first fun I've had in the longest time. And I like having fun. I even miss having fun. Were you having fun over there, Mr. Atwater?"

"Not much. We were discussing business."

"Let me ask you this," Anna said, her eyes engaging his in a flirtatious way. "Have you *ever* had any fun?"

"Yes, I have. I used to specialize in it."

"Care to describe how?" She pulled away from him for a second, took in the hurt look on his face, and quickly altered her tone. "I'm sorry, Arthur. I have no right to be teasing you. The wine's gone to my head."

"It's okay. You're not the first person who's ever teased me."

"Let's change the subject, shall we? How're your grapes doing?"

He smiled at her. "There aren't any grapes yet, Anna. They're busy being born."

"I never thought of it like that," she said, musing. "That's very clever! There must be a poet in you somewhere."

"If there is," said Atwater, "he's been hiding."

"What about the vines, then. How is the pruning going?"

"We're pretty much on schedule. One fellow on the crew slows us down a bit. I might have to get rid him."

"Can his ass, you mean?"

"You could put it that way."

Anna floated close to him again as they swung by the bandstand, where an accordion player now occupied the fiddler's spot up front. "Much better," she congratulated him. "You're loosening up. Am I talking too much?"

"No, I like it, actually."

"That's good. Because I haven't talked to anybody in the longest time. Can you believe I've been here almost three weeks already? I've been so busy there hasn't been any time for you to educate me about wine grapes."

"I don't know that I'm much of an educator. How has your mother been feeling, anyway?"

"Tonight she's fine. A neighbor is with her. But she's not getting any better." Anna's sparkly mood was going flat. "It's hideous, this disease, and nobody can do a thing about it. I was so arrogant, Arthur! I thought I could come out here and make a difference, but I'm as helpless as everybody else."

"You've been a big help, really," Atwater said, trying to revive her playfulness. "I've heard Victor say as much."

"I did feel that way at the beginning," she agreed. "Running errands, doing chores, putting their house back in order. You throw yourself into action so that you don't have to think. Then one day you look up, and nothing has changed. We're all just treading water."

"You sound ready for a break."

"You're probably right. I'm angry at the world, and when I get angry I get reckless."

Reckless? Atwater liked the ring of it. "Well, it's best not to burn out. Why don't you head down to San Francisco and check out some of those bookstores, like you said you were going to do. Treat yourself to dinner at Fisherman's Wharf, ride a boat to Alcatraz, and have yourself a wild old time."

"A wild old time?" Anna asked, flirtatious again. Had she read his mind? Why couldn't she be a little dumber?

"A vacation, then."

"Oh, I don't know what I'm going to do with myself," she sighed. "It makes me guilty to think about leaving even for a day. I'm just so confused!"

"You have every right to be," Atwater told her in a heartfelt rush, remembering the death of his own parents. "It's terrible to watch somebody you love suffer like that."

"Thank you, Arthur." Anna was looking at him differently now, more soberly. "That's very kind of you to say."

He danced another dance with her, looser still, and even spun her under the bridge of his arm once or twice before Jack Farrell stepped up and bellowed, "Rules are rules!" to cut back in. He retreated to the pie-and-cake table after that and ate two orders of cherry cobbler. It was almost eleven o'clock, way past his bedtime, but he stayed around for the grand finale anyhow, a raffle drawing for an all-expenses-paid trip to Puerto Vallarta, courtesy of Carson Valley Travel. The winner was Dr. Irwin Poplinger, and that sent Charlie Grimes into another stomping tirade about how all the tax-shelter farmers ought to be rounded up and beaten to a pulp. Atwater left right after the drawing, off into the night, his weary body truly relaxed for once and warmth of an unexpected kind flowing through him.

4

The first flush of springlike weather washed over Carson Valley later that month. A run of warm, dry, balmy days had the sap rising in every vineyard. Growers spread the word that their grapes were moving, pushing toward the light. Even the wine stored in barrels and tanks sloshed restlessly about in cellars, tugged at by the same natural forces. The brief period before budbreak was an optimistic and vaguely lazy time for most farmers. Some men couldn't tolerate the boredom at all and started on projects that they would never complete or instead took up a hobby they were certain to abandon once the grand cycle of growth was underway. The sight of Pepper Harris buying a mountain bike in town was frequently mentioned as a case in point, and so was Fred Vescio's sudden itch to learn a foreign language when, it was said behind his back, he had enough trouble speaking English.

Claire Torelli was especially grateful for the burst of heat. It helped to ease the aching in her bones. On most days, she was strong enough to sit in her bedside chair, at least for an hour or two, and read magazines, watch TV, or merely gaze out the window at a world that was gradually slipping away from her. She had started writing letters to friends she hadn't seen in years, prompted by a powerful recollection of one sort or another that seemed almost to emanate from the very person she was thinking about, a vibration echoing in space.

The letters were a way of saying good-bye, she supposed, but they still gave her such satisfaction. She would not go to her grave with any reserves of unspoken affection weighing on her heart. What was left unsaid did not exist, Claire believed.

After months of denial, she had come to accept the fact that her illness was probably terminal. That had given her some peace and led her to discover a pleasure that was new to her, the pleasure of doing absolutely nothing. She was frankly astonished at how much nothing a hardworking, floor-scrubbing, churchgoing person like her could do. Hour after hour she simply meditated on things, roaming around in her head and exploring. She had an odd sensation, too, that her mind was expanding as her body diminished. Her mind had a vastness that she had never suspected before—it was jammed with dreams and visions she couldn't account for having, and she drew from this a suggestion that the universe itself must be infinitely vast and intriguing and wondered why she had always been taught to narrow rather than broaden her focus. Where was the threat? Now in the fading tick of time, she wished that she had been braver and opened every door.

Anna still came to the house every afternoon, as prompt and dutiful as ever. Sometimes she brought flowers with her, sometimes a pile of new magazines. She changed the bedding, did the ironing, cooked dinner for her father, and made sure that her mother was comfortable. There were hampers of laundry to be washed, cupboards to be stocked, and rugs to be vacuumed, a hundred little details that combined to form the substance of a household. Claire was very thankful for all the help, but she felt that Anna was sacrificing too much, making a martyr of herself, and neglecting her own young life, so she was pleased when her daughter broached the subject of taking a break and spending some time alone in San Francisco.

"I wish you would," Claire told her. "There's no reason for you not to. I'll be fine with Victor. He can get me to the doctor on Wednesday."

"It would only be for a little while, Mother. I need to recharge my batteries."

"Don't make excuses. I understand, dear."

Anna smiled. "You always did understand, didn't you?"

"You're putting me up way too high," Claire said, waving a hand to protest. "I had no idea what you were doing half the time. You had me totally baffled."

"But you let me make my mistakes, didn't you? And then you forgave me. I owe you so much for that."

"There's no credit in being forgiving. What else was I supposed to do?" She thought about San Francisco, where she had only been a few times herself. "Where will you go in the city, Anna? Are you excited? Tell me what you'll do."

"Your vineyard manager ordered me to have a 'wild old time.' "

"Somehow that comes as no surprise," Claire said dryly. "Will you follow his orders?"

"We'll see. He told me to eat at Fisherman's Wharf and ride a boat to Alcatraz. That's my assignment."

"It doesn't sound so wild to me."

"Mr. Atwater was pulling his punches, I think." Anna kissed her mother on the forehead. "I'll phone you every day."

"You don't have to do that. Just go, Anna. Go, dear."

Claire was happy about her daughter's decision. The last thing she wanted was to be a burden to her family. She was the only child of second-generation Swedes herself, Bible-thumping moralists who had farmed walnuts and pears in the valley, and she knew how controlling a parent could be with just a few well-chosen words. She had tried never to be overbearing with her own children, partly to compensate for her husband's gruff manner. Victor loved both kids, but he could be distant, shut off from any close emotional contact. He was in his forties when they came along and already rigidly set in his ways. She had fought with him about his aloofness early in their marriage, but he couldn't or wouldn't change, and eventually she had dropped the matter. It had fallen to her, at any rate, to nurture Roger and Anna, a task that she quickened to, for which she was ideally suited.

Some of her fondest memories were of the evenings that she and Anna had spent together in the kitchen after supper, doing the dishes and trading confidences. Anna was in her teens then, a lovely but challenging girl who liked to show off by telling her mother stories from the library books that she was gobbling up, six or seven at a time. Anna raved on about famous writers and composers, she recited poems and spoke in wonder about a strange painter who had cut off his ear with a razor and another man who had ridden a camel across the Arabian desert. She was describing a world that she was attracted to and hoped to join someday, although Claire didn't recognize it at the time. It still puzzled her that her son should be so at ease with himself from the very start, while her daughter had always struggled to forge an identity. So much must be established at birth, she thought, in sheer innocence, in the random choosing of a name.

Claire kept her doctor's appointment later that week. She had not told Victor about the new pain in her legs or the lump near her spine, but she confided in Ed Sawyer, her gynecologist for many years, and he dispatched her to Carson Valley Hospital for some testing. The tests weren't strenuous, but they sapped so much of Claire's precious energy that she was kept overnight. Sawyer dropped by the next morning with a staff oncologist, while Victor was in attendance. The news they delivered was devastating. The cancer had metastasized and spread from Claire's ovaries to her lymphatic system. She was being ravaged from within, attacked, used up. Worse still, nothing could be done about it. She had lost too much weight to tolerate another round of chemotherapy, and radiation would serve no beneficial purpose. All they could do was to send her home.

"Ah, for Christ's sake!" Victor was hunched in his chair, his elbows on his knees and his hands buried in his hair. "She's only sixty-eight years old."

"We don't have to tell anyone yet, do we?" Claire asked him, a note of pleading in her voice. It would only interrupt Anna's holiday and disturb Roger at work.

"Not if you don't want to."

"I don't."

Claire had to comfort Victor the following day. He looked depleted. His eyes were red-rimmed, and his hands shook so badly that he could barely hang onto the cup of tea he'd brought her. It was another gorgeous morning, with sunlight pouring into the bedroom, and she had an impulse to pay a last visit to the farm, just the two of them together, while the weather was still so fine. She didn't say "last visit" when she put the request to Victor, of course, but he was skeptical about it anyway, concerned that it would be too taxing for her. Her resolve gave her courage, though, and she pressed him until he relented. With his help, she managed to get into a cotton dress that hung loosely on her ravaged body and wore a sweater and an over-coat on top of it. The drive out to the farm was the first trip she had made anywhere in months, and she relished it and took in the familiar landscape with appreciative eyes, alive to every sparkle.

On Carson Valley Road, she rolled down her window and sniffed at the air.

"Smell that, Victor," she said, her nostrils flaring.

He sniffed and frowned. "What is it?"

"Spring."

The willows and cottonwoods along every creek were in bud, all supple and showery green. The plum, pear, and apple trees had blossomed, too, in delicate pinks and whites. There were daffodils and narcissuses sprinkled in the meadows and a solitary California poppy, intensely orange, glowing in the weeds of a farmhouse yard. Claire watched some barn swallows flitting about and building nests under a bridge, tiny cups of mud lined with feathers. The swallows sailed and dived and flashed their spotted tails, and she thought that she had never seen any creatures so spirited. The sky was blue and endless.

She leaned forward in anticipation as they turned into the farm, smiling to herself as she recalled her first ride down the old dirt road and how her boyfriend of the moment, one Victor Torelli, had picked her up at the Ben Franklin Store in town, where she had a job as a check-out clerk, to bring her home and introduce her to his family. Nervous to the soles of her best patent leather pumps—and not at all certain what the visit might mean—Claire almost bolted when she saw how many Torellis showed up for dinner. It was like that famous circus act where all the midgets emerge from a single car. Torellis clomped down from the upstairs bedrooms, dashed up from the base-ment, materialized out of closets and bathrooms, and even jumped in through an open window—that was Victor's brother, Rudy—all of them huge and big-boned and amazingly loud and uninhibited, grab-bing beers from the fridge or splashing wine into glasses, nudging one another and scratching themselves in private places, the women along with the men.

Claire was accustomed to the tormented mealtime silence of Swedes, but these Italians all talked at once! They argued and harangued on various subjects, exchanging hugs and pinches. They laughed and yelled and even blew their noses in the sink. Their rowdiness intimidated her at first, but she got used to it over time and gradually learned to give as good as she got, although she never did adjust fully to Giovanni Torelli, the cranky paterfamilias, who was in the habit of recounting his bowel movements in excruciating detail. In his collarless shirts and an aged vest that he favored, with particles of food always clinging to his mustache, Giovanni was hardly the picture of intelligence—he played at being dim-witted, in fact, when it worked to his advantage—yet it was his cunning that had established the Torellis' fortune. Fresh off the boat from Genoa, at the tail end of a lengthy migration to California, he had headed for Carson Valley on a tip from a dockside hustler and began buying up the cheap benchland that local fruit and nut growers considered worthless, aware that certain wine grapes performed well in similarly stingy soil in his native Tuscany.

Victor drove on. The vineyard loomed ahead of them, dramatic now with clumps of brilliant yellow mustard flowers between the rows. Pruning was almost over for the year, but two field hands were working in a block of Cabernet Sauvignon by the house, and the old man braked to greet them.

"Hello, Antonio," he said, gesturing at Lopez's companion, a forlorn-looking fellow who avoided any eye contact. "Who's that you got there with you?"

"Eloy Hidalgo," Lopez told him, wiping sweat from his brow with a bandanna.

"He isn't much of a talker, is he?"

"No, he's better at being quiet. He likes to count. He counts up the lugs when we're picking."

"How's Atwater been behaving himself?"

Lopez brightened. "He's been real good, Victor. He hooked a steelhead after we quit yesterday. Eight pounds, he says."

"What do you say?"

"Maybe seven."

Atwater was down by the river on his tractor, dragging a brush chopper between some vineyard rows to chop up the pruned canes where they lay. The brush would be plowed under later with a disc harrow, along with the mustard and any weeds. Claire watched him as he maneuvered, admiring the skill with which he handled the tractor on soggy terrain while he pulled some twenty feet of clattering metal behind him. He had no room for error, either, because the rows were only about eight feet apart. A black-shouldered kite, high up, its wings flapping, trailed him on his route and feasted on the field mice that were escaping from the rodent villages destroyed by the chopper's churning teeth.

Claire got out of the truck without too much difficulty. She leaned on her husband for support and approached the house on brittle and faltering legs, settling gratefully into a wicker chair on the porch, her coat drawn close around her. She felt as though she had walked a mile through the mud and was unable to speak for a minute or two, gasping until she caught her breath.

"There's no need to go inside," she said, when Victor reached for the doorknob, knowing that the dust and disorder would upset her and knowing, too, that the house itself had already toppled into the past and belonged to no one now. "We'll be warmer here in the sun."

"All right." He carried over a chair and sat next to her, his feet up on the balustrade as he loftily surveyed his domain. "So how does the old place look to you, Claire?"

"The same as ever," she said, with contentment.

"Right about now, we'd be cutting twigs from the willows and planting them along the creek. Erosion control, you called it. You remember that?"

"I do."

He turned toward her and gave her a fond pat on the arm. "You were good at it. Better than me."

"That's not much of a talent, is it? Can't you think of a nicer compliment to pay me?"

"You kept the farm from washing away."

"Hardly."

"I should have let you do more around here, really," said the old man. "Probably I should have let you run the whole goddam show."

"Ha!" Claire exploded. "Fat chance of that, Victor! You wouldn't have been able to stand it."

"Well, I never did take to farming all the way, did I?" He stroked his chin moodily. "Not like my father did, anyhow. He was glued to the fields. They had to send me out to drag him in for supper. Come the harvest, he'd take me down to Frisco, and we'd sell our grapes over there in North Beach, where the Italians lived. Those paesanos all made their own wine. That was the most goddam fun. I never saw such a ruckus in my life."

"What would you have been instead of a farmer?" Claire asked him, although she couldn't picture him as anything else, try as she might. "If you could start over."

"A movie actor? Joe DiMaggio?"

"No, really, Victor."

"If I had it to do all over again," he said, his tone philosophical, "I might go to college."

"And study what?"

"Biology. How nature works."

She looked at him doubtfully. "That might have made you happier, I guess. But you would have found something to complain about sooner or later."

The old man took umbrage. "That's a hell of a thing to say, Claire."

"Well, it's the truth," she told him, with a coarse laugh. "I'm the one who's had to listen to you bellyache for the last forty-two years."

"Was it really so awful?" He had the look of a boy in need of reassurance.

"Only at first. I got so I didn't notice it anymore. It was like the noise of an airplane flying by."

"You should have told me."

"As if I didn't."

She saw that she had offended him and took his hand in hers to appease him. Her feelings toward him had fluctuated in exactly this way down all the years, forever altering, waxing and waning like the moon. The love she had for him at the start of their courtship was one-dimensional and centered in the flesh, quick to ignite and just as quick to gutter out, a sharply sexual flame that left her thrilled but also with a disconcerting sense that he had carried her up to a mountaintop and abandoned her there. She could sense him pulling away from her afterward, flowing back into himself and re-establishing his boundaries, until after they were married. Then her original love for him began to deepen. She was more trusting as she learned what she could and could not expect from him. Victor never surprised her in bed, for instance. For all his physical prowess, he was too timid for her. She wanted him to be rougher, more experimental and free, but she never dared to tell him that. Once, after too much wine at supper, he did some things to her that she had always craved, but he seemed ashamed of himself in the morning and never repeated them despite her reinforcing praise.

Next came the love that streamed into them both when their children were born, an enriching love whose source appeared to be planetary and universal. It made certain difficult aspects of Claire's life more tolerable and others less important. The children granted her some perspective and changed her relationship to passing time, slowing everything down. It was best when they were little kids, splashing around in the pond, chasing after the ducks, and bumping about in the big green paradise that was the farm. She had loved Victor as her dearest friend then, her partner and coconspirator, somebody who understood her every reference, with whom she could battle and debate and yet stand firmly beside when she was confronted with the treachery of the swirling world outside. She could not have imagined a further ripening, but as his brothers grew older and died off one by one, she felt a new and different love between them that was rooted in sadness, the love of comrades united in grief, bound together by their losses, by all that they had witnessed.

That had been her gift, Claire realized—an ability to hold onto love through hardship and disappointment. She had many chances and sometimes very good reasons to despise Victor, but she had remained steadfast in her affection.

"Was I really such a rotten husband?" he asked her abruptly, still licking his wounds.

"Of course you weren't," she told him. "You know better than that, don't you?"

His head was sunk in gloom. "I see my mistakes. I think about them at night."

"I never did anything wrong myself, did I?" Claire asked him coyly, sorry now that she'd hurt his feelings.

"Oh, I'm not so sure about that!"

"Here's what I remember," she said, with as much cheer as she could muster. "I remember the evening we met. I was out for a stroll with Maude Vescio, and you were sitting on a bench in the square with Tom Atwater. I believe you two were looking for girls."

Victor seemed heartened by the image of himself as a young rogue on the prowl. "Probably we were," he said. "Probably you're right."

"Do you recall what I was wearing?"

"Yes, ma'am, I do. A pretty blue dress."

"What a memory you have!" The dress was in fact a rose-colored blouse and a gray skirt.

"That's one good thing about me, anyhow," he said proudly. "My memory's like a goddam steel trap. Maude Vescio, did she ever have any interest in me?"

"Oh, you were the prize catch of the valley! But we girls had you figured as a bachelor for life. We didn't think anybody would ever land you."

"It's crazy when you come right down to it. There I was closing in on forty, and I thought I was so goddam old!"

"You were my first 'older' man."

"And I stayed that way."

"Yes, you did. You did indeed."

He got up to stretch and stood looking downriver toward the great oxbow of the Russian. She could tell that he had something on his mind and waited patiently as time had taught her to do while he circled around it and fumbled for a way to speak. "I've been considering that deal with Consolidated Vintners," he said finally. "Wade Saunders, he sent me over a sample contract."

"And?"

"Well, I go back and forth on it. The security angle appeals to me. It'd set up the kids real nicely if it worked out the way it's supposed to. They'd earn a dividend on the harvest every year, and Consolidated would supervise the vineyard work. Meanwhile, the value of the land would keep appreciating."

Claire pushed him in the direction he was going, toward what would be best for Roger and Anna. "Why don't you sign up, then? What have you got to lose?"

He shrugged. "Quality wine grapes, they're in short supply now. Some of the wineries around here, I've been selling to them forever. I'd hate to pull the rug out from under those fellows."

"You'd just be looking out for your family," she said, urging him on. "People understand those things. They'd do the same if they were in your shoes."

"I'm not so sure of that."

"Why don't you talk it over with the children? They might surprise you. I believe Anna's had enough of New York, really."

"Not that I've heard."

"Promise me you'll involve them, Victor. Will you do that for me?"

"I will." He sat next to her once more and put an arm around her shoulders. She felt the heated press of his blood and saw that his eyes were again rimmed in red. "You want to know the honest truth, Claire? I'm tired. This is too much work for an old man like me. They'll be carting me off to the boneyard before long."

"Dear Victor," she said, his hand in hers again. "Don't you know you're going to live forever?"

"It won't be living without you."

She wished that she could offer him some solace, but her strength was flagging. She was operating strictly on willpower, and that, too, was running low. "We'd better go, dear," she told him. "I'm getting chilly."

The trip to the farm proved to be Claire's last respite from the downward spiral of the cancer. She fell seriously ill again a week later and was unable to keep down any food at all. Her pain intensified and became the sum of what she was, so Ed Sawyer moved her to the hospital for the constant care she required, starting her on Demerol and soon escalating to morphine. The drug soothed her, but it also kept her in a hazy stupor, and often she failed to respond to the people who came to visit, old friends paying their final respects. Even Anna's identity slipped in and out of focus for her, but she always knew Victor and had no problem recognizing her son when he arrived.

"Roger's here," the old man informed her one afternoon. "He'll sit with you for a while."

Claire glanced up from her pillow and through heavy-lidded eyes saw Roger at the foot of her bed. She was struck as ever by how little he resembled his sister, being round where she was firm, shorter and much fairer in complexion, and even-tempered where she was passionate. He had a crooked nose that he had broken in a football game, badly needed a haircut, and wore a small gold hoop of an earring in his right ear. A part of him would surely remain boyish forever, she thought. He had been that way even as an infant, intrigued by every shape around him and every shaft of light, giggling as she changed his diapers, never crying or throwing a tantrum, comfortable in the hammock of his own skin.

She could not stay awake very long in spite of his company and dozed for about an hour. It was dark outside when she awoke, and there was a gusty breeze that signaled rain and rattled the hospital windows. Roger sat reading by a lamp. He was so engrossed in his book that he didn't notice she was watching him. She watched as mothers do, observant and indulgent, appreciating the opportunity and marveling in a primal way that she had ever given birth to him.

It took a forced cough to break his diligent studying. "I'm sorry, Mom," he said apologetically. "Can I get you anything?"

"Some water would be nice. Not too cold, please."

He poured her some water from a plastic pitcher and held the glass to her mouth. "Drink it slowly," he cautioned her. "There you go."

"I'm so pleased you're here, Roger." She was aware of his touch, of its delicacy. "You have such soft hands."

He stroked her damp brow. "It is from avoiding hard work," he told her with a smile. "Those vegetables don't fight back."

"What's that funny little book you're reading?"

"This?" Roger held up a miniature paperback, almost perfectly square, five inches to a side. "A book of Japanese poetry."

"Can you speak Japanese?"

He shook his head. "But I'm taking a class in it now. This is a bilingual edition. The poems are translated into English."

"Will you read me one?" Claire asked.

"Sure," he said, flipping pages. "See what you think of this."

She listened to him intently. His voice was round and deep, rich with respect for the lines he was reciting, and she felt proud of him simply because he was her son and no one else's, a young man who was learning Japanese. She heard a strange but beautiful music in the poem, like the chiming of a bell, but its meaning escaped her. "It's beautiful, Roger," she told him. "Who wrote it?"

"Ikkyu Sojun. He was a monk in Kyoto in the fifteenth century.

When he was seventy, he fell in love with a blind singer who was just forty and moved her into the temple with him."

"I've been thinking about love," Claire said softly.

"What about it?"

"How it changes."

"And how does it change?" Roger asked, stroking her forehead again.

"Like the wind."

Her eyes closed then, and she napped for a short while. When she stirred once more, she was bewildered and couldn't see very well. There were only shadows lacking in any detail. "Roger?" she asked, groping for him. "Are you still here?"

"I'm here. Would you like me to come over and sit by the bed?"

"Yes, please." His nearness consoled her. "Everything's getting all mixed up."

The bedroom appeared to be crowded when Claire opened her eyes again. She saw Anna sitting where Roger had been, and it was as if her two children had become one. They were undivided, both parts of a seamless whole. She heard Anna speak to her and thought with all the concentrated power that she could bring to bear on the situation what she should say in reply, but there was nothing. She had run out of the language for such emotions if ever she'd had any, and yet she felt a comforting clarity between herself and Anna, with no interference of any kind, and that gave her peace. Then it occurred to her quite suddenly that she did have something to say, and she touched her daughter's cheek and said, "Don't cry, Anna. Don't cry."

A delirium swept over Claire in the next few hours. Ed Sawyer worried that she would drop into a coma, but she hung on for three more days. Only in rare moments did she know herself still to be a presence on earth, orbiting instead through the hyperspace that separates the living from the dead. She slept dreamlessly now, in a state that wasn't really sleep. "This is a relief," she whispered to Victor on her last night, unable to see his face anymore but feeling the powerful grip of his fingers. She heard him walk away and heard some other voices in the room, but she was not connected to them now. Then there were no sounds at all, only silence as she drifted off a final time.

5

The cemetery at St. Brigid's Roman Catholic Church in Carson Valley occupied a grassy hillside overlooking town. About forty mourners gathered there for the funeral of Claire Torelli, a Lutheran convert by reason of her marriage, who was to be buried in a family plot where some of the chipped and blighted headstones were almost a century old. Claire had not attended services at the church for at least six months, and Victor had never attended them except under duress, so it fell to Anna to handle the arrangements. She moved with the dullness of a sleepwalker through a host of detailed work, discussing an obituary notice with a cub reporter from the *Herald,* who used the word *homemaker* anyway, and talking with a new young priest about a simple ceremony to be performed at the gravesite.

It was early in the afternoon when the mourners began their slow march up the hill, following a team of pallbearers led by Roger Torelli, who had nicked himself while shaving and wore a faded blazer with dull gold buttons. The older men and women were perspiring heavily in the spring heat, audibly chastising themselves for forgetting to bring their hats. One sound in particular stood out for Anna, a locomotive chuffing that Jack Farrell produced as he wrestled with his paunch against gravity, grunting with each thudding step. He was dressed appropriately in black, but not everyone in the funeral party had been able to honor that tradition. Arthur Atwater had on a ravelly Harris tweed sportcoat, dark brown and missing an elbow patch, while Fred Vescio was dressed in a pinstriped suit of blue serge that must have dated from the 1930s and made him look like a gunsel for the Capone mob. Wade Saunders, a newly signed CV contract in his pocket, could have been on his way to a rodeo in his bolo tie and fringed suede jacket with a Rotary Club pin fixed to his lapel.

Anna, in a simple black shift, walked with her father, an arm linked loosely through his. She shortened her stride to accommodate his limp and heard him swear every time he stumbled. The anguish on his face was too distressing for her to absorb. She was washed out herself, sunk in a sorrow deeper than any she had ever known. She had wept in church and was teary-eyed again, her heart on the point of breaking whenever she imagined the whittled-down old woman in the closed casket. She had no use for formal religion, but she was still affected by the dark and bloody symbols that had frightened her as a child—the nails in the flesh, the crown of thorns, the terrible dripping wounds on Christ's body. It hurt her, too, that the weather should be so perfect, sunny and cloudless, precisely the sort of day when her mother would roll up her sleeves and start digging in the garden, planting annuals in beds and using a pitchfork to turn over the soil for vegetables.

The young priest kept his remarks brief and unfancy, as Anna had requested. He spoke of things about which he had no firsthand knowledge, but at least he did it convincingly, commenting favorably on the Torellis' long marriage and their importance to the community. He seemed resigned rather than saddened, as though he had already dealt with many deaths in his brief service in the clergy and understood that he would have to deal with many more before he confronted his own. Yet at the same time he looked so clean and fresh-faced, just out of the seminary, that Anna, still weeping, believed that he had no real experience of suffering. She felt inducted into mysteries he couldn't possibly fathom, and her shoulders heaved desperately when her father, his teeth gritted, approached the grave and tossed in a handful of dirt.

Her turn came next. Emotions cycled through her—rage, emptiness, and a sense of incalcuable loss, above all else. She saw how badly she had underestimated the power of grief, saw how it could command the entire stage of a person's existence, crippling a bereft spouse or a stricken parent. What was it that Atwater had said about getting over things? *Some do and some don't.* Her own innocence, a quantity she had assumed to be nearly exhausted, was in fact apparently bottomless. Anna was learning so quickly there in the cemetery under the treacherous sun that she became a little unmoored and almost fell as she started downhill. Betty Chambers came to her rescue and took her by the elbow, offering condolences, and together they trudged past a stony mausoleum atop which a cherub stood guard over the privileged remains of Angelo D'Annunzio, 1883–1969, who had sired eleven children and was beloved by them all, according to the chiseled inscription.

The Torellis had not hired a limousine. That would have been too showy and expensive for the old man. He had driven his truck to the church instead, so Anna rode with him back to the house on Quail Court, while Roger trailed them in the Taurus. A number of close family friends dropped in soon afterward with food for a buffet, cakes and cookies and pies, fried chicken and bread fresh from the oven, pots of soup and stew, an age-old valley custom still commemorated. Anna served coffee distractedly, pestered by Jack Farrell, who seemed to have romance on his mind, oblivious of his impropriety. She put out some wine and beer and a bottle of brandy, as well. Nobody was comfortable at first. The guests huddled in knots, as if they needed protection, and chatted about blameless subjects in hushed voices. They were like children who were trying to be good, Anna thought. They were afraid to make any noise or cause any disturbance, being overly reverential, still intimidated by the nearness of death and unwilling to insult it, not yet returned to their human selves.

It was Charlie Grimes who finally broke the unnatural quiet. "Here's to a helluva woman," he blurted out, raising his brandy glass with one hand and swiping at his eyes with the other. "She's up there with the angels now."

"Amen to that," said Pepper Harris, and there was some scattered applause.

The positive reception encouraged Grimes to say more. "She was a wonderful gal to be with," he continued, after fortifying himself with a big swig from his glass. "One time, we all took a vacation trip to Reno, and we just had the best time ever. Claire even won a five-hundred-dollar jackpot on the slots."

"They took her picture with the manager of Harrah's," Fred Vescio boasted. "Then they threw in a free steak dinner for us all. We never had it so good. Isn't that right, Victor?"

Torelli offered a melancholy smile. "That's right."

"Did you win that suit up there, too, Fred?" Farrell asked.

Vescio plucked defensively at his pinstripes. He'd been paid a brutal abuse. "Don't you dare make fun of my outfit," he warned. "This is the very suit I got married in."

The story about Reno opened up the floodgates of memory. In turn, Claire was celebrated for her kindness and generosity, her compassion, her hybrid tea roses, and—by Grimes again—her ability to live with Victor for so many years without going over the wall. When there was nothing left to relate, when every anecdote had been shared and every bit of praise doled out, the guests filtered into the twilight, singly and in pairs. Anna experienced their absence as an echoing void. She began collecting the dirty plates and cups and stacking them in the kitchen, glad to be doing something again and recapturing a sense of purpose that had deserted her during her mother's final days. Her father observed and advised her from the kitchen table, pouring himself liberal doses of wine, while Roger sat on the living room couch and watched a cop show on TV. The ancient family dynamic was locking into place, Anna realized with chagrin. Nothing would ever be addressed, nothing would be confronted directly. Nothing would be settled.

"Well, she had a good life," the old man said morosely. "Up to the end of it, anyway."

"Yes, she did," Roger agreed.

"She was a wonderful woman. One in a million."

Anna felt sympathetic toward her father, but she knew also that he would descend into sloppy pools of self-pity if she gave him half a chance, so she joined him at the table with a pad and pencil. Her need to break the stalemate was so strong that it affected her like a rush of adrenaline. "We have to get ourselves organized," she said urgently, brushing the hair from her face. "I'm going to make a list of things to do. What about Mother's clothes? Do you care where they go?"

"Donate them to the Salvation Army or somebody," her father growled, throwing a hand in the air. "I don't give a good goddam either way. Her jewelry's all yours. Roger'll just have to wait."

"For what?" Roger wondered, turning his head to look.

Torelli pulled out his grandfather's pocket watch, sterling silver and bearing the insignia of a famous jeweler on the Ponte Vecchio in Florence, and let it swing by its chain. "For this," he said smugly.

"I can wait."

"Then you're in luck. Because I'm not planning to die any time soon."

"Nobody wants you to die, Pop."

"That's good. Because I'm not going to."

"I'll start getting things ready for you out at the farm tomorrow," Anna interrupted, again with undue haste. Her mind was churning. "It shouldn't take me more than a week."

"You can save yourself the trouble, Anna. I'm not going back out there," the old man told her.

"Sure you are. You're just too tired to think about it right now."

"Don't you be telling me how I feel! I've had it with that goddam valley. Can't you see that it's got nothing to offer me anymore? I'll stay where I am." He banged the tabletop with a fist. "In town."

Anna tried to reason with him. "But you can't just let that lovely old house rot and fall apart, can you?"

The old man glared at her. His eyes were cold. "I can do whatever the hell I please."

"Well, I won't let you!" She was on the verge of losing her temper. "It's just plain stupid. The house, the vineyard, you're letting everything slide. I won't stand for it! You're not the only one involved here."

"But I'm the one who makes the decisions."

"Not anymore. You're wrong about that. We're all in this together now. Aren't we, Roger?"

"I don't know," Roger said, still staring at the TV.

"Of course you know!" Anna shouted at him. "Jesus, you're a wimp! Why can't you ever take a position?"

"It isn't up to me."

"You're such a fucking coward, Roger." Anna was whipped into a frenzy, on the attack, and though she hated herself for it, she couldn't stop. "You'll own that farm someday! Give me a little support here, will you?"

"We'll discuss this in the morning," the old man said.

"No, we won't," Anna told him. "You'll ignore me. That's what you always do. You'll pretend that it never happened!"

Her father smashed down his glass in a fury, and it shattered into fragments and bloodied his index finger. "I've heard enough of this bullshit for one night," he shouted, spitting out the words. "No more of it now! Have some respect for your mother's memory."

"I'll get you a Band-Aid."

He was staunching the cut with a paper napkin. "I don't need anything from you, Anna! I can take care of myself." Down the hallway he rolled, heading off to bed as wobbly as a sailor on a storm-tossed deck, his hands braced against the hallway walls to keep himself from collapsing.

Anna's cheeks were hot. She looked at herself in an ornate mirror over the fireplace and saw a mad flame burning in her eyes. *Oh, Anna, you lost it there, you were out of control!* How badly she had underestimated the power of grief! She sat for a time in the vacant kitchen and talked herself down. She was a capable person and would eventually figure out a way to resolve the situation to everyone's advantage. That's what she told herself, and slowly her anger subsided. The anger was about so many things—not only the disposition of the house but also about her mother's pain and the various injustices that would be shoved down her own throat as long as she was alive—but it still had no chance against sorrow. Sorrow would always outlast anger, Anna thought. Sorrow was eternal.

After she had cleaned up the broken glass, she went searching for her brother to apologize for her outburst and found him in the back-yard. The evening was mild, and he was stargazing and smoking a joint. He extended a languorous arm.

"Want some?" he asked.

"Yes, I want some. I haven't smoked dope in years." Anna pulled a lawn chair next to his, pried the joint from his fingers, and took a deep drag. "This is potent stuff," she said, coughing through the smoke.

"Mendocino homegrown." Roger had another hit himself. "Guaranteed to cure what ails you."

"It's the farmer in you, Roger."

"I don't doubt it."

Anna slunk down and let her head rest against the chairback. The marijuana relaxed her, and she observed her brother as if from a great distance. Roger couldn't be other than he was, and she knew better than to fight it. "I'm sorry I yelled at you," she said. "I just lost control."

"No, you were right, Anna. I was laying low. I didn't want to get into it with him."

"How're you feeling?"

"Pretty lousy," he told her. "It really upset me to watch her die like that, wasting away. And then to have to listen to that priest go on and on. What an asshole! I swear, I'll never set foot inside a church again."

"You better be careful, Roger. Those priests have big ears. You're going to burn in hell."

"I'd just as soon. Try carrying a coffin sometime, too."

"Was it heavy?"

"No, but I got real paranoid." He shivered. "I was sure I'd drop the damn thing. I kept having visions of it tumbling downhill to the river and making a huge splash."

"You would have hit the front page of the *Herald*."

"That's all I need." Roger gave a sarcastic laugh. "Hey, who was that fat guy chasing you around?"

"Jack Farrell," Anna said curtly. "He's with the Chamber of Commerce. Would you like one of his cards? I have about a dozen of them. He had the nerve to ask me for a date."

"In the middle of a wake?"

"Indeed. He doesn't give up easily, either."

"Did you accept?"

"I might have, just to get rid of him," she said. "I'm unclear on the point. It's some sort of new low for me."

"Maybe it'll be a love connection."

"Stop it, Roger. You can be quite an asshole yourself, you know?"

Anna passed him the joint. "But what about Dad? Is he serious about staying in town?"

"I believe he is. He's told me the same thing before. He has about six months left on his lease. Maybe he just wants to get his money's worth."

"He'd be awfully lonely out there on his own, I guess. I get lonely out there myself," Anna said. "You think he'll manage?"

"He should. He's a tough old bastard. He still eats nails for breakfast." Roger sucked in more smoke. "When are you going back to New York?"

She thought about it. "I haven't decided for certain yet. I do want to get the house in decent shape and learn something about the business before I go. It is all going to land in our laps someday, whether or not you're ready."

"I wish I cared about it, Anna," he said. "But I don't. You can buy me out anytime."

"Some things never change." She reached out to ruffle his hair. "You look about sixteen, Roger. Honestly, you do."

"That's part of my plan. I'm traveling backward in time. Mentally I'm about twelve." He made as if to get up from his chair, but then he sank back into it. "Did I tell you Shelley and I might go to Japan if we can save up the money?"

"Is she the girl you've been seeing?"

"Woman, Anna. Shelley is a woman. She's almost thirty."

"Are you going to marry her?"

Roger seemed alarmed. "Why would I do a thing like that?"

"A fair enough question," Anna told him. "I should have asked myself the same thing years ago. I doubt that I'll ever get married again. I may never even fall in love."

"You believe you can control it?"

"To some extent, yes."

"What do you do for sex these days?"

She felt herself blushing. "I'm not going to talk with you about that, Roger. I mean, really! You're my brother. It's personal."

"I was just curious," Roger said slyly.

Anna didn't return to the farm that night. She was still too unsettled to be out there by herself. She couldn't bring herself to sleep in her mother's bedroom, though, and neither could Roger, so he gave her the couch and slept in a sleeping bag on the floor. They were camped like that when the old man woke them in the morning, grumbling and hacking as he peed thunderously in the hallway bathroom. Roger had to leave right after breakfast. His job awaited him at home in Mendocino, but he was reluctant to go and dragged out his goodbyes. He looked broken in spirit, Anna thought, and would probably be crying the minute he was around the corner. But Roger was fortunate in that his feelings cycled through him quickly. He did not dwell on them the way she did.

Her own day stretched out lazily before her. She sat reading the paper over coffee, uncertain about what to do next, dawdling over the comics until her father startled her by inviting her to his office. They had some things to discuss, he said, and Anna almost keeled over. He was very formal and solicitous and seated her in a chair across from him as he might have seated a prospective client in the enlightened epoch when clients actually came to call and even asked her permission before he lit his cigar. There he is at last, she thought in amusement, the father I always wanted.

"What do you know about Consolidated Vintners?" he began.

"Not a whole lot. I know they're a big corporation. My liquor store in Manhattan carries their jug wines."

He explained to her how CV operated, showed her a copy of his contract, and told her why he had signed it. She listened to him without interrupting, and he appeared to be pleased when she agreed with him that it was a good idea, especially in light of his current aversion to growing wine grapes.

"Aversion, hell," the old man groused. "I hate those sons of bitches."

"I'm going to try and learn something about the business in the next few days," Anna told him. "Roger doesn't seem to have much interest."

He gave her a funny look. "It might take you a bit longer than that," he said. He opened drawers and filing cabinets and loaded her up with pamphlets from the University of California's division of agricultural sciences. The pamphlets covered everything from proper pruning techniques to wine grape varieties and their potential yield. The stack was a foot high.

She was impressed by the volume of material. "Did you read all this?"

"Once upon a time."

Anna proceeded to throw herself into a flurry of activity. She was hungry for life, bursting with freshened appetites, and gifted with a new awareness of her own mortality. Her senses all felt sharpened, honed to a fine edge. It was as if she were waking to her true self again as the blur of her gray mourning days began to pass. The sorrow still struck her out of nowhere at times and stopped her in her tracks, but it did not go on relentlessly. It didn't paralyze her. She had expected the job of parceling out her mother's belongings to be traumatic, but instead the fading scent of powders and perfumes that rose from the garments as she packed them away evoked a string of tender memories. She was at peace with her mother, it seemed. There were no issues to be resolved between them, only love unalloyed. She saw that her soul's great turmoil would come with her father's death. They were alike in so many ways that it was bound to affect her like a wounding.

Full spring had captured Carson Valley. Anna luxuriated in its seductive warmth as she shuttled from the farm to town and back again. She found herself dreamily recalling other springs from her adolescence, virginal girlish springs when the sweetness of the air made her nipples tingle on the bus ride to her high school, in weather so heady and frankly sensual that she couldn't concentrate on anything but boys. She would steal glances at their crotches and buns and wish that she could press up against them and sample them as if they were different flavors of ice cream, particularly Eddie Santini, her first love, a lanky pitcher for the baseball team, who walked with her in the meadow one evening and lay down with her in the grass, his tongue in her mouth as he unzipped her jeans and snaked a hand under her panties. She was fifteen at the time and wildly wet and excited and came before she could push him away. Then she touched him, too, and thrilled to hear him moaning, although it also scared her to be enjoying herself so much and to recognize the extent of her womanly powers.

And where was Eddie Santini now? He had been a horrible student, as dumb as a rock. His sole ambition was to own a hardware store someday. Driving back to the farm one afternoon, Anna smiled to think of him in a red Ace apron with the front of his pants jutting out. Eddie was a human hard-on, a lump of mutant erectile tissue with only one thing on his mind. Surely he would be blind to the poppies and lupine in the fields along Carson Valley Road, all the wildflowers flowing in a swelling tide of petals to the base of the hills. The budbreak of grapes would soon follow—the growth cycle was that predictable. Anna had witnessed the juicy eruption up close just once, when a field hand had snuck her into the vineyard and showed her a trickle of clear liquid leaking from a pruning cut. She had touched a finger to the stickiness and rubbed it on her lips. The scales around the tiny buds were puffy and white, and the buds themselves looked fragile and not quite ready to emerge, but she could still feel the rampant energy in them, an aura of what was to come.

As she turned into the farm, she had to hit the brakes to let Arthur Atwater squeeze by her in his Jeep. She had not spoken a word to him in the week or so since the funeral. He was always busy these days, constantly in action from dawn until dusk. She had seen him on his tractor earlier that morning dragging a disc harrow along the rows and plowing under the chopped canes, the last of the mustard, and the weeds and grasses that threatened to suck nutrients from his vines. The intruders that he couldn't reach with his harrow, those in the little spaces between the rootstock, he sprayed with herbicides by hand, wearing a respirator over his nose and mouth and a tank on his back, somewhat Martian in appearance.

"Hello, stranger," Anna called to him affably. He stank of gasoline, and his hair was powdered with dust. "Where you headed?"

"The frost-protection pump needs a new gasket," Atwater told her. "I'm already late getting it into the creek. The water's been too high. If it isn't one thing, it's another."

"A hardworking fellow like you deserves a decent meal," she said, on an impulse. "How about dinner on Friday? We'll talk about wine grapes. Are you free?"

He paused to compute the question. "Free?" he laughed, scratching his head. "Why, yes, I am. I am free."

"Seven o'clock, then. Don't be late."

When Anna had finished getting rid of her mother's things, she started in on the house. It turned into a major campaign because of all the junk that her parents had managed to save over the past half century. She came upon objects whose very existence was barely credible, such as a crocheted item in a kitchen drawer that was either an odd-shaped beret or an artistic potholder. In an upstairs bedroom, there was a wooden rack with holes too small for wine bottles that somebody had stuffed with rolled-up magazines, here a *Sports Afield* from 1969 featuring duck hunting in Wisconsin and there a copy of *Life* with Dwight D. Eisenhower on the cover. To the good, she unearthed a trove of old 78 rpm records from a closet, mostly show tunes and dance music from the big band era, and an antique dealer in town paid cash for them off the books. She split the take with her father, who praised her to the heavens and called her a goddam genius.

There was a pleasant rhythm to the work. Anna felt that she was in gear again after weeks of being stuck. The playing field looked wide open. She had a sense of renewal and self-discovery as she dug up fossils from her teenage years—clothes, record albums, yearbooks, and even a secret journal with a tiny gold key. She had drawn hearts in it and pierced them all with arrows. Could she really have covered five whole pages writing, "Mrs. Eddie Santini, Mrs. Anna Santini, Mrs. Anna Torelli Santini"? Apparently so, judging by the evidence. Her other observations were noted much more succinctly: "Tom H. is cute but stuck-up. He thinks he's so hot just because he has a fast car. Wait till he has an accident." "I got the highest grade on the math exam. Too bad for Jenny di Grazia! It serves her right." Who in the world was Tom H.? Why did she have it in for Jenny di Grazia? The riddles were plentiful, she admitted, but the answers were few.

Another afternoon, tired of washing windows, she treated herself to a cold can of beer and sat cross-legged on the parlor floor to listen to some of her old albums on the ancient family stereo, a blond mahogany Zenith console. The needle, worn to a nubbin, robbed the records of their fire. Blondie, Talking Heads, and The Clash were made to sound historical, an insult to the very spirit of rock 'n' roll. But Anna kicked off her shoes and cranked up the volume anyway, remembering how she had idolized Chrissie Hynde of the Pretenders, coveting the red leather boots, the motorcycle jacket with its hundreds of zippers, and those lace gloves that left Chrissie's fingers free for obvious reasons. She had shopped for the same dramatic eyeliner and had even tried on a pair of tight black leather pants in Santa Rosa— but no, Mrs. Eddie Santini wasn't bold enough to shake her ass for the world! Only at Berkeley did Anna have a brief fling as a babe, turning up at frat parties during her sophomore year in a short, semisee-through knit dress from a thrift shop. It was currently on a hanger in her bedroom and still almost fit, she had been satisfied to learn.

She brought in a janitorial service to complete the clean-up operation. Several silent Laotian men in matching orange shirts and brown trousers scrubbed away the last of the dust and grime and left every room smelling fresh and piney. Anna tore down the heavy drapes after they had gone and banished two tattered wing chairs and a pair of Ethan Allan end tables to the basement. She bought a brightly patterned bedspread imported from Malaysia and used it to cover up the scars and cigarette burns on the couch and later stuffed all the aged throw rugs in a garbage bag and replaced them with cotton dhurries. The improvements were minor and cosmetic, but the house took on an airy cheerfulness that even Arthur Atwater remarked on when he arrived for dinner on Friday evening, promptly at seven, before Anna was really ready for him.

"You've made it so nice in here!" he said, craning his neck to admire her efforts, a tourist in the Sistine chapel. He had on his dancing Levi's, the ones with a crease in them, and his shiny cowboy boots.

She was momentarily gratified, then reminded herself that this was a man who lived in a trailer. "I'm running a little late," she told him, brushing her hands on her thighs, unaccountably nervous. "Excuse me while I change, will you? I won't be a minute."

Upstairs, she took a quick shower and ran a brush through her hair. Her nervousness had tipped her off to the fact—one that might never have arisen consciously—that she was again feeling a physical attraction toward Atwater, as implausible as it seemed. Probably it was just loneliness, she thought, or maybe a simple biological urge for some intimate human contact after the distancing effect of the past few weeks, so she warned herself to be careful. On the other hand, though, she hadn't been to bed with anyone except Sam McNally recently, and that prompted her to do some mental arithmetic and add up all the lovers she'd ever known. The disappointing total was six, most of them during an experimental period immediately after her divorce, when she was determined to compensate for what she believed she'd missed by squandering her youth on Bud Wright. Not much, as it happened.

Anna saw the knit dress where it was hanging, and the matter was decided. She would not play it safe tonight. She slipped into it for fun to see if she could make Atwater's eyes pop. It wasn't a problem.

"Wow," was all he said.

"I'm just fooling around, Arthur." His enthusiastic response made her shy. "I'm pretending to be a teenager again."

"I'd say you're doing a real good job of it."

Anna led him into the kitchen. She had fixed them a supper of roast chicken and mashed potatoes with a salad of mixed greens and a crusty baguette from the French patisserie. She directed Atwater to the table and passed him a wedge of Brie and some crackers. Without any hesitation, he fixed himself a little sandwich and consumed it in two rapid bites, crumbs falling in chunks down his shirt.

"Sorry," he said, looking sheepish. "I skipped lunch today."

"Will it bother you if I open some wine?" She had brought up a bottle of Zinfandel from the basement rack.

"No, it's fine. I'll even have a glass with you. I can drink a little wine when I'm not feeling crazy."

"And you're not feeling crazy now?"

He shook his head. "No, I'm way too busy."

Anna still had trouble reading him. He played it so deadpan and close to the chest that she never knew whether or not he was being serious. "You are a man of many mysteries, Mr. Atwater," she said, toasting him with a clink of her glass. "You must tell me the story of your life sometime."

He surprised her by saying, "Would you like me to do it right now?"

"By all means. What better time than the present?"

Anna leaned forward on her elbows to listen. She would never have taken Atwater for a college graduate, but he swore that he had a degree in English from San Francisco State. He had lived in the Bay Area for a while, he said, and also in Truckee, Big Sur, and Juneau, Alaska. His work experience was extensive, spotty, and entirely uninspiring. He claimed to have been a roustabout, a carpenter, a cabbie, and a plumber. He had no ambition at all, he said, although he confessed with some embarrassment that he had tried to write a novel once. He had done a lot of traveling as a young man, often to escape from one misadventure or another, and had spent a whole summer exploring Canada and later a winter bumming around the U.S. in a beat-up VW van. As he warmed to his tale, he described for her the high points of that journey, like the snowy morning in Boston when he had strolled around for hours on Beacon Hill among the lovely old brick buildings and felt a contentment he could hardly believe.

"You make me so envious." Anna carved the chicken. "All that experience. I haven't been anywhere since college."

Atwater refused to accept any credit. "I was just lost, really. Whatever I was looking for, I never found it. I always came home to the grapes."

"Did your family own a vineyard?"

He laughed. "No, they didn't own much of anything. My father was an auto mechanic who played the horses. I was lucky to have a pair of trousers! It was my grandfather who got me started in the fields when I was fourteen. A friend of his over in Napa hired me to sucker some vines and do all the shit work." He dabbed at his lips with a napkin. "Pardon my language."

"What was your novel about?"

Atwater groaned theatrically. "Do I have to answer that?"

"Oh, yes. Absolutely. That's the deal."

"This is pretty terrible," Atwater said, squirming a bit. "I wrote it when I was down there in Big Sur. Everybody I met was some kind of artist or other, so I figured I might as well be a novelist. Why not? I had a journalism class to my credit." He took a sip of his wine. "I set the thing in Spain. I'd never been there, of course. My hero was a bullfighter."

Anna clapped her hands in delight. "A bullfighter!"

"Yeah, Juan Romero was his name." He was getting his teeth into it now, she could tell. "Born in Seville to impoverished parents. That's the exact first line: 'Juan Romero was born in Seville to impoverished parents.' Juan, he kept getting gored. He just couldn't get out of a bull's way come hell or high water. He got gored in Madrid and

Barcelona and Málaga. I must have gored that poor bastard about twenty times before he finally died, but he never stayed on the floor of the bullring for very long. It was a novel about courage, see?"

"Did you ever submit it to any publishers?"

Atwater looked at her skeptically. "No way. I may be crazy, lady, but I'm not insane. I stood on a cliff and fed it to the ocean, page by page."

After dinner, Anna sat with him in the refurbished parlor. She had made coffee for herself and a pot of tea for him. Atwater seemed touched that she had remembered his preference. He was acting restrained again and all talked out, back on his best behavior. She liked his presence in the house, the simple fact of his company, and she was reminded of the comforting times she had spent with other men, with Bud and Sam when things were going well, those evenings when they had settled together into an enveloping silence and all was right with the world.

"You really did a super job on the house," Atwater said, complimenting her again.

"Thank you, Arthur. I enjoy being here. I feel useful and connected."

"Those are nice feelings to have."

Anna spoke with him about the vineyard. She had been studying the pamphlets her father had given her and asked whether it might be worthwhile to diversify into some of the newer varietals. "Like Mouvedre," she said. "Or Sangiovese or Cabernet Franc. They're in demand, aren't they?"

"It's worth considering," Atwater said. "We've got a block of older Chardonnay down by the river that isn't producing the way it should."

"Would it be difficult to do?"

"Not difficult. But expensive. It can run you up to fifteen thousand to replant an acre. Victor might not go for that."

"Let's look into it, anyway, shall we?"

"You're the boss."

"No, I'm the boss's daughter."

"So you are." Atwater finished his tea and got to his feet. Anna wondered if he would try for a kiss. That was the most she would reward him with for now. "It's time for me to go, but if you come out-side with me, boss's daughter, I'll show you something special."

She didn't hesitate. If this was his romantic ploy, it wasn't bad. "Let me get a sweater."

He walked with her out to the porch and down the steps into the vineyard. The moon was almost full and held them in the light. He touched her arm to stop her in the middle of a row and motioned for her to be quiet. But that was all he did. "Can you hear it?" he asked her. "That little rustle? It's the sound the vines make when they're growing."

"Oh, please!" Anna couldn't contain herself. "I'm not that naive! Charlie Grimes used to pull that on me when I was a kid. It turned out he was just rubbing his fingertips together."

"No, no, it's true," Atwater insisted. "Listen, will you?"

Why didn't he come any closer to her? "I *am* listening. I hear frogs. That's what I hear, Arthur. A bunch of frogs."

"There's another sound underneath them. Really listen, Anna."

"You better not be joking."

"I'm not."

Once more Anna listened, a hand cocked to her ear. She was aware that Atwater had not moved toward her, aware of his breathing and the steady pulsing of her heart, and she heard it then at last, a barely perceptible rustle of the grapevines as they grew.

6

It would be well into March before a bud showed itself on the Torelli farm, in a block of Chardonnay planted to riverside ground. Atwater found it while touring the vineyard in his Jeep and searching for just such signs of life. He bent to examine the little knot of tissue and nudged it with a finger, glad for its appearance but also numbed by the thought of how much work lay ahead of him over the next few weeks. Soon buds would be popping everywhere like firecrackers, and they would require his constant attention and protection. He passed the day on his tractor discing between the rows and almost fell asleep at the throttle during the afternoon, veering ever so slightly off course before the screeching cry of a red-tailed hawk woke him. He could have used a nap, but he was out of luck. There would be no rest for him now, not with the great cycle of growth underway. He would spin with the sap. He was its prisoner.

Trudging home at twilight, he sat on his ruined, bat-haunted deck to update his log.

TUESDAY, MARCH 17TH. Budbreak, riverside Chardonnay. 62 degrees at noon, everyone can feel the push coming on. Talked to D. Rhodes in town today. His hilly ground all dried out and Zinfandel breaking. Ours next. *Must* get the pump into the creek in the morning. A frost would be a killer.

He limped going inside, having stepped in a gopher hole and turned an ankle. Rosie, his dearest dog, licked his hand when he came through the door, while Prince snorted and ignored him. The puppy merely dozed. Atwater sat for a time before dinner pondering the intricacies of the CV contract that Victor Torelli had recently sent him. It was a document dense with language and numbers, scientific as all get out and specific in a way that grated against his own style of vineyard management. He hated science, really, and he also hated math and had flunked both chemistry and geometry with aplomb. Measure this, measure that—it struck him as such rudimentary bullshit. He preferred to rely on observation, intuition, mojo magic, and the techniques he had acquired not in high school but in the School of Hard Knocks, so he was distressed that the contract spelled out everything in such petty detail. The vision at its core bothered him, too, with its suggestion that every variable involved in the risky craft of growing wine grapes could be controlled. Yet for the old man's sake, he had promised not to stage a revolution. He would cooperate and do his best.

He ate and read and slept. Dawn woke him before he knew it. His bedroom was alive with birdsong, goofy mating tunes being crooned in a tangle of branches against a vibrant blue sky. He plucked his jeans and socks from the carpet, put on a ratty wool sweater, got an aromatic whiff of himself, and vowed to take a shower that evening, regardless of how tired he might be. He opened a package of glazed doughnuts and ate two for breakfast, then wrapped another pair in a paper napkin and stuffed them into his jacket pocket as a snack for later. He added a small box of raisins, gazed at the comely Sun Maid, and was distressed to find her so fetching. Before leaving, he dialed the National Weather Service in Santa Rosa to get the forecast. It would be mild again, the taped recording said, with temperatures in the high fifties and showers developing in the early afternoon. The chance of a freeze was only 30 percent, but a clearing trend would follow. That was not good news. If the sky was clear on a cool and windless day in spring, a farmer could be fairly certain of a frost.

Atwater gimped his way over to the barn, favoring his puffy ankle. The barn served not only as a machine shop and a storage space but also as a reliquary for the pack rat Victor Torelli, who was as acquisitive and tenacious as any other hoarder in the valley. Rusted harrows, cultivators missing teeth, a dented canoe, pitchforks with bent tines, they were all accorded a place of honor in the old man's grand design. His collection was a tribute to wrongheaded preparedness. He had refrigerator coils for a Kelvinator, spark plugs for a Kaiser Vagabond, and a ream of carbon paper. He had saved beer cans from defunct breweries, a few buffalo nickels in a glass jar, and the skulls of several small mammals, all unidentifiable to Atwater. There were honest trophies, too, racks of antlers and photos of giant steelhead and, most striking, the stuffed head of a marauding wild pig that Torelli had shot in 1953, his feat celebrated in a yellowed press clipping that was still on display, tacked up next to a mottled toilet seat that bore the caption "Italian Life Preserver."

The frost-protection pump was on an elevated wooden platform in a corner. It was a fairly expensive Berkeley model about fourteen years old that ran on diesel fuel through three-minute cycles. The pump showered the vineyard with water during a frost, creating an artificial rain that raised the ambient air temperature and prevented the delicate cells inside the vines from dying. Thermometers mounted at strategic points on the farm triggered an alarm whenever the mercury fell to 34 degrees, and Atwater would hear it buzzing in his trailer and have to drag himself from bed to switch on the system. He regarded the pump as his nemesis and not only because it would cost him some sleep. It was just too worn out to be dependable. He had lobbied for a new pump—he could have used two or three of them, really—but Torelli, trained by his stingy forebears, believed that any skilled vineyard manager ought to be able to hold his equipment together with chewing gum and baling wire. The Berkeley only ran for ten or fifteen hours each growing season, so it ought to last forever, according to the old man.

While Atwater was checking over the pump a final time, oiling it and testing the couplings, he glanced up and saw Antonio Lopez loitering by the barn door. Something was wrong, he could tell right away. There are men for whom work is as essential as blood, and Lopez was among them. Antonio was never desultory and always ready to get his hands dirty—tough, skilled, and dogged. He simply never quit. Today, though, he looked preoccupied and out of sorts.

His robust face was pale, and his ordinarily buoyant spirits were nowhere in evidence.

"'Morning, Antonio," Atwater greeted him. "How's it going?"

"I started the crew hoeing," Lopez replied dully. "You didn't get all the weeds, man."

"Nobody gets all the weeds, my friend. The weeds always win." He offered a sympathetic smile. "Sit down, why don't you? Take a load off your feet and relax. How's life been treating you?"

Lopez grabbed an old milk crate from Carson Valley Dairy, a long-gone enterprise, pulled it close to Atwater, flopped it over, and sat. "I don't know, Arthur," he said, sounding fatigued. "I think I got some problems at home. You still worried about that pump?"

"You want to know the truth?"

"Sure."

"I'd like to drop this pump off a bridge somewhere."

"That's not a good solution."

"Tell me about it."

"My stomach hurts," Lopez complained. He lifted his shirt and indicated a spot above his navel. "You ever have a pain right here?"

"It's all those beans you've been eating," Atwater told him, venturing a joke.

"It's not any beans, man. Elena, she gave me this pain. It's from stress. She wants to quit her job and only be a mother."

"When did she say that?"

Lopez was downcast, invested in his perceived abuses. "Last night. And on Saturday. And on Thursday." He spoke with anger. "You can name any day, Arthur, and she said it then. She doesn't understand anything about money. She thinks it's just laying on the ground for me to find."

"Women have their moods," Atwater advised him, edging toward a topic he could not in good conscience claim to have mastered. "I went with a girl once who cut me off for a whole month because I said her cat was ugly."

"Was it?"

"Let me put it to you this way, Antonio. If you were driving down the street and you saw that cat, you'd go out of your way to run it over."

Lopez wrung his hands. "Sometimes I want to run over Elena."

"You're taking it too hard, amigo. Give her some space. Leave her alone for a while. Don't be messing around in her kitchen. It'll probably blow over."

"You ever met a woman, once she has her mind set on a thing, it goes away?"

"Nope."

"At least you're honest." Lopez slumped forward on the crate, his elbows on his knees. He was sullen, brooding. "It's a good thing for her that I can control myself. Some guys, they wouldn't put up with her shit."

"Well, you don't want to resort to violence." Atwater gave him a severe look. "That's for the monkeys."

"I'm not a monkey, Arthur. I never hit a woman in my life. I never hit anybody at all unless he hit me first."

"That's the noble way."

Lopez grinned self-consciously. "I stabbed a guy once, though."

"Did he stab you first?"

"No." Lopez fingered the scar on his throat. "That was another guy."

"How about a day off?" Atwater asked with a burst of enthusiasm, seized by his own brilliant stroke. "We're going to be real busy around here pretty quick, and you won't be worth a damn to me if you're sick. Why don't you go home and take it easy? Do some recuperating."

"It could be a good idea," Lopez said haltingly.

"Sure, it is. Go on home, sleep a little, and have yourself a bath. Tonight you'll be nice and fresh. You and Elena can have a talk."

"What's left to talk about?"

"Soften her up a bit, Antonio," Atwater coached him. "Ask her to a movie. Buy her some flowers or some candy. Surprise her with some fancy underpants. There are a million things you can do to cheer her up."

"Why should I buy her anything? She's the one causing all the trouble. She doesn't even appreciate me. She takes me for granted."

"Try it, anyway. She'll fall for it, I swear! They all fall for that stuff." Atwater wiped some oil from the pump with a rag. "It beats the hell out of me, but they fall for it."

"God must have made them that way to torture us," Lopez said, standing up and smoothing out his jeans. "They're not stable like we are, Arthur. Everything pulls on them. You ever go to bed with a woman on a full moon night?"

"Not that I can recall."

"If you did, you'd remember. The moon, the stars, the sun, the waves, the comets. Everything in the world pulls on them."

"Go on and get out of here," Atwater ordered him with mock authority. *"Vaya con Dios!"*

He tackled the pump again after Lopez had departed and put it through a close-order drill, inspecting the filters, the screen, and the foot valves. He removed the nozzles and cleaned them thoroughly, mumbling to himself, *Ah, women!* It occurred to him that he hadn't gotten laid for a while now, not since his wild flight to Redding, and that made him think fondly of his student nurse. She was wholesome, disease-free, barely legal, and exceptionally horny, but all he could recollect of her was the butterfly tattooed just above her pubic hair. Such one-night stands—two nights, in this case—were a rarity for him at present, except when he was whacked out and on a tear. The times mitigated against such risks, of course, but it was actually his wife who had spoiled him for the casual affairs that he used to favor, showing him how love could fan the flames of passion and take it to a higher level. He needed to feel a deeper attraction these days, a special spark, some electricity in the mix. That he felt it for the boss's daughter was a bothersome sign.

Atwater had not yet worked up the nerve to make a play for Anna, regardless of his desire. The moment just never seemed right. Often she came to him in the fields with her questions, bright and amiable, and he would ignore her legs and her ass and adopt the icy veneer of a viticultural scholar for whom any pastime as base and squalid as sex was beneath contempt. He told himself he was too old for her, which was false, and that she was too smart for him, which was doubtlessly true. Besides, if he started flirting with her, he had nothing to gain from it but a sticky and potentially destructive situation. And she hadn't encouraged him either, had she? She had not invited him to dinner again in spite of the superb bit he'd pulled about the sound of grapes growing, a stunt that had worked beautifully for him with other women. The sad truth, he thought, was that Anna was indeed way above him. She could do far, far better than to take up with a guy who had failed chemistry and geometry, and yet at certain times, when the light was right, he had a hunch that she liked him. He saw it in her eyes, a little glow. Probably he could fuck her if he really tried.

Quit it, Atwater! But people knew these things, didn't they? There were no secrets in the end. It was a similarly subtle recognition that had led him to his wife—a seductive way she had of inclining her head to demonstrate her interest in him. He still thought of her with great affection at times, although all he had of her now was an address and a phone number in Seattle, where she had moved. Laura was a pretty, intelligent brunette as uncomplicated as any woman he had ever known, and Atwater was convinced that she had loved him much more fervently than he had deserved. He couldn't say exactly what had gone wrong for him, or why after their six years together he began to stay out late and tell her lies of a sort he'd never told before, except that it seemed to him in retrospect a purely biological uprising he could not have willed himself to avoid. He was, for reasons he could never articulate very well to Laura, all at once bored and unhappy, gone haywire, and he had blown apart the marriage with a dumb and toxic affair conducted in full public view as an irreparable insult. His regret was still profound.

When Atwater had finished tuning up the pump, he retreated to his trailer and grabbed the insulated rubber chest waders he wore while fishing for steelhead. He knotted together the laces of his cleat-soled wading shoes and tossed them around his neck. In the barn, he uncoupled the disc harrow from the tractor and rigged it for transporting the Berkeley to the creek on a little sled. The trip took about fifteen minutes as he inched forward at two or three miles an hour. He stopped on the bank by a grove of willows and saw to his annoyance that the creek had risen during the night, surely from a storm to the north, where the rainfall was always much heavier. He would need help in placing the pump and wished that he hadn't sent Lopez home, but he could not postpone the job any longer. *Thirty percent chance of a freeze.* The weather could really bust a grower's nuts at this fickle time of year.

His crew was weeding nearby, four men clinking their hoes against pebbles, stones, and the midden of shells that birds left behind when

they cracked open black walnuts against the metal grapestakes. Atwater sized up the men. The biggest was Ernesto Morales, who had
arms that were thickly muscled from a lifetime of manual labor and a
broad peasant's chest.

"Morales!" he shouted.

Ernesto Morales leaned his hoe against a stake. He did it slowly.
He did everything like that, slowly and with infinite attention to the
task of not overextending himself. He was the most lugubrious fellow
Atwater had ever worked with, greasy haired and shifty eyed, acceptable only because of his bond with Antonio.

"You will help me with the pump." Atwater knew that Morales's
English was limited and enunciated each word carefully. "Okay?"

"Okay."

They walked together to the tractor, Morales staying a diligent
stride or two behind. Atwater felt the horrendous weight of the man,
his absolute gravity, and attempted to lighten him up. "*Qué paisaje—tan
bonito*, eh?" he said, in praise of the landscape. "*La granja, los campos, los
pájaros.*" The farm, the fields, the birds.

"*Preferesco el mar.*"

That figured, Atwater thought. Of course, Morales would prefer
the ocean. Morales would be nothing if not contrary. "So you like to
swim?" he asked, doing a breaststroke in the air.

Morales shook his head. "No, *señor.*" His eyes were focused on the
ground, burrowing into it and worming toward the center of the
earth.

"Ah!" Atwater exclaimed, as if he'd solved a puzzle. "*Pescador!*"

"*No.*" Morales did not fish.

Atwater gave up. He could do nothing with anyone so lacking in
basic bonhomie. When they reached the creek, he stood by the willows and studied the flow. The water was a milky green color, silty
and fairly opaque. There were many such creeks in the valley, seasonal streams that roared all through the winter and carried off acres
of soil only to be dead dry by June, parched and coated over with a
brownish white crust of scum. The riparian rights to Wappo Creek
had belonged to the Torelli family for nearly a century. They had
shored up its banks by dumping in riprap and bulldozing some grape
brush on top of it, creating a mass of rock, chunks of cement, and in-

terlocked canes that gripped the porous earth and held it reasonably fast, but they still lost a little more soil every year, their property vanishing bit by bit, flowing into the river and on into the ocean—a lesson, Atwater thought, in what men could and could not hold onto.

"You wait here," he instructed Morales, as he climbed onto the tractor seat. A wide path ran through the willows at a tolerable grade to a flat landing where the Berkeley would sit, and he negotiated it with extreme caution, crawling forward with the pump behind him and idly wondering why it should be his lot to endure such trials. Other growers had cranes to set their pumps, they had guy wires and cables. Unlike Arthur Atwater, they were fully equipped professionals. Still, he persevered. He would have liked the ground to be less wet, but the huge corrugated wheels of the tractor dug in and held. When he got to the landing, he gestured for his assistant to follow him. Morales braced himself against tree trunks as he descended, a look of extreme apprehension on his face. They used wrenches to uncouple the pump from the rig and edged it to the chosen site above the swirling green stream.

Atwater started the tractor again and drove it back up the path. He shut off the engine, stepped into his waders, and cinched an old leather belt tightly around his waist. The belt was his insurance against a fall. It would keep his waders from filling up with water and becoming an anchor that might drown him. He took off his rubber boots and put on his wading shoes. "Now comes the tricky part," he said. "*Listo,* Ernesto?"

"I am ready."

He gave Morales a rope and asked him to grip one end tightly. The other end he tossed down toward the pump site. "Don't let go of that. I might need something to grab onto if I slip. *Por las manos,* okay? *Comprende?*"

"I understand."

Two suction pipes were on the bank, each about a foot in diameter, flexible and not too heavy. Atwater's plan was to sink the first pipe into the creek, then attach the second to the pump and couple them both.

He began his downhill journey with relative ease, his cleats providing traction as he dragged a pipe behind him. He got to the landing without incident and bent to retrieve the rope he'd tossed there, threading it between his belt and his waders. The ground below him was steeper and muddier. His shoes sank into the muck as he walked, one cautious step at a time. He had the pipe in front of him now and let the tip sink in a little, leaning into it for balance. The creek rang in his ears, an ominous noise, and he was briefly overwhelmed and felt his legs shaking, but he controlled himself and continued down to the water. His pulse was racing despite his intention to be calm.

He pushed the pipe into the stream. It hit bottom, but it wouldn't stay put. The current was much too strong. Atwater pushed harder, hoping to make it stick in the sandy bottom, but his effort was fruitless. He was forced to admit to himself that he had gone about the job wrong. He would have to reverse the order of things and fit a pipe to the pump first, so he began retracing his steps up the muddy rise. He hauled the pipe along behind him, but it was wet, and it slipped from his hand and splashed into the creek. He scrambled after it as fast as he could and caught it before it was swept away, but the racket of his pursuit spooked a pair of wood ducks from their hideout beneath some trailing cottonwood branches. The ducks honked sharply in alarm and took furiously to the wing, flapping over Atwater's head, surprising him, and causing him to lose his balance.

He grabbed for the rope at his waist as he fell, but there was no tension on it, none at all. Then he was rolling down into the creek and watching the entire length of rope tumble after him in slack coils. He saw through spatters of mud Ernesto Morales on the bank above him frantically trying to repossess the end that he had so carelessly released. Atwater crashed into the stream and felt the shock of cold water drench his sweater. The water trickled past the barrier of his belt, spilled into his jeans, and washed over his privates. His balls shriveled up on contact, and the creek turned him over twice before he fought his way to his feet. Miraculously, the pipe had lodged against some grape brush, so he sloshed over to get it, only to fall once more and crack his bad ankle on a boulder.

With the pipe rescued, he sat down where he was and ordered himself to take it easy. The danger was over. Soon he heard the crunch of twigs and leaves behind him. Morales stood on the bank as wordlessly as ever, incapable of formulating even a simple apology.

"Ernesto," Atwater said quietly, without looking at the man, "I asked you to hold the rope."

"I did," Morales told him.

"No, you did not. You didn't hold it at all."

"It escaped me."

"It escaped you?"

"From my hand. It escaped me."

Atwater didn't have it in him to pursue the interrogation. "Go do some more hoeing, Ernesto. When you're done for the day, you come to my trailer, okay?"

"Okay."

Atwater stared at the creek. From his stable position, the roar of it no longer seemed threatening. He was apart from it now, saved and spared, restored to his proper element, back on dry land. He felt diminished and cowardly. By worrying about falling, he had caused himself to fall. That was how the universe worked, he believed. It was an immutable law.

He left the pipe he'd rescued on the bank, securing it to a bay laurel with the rope, and rode over to his trailer, where he stripped off his soaked clothes and took a long hot shower. He wrapped his ankle, purple with bruises, in an Ace bandage, swallowed three aspirin and a Tylenol, and phoned the weather service again. There were no changes on the tape—chance of a frost, 30 percent. He would tackle the pump placement again tomorrow, this time with Antonio's help. He passed a miserable afternoon hobbling around the barn and mixing herbicides. The showers started at about two as predicted, with clouds in towering gray columns marching across the sky. Atwater welcomed the humidity. It meant that he would live to see the morning.

He was fixing himself a few peanut butter and jelly sandwiches for supper when Morales knocked on his door at about six o'clock that evening.

"Come in, Ernesto," he said wearily. Morales was dispassionate, unmoved, ever silent, his rage buried and probably explosive. "How many days did you work this week?"

"*Dos.*"

"All right." Atwater went to his bedroom and took fifty dollars from the emergency hundred he kept under his mattress. He did not want to bother with writing a check—he just wanted Morales gone from the farm and preferably from the planet. The old man would reimburse him down the line, anyhow. "Here you go. I'm sorry about this. I know you're a friend of Antonio's."

"*El mismo pueblo.*"

"I know, I know. The same village."

Morales stared at the bills in his hand as if they represented some unusual type of currency. He seemed to comprehend that he would never see their like again, and he lifted his head, looked Atwater in the eye, hawked up a lunger, and spat it on the carpet. "*Gracias por nada,*" he said, with a malign grin.

"Ernesto, I don't want to listen to your shit." Atwater fought to contain himself. "You almost got me drowned today. I want you out of here now. Have you got a ride home?"

"Hidalgo. He waits me. I ride with him."

Atwater pulled another ten from his pocket, his own entire supply of petty cash. "Here you go, Ernesto. Maybe you can come back and pick during the harvest. I really am sorry it didn't work out."

"*Por nada,*" Morales said again, slamming the trailer door behind him.

Atwater fed the dogs and ate his supper. Their bowls of chunky Alpo looked better than his sandwiches did, more meaty and substantial. The gradual dying of the light brought him some relief, a satisfaction that this pitiful day was ending. He had known other days just like it and was certain that he would know still others in the future, days when nothing at all went right, when a man felt cursed and blighted and wanted only to sleep. He tried to console himself further by reciting hackneyed proverbs to himself as he cleared the table and washed the dishes: *Tomorrow is another day; Seek and ye shall find; God helps those who help themselves.* He was exhausted and his guard was down, so it pained him severely when he saw a pair of beaming headlights cut through the dark of the farm and watched Jack Farrell bound up the back steps of the big house and pound on the door with his chubby fist until Anna opened it for him and let him in.

7

Antonio Lopez spent his day off moping. He drank some Pepto-Bismol for his stomach, bounced a rubber ball against a wall, said hello to the mailman, helped a neighbor bring down a dead tree with a chain saw, and eventually went into his straggly backyard and began raking such leaves as there were into neat little piles. For this lawn and this house, he and Elena paid nine hundred dollars a month in rent, a fact that caused him to feel both substantial and devastated. He could see the cash that they had given to their landlord over the past two years piled up to form an immense green column soaring into the sky. The column represented more money than anyone in his family had earned in a whole lifetime, a dizzying structure that dwarfed and made insignificant the efforts of those who had labored to build it. He was depressed to think that it would only grow taller.

Lopez had a twenty-dollar bill in his wallet and took it out to examine it. A president named Jackson was pictured on one side with a rippling banner over his head. Jackson had wavy white hair like Victor Torelli and eyebrows as bushy as caterpillars, but his face was very stern. Jackson was obviously a punishing-type man, and Lopez could easily imagine him wearing a badge, riding a motorcycle, and doling out an endless stream of speeding tickets. Counting aloud, he found that the number 20 was printed on the bill eight times. The

White House where Jackson and every other U.S. president lived was depicted on the other side of the bill, a huge palace surrounded by trees and hedges. There were no animals or people anywhere near it. Above the White House it said *In God We Trust,* which was something Lopez had always tried to do, although he had not always succeeded.

He was still deeply troubled about his relationship with Elena. They seemed to be drifting apart and he wondered if he had made a bad mistake by becoming involved with her in the first place. In his supreme ardor, he had ignored the great difference in their back-grounds and the problems that it might present. Elena had been born in Santa Rosa, the child of Mexican-American parents, and her father, Ed Rodriguez, had worked for the post office for many years now. The Rodriguezes were comfortably well-off and owned a nice house in a much better part of town, and Lopez felt increasingly that Elena expected the same from him someday. She had an easy part-time job at Kmart herself, putting in just twenty hours a week, yet her paycheck roughly equaled his own. Without it, they might not be able to afford the rent at all, but Elena still kept harping about how tough her life was, on and on and on.

Lopez returned to the farm on Saturday. He heard from Atwater about Morales's firing and knew that it must have been fated. Then he and Arthur put in a long depleting afternoon wrestling the pump into position. Lopez wished Elena could be there to see what real work was like. The women in Mexico labored as hard as the men did, Antonio remembered, with the same tireless fortitude. They scrubbed floors, ground corn in their *metates,* and cooked laborious *moles,* while simultaneously taking care of their husbands and children. Sometimes they even helped out in the fields, and they were always grateful for the smallest things. In Lopez's opinion, Elena was spoiled rotten. She acted like some kind of princess. He evolved a delicate way to explain this to her on his drive home and was disappointed to find that she had already gone to bed. He ate the plate of fried chicken that she had left out for him and looked in on Dolores, who was curled up in her crib with a menagerie of stuffed animals. It never ceased to amaze him how tiny and fragile she was, how dependent on him for protec-tion. He smiled as he watched a dream shoot through her. Her body wriggled, her eyelids fluttered, she drooled and kicked her feet, and then, all at once, she was calm again. The dream had run its course.

"*Mi hija*," he said tenderly, stroking her little body and contemplating his woes. "*Creo que estamos perdidos, no?*"

Waking early on Sunday morning, rested and relaxed, Lopez felt much better. His bedroom was warmed by a rosy wash of sun, and his mind was unburdened in the moment. He rolled over to be closer to Elena, who lay on her side with her back to him, and pressed his lips to her hair and sucked a few strands of it into his mouth. He turned his head so that his own hair mingled with hers in a glossy pool that he found quite stunning. He put a gentle hand on her hip, then slid it down her thigh and under her nightgown. She was hot to the touch, very soft and moist. When she stirred he moved closer still, but she slapped at him and pushed him away.

He nuzzled her ear. "What's the matter, baby?"

"Leave me alone, Antonio. I want to sleep."

"But you went to bed so early last night." He renewed his exploring. He was committed to it. It was the right thing, the only thing to do.

"Stop it now!" Elena yelled at him. "Don't be touching me there! I mean it."

Lopez got reluctantly out of bed. He was naked and stared down at himself, sighing a loud and pointed sigh. He dressed, grabbed a Coke from the fridge, and sat alone in the toy-cluttered living room. It was just seven o'clock, but he was used to rising at dawn. He turned on the TV and was pleased to find a soccer match from Italy on a cable channel. He didn't understand everything the commentators were saying, but he knew the game well and could judge its progress for himself, having played it all through his childhood on paved streets and unforgiving dirt fields that rewarded any tumble with a bloody nose or a nasty cut, although he had never suffered any injuries himself. He had grown up in a dusty settlement of Guadalajara, in canyon country not far from Barranca de Oblatos, the sixth of seven brothers and sisters, but even as a boy he had been separate from the others, the only one in his family who was blessed with good luck.

Lopez had learned about his luck on the auspicious occasion of his eighth birthday. His grandmother, who doted on him, treated him to a trip into the city for a big festival that was held every October, with bullfights and folk dancing. They rode a crowded bus from the canyons to the *centro* and wandered about in the *plaza de armas* where women in brilliant costumes were throwing flowers to people. He saw couples kissing in doorways and applauding *mariachis,* while drunks reeled about, frightening in their abandon. He ate tacos heaped with salsa and part of a tamale and begged his grandmother to stop on a corner where a fortune-teller had set up shop. The man had a canary in a cage and also a wooden box on which some flames were painted. The box was stuffed with hundreds of cardboard squares. If you paid a peso, the fortune-teller released his canary, and the bird would hop to the box and use its beak to pick up the square on which your future was written.

His grandmother had paid the required peso. Intensely excited, his eyes wide, Antonio looked on as the canary hopped to the box and pecked at the squares. The bird plucked one fortune, seemed to read it, rejected it, and plucked another. The second piece of cardboard had not a stroke of writing on it, only a heart tinted bright red with ink. The fortune-teller held it up for everybody to see. He was a fork-bearded fellow with copious hair sprouting from his ears.

"Ah, corazón!" he cried. He pounded his sternum with a fist and returned Lopez's peso. *"Tiene la suerte."*

In the aftermath of this divination, Lopez came to believe that good luck was truly his. He put his trust in it. It was his faith. His luck had allowed him to be first in his class at school, it had spared him from the pneumonia that carried off one of his brothers, and it had showed him where to hide whenever the older boys of the settlement ganged up on the younger boys and stole from them. Luck had assisted him in crossing the border and had directed him to his cousin in Sonoma County. He would never have met Elena without good luck, and it was his luck that had granted them a glorious child, but in the past few days, starting with the pain in his belly, he had been bothered by the notion that his luck might be perishable, not meant to last.

Lopez escorted his family to mass that morning. When Elena emerged from the bedroom in a simple black skirt and a steel blue blouse, her hair in an elegant braid, she stopped his heart. He knew again what he had known all along, that he would do anything for her and anything to keep her. He loved her that much, more than himself, more than any other creature. In her radiant presence, he felt like a man of honor.

"What are you gawking at?" she asked him, with a smile.

"A beautiful woman."

Elena let him hold her hand as they walked to the car. Their church was on the outskirts of Santa Rosa, but it was nothing like the imposing cathedral Lopez remembered from home. It had no spires or balconies, no pipe organ, no ornate altars. It lacked a vaulted ceiling to scrape against the floor of heaven and didn't have the power to intimidate him. In such an insignificant church, God himself was reduced in size, Antonio thought. He paid scant attention to the priest and instead gazed at the windows of stained glass and pictured himself repatriated to Jalisco, a landowner of substance with his own *ejido* and five—no, six—children divided evenly by sex. In fact, he had not been back to Guadalajara for almost three years and missed it terribly. His last visit had coincided with the Feast of the Immaculate Conception, and he happily recalled how he had attended a raucous party and had impressed his many cousins and friends with elaborate tales of his glamorous new life in Carson Valley, going on around a bonfire until well after midnight.

They had lunch with Elena's parents after church, as they did every Sunday. These occasions were rather formal and stuffy, and Lopez would gladly have skipped them for a meal at Burger King. Ed Rodriguez didn't really like him and had objected strenuously when his daughter first brought him around, screaming at her for dating a lowly farmworker, but Antonio was tenacious and in love and refused to be scared off. He had even gone so far as to buy her a dozen red roses once at a cost of forty dollars—enough money, he had reflected at the time, for a pair of good pruning shears—but the gesture failed to elevate his status. Only with the birth of Dolores, the first Rodriguez grandchild, did Ed make the slightest move toward accepting him.

"She's going to sit by me at lunch!" Ed cried, as he bent down to embrace the infant, who was done up in a cute corduroy outfit. "Come here, Dolores, and give your grandpa a kiss!"

They convened at a table in the dining room. Lopez was alarmed when, within minutes, the subject of Elena's health came up. Her mother was fretting over her, asking why she looked so pale. Had she lost some weight? Wasn't she getting enough rest? Did she take her multivitamins? Should she consult a doctor?

"She's just a little tired is all," Lopez said, butting in on her behalf.

He felt that he was being unfairly accused again, convicted of a crime he hadn't committed.

"I don't blame her," Tina Rodriguez said with emphasis, casting a negative glance his way. "It's hard to care for a baby and hold down a job at the same time. I'd like to see a man try it, Antonio."

"I'm fine," Elena protested to her mother, though her weak voice seemed to imply otherwise. "Really I am. We've had a busy few weeks."

Lopez saw that he had to do something before they ganged up on him completely. "Anyway," he volunteered, "she might be able to quit working in a while. They might be going to promote me out at the vineyard. To be like the assistant manager." He was surprised by his own boldness and creativity.

"Hey, that's great!" Ed clapped him on the shoulder. "Is this your boss Victor you're talking about?"

"Yeah, Victor. It's a big responsibility, but Victor, he thinks I can handle it." He paused to let this sink in, then he hit them with a silver bullet. "He has a lot of confidence in me."

Elena was regarding him with a certain disfavor. "Why didn't you tell me that, Antonio? You're always keeping secrets from me."

He had a bite of turkey and shrugged. "I didn't want to say anything until it was for sure. So you wouldn't get your hopes up in case it doesn't happen right away."

The conversation turned to Dolores and what sort of Easter dress her grandparents were going to buy for her, whether it ought to be pure white or maybe pink to match the pumps they had given her at Christmas. Dolores would stay with them through the afternoon and evening, while Elena worked her shift. On the way to Kmart, she cuddled up to Lopez, pinching at his sleeve in fun and fooling around in his pants, pressing him for more details about his promotion.

"Hey, girl, slow down a minute, will you?" he told her lightly, removing her hand from his unzipped fly. "I didn't say it's *absolutely* for sure. Only *probably* for sure."

She gave him a look of serious scrutiny. "You're not just making it up, are you? Because you do that sometimes, Antonio. You know you do, so don't make faces at me."

"I'm not making any face," he said. He did not want to lie to her, so what he told her next did not seem like a lie. "It's going to happen. The only thing is exactly when."

"You mean it could be next year?" She sounded discouraged. "What are you telling me here?"

"No, not next year. Way before that, probably." He thought about the vineyard and imagined a harvest of record proportions and the generosity that would be obliged to flow from it. He would demand a bonus like Atwater's. That was the obvious answer, the perfect solution.

"Can you ask Victor when it will be? Because then I could do some planning. I have to give my notice at the store and all that."

"Victor, he gets mad if I ask too many questions. But probably it'll be around the harvest."

Elena kissed him sweetly when he dropped her off, and he had a sense of being restored to his proper role as her husband and defender. The afternoon lay before him rich in promise, but he couldn't decide what to do with his freedom. He considered taking in a bargain matinee, but the day was too warm and pretty to be wasted indoors, so he bought himself an ice-cream cone instead and flirted briefly with the blond behind the counter. He drove about town in a mellow mood, glad for the sunshine and for the girls parading around in their shorts to celebrate the fine spring weather. In time, he came to the 7-Eleven where he and Elena had first met. There were a few men hanging around outside it and hoping for piecework, a lawn to mow or a basement to clean out. They were all full-blooded Mexicans, and though some of them were in California legally, others were not. The 7-Eleven was both their social center and a hiring hall.

Lopez knew a couple of the men and stopped to catch up on things, falling effortlessly into their banter. "*Está bien?*" he asked them.

"Nah, it's been real slow today," a rowdy, beer-bellied fellow called Tío told him. "No cars come in here at all except to buy shit."

"Sundays are bad, *hombre.*" Lopez fiddled with the rubber band holding his ponytail. "Families, they're busy going to church and having picnics and like that. God ordered them to take it easy for one day out of seven. It's right in the Bible."

Tío grinned. "You believe in that shit, man?"

"I'm not saying I believe in it. I'm just saying how it is."

"Anyway, the new kid, he's been getting all the breaks," said an idler known as Jorge. "He blew in here from Ensenada just last week, he went out with a roofer right away and got paid fifty dollars."

"*Estupendo!*" Lopez said, whistling. "How many days did he go out?"

"All week long, man. Three hundred dollars he made."

"That's good money. They pay that much? *Es verdad?*"

"*Es verdad,*" Tío replied. "My uncle, he works for a roofer in San Jose. If he gets on regular, he can make thirty thousand a year."

"*Trabajo feo,*" Jorge put in, his mouth wrinkled in disgust. "You fry your ass up on a roof all summer. You sweat like a fucking pig. You get tar in your hair, and it won't come out. Me, I'd rather be poor."

"Like you really have a choice, Georgie," Tío joked.

Lopez walked over to the kid from Ensenada, a squat and curiously symmetrical youth no older than eighteen. He hated the kid on sight. There was an arrogance about him, as if he didn't understand that his success had nothing to do with his talents—fortune was just running in his favor. Lopez asked about the roofer and heard that the story was true.

"*La carta de negocios.*" The kid haughtily showed off a business card with embossed letters. "Coronado Brothers Roofing Company, man. They the best."

"*Es conocido, esta compañía?*"

"*Sí, muy conocido. Tiene, amigo. Un regalito.*" A little gift.

Lopez noticed an abrupt alteration in the atmosphere as he accepted the card, the same intensifying of the elements that precedes an electrical storm. It was as though the wind had kicked up to blow clouds of dust across the parking lot. Somebody dashed by him shouting, "*La migra! Ándale! Ándale!*" and he looked up and saw two INS vans at the curb. Uniformed agents spilled from them, each carrying a nightstick and brandishing it to round up the loiterers and herd them away. The agents poked and prodded, they grabbed the men by their shirt collars and the seat of their pants and shoved them into the vans. They were fast and efficient and followed an arc of brutal energy that did not allow for interrogation.

Lopez was fishing out his green card when an agent confronted him. "I have my papers, sir," he said politely.

"Get in the van." The agent nudged him with a nightstick.

"But I am documented, sir."

"Get in the van now."

"Sir, please, I—"

The agent smacked him in the ribs. "You want more? I'll give you more. Get in the van."

The van held five detainees huddled together on benches in the caged and feral dark. Lopez joined them, angry with the fates and wounded that his rights as a guest of the American government were being violated. He realized to his added dismay that the kid from Ensenada had managed to escape. He saw Tío sitting in the back, and Tío kept grinning his stupid grin and made a gesture as if to say that such arrests were normal, a routine aspect of life in the United States.

"I'm legal here, Tío," Antonio told him hotly. "You want to see my green card?"

"Sure, *amigo*."

"Check it out, man."

Tío took the card and threw it on the soiled floor of the van. "Fuck your documents, Lopez. You're no better than the rest of us."

For three more hours, the agents conducted raids in the poorer neighborhoods of the city until the vans were filled to capacity. Lopez could hear the agents chatting in the front seat. Their voices drifted to him through the steel mesh that separated the prisoners from their captors. He was pressed in so tightly that he couldn't move. Smells were overpowering in the cramped quarters and sickened him a bit— tobacco, sweat, stale beer, farts, and an odor of terror, too, even though the penalty for being an illegal alien was not severe. He wondered what the men had really done wrong. Nobody ever asked to see their papers when they were hired to trim a hedge or paint a bathroom.

At an INS holding facility, the men sat in a big room from which, one at a time, they were summoned for processing. Lopez began walking anxiously in circles. He watched for a higher authority to whom he could appeal his case, but none ever appeared, and he was forced to wait with the others.

"Quit that walking all the time," Tío yelled at him. "You're pissing everybody off."

"*No me siento bien,*" Lopez said. He didn't feel well.

"*Dios mío! Llama una ambulancia!*" They would call him an ambulance.

It was nearly eight o'clock before Lopez heard his name at last. He was led to a much smaller room, where an agent sat at a desk littered with official-looking folders. Antonio refused to be scared off by the many signs and symbols of majesty and did not hestitate to present his documents. He was a victim, not a crook.

"I am legal," he said with bravado.

The agent checked over everything. "I'll have someone look at your card."

"It's real, *señor.*"

"We'll look it over. It'll be just a few minutes."

He waited for another forty-five minutes, his eyes on a wall clock and his spirit sinking. He would be late to pick up Elena for sure. The agent released him in the end and apologized for any inconvenience. Lopez was too rushed to even consider filing a complaint. And what if he did file one? His would be just another form added to a column that was already much taller than the column of wasted rent money.

"My car?" he asked. "You'll take me to it?"

They dispatched Lopez in a van. He was its only passenger this trip and was permitted to ride up front with the driver, who spoke Spanish fluently and offered an idiotic and inappropriate account of a recent vacation in Zihuatanejo. His Toyota was where he had left it, and he sped across town to Kmart where, at nine-thirty, Elena stood all by herself, a solitary figure in a circle of light. He raced to her side, eager to share the tale of his unlawful arrest and the horrible way he had been handled.

"*La migra,*" he said bitterly, holding the door for her. "They picked me up at the 7-Eleven."

"Why would they do that?" Elena asked him. "What did you do wrong, Antonio?"

"Nothing. I didn't do a thing."

"Come on. Be straight with me for once. The cops don't hassle people unless they do something wrong."

She isn't a Mexican, Lopez thought. She doesn't get it. He was twice bitter. "I was with those guys, Tío and Jorge," he said listlessly, hoping she would have some sympathy for him. "We were just goofing around. *La migra,* they made a sweep. They didn't ask one question. They hit me, too." He lifted his shirt to show her his bruised ribs.

Elena would have none of it. "You're a liar, Antonio, you know that? Why were you at that 7-Eleven in the first place? Were you trying to hook up with a girl?"

"No girls were there. Not even one girl."

"That doesn't make any sense. Why else would you be hanging out with those low-life creeps? Either for girls or for drugs. And you probably got into a fight."

"I didn't fight anybody. Why can't you be on my side one time, Elena?"

Her eyes were murderous. "Because you lie to me, Antonio. It's the same with your bullshit about a raise. You're not getting any raise, are you?"

"I *am* getting one."

"Well, I don't believe you. You liar. Take me home."

They reclaimed Dolores from her grandparents. Elena put the child to sleep and immediately went to bed herself. Lopez was saddened by what had happened to him. How could he have begun the day with his lips brushing Elena's hair, only to have the day conclude in this way? It was an awful situation. Elena failed to understand his problems and yet he loved her more than ever. This love is like a knife, he thought. It will kill me someday.

He was up at dawn as usual and soon gone from the house. The rolling green vineyard country brought him some comfort. He was always in harmony with the farm. Its laws were simple, clear, and immutable, yoked to the seasons and understandable to anyone in touch with the cyclical rhythms of the earth. All morning, he weeded one row after another with his hoe. He was steadied by the work, an ear close to the whispering leaves and shoots, his head lowered in an act of concentration so devout that he didn't see the two white men until they were almost upon him. For a few seconds, he figured that they must be border patrol agents out to question him again, but they weren't wearing any uniforms and had no revolvers or nightsticks.

"Boss man around?" The speaker had wooly sideburns and a toothpick jutting aggressively from his mouth.

"Victor or Arthur?"

"Already spoke with Victor."

"Arthur's in town," Lopez told them. "He'll be back by noon."

"We're from Consolidated Vintners," the toothpick man said. "This here's Rawley Kimball, your new field agent. You'll be seeing a lot of him this summer."

Kimball made no move to shake hands. His right one was mangled, the fingers bent in on themselves, and he hugged a clipboard to his chest. "I had a little accident involving a chain and a drive-shaft," he explained, in a friendly way. "We're just here to visit with the grapes, son."

"They're pushing real good," Lopez said with pride. "Those are happy grapes."

"Why don't you let us be the judge of that?" said the toothpick man.

They set off to tour the vineyard on their own. Antonio saw them put their heads together and write notes on the clipboard for an hour or so before they left. He went back to his weeding in earnest then and hoed until the sky was streaked with fading clouds. He bid farewell to Atwater, who was up on his tractor for a last pass at tillage before dark, and started along the dirt road he knew so well, having been its virtuous traveler now for eight full years, a master of its every rut and bump. As he drove on, though, he felt his worries begin again, plaguing him in the way of a recurring nightmare, so at the top of the road he turned left instead of right, away from Santa Rosa toward Carson Valley town, thinking that he would stop at La Perla Roja, feed some quarters to the jukebox, and shoot a few games of pool before he went home.

8

In a meadow off Carson Valley Road, on Pepper Harris's ranch and by his invitation, Anna Torelli went hunting for mushrooms on a warm April morning after several days of light drizzle. Harris, his graying porcupine crewcut in sharp contrast to his yellow rubber boots, led her through the damp ankle-high grass and showed off his expertise by pointing out some inky caps and some puffballs, although he passed them up. He also ignored a few jelly ears on a fallen oak. It was clear that Pepper had something else in mind altogether. Anna stayed close to him, moving along almost at a trot, and followed him down a modest slope and across a runnel. The sun brought up a loamy smell and cooked to pungency the horse manure in a small corral nearby, where an old roan mare was trying to get at some milkweed just outside her fence.

Harris hiked another ten paces at double time, stopped abruptly, cast his eyes about, and dropped to his knees. His Swiss Army knife flashed out from his pocket, and he used the saw blade to part the grass and reveal a half dozen agaricus campestris—he knew the Latin name and was obviously delighted to recite it—grouped together in tight formation.

"Ah," he said lovingly, with a gentle exhalation of breath. "Pinkies. The last of the season. Aren't they pretty?"

Anna knelt to have a look. They resembled supermarket mushrooms, but when Harris dug one up and turned it over, she saw that the fluted gills underneath were a delicate pink.

"That's the perfect color. It means they're real young," he told her. "I like to slice them thin, cook them in butter, hit them with a splash of sherry, and sprinkle on some parsley and a little salt and pepper. I mean, you're in for a serious treat."

"Thank you, Pepper."

"Don't thank me. It's my pleasure."

They scoured the meadow and collected about thirty more mushrooms before they quit at last. Harris, ever the gentleman, insisted that Anna take the lot of them. She was enjoying an overflow of attention from her father's pals these days, not a few of them bachelors or widowers, kindly old men with a hole in their lives that she was able to periodically fill. That wasn't a bad role for someone on the mend, she thought. Only three weeks had gone by since the funeral, and she was still in the process of healing. The old men were enamored of her company and felt duty-bound to introduce her to every last aspect of the valley, believing that they—and they alone—held title to it. It was their way of expressing their concern over her mother's death, Anna supposed. They had adopted her as they might have an orphan, and she was thriving on it, as silly as it seemed. By accident, she had landed in the middle of a pastorale that was doing wonders for her spirits.

The beauty of Carson Valley, its colors and flowing contours, newly revealed at all hours in the everchanging light, had become a source of great nourishment to her. Often she indulged in extravagant fantasies about what the Torelli farm could become someday, imagining a fieldstone chateau and a prize-winning cellar. She would turn the vineyard into a grand estate on the Provençal model, she would wear long dresses and wide-brimmed hats and plant bougainvillea and hibiscus as a floral border along the deer fence. Preposterous, yes, but this was a time in her life that she had set aside for dreaminess. Anna wanted no commitments beyond the moment. She had not felt so free in years. Sometimes she thought she would prefer to rusticate forever, although more often she diagnosed herself as just another victim of spring fever. Come the hard sun of early summer, and her enthusiasm would surely wane.

At any rate, she had bought herself a bit more time away from the bookstore and New York by inviting Jane Weiss out for a visit later in the month. As for the farmhouse itself, Anna had concluded her labors on it for now. She had done everything she could do short of painting it and undertaking some major repairs and renovations. Every bathroom still had peeling wallpaper in a wide variety of grotesque patterns, as well as porcelain fixtures that were permanently grimed with streaks of oil, grease, and ground-in vineyard dirt. In spite of such nuisances, she took a measure of satisfaction in having saved the old homestead from a sorry slide into oblivion. She had recently splurged on a pair of handsome Adirondack chairs in hunter green for the porch and sat out there on balmy evenings to soak up the sunset. Here she and Jane would convene to discuss the future of their business and would no doubt wind up discussing plays, movies, politics, and the sex lives of their mutual friends instead.

Anna was feeling starved for some female companionship after being so often surrounded by men. True, the old guys were sympathetic, earnest, and never overbearing, but they were of another species entirely. There were some things that she simply couldn't talk to them about. Once she had alluded casually to her menstrual cramps while Fred Vescio was in the vicinity, and Fred had stuck his fingers in his ears and almost fainted. The only woman Anna saw regularly was Betty Chambers, her occasional tennis partner, but Betty could seldom spare more than a couple of hours on account of all those children, who relied on her to be their transportation coordinator. On her own, Anna swam laps at the public pool in town, took walks around the property and up into the hills, slept in if she felt like it, and was a constant patron of the Carson Valley Library, where she indulged in long leisurely afternoons of reading.

She brought home the mushrooms and scrubbed them at the kitchen sink. From her window, she could see acres of glowing grapevines and swore that the leaves and tendrils were unfurling before her eyes, inch by inch, at an incredible rate of speed. The push was on for fair, as the farmers liked to say, and it had Arthur Atwater hopping to keep up. He was a regular whirling dervish these days. Rarely did he have any spare time to field her questions now. With the help of some field guides and some dog-eared Boy Scout manuals from his youth—Anna cracked up whenever she thought of him in his Webelo uniform, a sash of merit badges across his chest—he had schooled her in the local flora and fauna and had also taught her a bit about wine grapes, always stiff and formal in her presence, but he was apparently incapable of cutting loose, still as tightly wound as he was on the morning she had first met him. What would it take to shake him up? And did she honestly want to tackle the job? It was something she had pondered more than once.

In private, she had to admit that Atwater continued to intrigue her. He reminded her of Gary Cooper in one of those grainy Technicolor westerns that her father liked to watch—stoical, honest, reserved, and devoted to a code of behavior from centuries past, with a few probably not very riveting secrets that he was loath to reveal. It was a physical thing that Anna had for him, really. He came freely to her in fantasies, but in the flesh he remained inhibited. He had yet to show an iota of romantic interest in her, in fact. There were no dinner invitations, no flowers, cards, or flirtatious gestures. He had not made the tiniest move toward her that could be interpreted as extracurricular. Atwater was merely a cold fish, Anna thought at times, a loner content to wallow in his dump of a trailer, but she knew it was far more likely that he was already screwing some short-skirted, empty-headed barmaid in town on the sly. She and Arthur were apples and oranges, pears and tomatoes, X's and O's. He clearly had the right idea in leaving her alone.

Jack Farrell, on the other hand, was boiling over with misdirected lust after their single never-to-be-repeated date. Jack had squired her to The Rib Room for drinks at the piano bar and dinner in the restaurant, where he consumed a gargantuan surf-and-turf combo and coaxed Anna into hauling away a half pound of scorched sirloin in a doggie bag. As a topper, he had served up a massive good-night kiss in the French style that she was too surprised to fend off—full on the lips with his mouth wide open, the whole dismal bit. It was a measure of her bouyant mood that the kiss hadn't thrown her into a suicidal depression. She had turned down all his subsequent requests for further assignations, usually with considerable vehemence, but Jack kept calling every few days anyway to "shoot the breeze," parceling out the hot gossip and regaling her with his many addled schemes to promote Carson Valley as a tourist destination, including a plan to fly to Italy and convince the mayor of Florence, if there was one, to agree to become a sister city.

Anna wrapped up half the mushrooms in a cellophane package tied with a bow and gave it to her father the next day. They had fallen into the habit of having lunch together once or twice a week. It was a more enjoyable ritual than she ever would have guessed. "Ah, pinkies," he said when she arrived, echoing Pepper Harris. The old man, too, was in salutary shape and remained resolutely uninterested in vineyard affairs. His command of metaphors to describe the extent of his uninterest was also increasing. He would rather suffer a double hernia, he had told Anna at their last lunch, than ever discuss wine grapes again. His major concern at present was the dime store adjacent to his office, whose aged owner had sold out and retired to Palm Springs. Carpenters were dividing it into four smaller retail spaces, and Torelli had a hurtful paranoid vision of the trendy shops that might occupy them someday.

"Maybe you ought to open up a bookstore next door, Anna," he suggested, while he was slipping on a coat. "It's a good location. Better than San Francisco."

"Thanks, but no thanks," she told him. "You'd be yelling at me over the fence all day long. Has there ever been a bookstore in Carson Valley?"

"Yes, ma'am. A Christian lady ran it."

"How did she do?"

"She was finished in less than a year. Those video stores ate her alive. Put a book up against a video, and the video will win nine times out of ten."

"They say the Bible is the best-selling book in history."

"It didn't help her any."

For once, Anna persuaded him to forego his restaurant of choice, The Country Kitchen, where the Senior Citizen's Lunch cost just $2.99 and at least five kinds of pie were on the menu, to try Patisserie Parisienne. They had a sunny, two-block stroll over to it. The cafe was crowded with people grabbing a bite to eat between visits to wineries. There were Toulouse-Lautrec dancehall scenes on the walls and a scratchy tape of Edith Piaf playing over the sound system, her vibrato cutting through the clatter of dishes. Anna was afraid her father might bolt in the face of such effeteness, but instead he ambled awkwardly toward a table in back, the unwieldy bulk of him threatening to upset the delicate balance of the place.

They began a long wait for service. The only waitress, a tormented farm girl, couldn't cope with the traffic. "Don't be so antsy," Anna said, patting her father's hand to calm him.

"They come to you right away over at The Country Kitchen."

"Why don't you look at the specials on the board?"

"I can't read writing that small," the old man griped.

"I'll read them to you, then. They have a sausage plate with red cabbage, a *salade niçoise* with potatoes, green beans, and tuna, and a *croque monsieur*. That's a fancy grilled cheese sandwich."

Torelli smiled in a nostalgic sort of way. "Your mother liked a grilled cheese sandwich, you know. With those bread-and-butter pickles she used to put up."

Anna was still astonished at how quickly he seemed to have recuperated from the trauma of losing his wife. She had expected him to wallow in self-pity—and he did, although not for very long. He came out of his funk very deliberately, by incremental degrees, as someone might crawl up from a deep well into which they had fallen, and when he spoke of Claire now, it was always with supreme affection. She appeared almost to exist for him, re-created from a list of loving particulars that he had stored away in memory and invoked at appropriate moments.

"I heard this music for the first time my freshman year at Berkeley," Anna told him, listening to Piaf with a wistful smile. "We'd get a bottle of cheap Burgundy, lay around the dorm, and pretend we were in Paris." She noticed her father's dour look. "No, Bud Wright wasn't with us, Dad."

"There's a fellow who can go jump off the Eiffel Tower for all I care," the old man said.

"Bud wasn't so bad. We were just kids. We made mistakes."

"Well, you were bound to. You wouldn't take any goddam advice from anybody, that's for sure."

"What sort of advice would you give me about Jack Farrell?" she asked him lightly.

"Jack Farrell? Has he been sniffing around you?"

"Like a stallion in heat. He's pursuing me."

"I hope to hell you're a fast runner," Torelli said.

Anna laughed. "I did go out on a date with Jack. He held me to my word. He's one forceful kisser, I'll say that for him."

"Lord, have mercy!" The old man shuddered. "I'm glad it isn't any of my business who you sleep with anymore."

"I did not sleep with Jack Farrell! What a thing to say!" Anna was vastly amused. "And from the mouth of my own father!"

"Sometimes I wish I'd slept with more women before I got married," Torelli confessed without any shame. "I had the opportunities. What's the big deal about this sex thing, anyhow? People should have more pleasure, not less."

"I don't believe what I'm hearing."

"Well, that's how *I* feel, anyway. Why do they make sex out to be so dirty? I don't see the point of it."

"It's a threat to the established order," Anna said, wondering what act of God had transformed her father into the valley's own Wilhelm Reich?

"You can learn a lot about a person once they take off their pants," he carried on, teasing her now. "When somebody's naked, they don't have much to hide, do they? Old Jack, he's an ace ladies' man. He might have something special down inside his trousers."

"Enough, please."

The waitress finally came to their table, strands of wilted hair escaping from under her beret. They chose not to consult the menu, sure that the overextended child might never reappear. The old man ordered the sausage plate, Anna the *salade niçoise*.

He started in again as soon as the waitress left. "Here's a bet I'll make with you, Anna. I'll bet you've slept with more men than I've slept with women."

She was ready for him. "What's the bet? The price of lunch?"

"You're on. Want me to go first?"

"It only seems fair. You proposed the wager."

"I have to think for a minute." He shut his eyes, and his lips moved as he counted. "Five, all told. That must be about average for a man of my generation, or maybe a little more. How about you?"

"I'd say right around twenty," Anna informed him, with a straight face.

"Twenty!" He pounded the table and nearly sent it flying. "You've been to bed with twenty different men?"

"It could be closer to eighteen. Let's see, there was Bud Wright, of course, and Eddie Santini and the Mexican guy who worked in the grease pit at the old Esso station—"

"Never mind, Anna." He was barely able to conceal his distress. "You don't have to name every goddam one of them."

Anna was pleased with herself. She would happily pick up the tab.

They ate their meal with good appetite. The old man made grunting sounds of approval as he cut up his sausages of duck, veal, and pork, washing down the food with a glass of red wine. It was mid-afternoon when they departed. The sun was still bright in a clear sky, but Anna could feel a chill in the air and turned up the collar of her denim jacket.

"It'll probably freeze tonight," her father warned her. "Arthur better be on the ball." He glanced across the square. "Who's that outside my office?"

She looked. "Charlie Grimes, I think."

"I'll be damned. That's three visitors in one day. Antonio, he came by this morning to ask me for a raise."

"Did you give it to him?"

"Hell, no. We can't afford it. He'll get a bonus like Atwater does if the grapes go well. The boy's all upset. Somebody put it into his head that he could earn more money as a roofer."

"Can he?"

"Maybe. But roofers die young."

Grimes was resting on the office steps and perusing a *Valley Herald*. His clothes were spackled with whitewash, and he had whitewash in his hair, his eyebrows, and his nostrils. It was as if he had jumped into a bucket of whitewash and swum around in it until every exposed portion of his anatomy was thoroughly coated.

"Old Charlie Grimes!" Torelli called to him. "What are you doing darkening my door?"

"I ventured into town for a cocktail," Grimes said. "I thought you might venture to join me over to the Bullshot."

"You been painting your barn?"

"I've been painting it for almost three days now."

"It's a bigger barn than you ever thought it was, isn't it?"

Grimes cackled. "I never encountered a barn so goddam big!"

"I ate French food for lunch," Torelli bragged.

"That don't make you the president of anything," came the reply.

Anna pecked her father on the cheek and left him with his ancient crony, a man Victor had once praised for his ability to string a line of bullshit from the valley all the way down to Bakersfield and not get caught. She was impressed by the duration of their friendship, a tricky relationship compounded over time and surviving for more than fifty years. It seemed to defy a law of nature she was gradually being forced to accept, that everything on earth was frail and fleeting, destined to crumble. All you could cling to in the end, she thought, were those loving particulars.

She stopped at the library on her way home. She browsed among the stacks and found a novel that looked intriguing, along with an old buckram-bound edition of James Carson's journals that a company specializing in Californiana had published decades ago. Anna watched the sun drop behind the western hills as she drove out to the farm. There was no wind and not a single cloud, and the afternoon grew colder. The landscape had an absolute clarity, each detail fixed firmly in space with none of the soft focus of a warm and hazy day. She kicked up the furnace in the house and carted in some oak and madrone logs, aware of an anticipatory silence in the valley. It was as if every farmer had shut down every piece of machinery to listen closely to what the elements had to say.

Antonio Lopez showed up on her porch at twilight and asked to use the telephone. The sky behind him was molten.

"Is anything wrong?" she asked him. It was unusual for Antonio to come knocking.

"No, it's just about what groceries to buy," he said. "I'm sorry to bother you."

"It's no bother at all."

She gave him her cordless phone and let him stand in the foyer while she busied herself in the kitchen, noisy among her pots and pans, but she heard the sounds of an argument anyway. It was being conducted in sibilant and fervent Spanish. *Lo siento. Como? No. No. Qué quiere decir esto? Estoy cansado, tambien. No sea tonto! Lo siento. Lo siento.* And then, "I'm done, Anna."

She walked him out. "The sky's on fire," she said, marveling at the glow.

"Poor Arthur," Lopez said.

"You think it will freeze?"

"It's gonna freeze for sure."

After a light supper, Anna sat by the fireplace to read Carson's journals. They gripped her with an unexpected force because the writing was so immediate and reflected such a grand passion for adventure. The American West still had a quality of myth and represented true danger as well as potential rewards to Carson and his team of explorers. There was a portrait of the author that served as a frontispiece and brought him vividly to life. Robert Vance, a famous photographer of the period, had shot it at his studio in San Francisco when James Carson was in the full bloom of middle age. He looked prosperous and well fed, wore a bushy black beard, and posed with his right hand resting on a globe, as if the planet itself could be counted among his possessions.

That evening, Anna learned how Carson, a wealthy furrier, had crossed the Mississippi River from St. Louis with a party of ten men. They were headed for Fort Ross on the Pacific Coast of what would later become Sonoma County, an outpost where some Russian hunters did a thriving trade in sea otter pelts. Carson had hoped to do some business with them, but the Russians had hunted the sea otters almost to extinction, so he left in disappointment and meandered inland through Miwok Indian territory until he came to the valley that now bore his name. The journals provided an illustration of the *diseño* that he had submitted to the Mexican government, a rough topographical sketch of the land he hoped to claim. He was awarded a *rancho* of six leagues on which to graze some cattle and described the property as being "fertile and glorious, very near to Paradise."

Anna closed the book at ten o'clock and checked the porch thermometer. The temperature was 36 degrees. Atwater's trailer was dark. He must be out prowling, she thought, on the alert.

She threw an extra quilt on her bed and slept fitfully for a few hours before waking to the loud barking of a dog. The house was entirely dark, and for an instant she didn't know where she was. But then a profound sense of recollection came over her, and she remembered how her father's heavy footsteps would wake her on just such frosty nights when she was a child. He would race by her bedroom and clamber down the stairs, and she would hear the front door slam as he disappeared into the vineyard to stand his lonely vigil. Sometimes her mother would get up, too, and make him some coffee to keep him going. The lights in the kitchen would go on, and Anna would pad down in her pajamas and slippers for a cup of hot chocolate or a glass of warm milk, standing by the stove and listening to the hiss of the sprinklers outside.

Again, the dog barked—two dogs, actually, Prince and Rosie. Anna stayed in bed and tried to go back to sleep, but something gnawed at her. She wanted to be included in the action, not kept out of it as she had been as a kid, when all she could do was to wait like a sentinel at her window, drowsy and yawning, for the sprinklers to stop and the crop to be saved. Shivering in her chilly bedroom, with goose bumps all over, she dressed hastily and went downstairs. She put on the old navy peacoat and a knit watch cap and grabbed a flashlight from a shelf. The time by the kitchen clock was three-forty. The temperature on the porch was now 34 degrees.

She walked hurriedly toward the creek, where she could see another light shining. The cold air rose from the ground and climbed above her knees and then up to her breasts, making her nipples hard. That was high enough to damage the tender buds and shoots of the grapevines for certain. The new growth would begin to wither and die in a matter of minutes without the water necessary to protect it, Anna knew. She was in the middle of the vineyard when she realized that the sprinklers might start at any time and drench her, so she began jogging. The rush of frigid oxygen through her lungs energized her, and when the dogs picked up on her scent, they dashed toward her, two panting shapes in the dark, and Anna let them smell her and lap at her hands, their saliva hot and slippery on her icy skin.

The light by the creek converged on Atwater in his fishing waders. He was knee-deep in the stream and using a wrench to tinker with the Berkeley pump. He was so dedicated to the task that he failed to register her presence on the bank. "Arthur?" she said faintly, not wanting to scare him. "Arthur?"

He raised his head and looked up at her. She had never seen anyone quite so isolated, a solitary human being struggling in the night and on the verge of being swallowed by it.

"What are you doing out here?" There wasn't any anger in his voice, only wonder and confusion.

"Can I do anything to help?"

He took a few seconds to answer. "Yes, you can. Scuttle down the bank and steady that beam for me, will you?"

She did as he asked and took hold of a nine-volt lantern. "Where should I point it?"

"Right down here, where I have the wrench."

"What's the problem?"

"I wish I knew," Atwater said, in disgust. "It could be some dirty fuel clogging the line. It could be the battery. It could be the same damn foot valve as last year. I ought to let the grapes freeze just to teach Victor a lesson."

Anna watched him tighten the valve with his wrench, then step out of the creek to reflect on what he'd done. His fingers in the lantern beam were smeared with oil. From the hills across the river came a howling cry.

"Coyote?" she asked.

"That's a coyote, all right." He pronounced it the cowboy way, *kai-yote*. "Somebody's sheep are in big trouble." He slid down the bank and knelt by the pump to try and start it again. "Here goes nothing."

Anna was supremely conscious of the stillness of the night. Even the dogs had stopped their dashing around and lay attentively on the ground, as if their fortunes, too, were riding on the moment. Atwater checked the level of the diesel fuel and applied his wrench to the foot valve a final time, but his attempts to get the motor going only resulted in a series of coughing chugs, little sputters that spiraled toward ignition and faltered on the brink.

"Turn over, you useless bastard," he muttered, kicking the pump in his frustration.

It seemed to Anna that he truly believed the machine had a will of its own and was withholding its services for reasons no mere mortal could comprehend.

"Be nice to the pump, Arthur," she advised him. "Give it another try."

He stood staring at her with his fists on his hips. "Anna, that is the stupidest piece of advice I've ever been given," he told her. "The pump doesn't have any feelings. The pump is just a pump."

"*You* act as though it had feelings."

"Oh, this is comical, indeed!" Atwater shouted, throwing down his wrench. "In blackest night, heaven has sent me a pump expert!"

"I didn't say I was an expert," Anna corrected him. "But I do know that kicking a pump won't fix it."

"Well, what the hell! What have I got to lose? Some woman's stupid goddam advice might be just the ticket." He bent to the Berkeley as a doctor would, as if to apply a stethoscope to its faltering ticker. "I'm sorry if I offended you, pump," he began, stroking it and glancing up at Anna. "How's that sound? Am I doing okay?"

"Just get on with it. I've got my fingers crossed."

"That's another big help. How did I ever get along without you? Now if we can find a rabbit, we ought to cut off a foot."

"Get on with it, Arthur."

Atwater gave her a sour look and launched into his speech again. "I apologize for kicking you, pump, but I've been up to my ass in freezing cold water for about an hour out here, and I'm worried that my whole crop of grapes is going to die on me because you won't work. We're talking about hundreds of thousands of dollars here, pump. I'm sure you understand. You're so goddam old, you must have seen it all by now. Most pumps your age are in the junkyard, aren't they? Anyway, I promise never to kick you again. Now start, you little fucker!"

The pump erupted with another coughing chug, but something clicked this time. A plume of smoke shot up in a puff, and there was a resonant noise as the water from the creek filtered through a network of underground pipes to the sprinkler heads, and the heads began spraying water in rainbow arcs. Anna almost applauded, but she caught herself because the ordeal was far from over. The pump might still break down, and if that happened, the water on the vines would turn instantly to ice, and the ice would be every bit as disastrous as a frost.

"You can go back to bed now," Atwater said wearily, standing on the bank and stripping off his waders. "I'll be fine on my own." He offered her a conciliatory smile. "You were right, I guess. The pump does have feelings."

"I'll bring you a Thermos of coffee if you like."

"I wouldn't refuse it."

The night dragged on. Anna read by the fire and listened to the music of the sprinklers. The coldest hour was right at dawn, and it posed the last and greatest threat. She went out to the porch and watched the sky go from black and starry to the palest gray, a color unique unto itself, the color of first light, and when the Berkeley kept pumping, she experienced a slow release of the tension that had put a knot in her stomach. To the east, toward Napa and a spiny mountain ridge, the sun was on the rise, and as its warmth hit the farm, she and Atwater and the grapes were relieved of their burden. The vineyard was all shimmery with droplets of water pearled up on the green buds and shoots.

By eight o'clock, the temperature had risen to 39 degrees, and Atwater was able to shut down the frost-protection system. Anna intercepted him as he walked back to his trailer. She had a desire to stay connected to him, wanted a continuity between them. She was acting on an impulse, trying not to think her way around him. Up close, she saw that he had a three-day stubble and tired old eyes. He seemed battered and beaten.

"You did a superb job," she told him.

He eyed her with distrust. "That's a bit of an exaggeration."

"That pump has to be replaced. You shouldn't have to put up with such nonsense. I'm going to talk to my father about it."

Atwater didn't speak. He looked at her and through her.

"What would you say to some breakfast?" Anna asked him, with more urgency than she intended.

"Breakfast?"

"I mean, I'd like to cook you some breakfast. If you're hungry, that is."

"I'd say yes to breakfast. That's what I'd say."

They walked to the house together, and Atwater insisted on taking off his boots in the foyer. His thick wool socks, two on each foot, had several holes in them, but it didn't appear to bother him. Anna cracked open a half dozen eggs and set some strips of bacon to sizzling in a cast-iron skillet. She could feel him staring at her from the kitchen table and knew what was in that stare, the tempered heat of it.

"Bacon frying is one of the best smells there is," Atwater said, relaxing now with his hands locked behind his head and a smile on his face.

"What else?" she asked.

"You want my list of top ten smells?"

"If you've got that many."

"I'm not so sure I do. There's the smell of grass after somebody mows a lawn. Coffee brewing. Bread baking. The smell inside a dry cleaning store." He paused to think. "How many is that?"

"Five."

"Maybe I'm not as smart as I used to be."

They made a feast of the scrambled eggs and the crisp bacon, some buttered toast, two kinds of jam, and some leftover potatoes fried with onions and green peppers. The sun was roaring through the kitchen, and the room was all ablaze. Anna felt a profound need to be close to Atwater, to hold him and be held by him, a need to extend the moment that they were sharing. It was that simple and natural, and yet it intimidated her so. The plates clattered in her hands as she cleared them away, and she dropped a juice glass in the sink and broke it and almost cried out in joy when she saw how bold she was going to be, stealing up behind him, too bashful to confront him directly, and lowering her lips to his ear.

"Come to bed with me, Arthur?" she whispered. She was struck dumb after that, and she became anxious and wished she could take back her words, certain that he would reject her and thinking she had never done anything so foolish in her life. She wanted to run and hide somewhere, but that sensation passed in a few seconds, and she felt brave again, strong within herself and convinced of the rightness of her need as she circled his chest with her arms. Her lips were still at his ear, and she asked him once more, with real confidence now, "Would you like to come to bed with me?"

"Yes, Anna," Atwater said, shy himself as he reached up to her. "I'd like that more than anything."

9

Atwater on his tractor rode the fields in turmoil the next afternoon, semiconscious and trying to dismiss what had happened to him. It was all wrong, it made no sense. He did not belong with a woman like Anna Torelli, a worldly woman with perfect legs and the softest lips and no tattoos anywhere. They were never meant to be. Two lonely people on a lonely farm on a cold and lonely night—it had been an accident, pure and simple. Only a simpleton would believe otherwise. He vowed to call Anna that very evening to set matters straight, sure that she would understand and probably be relieved. In a moment of weakness, they had committed an error in judgment, one that was forgivable but not to be repeated. He was the man, after all, and he would put a stop to the affair before it got out of hand.

He entertained such thoughts while squeezing cautiously between the vineyard rows. He was involved in a second phase of tillage now, turning over the soil another time to hasten the mulching of decaying weeds and grasses. The ground was harder than he liked it to be and bricked up on him in clayish lumps. He was so beat after his sleepless night and idyllic morning that he had trouble keeping his eyes open. His mind drifted again and again toward sublime images of Anna naked in her bed. *Too bad, buddy.* He would just have to suffer for a while. That part of it he couldn't control, any more than he could erase what his field hands, including Antonio Lopez, had witnessed earlier. They had all watched him slip out of the farmhouse just before noon, and as he had slunk past them they had snickered and joked about him in Spanish, a perpetrator of lewd and lascivious acts caught out in broad daylight.

He could see most of the crew from his perch on the tractor, four men thinning and suckering vines in a block of Zinfandel at the foot of a hill. They pinched off every shoot that had failed to produce a cluster of tiny embryonic grapes, rerouting the vegetative energy to the other shoots, the Darwinian survivors. It was a job that most men enjoyed, slow-paced and not very tough, and it earned them some money in a season when work was beginning to be scarce. Lopez was not among them at present. Atwater had dispatched him on a special reconnaissance mission, ordering him to tour the vineyard and check it for frost damage, and Antonio flagged him down at about five o'clock to deliver his report.

"Well?" Atwater cut the motor to listen.

"The Chardonnay got hit." Lopez held up a black shoot, dead and gone. "The other vines are fine."

"How many plants?"

"I didn't count them all. Not exactly. About twenty?"

"Why are you looking at me like that, Antonio?"

Lopez's eyes shifted into the distance, as if he'd been distracted by an insect flying by. "I'm not looking at you any kind of way."

"Yes, you are. Did I say something funny?"

"No."

"Then why do you have that shit-eating grin on your face?"

"Could be I'm happy for you," Lopez admitted. He failed to rub out the grin with a fist. It was too grand, too appreciative. "Congratulations, *amigo*. Anna, she's not above you!"

"Don't you be congratulating me. It's none of your business. You better shape up, brother," Atwater warned him. "Because that shit-eater makes you look like the village idiot of Carson Valley."

He fired up the tractor and proceeded in a foul and mulish mood to the barn. A trail of clods unfurled behind him, solid lumps that would require another pass with the cultivator before they crumbled. He attended to the Chardonnay vines himself and added up the

damage, sixteen plants with varying degrees of injury, some never
to recover in time for the harvest and others that still might yield a
reduced crop. He retired to his trailer after that, heartened by the
sight of a cloudy sky, and phoned the National Weather Service in
Santa Rosa to confirm what he already suspected. No frost was in the
forecast.

TUESDAY, APRIL 8TH. Lost some Chardonnay during the freeze,
nothing serious. Cool today, good for keeping down botrytis. The
crew is thinning and suckering. I have to start sulfur dusting soon.
I'm behind on it, always behind on something.

While he heated up his supper, he stole peeks at the big house and
stared dreamily at the lighted kitchen, a room he had only lately va-
cated, one that served him now as an emblem of how incredibly sweet
life could be. He ate spaghetti and meatballs prepared for him in advance by the fabled Chef Boyardee, second only to the wizard Irish
gourmet Dinty Moore in Atwater's opinion, and reminded himself of
his vow to do right by Anna. He would be patient and wait for a mystical bolt of intuition to let him know that the moment had come to
make his phone call. Tense and cracking his knuckles, with the chef's
cuisine sloshing around in his belly, he trod a familiar circular path
that he had previously worn into his shag carpeting in periods of
duress. *Sit down, Arthur,* he told himself. He did. Rosie joined him and
stretched out on the floor, spreading herself like a comforter over his
bare feet.

His own phone rang. That was a rarity, except when his creditors
were after him. The sound affected him like a stick of dynamite ex-
ploding under his butt, and he leaped almost three feet into the air.
Don't answer it, Arthur! He let it ring a few more times, allowing his
pulse rate to return to normal and assuring himself that he could deal
with it if it should be Anna. Nonchalantly, as if he had been on holiday in Greece and had only that minute arrived home, a jaded bon
vivant to whom no message, however obscene or blasphemous, could
be upsetting, he lifted the receiver.

"Hello?" His voice cracked like a juvenile's, all deception fled
from it.

"Is this Mr. Arthur Atwater?"

"Yes, it is."

"This is Darlene at the *Valley Herald*. How are you tonight, sir? I'm calling about the half-price subscription offer we have going on right now? You can win a brand-new home and garden patio set from Wallace Furniture simply by—"

Atwater hung up. Darlene was history. He started walking the circular path again, round and round, and noticed that Anna's kitchen had gone dark. He pictured her reading in the parlor with a fire burning, the smell of woodsmoke in her hair. What would she be wearing? Had she taken a shower and put on her robe? Probably. He imagined her that way, anyhow, sitting by the hearth with the robe open slightly to reveal a little of the creamy, upturned, small-nippled breasts he had sucked, licked, and gently bit that morning. His cock began to stir. *Sit down, Arthur. Be still!* He did and was. He ridiculed himself for acting like a teenager and behaving precisely as he had in junior high school when his hormones went utterly wacko and forced him to jerk off three times a day, too frightened of rejection to speak a single sentence to the girl he most coveted, Sharon Somebody—her surname was lost in the mists of the 1970s—who had the desk next to his in algebra class and let her skirt ride up so relentlessly that he was nearly crippled by a perpetual hard-on.

Get a grip on yourself, man! He waited another ten minutes and picked up his phone. He dialed five digits and put the receiver back. He picked it up again right away, replaced it, went into the bathroom, combed his hair, brushed his teeth, peed, and burst out of the trailer to rush with gigantic plummeting strides toward the big house, where he knocked loudly on the door and heard his nervous breathing and the alarmed cry of a great blue heron startled somewhere in the downriver night.

Anna was at the door in an instant. Her eyes were very green and innocent. She had put up no barriers between them—he could see right into her, in fact. "Listen," he began, his head lowered in a semblance of shame, "I feel real bad about this morning. I—"

She came into his arms, her cheek against his chest. "Don't talk," she said softly. "Don't ruin it."

"Oh, Jesus." Atwater was stunned by the passion he felt. The press of her body against his eroded the infinite space of his loneliness, and he held onto her tightly, clutching her to him as if she and she alone could save him from some awful destiny. She took him by the hand and led him into the parlor where, by the fire, she unbuckled his belt, knelt, and took his cock in her mouth. He wasn't used to such directness and anxiously stroked her hair, thinking that this was the most beautifully undeserved experience he'd ever had. He couldn't contain himself and tried to push her away, but Anna wouldn't go and instead held him forcefully, gripping his thighs, her fingers digging in. He was surprised by her strength, by the many dimensions of her power.

"I want this." She looked up at him with those innocent eyes. "It's for me."

"All right," he said, as his legs went weak.

He was completely in her thrall, without any will of his own, a captive of the senses. She walked him upstairs afterward and lay next to him in her bed. He could feel her skin so hot everywhere and her cunt against his thigh dripping wet, and soon he was hard again and ready to fuck her. He did it in a way that surprised him, unguardedly, for his own delight. He had not been aware of the depth of his hunger and worried for a brief few seconds that he might hurt her, but her tongue lapped at his neck in encouragement, so he went at it faster and faster, flying out of his brain, each new thrust causing Anna to moan and scratch his back as his pelvic bone banged against hers almost painfully, and when he came this time he felt emptied of something long in need of release.

"That was so lovely," he heard her say, as if from far away. He was exhausted himself and dropped immediately into a heavy slumber, waking later in a daze, staggered to find himself in her bedroom again. Anna was asleep by his side, her legs tangled in the sheets. He nudged her shoulder with his lips, but she didn't move. It was nearly midnight by the bedside clock. He set the alarm for three A.M. and slept solidly until it rang, smothering the buzzing with a pillow. He was already up and dressing, aching in muscles long unused, when Anna reached out to him blindly in the dark, her hand fumbling about behind her.

"Don't go, Arthur," she urged him. "Stay the night with me."

He didn't want the crew to make fun of him again in the morning. Caught out once you were a philanderer, he thought. The second time you were a fool. "There might be a frost," he said as an excuse. "I've got to go out and see."

"Come back when you're done, will you?"

He crouched by her and petted her forehead. "This is all wrong, Anna," he said without much enthusiasm.

"Only if you want it to be."

"I can't be sleeping here. The men already know about us. Everybody in the whole valley will hear before long."

"Do you care?"

He searched his heart. "No. Not really."

"Kiss me, please," Anna said, a finger to her lips.

Atwater leaned down and tasted her mouth, all sour and fuzzy from their intimacies. He drew away from her then, laced up his boots, and marched out to patrol the vineyard. The porch thermometer was stable at 43 degrees, but he stomped around for a while anyway, alert to the flow of cold air and making sure it remained below the level of his knees before he permitted himself to go back to his trailer, where he collapsed into bed in his clothes.

He didn't see Anna the next day. He was busy with minor emergencies in the fields and felt the need when evening came to establish some distance. He was reluctant to impose on her and still fighting his emotions, denying their legitimacy. Yet he missed her so badly in the morning that he stopped by her house on his lunch break, sheepish about his lust and expecting her to send him packing, but instead he floated upstairs with her in a helpless, swooning surrender. They were lovers after that by tacit agreement. All pretense of the accidental fell by the boards. There were never any discussions of their affair and no formal rules of engagement. Sometimes they wouldn't talk for a couple of days, while at other times they couldn't bear to be apart. Whatever was going on between them had a rhythm of its own, as well as an intensity that was very nearly overwhelming.

Atwater's emotions were all over the map during the following week. By turns, he was thankful, astonished, fretful, and perplexed. He had a farmer's desire for simplicity and order and wondered in his idle moments where the two of them were headed. Anna was unlike any woman he had ever met. She was flighty, independent, aggressive, and full of surprises, capable of evoking both his bliss and his wrath. She tested him and pushed him to his limits, drawing out a part of him that he had never investigated before. It was, he confessed to himself, a thing of beauty, but he still had a superstitious fear that it would end in disaster. He couldn't say why this should be, except that he felt in some general sense that he did not merit her attentions. She would tire of him, sooner rather than later, and would be forced to dump him. What did he have to offer her, really? He was nothing but a passing fancy to keep her occupied until she departed for New York.

Then Atwater would catch himself in the midst of such dour deliberations and realize that it was all in his head! Anna gave him no cause to worry. *Lighten up, buster!* In fact, she was a ceaseless pleasure. He was like a giddy kid around her, a balloon tethered to the earth by the skinniest of strings. So smitten was he that he even cleaned up his act on her behalf, changing his underwear regularly and laying in his first-ever supply of dental floss. His impulse to lavish gifts on her was extreme in spite of his paltry budget. He bought her a box of Mrs. See's finest caramels and a fancy old-fashioned silk scarf that he saw in an antique store window. He drove her over to Geyserville one night and took her to his favorite Italian restaurant, where the recipe for ravioli was purportedly a secret of such international repute that wars had almost been fought over it somewhere in Sicily. In his rapture, Atwater could not be roped in. He bought her flowers, of course, and a funny key chain in the shape of California and gave her his goofy pup for company. Anna laughed at his excesses and named the little dog Daisy.

Their fucking remained incendiary. They usually got together at the big house because it was a lot neater and more comfortable—the sort of place where an adult might live, Atwater often reflected—but Anna visited him at his trailer once, too, arriving unannounced on a drizzly evening. She held an umbrella over her head and wore a threadbare raincoat buttoned up to the neck.

"You'll never guess why I'm here," she said, a coquette if ever he saw one.

"Cup of sugar?"

"Something like that."

"I'll put out the dogs." He rounded up Prince and Rosie and shoved them onto the deck. "Okay, I'm ready for instructions."

She stood before him, a challenge. "Unbutton me, then."

His fingers fumbled with her coat. "My goodness!" he said, a stagey hand to his cheek. Anna wore lingerie such as he had only seen before in catalogs and magazines, a lacy bustier and black net stockings that the devil himself might have designed to snare such wayward souls as Arthur Atwater. "Where in the world did you find that outfit in Carson Valley?"

Anna leered at him. "That's private, mister. On or off?"

"On, definitely."

"I knew you'd say that!"

He knew things about her, as well. He had begun to master the subtleties of her body and was learning to satisfy her in a number of ways, fast or slow, delicate or nasty, back or front or sideways. He did her bidding gladly, heroically, every ounce of him dedicated to it. She had to guide him at first and teach him what she most preferred, but he had gone on from there to invent new forms of gratification, a prize pupil whose own cleverness elated him in secret. He had never thought of himself as the artistic type, not when it came to the old in-out, yet here he was performing the erotic equivalent of cartwheels. The sex was always very good, always feverish and sloppy and crackling with electricity, and it left them entirely satisfied. It resolved their differences, their essential opposition. It was their common ground.

Atwater sipped a glass of water, his head pillowed on Anna's breasts. They were both dry on the inside and slippery wet on the surface.

"Everything about you is pretty," he said, tracing a line below her navel, a scar from her ectopic pregnancy. "Even this."

"I could do without it."

He kissed her there. "Poor Anna. Nothing bad should ever happen to you again."

"Did you and your wife want to have kids?" she asked him.

"I *was* the kid," he told her.

"No, really. Be honest."

"We never discussed it much. Not that I can recall, anyway."

He could recall, of course. There were many such talks. Laura would bring up the subject, and he would duck it with a stock set of semivalid objections. *We don't have the money, Laura. We're too young. It'd tie us down. It's too much responsibility.* He had nothing against children per se, just a mental barrier in the form of a lingering memory of his own difficult childhood. Sometimes he thought the stumbling block was that he had known intuitively that his marriage wouldn't last. Such things were possible, the mysteries were abundant enough to account for it.

"I wanted a huge family," Anna said, lazily stretching her arms. "I can't imagine why, but I did. I must have got it from books or TV or something. I planned to be the perfect nuclear mother with three perfect nuclear children. I even had names picked out for them."

"Let me guess." Atwater pretended to concentrate, his eyes closed and his index fingers jabbed against his temples, as if to consult the spirits. "Could it be Samantha, Jessica, and Dylan?"

She laughed. "Pretty darn close, Mr. Atwater. You can be a wicked fellow, can't you? I swear, you don't take me seriously half the time."

"Okay, what were their names?"

"That's much better. Now you're being nice. I approve of you." Anna paused to sip from his water glass. "Nora, Nicholas, and Susie." She broke down and laughed again. "I find it hard to believe myself."

"Two girls and a boy. How come you didn't give the third kid an *N* name?"

"Probably so people would ask me about it," she said. "That was my idea of being exotic back then. Nora was intelligent, Nicholas was dashing, and Susie was supposed to be the hell-raiser her mother never was."

"You never raised any hell?"

"Not until I met you."

Atwater shrugged off the compliment. "This is just a tiny bit of hell," he told her. "Big-time hell-raising gets hairy."

"Be that as it may, Arthur, I must tell you that I thought you'd never show your cards. You were the most tightly wound man I have ever seen in my life, bar none. You walked around as though you had a poker up your ass."

"That's how it felt," Atwater said agreeably. "I was trying to stay away from you. It's a bad business to take up with the boss's daughter."

Anna poked fun at him. "Such is the folklore of Carson Valley," she said. "You don't actually think that way now, do you?"

"Sometimes I do. But for a different reason."

She sat up, her arms around her knees, and gave him a puzzled look. "Why is that?"

"Well, one of these days Anna Torelli is liable to wake up, come to her senses, and fly back to New York as fast as she can. And I'll be plenty sad."

"I'm not sure what I'm going to do," Anna said quietly. "That's the truth of the matter."

"It doesn't help me much, does it? I like firm ground under my feet." As soon as the sentence was out of his mouth, he regretted it.

"Don't ask me for things I can't give you, Arthur."

"I didn't mean to."

"My life is just beginning again." Anna's voice had risen, and there was some color in her cheeks. "I couldn't stand to be fenced in. I've already done the marriage bit, and it nearly ruined me. Isn't it enough that we enjoy each other's company? I have such a good time with you."

"So it's a game?"

"No, it isn't a game!" she said angrily. "I don't know what it is exactly. But I do know that we shouldn't put any weight on it."

He cursed himself—*Atwater, you asshole!* He knew much better, knew that a man couldn't afford to wobble in front of a woman he cared about. It was useless to express any doubts. A man had to be the still point around which a woman orbited. He had to be the solid center, the one person on whom she could depend absolutely. A good woman ran from a man who pressured her.

Anna had calmed down by the time she left. They were lovers again, but he had lost some purchase. "Did you remember that my friend Jane gets here on Thursday?" She slipped back into her raincoat, a dream disappearing. "Maybe we can all do something together while she's here."

"I hope so," Atwater said. "But my week is pretty busy. I've got Kimball to deal with, for starters."

She kissed him at the door. "You'll do fine."

In the morning, submerged in his work, he was able to forget his mistakes. When he wasn't supervising his crew, tinkering with machinery, or speeding to town for a spare part, he had to contend with sundry other unrelated distractions such as Rawley Kimball, his CV field agent, who turned up every other Wednesday at two o'clock on the dot. Kimball was a combative, flat-nosed little elf, broad of beam and sober in manner, and he always had an abundance of pens and pencils jutting out of his shirt pocket and his mangled hand concealed in a trouser pocket. His sunglasses were the clip-on kind—a detail that said it all for Atwater, although the worst of it for him, truly, was that Kimball saw himself as a messiah of modern science out to save ignorant vineyard managers from committing any crimes against nature.

They rode around the farm in the Jeep, with Atwater in dire resistance to Kimball's every suggestion.

"Look here," Kimball said, stopping him in a row of the ancient Chardonnay vines that were slated to be replaced. "With this old rootstock, you ought to be checking for corky bark virus. Have you done that?"

"Not yet."

Kimball made a penciled note on his clipboard. "Leaf roll is another hazard. You ought to be inspecting for that, too."

"I will be from now on. Yes, sir." Atwater struggled against a temptation to salute and utter *Jawohl!*

"Have you done any sulfur dusting?"

"I started last week."

"Well, pay special attention to your Cab vines," Kimball commanded him. "Because you've got some real heavy foliage, and that dust is going to have a tough time penetrating through to the grapes."

"Thanks for the tip, Rawley."

"It's no skin off my nose, Arthur. I'm here to help. It's my job."

Atwater brewed a pot of tea that evening and took solace in his log.

WEDNESDAY, APRIL 23RD. Applied herbicide to hillside Zinfandel. Hidalgo and Antonio hoeing Cab block, lots of weeds still to get. Weather warmer, seventy-seven degrees at noon. Bloom coming on, the whole farm smells sweet. Kimball here talking about corky bark virus. I wished I could smack him in the head with a shovel and bury him six feet deep.

He flipped to another section at the back of the log that was marked by a turned-down page. It was a new section that he had just started—the equivalent of a diary, where he jotted notes and tried to sort out his confused feelings about Anna.

Anna here last night. Is the fucking so good because it can't last?

She asked me to take her on a canoe trip down the river. Talked about a raft she and her brother were going to build once. I said yes, of course. I'd do anything for her right now. Take me to Madagascar. Sure, honey.

Why am I so nuts about her? Because when I'm with her, I forget who I am? She makes me feel good about myself, like I'm another person. Maybe she sees a side of me that everybody else misses.

Only the brave deserve the beautiful. I read that somewhere once.

Worry about falling into the creek, and you'll fall into it.

Atwater fitted a weed knife to his tractor on Thursday and made some passes through the rows of old Chardonnay, dragging the blade deep beneath the soil to cut the roots of such hardy perennials as Johnson and Bermuda grass, both nuisances almost impossible to destroy. He wished that he didn't have such a hatred of chemical weed-killers, since the chemicals were very effective and easy to apply, but he feared that they might cause him to sprout a third ear somewhere down the line.

Toward dusk, he saw a bright red Mustang convertible pull up at the big house and assumed that the woman at the wheel must be Jane Weiss, Anna's friend. He watched Anna come out and hug her on the porch. He thought that she might call and invite him to join them for supper, but she didn't. They left together in the Mustang the next day and were not yet back when he turned in. Saturday, too, they were gone for hours, and he started to feel excluded and abused, as well as ridiculous for feeling that way. Only on Monday did Anna bring Jane around to be introduced, catching Atwater at an awkward moment while he was on his knees fiddling with the weed knife and covered from head to toe with dirt.

"This is Arthur Atwater," she told her friend. "Our vineyard manager."

"I'm pleased to meet you," Jane said. Her voice was chirpy, and

Atwater took an instant dislike to her. How dare she come between him and his lover? She had sharp features and short black hair in an unflattering bob and was not meant for the jeans she had on. "I love your ranch! Is that what you call it?"

"You can call it whatever you choose," Atwater said coolly. "We're not real picky about it."

"Anyway, I'm having a wonderful time! I used to think of New Jersey as the West. Anna's going to turn me into a cowgirl before I leave."

"She's good in the saddle, all right."

"Don't let us keep you, Arthur," Anna said, casting him a withering glare.

The rest of the day went by without so much as a message from her, and Atwater fell to circumnavigating his carpet again that evening. He was on a psychological roller-coaster, tolerant one minute and in an infantile rage the very next. Didn't Anna promise that they'd do something together? Was he such a dolt that she had to exclude him from all the fun? He became convinced that she must be ashamed of him, so he spied on her until Jane finally drove off alone in the Mustang on Tuesday afternoon. Then he got down from his tractor in a rush and broke straight for the house. Anna was in the kitchen, dressed for the heat in shorts and a halter top and arranging a bouquet of gladiolus in a vase. Atwater cautioned himself not to make a scene. Instead, he would be perfectly rational and convey what was troubling him in a mature fashion, but in fact his very first sentences betrayed him.

"Here I am," he bayed at her. "Your vineyard manager. Your *hired* hand!"

Anna turned to confront him. "Spare me, Arthur. You're being ridiculous."

"Am I? Isn't that how you introduced me the other day? I'm not beneath you, Anna. I'm not your goddam servant!"

"What would you prefer to be called?" she asked him in an ironic tone. "My boyfriend? My *swain?*"

He looked at her more closely. "Are you drunk?"

"No, Arthur, I am not, as you put it, drunk. Jane and I toured some wineries and did some tasting after lunch."

"You're a little high, then."

"What business is it of yours? Tell me that, please."

Atwater kept after her. "Here's what I don't get," he said, much more loudly than he intended. "Why haven't you included me in any of your outings?"

"Because I didn't want to include you." Anna spoke slowly, as if to the cretin Atwater increasingly understood himself to be. "I haven't seen Jane for ages. We've been catching up. And we have business to discuss. I've let my end of the bookstore bargain slide. Does that make any sense to you? Or do you need it explained again?"

"Explain it again. Vineyard managers are dumber than shit."

"You really are overstepping your bounds here, you know."

"Overstepping my bounds?"

"That's right. You have no claim on me. Jesus, Arthur, you're be-having like a husband! Besides, *you* could have invited *us* to do some-thing."

That had never occurred to him, of course. He felt that he had lost a crucial point. His argument was collapsing around him like so many unmortared bricks, and he had an urge to dive under the table to protect his head. "Like what?" he asked, stalling for time.

"Oh, who knows!" Anna was shouting at him now. "Let's see. How about fishing? Ha! Fishing would have been fucking brilliant!"

"The steelhead run is over for the year," Atwater said lamely. "There's only bass and suckers to catch. But we could go tomorrow if you want to."

"Arthur, this has got to stop. You're being much too serious!"

Fully blocked and parried, he accepted his defeat. "The other night, you told me I didn't take you serious enough."

"It's serious*ly*," Anna told him. "An adverb. You didn't flunk Eng-lish grammar, too, did you?"

The last brick had fallen. Atwater regarded her there in the kitchen, his noble adversary and demon lover, a beguiling half smile of victory on her lips. He swallowed the entire miracle of her with his eyes and wanted her more than anything.

"Anna," he said, moving toward her, "take off your shorts."

Her eyes were locked on his. He could feel them burning. She was testing him again, ready for any dare. The shorts dropped in a pool on the floor.

"Your panties, too."

"All right."

"Go sit on that counter."

She hoisted herself and waited with her legs spread slightly, taunting him. He went to her, buried his face in her crotch, touched her with his tongue, and heard her say, "Oh, yes, that's so good." She came for him swiftly and eagerly, and it excited him beyond any rapture he had known. He yanked his jeans down to his knees, sat on a chair, and lifted Anna astride him, feeling the wet slap of her against his legs and her hot breath in his ear. He was transported and yet keenly uneasy at the same time, certain as he plunged into her that he was overmatched, in trouble, in love, and no doubt doomed.

The only peace he could find now was in the fields, where his long laboring through the winter and spring was being rewarded in spades. There came a morning early in May when the growing shoots appeared to rise up in tribute, arching toward the sky in gratitude for his mindful nurturing. The shoots were almost three feet long and manic in their energy, and Atwater hiked the farm as though he owned it. He nodded at the vines and had such a renewed sense of self-worth that he decided to celebrate by buying himself some dinner at The Rib Room. He started down the dirt road at twilight, only to pass a dented Toyota hatchback parked on a shoulder, its hood up and Antonio Lopez's head thrust into its vitals.

"Battery's dead," Lopez told him when he stopped. Then Lopez began swearing, *chinga* this and *chinga* that. "And the guy I bought it from guaranteed me it would last for at least five years!"

"A warranty's only as good as the paper it's written on."

"There wasn't any paper, man."

Atwater fetched some jumper cables from the barn, but the battery wouldn't hold a charge. The other men on the crew had already gone home, so he had no choice but to offer Lopez a lift to Santa Rosa. He drove Carson Valley Road going south and cut across toward the freeway.

"Sears'll be open till nine tonight," he counseled Antonio. "Get yourself a new battery, will you? Used batteries are never worth a damn."

"The guy said it *was* new. Hey, Arthur?" Lopez asked, his attitude suddenly upbeat. "You're looking different these days! There's like this little glow around you."

"Like a halo?"

"What's that?"

"The thing around an angel's head."

"No, it's nothing like that," Lopez said with a laugh. "You're no angel, man. It's just a glow."

"Well, I feel pretty darn good, actually. I feel like a human being again."

"It's because of love, Arthur. What did you feel like before you had some love?"

Atwater considered the question, then laughed himself. "I felt like a dog, Antonio. There were four of us barking in my trailer."

When they arrived at Lopez's house, a modest stucco bungalow with some scrawny azaleas out front, Antonio asked him in for a beer. Atwater didn't really care for one, but if he refused it would be interpreted as a grievous insult. He had never been inside the house before and saw that it was very nicely kept and furnished with some newish furniture from Kmart. He paused before a framed portrait of a Madonna on a wall above the couch. "Who's this?" he said.

"The Virgin of Guadalupe," Lopez told him. "She brings me good luck."

"But she doesn't do batteries."

"I guess not, man."

They continued into the kitchen. Elena stood by the stove working a wooden spoon in several pots. Dolores was in a high chair spattering pureed green beans all over herself. She had green beans in her hair, her nose, and under her fingernails. Antonio brought out two cold Budweisers and hugged Elena, who returned his embrace, her head resting on his shoulder and an arm around his waist.

"You see?" Lopez said genially. "This is how it's supposed to be. The whole family is together! The wife is where she ought to be. She's cooking the dinner in her home."

The statement baffled Atwater, but he didn't comment on it. Instead, he made a joke. "My wife never cooked dinner for me."

Lopez looked at him with disapproval. "Maybe you picked the wrong woman, Arthur."

There might be some truth in that, Atwater thought. Nothing in the world seemed certain to him anymore.

10

There were always new people coming to Carson Valley from Mexico to look for work. They came from every state, from Chihuahua, Sinaloa, Jalisco, Guerrero, and faraway Tabasco and Campeche on the eastern Gulf Coast, from such big cities of the interior as Monterrey and Nuevo Laredo and little towns of the Baja California Peninsula as San Ignacio with its date palms and Indian laurels and San Borjita with its ancient cave paintings of war and hunting scenes. They would traverse any obstacle on their journey, be it the Sierra Madre Occidental, the Volcanic Highlands west of Mexico City, or the Plains of Sonora because they had friends and family in California, uncles and nephews and distant cousins who had spoken to them of the glory of the vineyards and the money to be reaped by toiling in them.

There was no single route they followed. They traveled by foot and by van, on horseback, in private automobiles, as hitchhikers and as unwanted passengers spread-eagled on top of boxcars, they would swim if they needed to—they would do anything at all once they had set themselves the task of crossing. They were freighted with the usual hopes and dreams of immigrants, nourished on fantasies, improbable success stories, and even tales of dominion, their curiosity whetted by the sheer implacable magnitude of the country to their north and by its abundant riches, the currency that dripped from the fingers of every citizen, dollars to be had for the mere mentioning of them, an

El Dorado where a man could get a job and then, with some ingenu-
ity, find an angle that would let him return to Mexico someday as a
person transformed, someone to be admired and emulated, a winner
in the great sweepstakes that operated continuously and eternally just
over the artificial line that was known as the border.

So it was that Omar Perez, a boy of fifteen, stood in front of a tin-
roofed shack in a dusty settlement between Zapopán and Tesistán,
northwest of Guadalajara, and dutifully kissed his mother good-bye
on a mild morning in May, while the roosters were still crowing. She
was sobbing and holding onto him by a shirtsleeve, pinching it between her fingers and crying, *"Mi hijo! Mi hijo!"* with such operatic despair that the neighbors were shouting for her to stop and had even
splashed down a bucket of water in an attempt to shut her up. Omar
was not unmoved, but he knew that her sorrow was bottomless, part
of her nature, a condition of her being. She would have wept as
mournfully if he had left at the age of twenty-five, he believed, so he
braced himself against her tears, broke away, and walked off with his
head down, determined to make his fortune in California.

He rode a bus into the city and then another bus to La Nueva
Central, a modern transport terminal of seven mazelike buildings on
the Zapotlanejo road. He almost got lost inside, but a clerk directed
him to the first building, where the cheapest fares were available, and
he bought a second-class ticket to Tijuana, a place he had never been
before. He was more excited than wary about the prospects ahead of
him, more thrilled than fearful. While he waited in the terminal,
chewing gum and smoking a cigarette, he studied the scrap of paper
on which his cousin Antonio Lopez had written an address and phone
number in the town of Santa Rosa, committing both to memory.
They had met at a big party during the Feast of the Immaculate Conception some three years ago, and Omar had been very impressed
with his cousin, who, after several shots of tequila, had invited him to
visit anytime.

He had thought about writing Antonio a letter in advance of his
trip, but he had decided against it. It would give his cousin a chance
to revoke the invitation, and he didn't want that. Omar Perez was
quite good at figuring the percentages and getting what he wanted,
in fact. He was a tough, cocky, durable kid, ambitious and a little
crooked, no more than five and half feet tall and gifted with an ability

to win the confidence of others. He had dropped out of school at the age of twelve to join a gang of youths who roamed around Guadalajara and cadged money in any way they could, becoming a competent petty thief and an occasional dealer of marijuana. His specialty was fleecing tourists, those elderly or innocent Americans who were susceptible to taking pity when Omar spun them a beggarly tale about his poverty and the beatings he'd endured at the hands of his mongrel parents. Once, he had so impressed a sailor on leave that he had been rewarded not only with some money but also an electric hair drier from the sailor's hotel room. He carried the drier with him now in a satchel that also held a change of clothes, a pair of sandals, and his radio.

The trip to Tijuana took almost two days. Omar dozed in his seat, his stomach uneasy. He couldn't eat the tamales or the fruit that his mother had packed for him in a paper sack. Sometimes at a rest stop he couldn't resist splurging on a soft drink, upset with himself for spending the cash because he had only forty American dollars to his name. His stomach settled down as the bus made its way up the coast, through Mazatlán and Culiacán along the pure blue waters of the Gulf of California. He was able to sustain himself with visions of Carson Valley and the wonderful grape farm that Antonio had described to him, a farm where he, too, planned to work and where he would become just as wealthy as his cousin. It was easy for him to imagine the treasures that would accrue to him—a better radio, a color TV, a camcorder, and, in time, his own car.

Tijuana offended Omar at first. It was not a colonial city like Guadalajara and had none of the grandeur to which he was accustomed, no eye-catching cathedral or majestic plazas. It lacked any aspect of welcome and seemed hard and fast to him, in a state of perpetual flux. He slept in an alley on the night he arrived, stretched out on a piece of crumpled cardboard with his money concealed in his underwear and his satchel serving as a pillow. Stray cats kept waking him by nuzzling against his face, and he heard music filtering down from windows and *cantinas* and the clatter of bottles and cans. There were cars roaring past him until very late, and toward dawn a drunk stumbled along the alley singing and crashing into the walls, pausing to piss down a stairwell before continuing on his oblivious march.

When a *panadería* opened nearby, Omar rousted himself and

bought a sweet roll and some coffee. He was stiff and sore and wished more than anything for a bath, but there were no facilities for the likes of him. The racket of the city picked up once more, dust and exhaust fumes rising everywhere to mix with the stench of garbage in the gutters, but he was committed to surviving the squalor and achieving his goal. He asked some questions of a girl behind the counter, counting on his good looks to win her sympathy, and she directed him to a brushy area above the levee of the Tijuana River, a murderous stream so poisoned with toxins that PELIGROSO signs were posted on its banks. Already, at noon, many people were gathered on the levee and preparing to cross the border after dark, groups of six or seven or a dozen men, husbands with their wives and children, and criminals armed with knives and revolvers. To Omar's surprise, they stood utterly revealed, their intent plain for the world to see.

He wandered through the crowd and made eye contact, nodding to his fellow pilgrims. He heard somebody hiss at him, a *coyote* promising to guide him safely, but he couldn't afford the price. Down the levee, he came upon some boys about his own age crouched in the shade of some mesquite bushes, each carrying a satchel or a bundle like his own. He joined them without being invited and sat at a polite distance from their circle, waiting for them to get curious, for one of them to speak.

"*Amigo,*" a boy called to him at last, tossing a twig at him. "*Qué quiere aquí?*"

Omar shrugged and acted amiable and harmless. "*No se.*" He pretended that he had nothing special in mind.

"*Váyase!*"

He would not go away. "*Yo no he hecho nada,*" he told them. That was so, he had done nothing to cause any alarm.

Another boy repeated the initial question. "*Dígame, muchacho. Qué diablos quiere usted?*"

"*Necisito ayuda. Quiero ir a California.*" Okay, he would tell them—he needed some help in reaching his destination.

They all laughed in his face. "*Taxi!*" yelled the first boy. "*Lleve el cabrón a California!*"

"*No soy un cabrón, amigo,*" Omar said staunchly. He would not tolerate insults.

He made a friend among them eventually, Martín Herrero, a

fellow *tapitío* from Jalisco who was a veteran of the border scene, twice arrested on a strawberry farm in Oceanside and twice returned to Mexico by *la migra*. Herrero was mightily conceited about his exploits, so Omar played up to him and flattered him with all kinds of questions. It turned out that Herrero planned to cross again that night—not at the levee, where Border Patrol agents were plentiful, but at a safer spot—and Omar asked to accompany him.

"*Por qué tu conducir?*" the haughty Herrero wanted to know. Why should I take you?

"*Porque tengo corazón. Soy un tapítio. Puede usted ayudarme, por favor?*"

"*Quizá.*" Maybe.

In the late afternoon, they left the levee together and rode a bus to a raw canyon scoured of all vegetation on the outskirts of Tijuana. The soil was a reddish color, very dry and rock solid, baked for centuries under the sun. Houses built of concrete blocks and scrap lumber were perched on the canyon rim, each in a different stage of completion, missing a door here and a wall there, not one of them wholly finished. Herrero led Omar down a dirt road notched with declivities to a spot where the ground was flat and stretched out like a plain. About two hundred people were assembled there, forming a little metropolis hidden from the authorities and patrolled by a few skinny pariah dogs, who yelped and moaned and nosed around in the underbrush.

"*Fenomenal,*" Omar said, in a whisper. He was honestly amazed. That morning, he had been alone, but now he was one of many.

He wandered through the camp with Herrero, his wonder growing. Vendors had set up some folding tables and had stacked used clothing on them in random piles, offering blue jeans, sweatshirts, and baseball caps to disguise those who intended to cross and give them the appearance of Americans. Omar spent two dollars on an L.A. Dodgers cap and wore it with the brim backward as he had seen actors do in movies. He walked over to a food stand on the other side of the canyon and treated his partner to some chicken tacos and a Coke. The atmosphere was almost festive. The woman who did the cooking had a big pot of beans simmering and a charcoal brazier on which she grilled strips of beef for *carne asada*. She was jolly and fat and wore her hair pulled back in a bun and several showy silver bracelets from Taxco.

The reddish color of the canyon deepened as the light began to fade, and the sky went from a hazy blue to a deep indigo. Omar felt exhilarated and also slightly anxious. He knew the sensation from his time in the streets of Guadalajara, an energy rush that always preceded the picking of a pocket or the snatching of a purse.

"*Cuanto dura la travesía?*" he asked. "*A que distancia está?*"

They had about ten miles to cover, Herrero told him. It would take them all night.

At dusk, the first few people set out, tentative in the face of the vastness before them, a plateau carved with ruts, potholes, and arroyos and made more treacherous still by clumps of sagebrush and thorny mesquite. No one dared to use a flashlight for fear of being detected. The moon was in its first quarter and afforded them little assistance. It was as if they were all being summoned at once, Omar thought, as if they were all responding to a signal only they could hear, moving off in units, three here, six there, each on a different path, their shoulders hunched, their bodies low to the ground, and their eyes constantly alert to any flicker in the immense blackness around them. The pariah dogs howled and chewed on bones and scraps of food, while the vendors packed up their wares and started up a bumpy road to their parked cars, only to return again in the morning to serve a fresh batch of customers.

An hour passed before Herrero was comfortable enough to take off. Omar followed behind him, not too closely. He found that he could make out shapes and see much more than he had expected. What he had expected was a kind of blindness. He walked carefully and watched the ground for snakes and scorpions, but he fell into a rhythm after a while and relaxed. The stars burned with a fiery brilliance, and he saw insects on the wing before him and once a panicky jackrabbit darting from behind a cactus. He was thirsty and wished for a drink of water, but he put the thought out of his mind and just kept walking, one foot after the other, toward California.

They came in time to a broad mesa. About two hours had gone by, Omar reckoned. He stopped in fatigue and looked across the mesa to the lights of a distant city. The lights were blinking and dancing.

"*Cigarrillo?*" Herrero asked, holding out a pack.

"*Gracias.*"

They rested for a few minutes before going on. Omar walked with a steadiness of purpose now, a resolve. He stared at the horizon, where the lights refused to budge. The lights were never any nearer to him and seemed actually to be receding into the distance. *You are imagining it,* he told himself. *You must be very tired.* He trudged on for another mile or so and began to get a second wind, his lungs capacious again and his leg muscles strong. At that instant, he felt that he could keep walking forever, from one end of the earth to the other without a break. He and his new friend Martín Herrero were two heroes scrawling their names across the globe, performing an act of bravery, men from Jalisco, *tapítios* who had met by chance on a levee in Tijuana and had forged an ironclad bond—brothers, then, in the mystical night.

They walked on. Yet another hour passed. The lights blinked and danced, more of them now, more discernible and individual. Omar lost any awareness of the landscape through which he moved. He became a hooded creature of the canyon fighting to stay awake, kin to lizards and spiders, and he did not hear the strange, whirring sound above him right away, a sound of metal blades slashing at the sky. It shocked him when a big cone of light fell from above to illuminate a wide sector of the mesa and every scurrying, furtive refugee on it. He shielded his eyes and looked up as a helicopter approached, its beacon searching the ground and causing people to freeze in place like statues, bathing them in an eerie white glow.

There was nothing to do but run. Martín Herrero had long legs and ran fast. Omar could not keep up with him. He watched in despair as his mentor and savior moved away from him, ten, fifteen, twenty yards ahead, growing tinier and tinier, diminishing. Herrero might soon have vanished from sight if the beacon had not cut across his path and forced him to duck and hide in some sagebrush, where Omar, panting hard, caught up to him. He grabbed at Herrero's trousers, a hand inside the waistband, and held him securely to prevent him from escaping again.

"*Silencio! No se mueva!*" Herrero warned him, and he did not so much as draw a breath.

Then they were running again. Herrero slipped free and swung to his left to avoid the helicopter beam. Omar trailed him, falling ever more behind, his spirits sinking as he realized that he would only be a bit player in the drama of Herrero's liberation. "*Espera!*" he yelled, but his friend would not wait and would not help. He knew then that he would surely fail in his mission. Instead of crossing safely, he would be arrested, thrown in jail, and herded back to Tijuana, where he would have to begin all over again. He cursed himself for trusting Herrero, a boy whose motives were at least as suspicious as his own.

Herrero was gone a moment later, vanished completely, not even a spectral trace of him left to be seen. His disappearance dealt a final blow to Omar's hopes. He simply gave up and quit running. There was a tremendous relief in his surrender, and he soon discovered that he was no more pursued than he had been on the fly. He could breathe at his leisure and didn't have to struggle. He walked briskly but without any haste and aimed himself toward the lights, which were not so distant now, stopping only when a loud whimper shocked him. He thought it must be an animal of some kind, but as he drew nearer he was sure that the whimper was human. It was the sound of somebody crying in pain, and it came from the pit of an arroyo just ahead.

He peered into the arroyo. Martín Herrero lay on the ground, clutching his right leg.

"*Amigo,*" Herrero begged. "*Creo que tengo una fractura.*"

Omar shimmied down the arroyo wall. Herrero released his grip to show off his wound. His ankle was bent at a sharp and terrifying angle, and a shard of bone had punctured the skin. The leg of his pants, his sock, his shoe, the ground, they were all drenched in blood.

"*Fractura, no,*" Omar said. "*Un hueso roto.*" A broken bone.

"*Me siento débil, amigo.*" Herrero's voice was quivering, imploring. "*Ayúdame, por favor.*"

To Omar, this was an example of cosmic justice in action. He was delighted to see Herrero groveling at his feet. "*No es posible,*" he said firmly, denying the request.

"*Soccoro!*" Herrero shouted. "*Ayúdame!*"

"*Adiós, Martín!*" Omar climbed from the arroyo and started running again, happy with himself and relishing his freedom, and as he ran the sky grew lighter. He felt then that he was blessed. He could see the actual buildings of a city now and also the other refugees who had eluded capture. They ran in a pack toward a chain-link fence that marked the border, and he joined them and got down on his hands and knees to crawl through a hole. Trash was strewn along the fence, dirty diapers and rinds of fruit and shreds of paper, the detritus of a mass and ceaseless migration, and he kicked it aside and made for a street not far away.

The city was not as big as he had imagined. It was more of a town, really, and everything in it, every house and every shop, looked new. Omar tried to be inconspicuous, but nobody was paying any attention to him. He didn't have to be afraid. He blended easily with the people of this place, who had the same dark eyes and dark hair, Mexicans once or twice removed from their homeland. He sat for a time on a bus stop bench, and when a wrinkled old lady sat next to him he asked her what the town was called.

"San Ysidro," she told him.

He had another question for her. "*Donde está* Carson Valley? *Es este el camino más corto?*" He wanted the shortest route to his cousin's house, but she gave him a cronish look of displeasure and left him alone on the bench. He didn't know what mistake he had made until he noticed that his clothes were smudged with grime and stained with Herrero's blood, so he went into a gas station rest room and washed his face and combed his hair. He changed into a clean shirt, traded his sneakers for his sandals, fluffed up the crown of his baseball cap, and strolled to the center of town, where the traffic was thick and congested at the port of entry, backed up in both directions.

Omar stood in the morning sun, his satchel at his feet. The shiny press of things enchanted him. There was a latent power in the endless line of cars ferrying passengers between Mexico and California, and he could feel a thrumming in his chest, as if an engine had kicked into gear, and he looked away to the desert, so near, where the air was heavy and brown and a few buzzards were circling around something dead.

A man came up to him. He had an insinuating smile, and his shirt was soaked with sweat. "You're new here," he said.

Omar returned the smile. "*No comprendo,*" he replied, pretending that he had no English, although he spoke it fairly well.

The man nudged the satchel with his foot. "You're new here," he repeated. "I can arrange some things for you."

They chatted in the shadow of the port of entry. The man offered to set up a ride to San Diego for Omar. San Diego was a true city, he explained, and it had a vast and teeming *barrio,* where a person could hide out and some other things could be arranged.

"Ten dollars," the man said.

"*Ay, no, eso es más de lo que puede gastar,*" Omar told him, bargaining. "*Acceptaría* five dollars?"

"Eight dollars."

Omar paid. That evening, he waited on a street corner as instructed, thinking that he had made another mistake, but precisely at six o'clock an old gray station wagon pulled up at the curb, and somebody threw open a door. Inside were a number of other people going north—two teenagers from Rosarito, a married couple from Oaxaca, and a girl whose aunt lived in Sacramento. Nobody talked during the ride, as if to speak would be to break a solemn treaty. Everyone shared the same secret, everyone was nurtured by the same dream.

Omar fell asleep for a while. He woke to find his head resting in the girl's lap. "*Pobrecito,*" she said, in a kind way, as she might have to a child.

He yawned. "*Estoy cansado,*" he told her.

"*Claro.*"

"*Conosce usted* Carson Valley?"

She shrugged. "*No lo conosco.*"

They were released eventually into the *barrio* of San Diego. Omar was puzzled by the city's complexities, by its sheer volume and size. Not one person here cared about him, not one person knew his name. He asked the driver where he might find a telephone.

"Two blocks. Up that street."

"*Necesito fichas para el telefono?*"

"No tokens. American coins."

In a liquor store, he bought a bag of salted peanuts and changed three dollar bills for twelve quarters. He handled the transaction ineptly, in a manner that marked him as a foreigner, but the clerk ignored him. The telephone booth was occupied, though, and he had to wait yet again. When his turn came he deposited a coin and dialed his cousin's number, but nothing happened. Instead, he heard a mechanical voice saying something, so he fed in more quarters until the voice went away and a ringing noise began.

A woman answered on the other end. "*Puede hablar con* Antonio Lopez, *por favor?*" Omar asked.

"Just a minute."

The boy was skittish, apprehensive, overjoyed. The booth felt like a rocket ship to him.

"*Dígame,*" Antonio Lopez said.

"*Omar habla!*" he cried.

"*Con quien hablo?*"

"*Omar Perez.*" A blank silence greeted his words. "I say in English," he went on. "I am cousin to you, yes?" That provoked no response either, so the boy switched back to Spanish and described how he and Antonio had met and reminded him of his offer. "*Quiero trabajar contigo,*" he said.

"You should have called before you left, man. You should have written me a letter or something," his cousin said. "There's no work now, Omar. Not until the harvest."

"I can harvest, yes?"

"It's not until August at the earliest. The last part of August. *Agosto, comprendes? Más tiempo.*"

"I come in August."

"Does your mother know where you are?" his cousin asked him. "Where are you, anyway?"

"San Diego."

"You should go home, Omar."

"I come in August, please?"

There was a pause. "If you show up, I'll see what I can do. But I can't promise you anything. You should go home. You know that, don't you?"

"I come in August."

"Come if you want. I can't stop you, man."

"*Muchas gracias.*" The boy said his good-byes and moved off into the colorful swirl of the *barrio,* elated that the future had been decided in his favor.

11

The first field report from Consolidated Vintners reached Victor Torelli in his office mail on a Saturday in mid-May. He studied its six pages over a shot of Old Crow. He had never read a document so dense or data-strewn, its conclusions supported by numbers, percentages, and fractions that swam before his eyes, the work of a computer somewhere in the bowels of the universe whose intricacies he dared not contemplate. The news was depressing, if the report could be believed. The CV field agent, one R. W. Kimball, had employed an esoteric formula involving some advanced mathematics that Torelli could not fathom in the least to project an estimated yield for the vineyard of 4.2 tons per acre. That was far below his average yield of five-plus tons. Kimball listed several possible reasons for the problem, each of which, he suggested, pointed toward oversights on the part of the vineyard manager.

Torelli rolled up the report and stuffed it crankily into a back pocket. He could have done without such news. His mood was already bleak. He had spent another rough night tossing in bed, his sleep interrupted so often by various aches and pains that he felt as if he hadn't slept at all. His bum knee was as sore as ever, and his heart was bothering him, too. It kept jumping around in his chest and skipping beats, and he got so short of breath at times that a short stroll thoroughly tired him out. He was also subject to an extreme exhaus-

tion that swept over him every afternoon and made him want to lie
down wherever he was and rest for an eternity. The spell always
passed after a few minutes, though, so he wasn't ready to concede that
anything might be wrong with him. He had, of course, not mentioned
his worries to anybody.

The day was bright and burning, already in the mid-eighties when
Torelli stepped out of his office a little before noon. Catfish weather,
his grandfather used to call it. Giovanni Torelli chewed Red Man tobacco, had jug ears, and wore suspenders that slipped down his shoulders and threatened to take his trousers with them. He was renowned
for a special spaghetti sauce that he fixed with chicken livers, which
also figured in the horrendous bait he liked to concoct. Every May,
when the heat kicked in, Giovanni would head for the nearest butcher
shop to buy a few pounds of innards. Then he dumped them in a
metal pail, carried the bloody mess outside, and left it in the sun to
cure for a week or so. The innards festered, slimed, suppurated, and
reeked beyond belief, and when the stink got so bad that the family
pets ran from it, Giovanni would consider the bait properly cooked
and would try it on the lunker catfish lurking in the depths of the pond.

The streets in town were busier than usual, Torelli noticed. Tourist
season was in full swing again, with weekenders holed up in all the
quaint bed-and-breakfast inns, city folks who blinked and gaped at the
spectacle of an aging grape grower in baggy dungarees. *I ought to do
like the Indians do,* Torelli grumbled to himself, *and charge 'em a quarter to
shake my hand.* He felt the good heat penetrate his splintery bones and
was certain that summer had arrived, no matter what the calendar
date—the valley would be hot, dry, and ever more dusty right through
until the harvest. It was a time of year when the pace of things slowed
down at last, when farmers took a break to watch ballgames and odd-
shaped clouds and did the neglected household chores that their wives
had been after them to do since budbreak, a time given over in the old
man's mind to tranquil evenings on a bench in the square, where he
and Thomas Atwater, the closest of pals, sat waiting to meet some
girls.

Torelli slid behind the wheel of his truck. He had a social obliga-
tion to fulfill, one that he would gladly have swapped for a nap on his
couch, but Hazel Poplinger had put the screws to him. She was

throwing a huge gala and had phoned him herself, all sugary and phony, to be sure that he would attend. It would not be a true valley event, Hazel had said, unless Victor Torelli graced it with his presence. What nonsense! Her formal invitation was strewn among the detritus on the old man's dashboard, a fancy printed card trumpeting "A Celebration of the Bloom." It featured an artist's rendering of a grape flower in the form of a goddam tulip, when grape flowers didn't even have any petals. Instead, there was a cap of green tissue that dropped off to reveal four white stamens lightly powdered with yellow pollen at their anthers. The flowers were so fragile that Torelli's grandfather wouldn't set foot in the vineyard while the bloom was on. *Stai attento!* he'd yell at his grandson, who was fond of chasing butterflies down the rows.

The Poplingers lived on a high hill off Carson Valley Road. Although it was commonly asserted that Irwin Poplinger was a humble dentist, Torelli had more accurate information. The doc was actually a crack oral surgeon who practiced at a consortium of Bay Area hospitals and had earned a million dollars before his fortieth birthday. Poplinger was in his early sixties now, and the estate was a monument to his skill and his business acumen. The wrought-iron gate at the bottom of the driveway served him as a sort of trophy. Torelli had once been told that it had cost more than fifty thousand dollars. A filigree of tendrils were threaded in decorative swirls around a massive, sans-serif P. The mansion beyond it, up on a rise, was equally impressive with its turrets, fieldstone walls, and arched windows in the Gothic mode, a capricious estate praised in the leading architectural journals for its bravura style.

The old man turned over his truck to a valet parker and paused to get the lay of the land. Guests were convened all over the estate, some of them in very expensive and fashionable clothes—more city folks on the lam, Torelli gathered—and he could hear the clink of glasses, lots of yakking and laughter, and a clear and winsome bell-like sound that came from a set of wind chimes. Some musicians were playing a Haydn string quartet on the patio, while children splashed around in a big swimming pool below them and batted a pink beach ball into the air. Entering the foyer, Torelli stopped to admire the marble floor, the elegant porcelain vases, and an abstract painting that looked like the aftermath of a car wreck before he continued into a huge living room that afforded him a stunning panoramic view of the valley and its billowy green vines.

The Poplingers were receiving there. Hazel was short and vivacious, while Irwin was lanky and earnest and seemed honestly to respect the craft of growing wine grapes.

"How nice of you to come!" Hazel exclaimed, as though she had never made an importunate call.

"We're honored to have you," Irwin added.

"Wouldn't have missed it for the world," Torelli told them dryly. "You know that grape flower on your card?"

Hazel blinked. "Yes?"

"It shouldn't have any petals."

The old man excused himself and escaped to the patio, where he was accosted by a four-eyed gent with three cameras draped around his neck. "Photo for the *Herald?*" the fellow asked him.

"There's no need to shoot a photo of me," Torelli complained, although he whipped out a pocket comb and started right in on his wavy white hair.

Charlie Grimes toddled over, eager to be part of the composition, and edged his way into the frame. He was holding a full-to-the-brim flute and slopping champagne on a Navajo rug. "Hell, yes, take our picture!" he shouted, zooming a fist into the air. "We're the very pioneers of Carson Valley!" He put an arm around Torelli, pulled him close, and whispered, "Hold still, goddam it. I need the publicity!"

A flashbulb popped, and the photographer dashed off. "There now, that didn't hurt, did it?" Grimes asked. "Isn't it nice to be a celebrity for once?"

"Celebrity, my ass."

"What's eating you, Victor? You don't look so swell, you know."

"Neither will you when you're almost eighty."

"Don't you be pissing on my shoes," Grimes told him huffily. "I'm your friend, remember? Why don't you go out back and listen to those fiddlers in tuxedos? Maybe they'll cheer you up."

Torelli obeyed. Standing on the patio as the string ensemble cycled into a minuetto allegro movement, spritely and uplifting, he surveyed the festive scene on the backyard lawn. He could smell some beef and pork ribs cooking on a grill at a barbecue pit where a black man, the rarest of valley sights, tended them with a pair of tongs over ember-bright coals, his apron soiled with sauce. He wore a toque that had a red star on its crown and in script the words *Original Willie's BBQ*. Bowls of coleslaw, beans, mustard greens, and several kinds of salad were on a side table, and the old man took a place in line and helped himself to the food, accepting a heavy ration of ribs from the smiling chef.

He ate on his feet and observed the goings-on around the swimming pool. His daughter was reclining on a chaise lounge and chatting with Dick Rhodes. He had not seen Anna so mellow or carefree since she'd gone off to college. That her contentment was due, at least in some measure, to her affair with Arthur Atwater was difficult for the old man to swallow, but he had learned long ago that hearts were lunatic, not rational. Love of that sort had its own dynamic. It struck with the speed of light. He thought of stooping hawks, of a stone dropped from the top floor of the leaning tower of Pisa. Atwater was a pretty scuffed-up individual, but then Torelli had not chosen his own wife on the basis of her beauty. Claire had instantly touched something in him, an empty place that he had never before recognized as empty. He had been half a man and unaware of it, and she had made him whole.

It was the middle of the afternoon before Atwater himself showed up. Without so much as a hello to anyone, he dived straight into the chow line, commandeered a vacant table, and started eating ravenously, as somebody does when they've passed up their lunch hour to keep working in the fields. Torelli approached the table with a sense of foreboding, the CV report like a grenade in his back pocket. Why should he be drawn into the business of wine grapes again when he had done all he could to be liberated from it? And how would Atwater, who had a tripwire nervous system, react to Kimball's criticism? Well, he knew the answer to that one, but what if his vineyard manager went on the offensive? What if he had to let Atwater go? The unfairness of his predicament caused the old man's heart to do its little dance.

"Mind if I join you, Arthur?" he asked, with an abnormal blandness.

Atwater glanced up from his plate. "No, sir," he said. "I'd be glad for your company."

"You've got yourself an appetite."

"I could eat a horse, tail and all."

Torelli had a sip of his 7-Up. "Anna tells me you took the ladies fishing while her friend was here."

"Yes, I did, after Anna lit into me." Atwater grinned, and his eyes were jolly. "Victor, I wish you could have been there! The look on Jane's face when she hooked that bass! She jumped up and down, and the bass flopped and thrashed and ran on her, and she jumped again and landed on her butt."

"Did she keep the fish?"

"Hell, no." Atwater was nearly beside himself with mirth. "She's for animal rights!"

Torelli couldn't bring himself to share in the fun. The CV report was weighing on him, so he tossed it on the table. "Tell me what you think of that, will you?"

Atwater put down his fork and read it with close scrutiny. The old man could see his outrage mounting. When Arthur reached the last page, he turned back to the beginning and read it through a second time. "It's bullshit," he said finally. "Pure, one-hundred-percent, un-adulterated bullshit."

"This Kimball, he's a scientist," the old man replied, with a hint of doubt. "He's got a degree in viticulture. Wine grapes are his field."

"He hasn't ever worked our farm."

"That's not the point, Arthur. Nobody is questioning how much effort you put in. We all know how hard you try. Kimball just wants to improve things a bit."

"But it's all hypothetical, Victor!" He pushed the report away from him and crossed his arms. "It's nothing but graphs and projections."

"What about this section here?" Torelli flipped to the last page. "Where he says there's some mildew on our Chardonnay because you didn't do enough sulfuring?"

"Nobody in the whole valley did enough sulfuring! We had show-ers all through the first half of the month, and the rain washed the dust off the leaves. Every grower got caught."

"He says we've got leafhoppers and thrips, too."

Atwater snorted. "Those bugs aren't harming anything."

"Kimball believes you should do more spraying."

"Rawley Kimball doesn't know that vineyard the way I do, does he? A little more of this hot weather, and the thrips will die off. The leafhoppers have enough predators to keep them from spreading. We've got a good natural balance going. Why ruin it with chemicals?"

"This estimated yield here is low." Torelli isolated a column of numbers. "It's real low, Arthur. My Chardonnay vines always bear five tons or more. My old Zinfandel vine will go as high as six tons in a good year."

"We'll come close to that."

"Not by Kimball's estimate."

Atwater was fuming now. "I *guarantee* it. Measure this, measure that—he's just blowing smoke, Victor. It's only *arithmetic*. That's what he gets paid to do!"

"Suppose he's right?"

"I'm not going to argue with you anymore," Atwater said flatly. "You can trust a computer, or you can trust me."

Torelli returned the report to his pocket. "It's not a matter of who to trust, is it? This is science we're dealing with here."

"Okay," Atwater said. "I get it. You want me to quit."

"No, I don't want you to quit! That's the stupidest goddam thing you've said yet."

"You want to fire me instead?"

"No, I don't want to fire you either. Boy, you are a pain in the ass, Arthur! Why do you have to be so goddam sensitive?"

"That's how I'm made," Atwater said contritely. "I can't control it."

"All I'm asking you to do is to listen. Kimball, he's not a bad fellow. You don't have to take every bit of advice. Just take some of it. You can pick and choose. I—" Torelli's train of thought was abruptly derailed by some intense shrieking. "It's Vescio," he said, shaking his head. "Wouldn't you know he'd pull his stunt?"

The guests were scattering in the wake of Fred Vescio who, in customary fashion, was cuddling a piglet in a blue baby blanket and feeding it milk from a bottle. His sister-in-law Maude followed several steps behind him, a hand covering her mouth, half embarrassed and half enjoying the ritual, her hair, dyed a flame red color, alive in the sun. The piglet squealed, squirmed, and twitched its corkscrew tail whenever Fred thrust it into someone's face. The valley old-timers were fond of barnyard humor and took the performance in stride, but some genteel friends of the Poplingers were very uncomfortable and seemed to think that the poor little critter meant to bite them. Their reaction only egged on Vescio, and he released the piglet and sent it skittering toward a particularly fainthearted woman, who slipped and fell into the swimming pool.

"The day they handed out brains," Torelli sighed, scratching a mosquito bite, "Fred was last in line."

"Victor," Atwater told him, calmer now, "I'll make a deal with you. I'll listen to Kimball, but I won't take any orders from him."

"Nobody's asking you to take orders. Just to listen."

"You're the only one who has the right to give me orders. So long as that's clear."

"Fair enough," the old man said. "But don't go running away on me, Arthur. You'll never get a fourth chance out of Victor Torelli. I can promise you that."

"I understand."

Torelli offered his hand to seal the pact. While they were shaking, they were joined at the table by Jack Farrell, who sat glaring at Atwater with total aggression for a minute or two without speaking. Silence wasn't ordinarily Farrell's style.

"Well, Jack," the old man asked him. "Cat got your tongue?"

Farrell broke down. "All right, I'll state my purpose. I'm here to challenge my rival."

"Who might that be?"

"Him!" Farrell pointed at Atwater. "Arthur Atwater."

Atwater seemed to find this diverting. "It's news to me, Jack," he said serenely.

"You're the asshole who stole Anna away from me, aren't you?"

"I wouldn't put it quite like that."

"Maybe she prefers him," Torelli suggested.

"He stole her away from me, Victor! I never had a fair shot at her!" Farrell wailed. "If I did, she'd be in love with me. Hell, I can convince anybody of anything if I try! People from Hawaii have visited this valley on account of me. I've sucked in tourists from all over Europe. There's a delegation from Senegal due in November. That's a country in Africa. I *am* the Chamber of Commerce, friends. You better believe it."

"What's the challenge?" Atwater asked.

"A game of horseshoes. The winner gets to take Anna home."

"Like a duel, Jack?"

"Exactly! Except nobody has to die."

"Suppose Anna has her own car?" Torelli asked.

Farrell was flustered. He thought for a moment. "Sufficient unto the day are the worries thereof," he said, rather pleased with his biblical scholarship. "Will you play, or won't you?"

"Sure, I'll play," Atwater told him.

"Good. Fifteen innings, count-all. I pick Ron Santini for my partner. Who do you pick?"

"I pick Victor."

The men removed themselves to a pitching court at the side of a barn that was carefully concealed by some artful landscaping. The Poplingers' field hands maintained the court for their own use after work. A chalkboard hung from a nail on the wall for scoring purposes. Farrell tossed a coin and chuckled when it turned up heads and earned his team the hammer. His aim with the shoes proved to be erratic. The first two that he threw sailed past the stake by a good eight feet, propelled by the thrust of his anger, but Santini, a retailer of farm machinery, had once belonged to the National Horseshoe Pitchers' Association of America and recouped with five ringers in just six turns.

"Easy as pie," he bragged after the fifth one, showing off a primatelike forearm.

"Easy when you're a professional," Torelli growled at him. "Whatever became of that son of yours, Santini?"

"Eddie moved up to Bend, Oregon."

"What's he doing with himself up there?"

"He opened a hardware store."

The old man was having trouble with the game. The shoes only weighed about three pounds each, but they felt much heavier to him. His tosses kept falling short, and he didn't score a single point through nine innings. The fatigue and shortness of breath that had been bugging him added to his discomfort. The score was twenty to twelve, with three innings to go, when Anna walked up to him.

"It's a little hot for this, isn't it?" she asked. "I'll bet it's a hundred degrees in the sun."

She took to the heat herself, Torelli thought. Her skin was tanned to a lovely bronze. "We're having a duel," the old man explained to her. "Your affections are at issue. The winner gets to take you home."

"Ha!" Anna cried. "Did it occur to anyone that I might have my own car? As well as my own wishes?"

The game was decided in the next inning when Atwater's team failed to make a point. "Do you concede?" Farrell bellowed from his end of the court.

"I concede!" Atwater called back through cupped hands.

Farrell came toward Anna at a shambling trot, taking pitty-pat steps like Babe Ruth rounding the bases after a homer, but she was too quick for him and veered off in a different direction.

"Sorry, Jack," she said, a possessive arm around Atwater's waist. "Arthur's my guy."

"But he accepted my challenge!" Farrell shouted. "Tell me one thing he's got that I don't."

"Savoir faire."

"What's that?"

"It's French for *cojónes*," Anna told him.

"*Cojónes?*" Farrell asked. "You don't think I have *cojónes?*"

They all started back to the mansion through the lengthening shadows of early evening. Torelli trudged along by himself slowly and warily. He saw in his daughter's confident gait the same easy grace that Claire had possessed and recalled the strolls that they would take at twilight, just the two of them wandering around the vineyard and talking over the happenings of the day. How simple and yet how comforting, he thought. He realized how much he had depended on Claire and how much he missed her. All at once, with an utter certainty, he understood that the earth was wearing out for him. Though he was not a man who prayed, something like prayer gripped him, and he found himself hoping that he might die in relative peace, with no more pain than he could tolerate.

He sat at a table again to watch the ceremony that Hazel Poplinger had devised to conclude her gala. Two little girls in flowing dresses, nieces of the hosts, materialized on the patio and carried a huge rectangular cake down to poolside, tripping once on the flagstone steps before they reached the spot where a caterer stood at the ready with a stack of plates and an urn of coffee. The frosting on the cake was white and raised up in curlicues at the edges. A talented pastry chef had added some purple bunches of grapes in a field of green leaves. Above the grapes, in luminous orange script, were the words, "Long May They Bloom."

"Speech!" somebody shouted.

Irwin Poplinger was not cut out for speaking in public. He meant well, but he was terribly long-winded, and Torelli had to stifle several yawns behind a fist. He had almost fallen asleep when he caught a gamey whiff of perfume and saw that Maude Vescio had seated herself next to him and was applying lipstick and blotting it on a paper napkin.

"That dentist can go on, can't he?" she said under her breath.

"He has the gift."

Maude was staring at him oddly. "You look a little peaked, Victor."

"I'm tired, Maude." He surprised himself with the admission.

When the speech was over, Maude insisted on bringing him some coffee and cake. She belonged to a different generation than his, the same one as Claire, and he had always treated her as a kid sister, both flattered and irritated about how she fussed over him. She considered him to be an important person, somebody from a better class. The Vescios were a rough-and-tumble breed, private and secretive and possessed of abundant and sometimes malignant vices. Maude was a Vescio by marriage only, of course, and so was exempt from such character flaws, but the old man remained leery of how she had flourished after her husband's death. Her hair was too red, too optimistic.

"You still doing all that traveling, Maude?" He'd heard about her recent trips to Lake Tahoe and Disney World in Florida.

"Yes, I just love it!" She was a giddy sort, prone to outbursts of baseless enthusiasm. "And I'm off to Europe with my ballroom dancing club in the fall!"

"If you're going to Europe, you ought to visit Italy. That's where my people are from. A city in Tuscany called Montalcino."

"Well, what do you know about that!"

"Yes, ma'am," Torelli said, with pride. "I was just thinking about my grandfather this morning."

"Isn't that a coincidence!" She inclined her head toward him in a show of interest. "You must tell me all about him."

Torelli scoffed at the idea. "I'd bore the pants off you."

Maude ruffled her skirt with a hand. "But I'm not wearing pants!"

"You got me there," the old man said, admiring her quick wit and launching into his story.

12

On Memorial Day, the *Valley Herald* always ran a traditional front page photograph to remind its readers that full summer was just around the corner. The composition of the photo was based on a famous painting by Thomas Eakins, but no one except the town librarian, who was an amateur art historian, still remembered that. It showed a group of schoolkids, not a few of them in their underwear, cavorting on a bridge by the river, where a temporary dam of bulldozed earth had created a swimming hole that was known as Carson Beach. It was the paper's conceit that the children were about to dive into the water, a freefall of about thirty feet, but nobody had done that since the Markley twins had their accident, and the boys and girls were actually shepherded away right after the shoot and treated to some ice cream at a Baskin-Robbins.

The back pages of the same issue featured a few pictures from the Poplingers' gala, including a shot of Anna Torelli grouped among some other guests at a buffet table. When Anna came across it over breakfast one morning, she was astonished by her own radiance. She barely recognized herself at first—her tangled emotions weren't reflected anywhere on her face. She looked serene, relaxed, and younger than she had in years, despite a terminally overwrought Jack Farrell lurking behind her at the margin of the frame. Farrell's contorted expression bore a curious resemblance to a gargoyle that Anna could recall seeing on a church façade in Germany during her grand tour of Europe. "Visitor From Back East," read the caption above her head, but she didn't feel like a visitor anymore. Instead, she felt like someone whose true location, an aspect of the spirit, couldn't be pinned down on any map.

Slowly and with difficulty, Anna had accepted the fact that it was time for her to leave Carson Valley. Her sojourn on the farm had the texture of a pleasant dream from which she was reluctant to wake, but she had run out of reasons and excuses to prolong it. Jane Weiss was understandably tired of covering for her at the bookstore and kept pestering her by phone until she had agreed to return to New York at the end of June. She was trying to be sensible about the arrangement and told herself that there was really nothing final about her departure. If the valley still tugged at her when she got home, she could make the necessary changes in her life and come back. She hoped, too, that the distance might grant her some clarity, although she had a sneaky suspicion that her current problems wouldn't ever bend to logic. On a certain level, she understood that this particular idyll could not be reconstructed once it was undone.

Atwater was the sticking point, of course. Anna had no idea what to do about him. So far, she had dared to broach the subject of her leaving just once, while they were picking plums from an old orchard tree in the meadow. She mentioned it casually in passing as she might have an insignificant item of gossip, but the news seemed not to disturb him at all. "I always knew that," he replied simply, turning away from her. She was crushed by his detached response, but what had she expected? If he had gotten down on one knee and begged her to reconsider, would it have made a difference? Definitely not. Her plans were firm. Besides, Arthur wasn't the type to beg—under any circumstances—and Anna couldn't blame him for the bind she was in. Against her better judgment, she had allowed herself to develop feelings for him. She had assumed at the start that their affair, in its sheer incandescence, would quickly crash and burn, but she desired him more than ever now, and not merely in bed.

For Atwater, this difficult and eccentric man, had given her a wonderful gift. He adored her without reservation. Anna would never have guessed how satisfying that could be or how much she craved such attention. When she was married to Bud Wright, she had taken on the role of an adoring young wife, but it was just playacting, and extremely unconvincing at that. Often Bud must have seen that she was putting on a show for him; but in Arthur, there was nothing false. All his actions and convictions, right or wrong, admirable or despic-able—and he *could* be despicable—had a wholeness about them, a richness and a roundness, as if he had cast off every imaginary and fantastic version of himself long ago and could only offer up his es-sence. He was incapable of half measures and only knew how to love someone with the full screaming intensity of his heart. And Anna had no doubt he loved her that way.

As much as she doted on his affection and flattery, though, it could be overwhelming sometimes. Atwater—whose motto might have been "Damn the torpedos"—lacked the slightest talent for nuance. In his wild exuberance, he was insensitive to Anna's occasional need for pri-vacy and had a bad habit of intruding on her whenever she chose to be alone for a while, and she would have to withdraw from him to pursue her own interests. He resented it, naturally, but she felt that she was under attack. What *he* wanted was for Anna to be up to the pitch of his energy and ready for some high jinks at any hour of the day or night, while the last thing *she* wanted was to be grafted to him at the hip; but her efforts to explain that to him had fallen on deaf ears. Arthur drove her nuts, too, with his maverick streak, posing as the only sane person in a universe gone mad. *Go join the Foreign Legion!* she had shouted at him once, swearing that he deserved one of those wacky hats and a seven-year trek across some womanless desert in Arabia.

The vineyard was another bone of contention between them. Anna had lobbied for a joint venture, with her as the junior associate, but Atwater refused to listen to a word she had to say about wine grapes. He couldn't get it through his thick skull either that there might be something worthwhile, maybe just a single scrap of perti-nent data, in the biweekly CV reports that she read, annotated, and underlined for his benefit. Whenever she screwed up the courage to ask him about the progress of the crop, he answered her in monosyl-lables—fine, good, fair, shitty—he was a minimalist genius at blocking her out. The only job he had let her handle was to investigate what kind of rootstock to plant when they ripped out the old Chardonnay vines. Anna was determined to prove her mettle and went at the research in her own predictably maximalist way, and when after countless calls to nurseries and a road trip to Foundation Plant Material Services at UC Davis she had presented him with the results of her survey—Ganzin Number One—his response was less than satisfactory.

"Ganzin Number One, eh? Yeah, I can see that. It does well on the valley floor."

Thank you so very much, Mr. Atwater! After such patronizing dismissals, she was ready to pack her bags and head straight for the nearest licensed clinical therapist to get the counseling she so evidently required, and then, out of nowhere, Arthur would charm her again just by being himself. That was what she liked best about him, actually—Atwater was Atwater, secure in his identity and never putting on airs. She respected his integrity in facing the world as he truly was, without any mask. Because he wouldn't refashion himself to suit her, or even entertain the possibility of altering any of his most offensive traits, they'd had some terrific arguments, real knock-down drag-outs of a sort that Anna had never participated in before. Oddly enough, she enjoyed them—not for the arguing itself but because she didn't have to hold anything back. Arthur could take her best shot. That was a corollary to their fucking, she supposed, and it made her think that perhaps he *was* her equal and, further, that equality wasn't a given in any relationship but rather something to be struggled for in the ceaseless dance of yin and yang.

So, day by day, Anna's confusion was mounting. She saw that she had built an elegant trap for herself in Carson Valley, and to escape from it she put in long hours working in her vegetable garden. The garden was her Back Forty, her guru, her mantra, her salvation. She had planted it close to the house in a big rectangular plot rototilled for her by Dick Rhodes and fertilized with compost, bonemeal, nitrogen, and ample loads of horse manure from Pepper Harris's paddock. Her selection of crops was decidedly cornucopic. Anything she could find a seed for she had sunk into the ground: Golden Bantam corn, green and wax beans, several exotic lettuces, some spinach and Swiss chard, Early Girl and Ace tomatoes, and more Chefini hybrid zucchini squash than could be eaten onsite or laid off on her friends and neighbors, who already had too much Chefini hybrid zucchini of their own. Anna could have operated a truck farm out of her own backyard.

But the garden caused her some trouble, as well. Many nasty predators were attracted to its bounty, and Anna despised them all. She wasn't prepared for their vicious forays at first. Her most recent try at growing things, a larkish urban adventure, had involved two pots of cherry tomatoes on the fire escape of her apartment, where the only predator around was Sam McNally, who plucked them when she wasn't looking. This country farming was serious business, though, and it had turned her into a killer. She murdered slugs and white flies with abandon, but the pocket gophers had her stymied. One afternoon, she watched in horror as a mature bean plant disappeared down a hole. How very brazen! Anna scoured the barn for heavy artillery after that and found some old spring-loaded gizmos on chains. They resembled medieval instruments of torture and impaled their victims on a metal spike. Still, she sank them into tunnels with enthusiasm, only to blanch when she finally nailed a gopher and had to scrape away its crushed and bloody remains with a trowel.

That was more destruction than she could stand, so she called around the valley for advice. She heard support for rat poison from Rhodes, dog urine from Charlie Grimes, garlic cloves from Maude Vescio, and compassionate tolerance from Betty Chambers, who had taken a course in Tibetan Buddhism at Santa Rosa Junior College. As for Arthur Atwater, he swore to her that his grandmother had policed her garden with a handgun.

"She sat out there in her rocker smoking a cigarette and reading *True Romance,* just as patient as she could be," he told her. "And pretty soon one of those little guys would get careless and stick his head out of a hole to see what was going on, and *bam! bam! bam!*"—Atwater was yelling—"my granny would blow him away."

"What an exquisite tale. Thank you for sharing it with me, Arthur."

"Gophers are a low form of life. They steal from people."

"So they should be shot?"

"Correct. Shot or poisoned. It's the law of the jungle."

"Even in the garden?"

"Yes, even in the garden," Atwater said. "One time when I was a kid, we stuffed a firecracker . . ."

Anna chose to follow the Chambers approach and tolerate the gophers. She adopted a high-minded attitude toward them that was in no way natural to her, but when some blacktail deer crept down out of the hills one night and devoured a whole row of okra, she was indeed tempted to spring for a .357 Magnum and take to her rocking chair. Instead, she prevailed on Atwater to build her a fence. He did it in his free time, complaining about how tough it was to drive stakes into soil that was so hard and dry, but he got it done. The garden, once fenced, became a private preserve for her, where she could fall into the hypnotic and meditative rhythm every gardener knows and cherishes, her thoughts ranging far and wide and generally in the opposite direction from her worries.

The field hands on the farm were baffled by her dedication. Eloy Hidalgo, Hector Cruz, and even Antonio Lopez couldn't fathom why a woman of means, a *gringa* with plenty of *pesos*, would voluntarily spend such long hours on her hands and knees in the same punishing dust that was their element. They seemed to believe that Anna was under the influence of a dark and compelling force and felt obligated as gentlemen and knights-errant of Mexico to offer their assistance.

"I can pull some weeds for you, missus."

"Would you like to borrow my hoe, Anna?"

"*Buenas tardes, señora.* I can do the watering. Why don't you rest yourself?"

She rejected them all. They were embarrassed for her and attributed her weird behavior to a configuration of galloping hormones and planetary alignment that was beyond the ken of any man. They began teasing her, too, muttering whenever they walked by the garden that she was "*un poco loca, una mujer peligrosa,*" and Anna would smile amiably and think, *Yes, it's true, I am a little crazy, I am a dangerous woman.*

Atwater reaped the benefits of her labors. She fixed him supper three or four times a week, often vegetarian meals that he ate without any protest over the absence of meat. She would sit with him on the porch afterward, neither of them talking very much, each grateful for the other's presence, in balance and harmony and pretending that the

end was not in sight. *Why isn't this enough?* Anna asked herself time and
again. Sweetly cradled in the imperturbable quiet of the farm, she listened for the sparrows that began singing just at dusk, birds whose
sorrowful music had a peculiar quality of resignation, even of vespers,
about it.

"That must be the saddest creature God ever made," Atwater said
one evening, sprawled in his Adirondack chair—*his* chair and *her*
chair, Anna realized, wishing she had never noticed. "They must have
broken hearts. Every last sparrow."

Anna took his hand. "Dear Arthur," she said fondly, looking at this
unlikely man who had become her partner through fate or by accident or plain desire and wishing that she could love him as he needed
to be loved, unconditionally, as another woman must once have loved
him, maybe his lost wife. "You're my own personal Saint Francis."

"I don't know about that. But if I could talk to the birds, I
wouldn't mind."

"But you have a penis."

He seemed puzzled. "What's wrong with that?"

"Nothing," she said, touching him. "Unless you're trying to be a
saint. You remember Saint Augustine among the fleshpots."

"We didn't study him over in Napa."

"Come to bed, Arthur."

In the middle of the night, Anna woke to the rustle of Atwater
rising from her side. She was accustomed to his nocturnal ramblings
by now. He was an accepted thing, a pale shape in the moonlight, his
body abnormally white except for his arms, which were tanned to the
T-shirt line on each bicep, and his face and neck. He looked lean and
fit and full of purpose. That he had no awareness of his own mascu-
line beauty only added to his appeal, she thought, letting her fingers
trail idly over her breasts and her nipples, which were exquisitely
tender. Her hand slid lower and nested languidly between her thighs.

"Arthur?" she asked him. "Are you going dusting?"

"Yes, I am."

"Have a good time, dear."

He laughed softly. "I'll try."

She watched him leave, off to spray the grapes with sulfur dust to
protect them from powdery mildew, a job best done in the dead black

hours when no wind blew. Dusting was an essential part of the vine-yard routine, and Atwater's sleep would be interrupted every ten days or so until the crop was ripe. She imagined him moving through the dark fields with a flashlight and waited until she heard the sound of his tractor, a dull gnawing, a severance, before she went back to sleep.

The next morning dawned with an awesome power. Anna stood naked by an open bedroom window, a gauzy curtain tickling her skin, and looked out at a hostile sky that was brown with haze and chemi-cal residue. It would be one of those days in early June when the sun baked the farm with a blistering ferocity. The smell of sulfur dust was everywhere, an odor she remembered from Roger's experiments with his chemistry set, that stink of rotten eggs all red-blooded boys feel duty-bound to concoct if only to disgust their parents and siblings. She saw, too, that the hills had lost their last trace of springtime green and were thoroughly dry now, gone to shades of tan and gold, a thatch of wheat-colored tinder at the mercy of any random spark.

She had a tennis date with Betty Chambers at ten o'clock. They played on a court at Carson Valley High once or twice a week, when-ever Betty could shake free from her family. The temperature was in the nineties when they began volleying, though, and they were worn out after a single set and sat in the shade to chat instead.

"I like your bracelet," Anna joked, sipping a lukewarm soda from her tennis bag.

Betty had a frayed lanyard on one wrist. She was a short, chunky woman in a white visor and a standard tennis outfit. "I forgot all about it." She stared at it bemusedly. "It's from arts and crafts class. If you don't wear what a Brownie makes for you, the Brownie gets pissed off."

The Chambers were busy preparing for summer, looking into camps and recreational programs. "How're your vacation plans going?" Anna asked.

"Not so great. I got voted down. Nobody else wants to lie on a beach in Maui for three weeks."

"Nobody else takes care of the children every day, do they?"

"That's a nonstarter, Anna," Betty said, shaking her head. "I tried that argument already. The kids are on Lloyd's side. He got them all cranked up for a wilderness expedition. He's a terrible man, really. He even read aloud to them from Eddie Bauer catalogs. Don't laugh, it's true."

Anna put her racket into a press. "Where will you go, then?"

"To Yosemite in August. The same as last year and the year before that. Lloyd is an accountant, honey. He does everything by rote." Betty grinned over a fresh insight. "Maybe he likes to count up all the people in the park."

"I wish I were more that way," Anna told her. "I envy you two sometimes. You're both so secure. You've made peace with your choices."

"I'd swap with you in two seconds flat!" Betty's earnestness was impressive. "All the freedom you have, what I wouldn't do with it!"

"Champagne and oysters, eh?"

"To begin with."

"It's strange that I don't *feel* free," Anna said. "And freedom was what I wanted most when I split up with Bud."

"Well, Lloyd and I will never get a divorce." Betty had a swig of the soda. "I'm stuck with him for life."

"How can you be so certain?"

"I've tried it on my own. We were separated once for about three months. I actually slept with another guy for a while."

"It wasn't any good?" Anna asked.

"No, it was fabulous! He was terrific in bed. A Lithuanian, if you can believe it."

"You must have missed the kids."

"Not that much. There weren't so many of them then! But I came back anyway, didn't I?"

"Why?"

"Time passed," Betty said wistfully.

The heat continued unabated through the day. Anna slept alone that night, restless and sweaty beneath a single sheet, with a dime store fan to circulate the still and sulfury air, and woke to another blazing morning. When the porch thermometer topped 100 degrees in the early afternoon, she went down to the river for a swim, eager for the cool and soothing caress of water on her skin. The dogs tagged after her, all three. Daisy was fatter, furrier, and even goofier now, always covered with ticks, burrs, brambles, and fleas. Prince and Rosie appeared to regard the pup as an object of fun, romping with her and forcing her to chase them. Anna led them along the path at the edge of the vineyard where the trellised shoots had hardened into canes heavy with fruit. Grapes in bunches showed beneath the lush awning of leaves, still tiny, hard, and green, but they were ripening by subtle increments as they captured energy from the sun and turned it into carbohydrates.

An outcrop of serpentine, grayish green and splattered with bird droppings, marked the spot where the Torelli clan had always gone swimming. Fishermen parked themselves on the rock in steelhead season and often forgot the gear they had stowed in its crannies—bobbers, lures, and sinkers that Anna had searched for as a child, encouraged by her angler uncles, who paid her a nickel for anything of value she found. The river eddied up against the serpentine, its force curtailed, and poured out into a deep bowl-shaped pool, and there was a scallop of pebbly sand and gravel that passed for a beach. Thick vegetation grew around it, not only the usual cottonwoods and willows but also some maidenhair ferns, wild roses, and a stand of ragged bamboo.

Anna stripped off her clothes behind the bamboo. She had never been one to test the water with a toe and instead plunged right in, diving from a ledge of the rock. The river was every bit as delicious as she had imagined it would be. She floated on her back for a while and remembered how on torrid summer days she used to beseech her mother to let her go skinny-dipping without a chaperone. She always had to plead her case, dragging out the certificate that she had earned in a Red Cross safety class, and if that didn't work she would whine repeatedly, her head drooping at a pitiful angle, like a wilting flower, "But, Mom, it's so *hot!*" until Claire relented.

Sometimes she got to invite her friends to skinny-dip with her, townie girls who had never been naked in public before. The girls would squeal with delight as they undressed, giggling and pinching each other, liberated from the tyranny of little boys and eager to compare their boobs-to-be and later their first sprinkling of pubic hair, inconceivably wiry and dark. The di Grazia sisters were especially forward. Once, when they were all in their teens, the sisters had tricked Anna into hiding with them in the bushes, while Roger and his jock pals were having a kegger party and drunkenly cavorting by a bonfire without their bathing trunks. The di Grazias observed the jocks with clinical detachment and rated each set of genitals, saying "dick," "cock," and "prick" without blushing, identifying this one as "just right" and that one as "really gross," as if they were infinitely experienced and well-versed in every particular.

Those di Grazias were bold, all right. It was Jenny who had jumped on that motor scooter in Montalcino, Anna wryly recalled, smiling at the thought of Guido the Renaissance faun in his crotch-hugging bell-bottoms. The sisters had both attended first-rate colleges, Susan to study political science and Jenny botany, and they would turn up in the valley every Christmas during those years with a handsome new boyfriend in tow, one per holiday season. And Anna Torelli, who lacked their talent for serendipity, would bring home her steady boyfriend from Berkeley, Bud Wright, a Phi Beta Kappa straight arrow whose dick was perfectly nice but unspectacular in action. From the very first, Bud was a panting lover and much too quick to satisfy her, able to leap from his bed to the formality of tort law with an amazing facility, but Anna would never have presumed to mention anything to him, assuming that the fault must be hers.

She swam laps to the opposite shore until her arms began to tire. Scrambling to her feet in the shallows, she noticed again how tender her nipples were, disconcertingly so. When was her period due? She did some mental arithmetic and figured that she was late by a few days. How many? Four, maybe five. She would have to consult a calendar to be sure, since she had never been especially punctual in that regard. She dressed, whistled for the dogs, and walked with them uphill, delivering Rosie and Prince to their master's trailer, where Rosie nudged at the front door with her nose.

"What do you want, girl?" Anna asked. She tried the knob and found that the door was unlocked. "Are you hungry?"

As if in reply, Rosie padded to the kitchen and bent her head to her empty food bowl. Anna followed her inside. Never before had she been in the trailer alone, without Atwater there to mitigate its shabbiness. She saw with a sad heart how diligently he had worked to remedy its condition, his paperback mysteries arranged in neat rows on a shelf and a quilt tossed over the stained cushions of his couch.

He had left his vineyard log out on a table, and she picked it up and thumbed idly through the flat, data-rich entries, *irrigated Zinfandel block, sprayed for spider mites,* until she came to a few pages at the back with their corners folded down. The reason was immediately apparent to her.

Why am I so crazy about this woman? Two lonely people, etc. Don't play the sap for her. We have *nothing in common.*

What if you tell her you love her? Do you? Yes and no. You liar. You'd walk six miles barefoot over broken glass just to get a glimpse of her.

Worry about falling into the creek, and you'll fall into it.

There were a dozen such jottings, all obviously scribbled in haste and probably against their author's will, if Anna were to judge by the cramped and very nearly illegible handwriting. She skimmed through them a second time, ashamed at her transgression and wishing that she had never peeked at the log. Atwater stood before her revealed, his confusion matching her own.

He called that evening, of course, and asked if he could drop by, but Anna put him off with various excuses. She could hear the ache in his voice when he hung up. She ate only a salad for dinner because of the heat and drank most of a bottle of Sauvignon Blanc in a leisurely fashion, while she wrote a belated thank-you note to Jane Weiss.

Dear Jane,

Sorry to be so late in writing. I'm behind in everything, just like the farmers. Thank you so much for your gift. It's too perfect! Never in my wildest dreams did I ever think I'd own a serving platter with a goddam leaping bass on it. (I've been here so long I'm starting to talk like them. I really am.) Only you could have found such a precious object in Manhattan and at Bloomingdale's, no less. I love you for it, and I love you even more for not being angrier at me than you already are.

We're in the midst of one of our notorious heat waves here. They always last for exactly three days. This is day two, and I'm suffering. I went skinny-dipping this afternoon and got sunburned where it counts, and my period is late and I feel bloated and too fat for any of my clothes, plus the dog ate my shoes. No, I'm kidding about the dog. But I *am* lounging around in my underwear and have almost killed a bottle of wine. Probably that says it all.

I'm looking forward to getting back to New York. I tell myself that at least, but I don't know what to do about goddam Arthur Atwater or even if there *is* anything to be done. Why can't I be a sophisticated lady for once and admit that I've had a sexy little fling that was great for my self-esteem at a time when I needed it and just let it go at that? Arthur's been good about not pressuring me to stay, but sometimes I wish he would, or is that my ego talking? I don't belong here, but it's so hard to leave! I spent most of my youth running away from my father, and now I worry about how much I'm going to miss him. Maybe we should move our operation out here and sell my vegetables on the side. We could wear bonnets and gingham dresses. I'll even toss in half of Atwater.

Don't mind me, Jane. It's just the wine talking. I'll be home by the end of the month. I'm looking forward to it, honest—

Your pal in Carson Valley,
Anna

The heat wave broke as Anna had predicted it would after one more sweltering day, but her period didn't start. She had some spotting, but nothing more. When another few days went by without anything happening, she became seriously anxious for the first time. She felt strange—light-headed, moody, and distant from herself—and yet she refused to believe that she could really be pregnant until the undeniable physical changes began. One morning, she looked in the mirror and saw that the lines on her face were much fainter and that her skin had a new vibrancy. Beauty of a special kind was taking hold of her, and it made her feel both invincible and terribly vulnerable. Often she gave in to brief crying jags that blew through her in minutes and left her trembling.

Even Arthur registered her altered appearance. While they were walking by the creek of an evening, he remarked in his offhand way that she had never looked prettier. Anna knew that it was true. She had put on some makeup and worn a favorite green silk blouse. In the nearness of her lover, a frightening thought came to her, *I am going to betray him.*

"You're awfully quiet tonight," Atwater said as they returned to the big house through the meadow. "You seem far away."

"I'm here. Really, I am."

"I brought you a present." He pulled a booklet from his back pocket, another of his dog-eared Boy Scout pamphlets, this one a manual on canoeing.

Anna took it in hand. "It's from the authentic private collection," she said, brushing dust from the cover.

"You better study it if we're going down the river."

"I will, captain. You're turning me into a first-class scout. Maybe we'll become blood brothers someday."

"Sorry, Anna. I already have a blood brother. His name is Junior Thompson. He was in my troop."

"What about a blood sister?"

"Blood sisters are like fourth chances." Atwater threw an arm around her and pulled her close. "There aren't any."

The next morning, Anna bought an EPT kit at a pharmacy, but she never opened it. Instead, for the sake of absolute certainty, she made an appointment with Ed Sawyer for later in the week. She had always liked him. Sawyer was the first gynecologist ever to examine her, gentle with his hands and aware of the absurdity and even perversity of the specialty he had no doubt chosen blindly in med school. He was in his sixties now, bearded and outgoing, and after some small talk he got her up on a table and eased her feet into the stirrups. Anna let her mind drift as she did when she was gardening.

"The texture of your cervix has changed," she heard Sawyer say. "Your uterus is enlarged. Are you tender here?"

"Yes."

"Your breasts are slightly swollen," he went on, touching her nipples. "How does this feel?"

"It tingles," Anna said, her face hot.

Sawyer took off his gloves. He met with her in a consulting room afterward and explained that he was 99 percent sure that she was pregnant. "We can do a blood serum test if you like," he offered. "That's as close to foolproof as it gets. It's none of my business, but I gather this was an accident?"

"I don't have a clue how it could have happened," Anna said, but she did know, of course, and could even pinpoint the very moment of conception—that spring afternoon when Atwater had burst in on her in the kitchen, when she was tipsy after her tour of wineries and prickly with desire, wet and yielding and wholly open to him. She had wanted him more than anything just then and hadn't bothered with her diaphragm.

"You have a little time to consider your options," Sawyer advised her. "But don't take too long. If you need to talk some more, please call me. We'll have to monitor this closely, given your history."

The streets in town looked foreign to Anna when she left the office. It seemed incredible to her that she could be carrying a child in this curious and random fashion, especially after all the fruitless striving with Bud, those precisely arranged matings that had involved body temperature, datebooks, and the approximate motility of sperm. She wandered around in a daze, mad at herself for being so careless and yet pleased in a purely biological way, high on the changes in her body. She thought about poor Arthur, her innocent accomplice, and felt that she ought to spare him from any damaging consequences. If she chose to terminate the pregnancy, there was no reason to tell him about it at all, and if she went home to Manhattan and had the baby, a daughter or a son—the words had a gemlike brilliance—she would tell him at the appropriate time. Anna played with those sentiments as she walked and walked, half conscious and half in dreams.

13

━━━◦◦◦◦◦━━━

They were sitting on a bench outside Roy's Market and watching the traffic go by on Carson Valley Road, three old men in denim and cotton as fixed in place as totems, very tranquil, contained, and thoughtful in the heat of the afternoon. They felt their age most keenly on such sweltering days when the air rested heavily on their lungs and made every minor infirmity seem major, but they were still quick to focus their attention whenever a car pulled up, competing in an undeclared contest as to who could be the first to name its occupants and earn bragging rights to superior mental agility. Strangers they ignored each in his own way, Charlie Grimes by eating M&Ms, Fred Vescio by chain-smoking Camels, and Victor Torelli by studying the drowned fly in the fizzy dregs of his Calistoga water.

Their conversation proceeded in fits and starts according to a ritual only they understood, one established over a half century or so of friendship. The silences among them were frequent, and after a fairly long one, Vescio introduced a new topic that was close to his heart.

"I got up to pee six times last night," he said. Fred had a face as wrinkled as a sun-dried apricot. "That's a record for me. And I hadn't drunk but a single beer. I'm so sick of it I might just pee in my bed from now on."

"You've got a condition there, all right," Grimes told him. "Proba-

bly I don't pee more than three times in a whole day. That's about average for normal people."

"But you fart all the time."

"Ah, that's just letting off steam! What about it, Victor? You been
doing a lot of peeing?"

Torelli's eyes were concentrated on the parking lot, ready to
pounce on the next car. "I don't keep count, Charlie."

"Well, estimate for us, then."

"I estimate I pee about as often as I have to."

They fell silent again. Grimes tossed up a red M&M and caught it
in his mouth. He tossed up a green M&M and caught it, and then an
orange M&M.

"You always eat those one at a time?" Torelli asked him.

Grimes nodded affably. "Mmm-hmm. And I never eat the same
color twice in a row."

"The hell you don't," Vescio corrected him. "You ate two straight
reds just a minute ago. I wish I had a videotape camera to prove it to
you."

Torelli sensed an opportunity. "Either of you boys ever seen one of
those adult videos?"

"No, but I saw the cops beat up a few Negro fellows on TV," said
Vescio. "They was really pounding on 'em."

Grimes looked away and feigned an interest in the wasps swarming over an open trash can.

"You can rent those tapes in town," Torelli went on, pressing his
advantage. "I rented one once."

"What was it called?"

"Titles aren't so important in the pornography line, Fred. But I'll
tell you this much. If you rent one yourself, you won't feel cheated.
'Course, you have to be brave to walk into the X-rated section in
broad daylight."

Vescio pondered this for a moment, then tamped out another cigarette and changed the subject. "I got leafhoppers in my vineyard," he
said. "They're leaving yellow spots everywhere."

"Nuke the bastards," Grimes advised him.

"I did twice. But they come back for more. They're pretty rough
customers. How are your grapes going, Victor?"

"It depends on who you listen to." Torelli swirled his bottle and watched the dead fly go around. "Atwater swears we're in fine shape, but those CV boys, they keep sending me reports to the contrary! I don't know who to believe."

"Atwater's an honest sort," Vescio said. "I'm not inclined to disbelieve him."

Torelli frowned. "CV's got all those goddam facts and numbers and graphs! How can you argue with that stuff? It's enough to rattle a person."

"Maybe they mean to rattle you." Grimes raised a haunch and released an echoing fart whose stale gases had an effect not unlike a mushroom cloud on those in the general vicinity.

"I told you so!" Vescio laughed and backed away. "Jesus, Charlie! Whoa! That's bad medicine!"

"Why would CV want to rattle me?" Torelli asked. "What's in it for them?"

"Some folks just like to show off how goddam smart they are," Grimes told him. "Take that Rawley Kimball. He can't be more than five feet tall! Plus he's so full of fancy scientific bullshit, it's running out his ears."

"That's true," Vescio agreed. "Rawley can be a righteous little bugger. But Wade Saunders, he's a decent enough sort. He's been buying my grapes for eight or nine years now, and we get along like peas in a pod."

"He keeps to his word, does he, Fred?"

"Old Wade's a company man, but he wouldn't cross the street just to kick you in the ass. He belongs to the Rotary Club, you know. They're not allowed to lie."

"Who told you that?"

Vescio picked at a wart on his ear. "Nobody," he admitted. "I just assumed it."

"I'd trust Atwater if I were you, Victor," Grimes put in. "He's got the practical experience. It could be you want to discount him because he's fooling around with your daughter."

"That doesn't come into it at all," Torelli said hastily.

"Well, it must stick in your craw a bit, don't it? The two of them being together? Having sex with each other and whatnot?"

"Anna's old enough to do as she pleases," Torelli said, thinking but not confiding to his mates, *What's the goddam difference? She's already slept with twenty other men!*

"She's a beautiful girl," Vescio said. "It's hard to believe you had a hand in creating her, Victor."

Grimes was smirking. "It wasn't his hand that did it."

"Why do you always have to be so goddam low?" Vescio asked him. "Everything with you is farts and smut! You just boil it right down, don't you, Charlie?"

They were forced to quit talking when a Ford Bronco as armored as a tank veered into the parking lot, and a perky woman leaped from behind the wheel, circled to the other door, and grabbed the hand of an apathetic buzzcut boy in a Little League uniform.

"There's Alice McLaren!" Torelli shouted, thrilled to have spoken first.

"We know who the hell she is," Vescio told him sourly. "If you're going to list every goddam person who drives up, I'm going home."

"Yes, and I'll go with you," seconded Grimes.

Torelli let his head rest against the wall behind his bench and asked himself, *Was I ever as small as that child? Did I ever really go to school?* He remembered the old Carson Valley schoolhouse, a clapboard building painted white with a gabled roof and a cupola where an iron bell lacking a clapper was stored. He pictured the playground, the ballfield, and the orchards that used to border the school in those ancient days before wine grapes had taken over the valley. There were pears, peaches, apples, plums, and prunes in abundance, and the sweet aroma of fruit would linger through the summer and on into September, filtering into the classroom where Mrs. Schmidt, a particularly strict teacher feared for her treacherous use of a yardstick, stood writing arithmetic problems on the blackboard. He felt the solid rungs of a ladder under his feet and knew again the excitement of climbing into the arching limbs of a tree and reaching up toward perfect ripeness, the rich scent of it nearly toppling him as he floated among the branches.

"Did you pick much fruit when you were a kid, Charlie?" he asked.

Grimes nodded and tossed up a brown M&M. "I surely did. I remember filling those bushel baskets and how good the apples tasted.

You can't find apples like that anymore. Gravenstein, Delicious, Mac-intosh, we had every damn kind."

"Bartlett pears were my favorite." Torelli's face looked relaxed, as if the memory had refreshed him somehow. "I'd eat so goddam many I'd get sick to my stomach."

Vescio stomped out his cigarette butt, grinding it under the heel of a worn work shoe. "We had some hops over to our farm when I was growing up. My pop sold off most of the crop, but he always kept out enough to make homebrew. That was powerful beer! This crap they're selling now, it just turns straight into pee."

"I never knew a man to be so concerned with his own urine as you are, Fred," said Grimes, with considerable loathing. "There's more to life than draining your bladder, my friend."

Vescio, immune to such criticism, studied his knuckles. "You figure Atwater's in love with Anna, Victor?" he asked.

Torelli didn't answer right away, although it was a question he had contemplated on his own many times. "I suppose he is. If you can judge by how he behaves, he must be. Arthur's not much for hiding his feelings. I'd say he dotes on her."

"You figure she loves him back?"

"I'm not so sure about that. Some women, they don't like to show what they're up to, do they? They like to keep you in the dark. Anna's that way. She's been careful since her divorce. She doesn't want to make another mistake."

"If those two wind up getting married," Grimes said, his voice full of glee, "Arthur Atwater will be your goddam son-in-law!"

"Aw, there must be a legal way to get around that." Vescio plucked a strand of tobacco from his lip. "If you went to court, you could get it, what do they call it?"

"Annulled," Grimes told him, rubbing it in. "You're mind's going on you, Fred."

"Yes, sir. You could annul Atwater as your son-in-law."

"Why is love so complicated anyhow?" Torelli asked. "It's the strangest goddam thing. Matter of fact, I've been having these dreams lately about the first girl I ever fell in love with."

"Who might that be?" Vescio asked him, his eyes narrowed.

"Do you remember Lucy Carpenter?"

"Lucy Carpenter!" Grimes popped up from the bench with a blast of jet-propelled enthusiasm. "She had the biggest tits I ever saw! I never met a girl so hot as her. Lucy lived to do the dirty deed!"

Torelli was shocked by what he heard. "I never knew you even had a single date with her," he said.

"A single date?" Grimes sat back down, enjoying his turn at having the upper hand. "Hell, Victor, I priced out an engagement ring for her and all that, and we were going to take a stroll down the aisle, but she broke up with me all of a sudden and ran off with some midget she met at a cafeteria in Santa Rosa. They landed in a trailer park in Honolulu, last I knew of them."

"A midget, Charlie?"

"I made up that part."

"You just can't ever tell with love, can you?" Vescio hacked to clear the phlegm from his throat. His voice was hoarse but emotional. "I had this piglet once—just an ordinary piglet, I thought—but when it keeled over and died from the swine flu, it hurt me so bad I pretty nearly didn't get over it."

"Maybe you should have wed that piglet instead of your wife," said Grimes. "Probably it was a whole lot better-looking."

"For a man who never *could* find a wife," Vescio replied, with cool detachment, "you do carry on."

Grimes spat on the ground. "Goddam that Lucy Carpenter!"

They were silent once more, watching the traffic flow and conserving their energy in the sapping heat. A flock of red-winged blackbirds flew by with a great rushing of wings, and they lifted their heads to look. The birds were bright black in a field of blue and formed a kaleidoscopic pattern as they sailed apart and then flowed together again.

"I've been thinking about those hunting trips we used to make every fall," Grimes said, starting in again. "We'd be doing our planning right about now, wouldn't we, Victor?"

"Yes, sir. We had that nice camp up by Chester one year," Torelli said, with a satisfied grin. "Up there in Feather River country."

"Oh, that was a gorgeous camp!"

"Fred, I wish you could have been with us. We were on a flank of the Sierra, way up in the pines and Douglas firs, and we could see

Mount Lassen just as clear as day. We had a good big tent and set ourselves up on a creek where you couldn't but cast a line and not catch a trout."

"They were in there as thick as bricks, Fred!" Grimes cried.

"That's the truth," Torelli confirmed. "And we both got our bucks the first morning out. If I'm not mistaken, Charlie's was an eight-pointer."

Vescio helped himself to another Camel from the crumpled pack in his shirt pocket. "I never did take to hunting," he told the others. "I couldn't bring myself to shoot a deer except if it was eating my grapes."

"It's different in the Sierra. Don't you think so, Charlie?"

"No comparison." Grimes looked rhapsodic. "I slept real good up there, too."

"I never saw a better camp in my life."

"We should go on up there again this autumn. All three of us this time."

Torelli swirled his bottle, and the dead fly went round. "It's a little late in the game for me," he said hesitantly. "I doubt I could handle the altitude anymore. The air gets awful thin in those mountains."

"Ah, hell, Victor. I never knew you to be scared of a little challenge."

"I'd go in a minute if I felt right. Trouble is, I get so short of breath! Maude's been pushing me to see a specialist."

"It's none of my business," said Grimes, "but I don't hold with those specialists. Their whole job is to test you and test you until they find something wrong."

"You better beware of Maude," Vescio whispered, glancing over his shoulder to check for eavesdroppers. "She'll pussy-whip you for fair. She pussy-whipped my poor brother until he up and died on her."

Torelli smiled. "I haven't seen a pussy in years, Fred. Much less been whipped by one."

He let his head rest against the wall again and thought about that camp on the Feather River, which was really every hunting camp he'd ever known rolled into one. He thought about the stony mountains and how the light fell through the Douglas firs, a piney fragrance everywhere and the little stream so bright and clear. Trout for breakfast, eggs scrambled over a wood fire, bacon frying, strong cowboy coffee, those long siestas in the afternoon, the deer gutted and hung out to season, blood on the earth, blood on his hands, and the blood washed off in the ice-cold water of the creek. Each detail of the trip lived in him as a nucleus resides in a cell, and it was the most disturbing aspect of his old age that he would soon be deprived of such sensations forever.

Torelli looked over at Charlie Grimes, who had consumed his last M&M and was studiously folding the empty packet into quarters for reasons that were no more discernible to anybody than the why of red-winged blackbirds passing in the sky. He had known Grimes and the Grimes family almost since his birth, and yet he felt that he didn't really know his friend at all, even that every other person in Carson Valley and beyond was an enigma to him finally, a code never to be cracked.

"I come up with a new way to promote my wine, boys," Grimes said, having concluded his labors on the packet. "It's a right smart one, too, if I do say so myself."

"Anybody got a match?" Vescio asked with a cough, still another in the infinite chain of Camels dangling between his lips.

Torelli held out his lighter and indulged in a Toscano himself. "So what have you got in mind, Mr. Promoter? Another painting spree?"

"No, my career as an artist is over. My lawyer, he tells me it was 'ill-advised,' " Grimes cackled. "What I have in mind is something new."

"Why don't you dive off the roof of your barn into a barrel of water?" Vescio suggested. "That'd get you some free publicity."

Grimes brushed aside the comment. "What if you saw an ad in the paper that offered you two bottles of wine for the price of one, Victor?"

"I'd wonder what the catch was."

"Suppose there isn't a catch? Suppose it's all on the up-and-up?"

"Well, I guess I'd be a fool not to take advantage of it, wouldn't I?"

"Goddam right you would be."

Vescio's brow was furrowed in an effort to ferret out the nature of the scam. "Do you get to choose which wines you buy? Is it any old wine, or just a certain kind?"

"Fred, you can be pretty clever for a dumb fellow," Grimes said, with grudging praise. "The customer gets to choose one bottle. The other I pick for him."

"It wouldn't be that old Burgundy blend you got in your cellar, would it?" Torelli asked. "That vinegary stuff?"

"It might could be." Grimes produced from somewhere on his person a copy of the ad he planned to run. "It looks real nice, doesn't it? I paid a professional to do it on her computer."

"Computers rule the world now," said Vescio.

Grimes touched a finger to a blank corner. "I'm tempted to put in a little Dumbo over here, just for the hell of it."

In the glare of the sun, Torelli made some not-entirely-heartfelt remarks about the elegance of the design and the sensitivity of the layout, as impressed as he always was by the sheer amount of deception in the world, people being deceived, deceiving other people, and deceiving themselves. There's no end to it, he thought as he rose from the bench achingly to make his way home.

14

In those slow blue ripening days of early June, Arthur Atwater pushed himself to the limit, heeding the demands of a clock whose ticking only he could hear. He was on the alert, ever vigilant for the tiniest sign of trouble, the first cane tip to wilt for lack of water or the first leaf to show the blotchy scabs caused by feeding thrips. He walked the vineyard rows and plucked the shot berries from his riverside Chardonnay, those seedless specimens that had died from an undetectable virus—plain misfortune, but just an ounce of it and not enough to cause alarm. Always he gave pep talks to the grapes and inquired after their health, remarking on how good they looked and wondering aloud if he could do anything to make their brief lives on earth a little better.

THURSDAY, JUNE 8TH. Hot enough to fry eggs. Dragged the disc all day cutting down weed seedlings, Bermuda grass and Johnson grass. Big pain in the butt, there'll be new seedlings in two weeks. Ate a ton of dust, too.

Atwater didn't have much company in the fields now. There wasn't enough work to support a full crew. Only Antonio Lopez still reported each morning as usual and then, with his boss's approval, left in the early afternoon to earn some extra cash clearing the land for a new vineyard going in off Carson Valley Road, up in the scrubby chaparral. The job was tough and crude. Lopez had to chop back prickly tangles of chamise, manzanita, and toyon by hand, roll around boulders, and dig up stumps six feet in diameter. His list of grievances was long and consistently expanding.

"Look at this, Arthur," he said that Friday while they were taking a break. His forearms were raw and blistered. "You ever seen it before?"

"I've seen it, and I've had it."

"Poison oak. This itching is too much. I'm burning up, like with a fever. Tonight I got to stop at the clinic." Antonio picked up a clod of dirt and tossed it morosely at a lizard, who darted away. "There goes half the money I already been paid."

"They're running you guys hard, aren't they?"

"Too hard for five dollars an hour. They treat us like Mexicans, man."

"Nothing worse than that."

"When I'm rich," Lopez said, his gloom receding as an invigorating fantasy blossomed in him, "I'll hire a whole bunch of white people to work for me. Really old white people with arthritis. They're going to scrub my floors and clean my bathroom."

"Who owns that vineyard, anyway?" Atwater asked him. "Somebody over at Roy's told me it's a Hollywood producer."

"Could be somebody from Hollywood. Could be just another dentist, too. They got a name for their wine before they even made any."

"What's it called?"

"Hawk Wind."

Atwater shook his head in dubious tribute. "Hawk Wind. That has a certain ring to it. Kind of like Thunderbird."

"I drank that stuff once," Lopez told him, shuddering at the memory. "It made me throw up all over the place."

"Better stick to the Budweiser, then."

"I do. Hey, you want to come up and have a look around tomorrow, Arthur? Their winery building, it's becoming like a castle."

"Can't do it tomorrow. I have plans."

"Yeah, sure, I know," Lopez joked. "You got to ride around on your tractor some more."

"No, I don't, Mr. Smart-ass. I'm taking Anna on a canoe trip down the river. We're having ourselves an excursion."

"You don't sound too excited about it."

"Well, I promised her a long time ago, and damned if she didn't remember."

"Cheer up, Arthur. It'll be fun for you. A lot of fun."

Atwater regarded Lopez with a skeptical eye. "I sincerely doubt it. It's supposed to be in the nineties again. Maybe you ought to go instead of me."

"She's your lady."

"Sort of," Atwater said distractedly. "How're things between you and Elena these days? You patch up your problems?"

"Yeah, we did," Lopez said. "Since Elena quit her job, she's being like a housewife. It makes her happy."

"Don't you miss the money she made?"

"A little bit. But we'll be okay once the harvest comes, and I get my bonus."

Atwater stood up. "Can you spare a minute before you go up to, ah, Hawk Wind?"

"Sure, *amigo.*"

"Come help me with the canoe."

They headed for the barn, a pair of slump-shouldered figures nearly lost in the swirling greenery. The sun bore down on them, and Atwater thought with extreme distaste of the broiling that he would get on the river the next day during this ill-conceived trip he had offered up in an instant of passion and had done his best to avoid and postpone ever since. He stopped as they passed a particularly handsome row of vines and lifted some leaves to show off several plump and lustrous clusters of Zinfandel.

"The harvest'll be early this year," he predicted, cupping the grapes and admiring the heft of them. "I'll need you full-time before long."

"One thing, Arthur?" Lopez shuffled his feet as he always did when he wanted something. "There's some good workers on the crew up there. They could be good pickers for us."

Atwater looked at him sharply. "Not Ernesto Morales, by any chance?

"No, not him. But maybe I might hire a cousin of mine? He might be coming up from San Diego."

"As long as he has his papers."

"He does."

Some violet-green swallows sailed out of the barn when they entered it. The canoe rested on a plywood platform that rested in turn on rafter beams draped with cobwebs and dotted with owl pellets. Where the canoe had come from Atwater didn't know for sure, although he suspected it had washed up in the willows by the river years ago, abandoned by some rowdy frat boys or a poor tortured sunburned soul such as he imagined himself soon to be. It was old, aluminum, and about seventeen feet long. On its stern, it still had the faintly lettered insignia of the company in town that rented canoes. It seemed paltry compared to the first canoe he had ever set foot in, his grandfather's Hiawatha, a beauty made in Canada of clear-grained Ontario white cedar. As a boy paddling down the Napa River in it, he had felt positively princely.

He climbed a ladder and wrestled with the prow of the canoe, sliding it forward at an angle and gently easing it along. He aimed it at Lopez down below, who stood with his arms awkwardly outstretched, as if to receive manna from heaven. Atwater balanced the weight well enough until more of the canoe was off the platform than on it, at which point gravity set in and caused him to lose his grip. He watched in horror as it hurtled toward the barn floor like a silvery missile. Lopez jumped out of the way just in time and let it crash. It rolled over once and rocked for a bit before coming to a stop. Atwater climbed back down, crouched low to inspect the damage, and found a huge new dent in a hull that was already dinged, epoxied, and scratched beyond belief.

"No holes, anyway," Lopez said, probing the aluminum with a finger. "What if this thing had landed on me?"

"I'd be very sorry. And so would you."

"Can I go now?"

"Yes, Antonio, you can go."

Atwater spent his evening in the barn, a radio plugged into an overhead socket so that he could listen to the Giants' game while he made provisions for the trip. He could by no means address all the dents, but he pounded out some of the major ones with a rubber mallet and applied duct tape to the splintery handles of three warped paddles. With some garden shears, he cut in half an empty plastic bleach bottle and threw it in as a bailer, adding a coil of rope and a faded orange life preserver. He liked the comforting background noise of the ballgame and the oblivious snoring of his curled-up dogs, recalling how in his Boy Scout years he would put his gear in order with a similarly rapt attention. What a sober, industrious lad he had been, the winner of countless merit badges and a budding anti-Communist in the service of God and country. It was an image of himself that gave him pause.

The lights were still on in the big house when he went to bed a little before ten. He faltered easily toward sleep and smiled to think of Anna in the kitchen tending to the last details of the grand picnic she had agreed to provide as her part of the bargain. She was roasting a chicken for him, his avowed favorite from her culinary repertoire. Love resided in the honoring of such pacts, Atwater supposed, and in the keeping of such promises, but she had never spoken the word *love* to him and had resisted his few fumbling attempts to speak it to her. That didn't bother him so much anymore, although he wished it could have been otherwise, even knowing as he did how absurd any declaration of love could prove to be. But he knew also that he loved her absolutely, with a painful intensity he could not in the least control.

He lived in utter terror of her leaving the valley, but he felt that he had no right to try and stop her. A part of him understood that Anna had obligations to fulfill, an entire life that she had deserted in a moment of crisis, deadlines to meet, and a business partner to placate, yet there was another part of him that resented her for not giving him something to hang onto. In his blackest hours, he accused her of being cowardly and escaping from her emotions. But who was he to know what was truly in her heart? He had no markers to call in, no IOUs. Anna had made him no promises. When he considered all that, he would change his mind and decide that *he* was the coward for not declaring himself more boldly. His only course of action now was to steel himself against her departure. He would be the still point, the solid center. It wasn't impossible that she would come back to him someday if he could stand his ground.

Yeah, right. Good luck, sucker.

So Atwater tossed and turned through a restless night, woozy from an overdose of circular thinking. He had planned on an early start in the morning to get a leg up on the heat and found Anna waiting calmly for him on her porch at seven o'clock. He was awed by how perfectly composed she was, a wicker picnic basket at her feet. She wore a blue cotton shirt, white shorts and socks, and new white sneakers without a single scuff mark. The sight of her, so simple and right, was doubly poignant for him because he already knew how its absence would affect him, depriving him of a joy that could never be repeated.

"Hello, Skipper," Anna said brightly. Her face looked freshly scrubbed, and the tips of her hair were still damp from the shower. "Fine day for a cruise, isn't it?"

"You smell great." Atwater came nearer and kissed her. He breathed her in. "All soapy and clean. Did you bring a hat?"

"It's in the basket."

"Sunscreen?"

"Yes, sir."

"Did you study your canoeing manual?"

"I'm ready for my test."

"What about Victor? You sure he doesn't mind meeting us in town and driving us back?"

"I'm sure."

"Then let's hit it."

He carried the canoe from the barn down to the water, jerking it up and ducking his head under the gunwales, so that the center thwart came to rest on his shoulders. Arms flexed and knees bent, he resembled a lost and struggling Atlas. Anna followed him with the picnic basket, a spin-fishing rod, and his rusty tackle box. The river where they put in was a dull green color and flowing slowly, ebbing toward its summer low. Killdeer dashed away with a frenzied piping as Atwater edged the canoe into the stream, steadying it for Anna to board. She grabbed the gunwales for support, stepped in, and sat in the bow, and he went up the hill again and returned with their other gear and the paddles. Then he pushed them off.

The canoe eddied into the current. Atwater felt a little flutter of excitement at their surrender. They were swept from their solid underpinnings into a world that was fluid, were ferried through it at a pace that was not of their own devising. Although they were undeniably in motion, it seemed the other way around at times, as if shore-bound things were gliding by them, unspooling like a ribbon of film. The trip from the farm to town would cover about eleven miles, and he counted on it taking about seven hours, including their stop for a picnic. He anticipated no danger. They had no rapids to run and only a few tricky stretches of white water. Instead, they would skim along on the surface of quiet pools and let the tractable current guide them around wide bends and through narrow, tree-sheltered channels, relaxing all the while.

Atwater oared with a basic power stroke as they set out. He switched to a J-stroke, digging more deeply into the water and twisting his paddle to apply some torque when they rounded the first bend and began a lazy glide down a still stretch that went on for several hundred yards. He saw to his surprise that Anna was paddling on the opposite side of the canoe, exactly as she should have been doing, in flawless harmony, without any instruction from him. The look that she gave him when he glanced back at her let him know that he ought to have expected as much. It was a look familiar to him now, at once daring and playful. He watched the landscape unfold and heard the rattling cry of a kingfisher and the bleating of some grazing sheep. No other boats were afloat, and there were no houses in sight.

Midway through the glide, Anna put down her paddle and reversed herself. She sat with her legs extended toward Atwater and a hand trailing in the river. Her head was pillowed on the bow, and her eyes were shut.

"You're right out of a painting," he complimented her as he paddled. "A French painting. One of those impressionists."

"Which one?"

"Now you're pushing it."

"How about Monet?"

"If you like." He smiled at her. "You look like a Monet, Anna."

"Thank you. The water's warm," she told him, swirling her hand about.

"It's warm on top. Not down below."

"We should swim later. Will you go swimming with me?"

"I forgot my suit," he lied.

"Then you'll just have to swim naked."

"Maybe."

"This is really excellent, Arthur." She opened her eyes to look at him, and he fell into the depths of them again. "I don't know why I haven't done this more often. I was about ten the last time I was in a canoe."

"The last time for me was when I was a Scout," Atwater said. "Troop Forty-eight from Napa, California. Panther Patrol."

"Did your blood brother come along?"

"Junior Thompson? No, he had the measles. Do you want to hear our patrol call?"

"Nothing would please me more."

Atwater put a fist to his mouth and blew through it. *"Keeok! Keeok!"*

"You don't put much punch into it, do you?"

"I did in the old days. Somehow it's not the same."

They passed a snowy egret stalking the shoals, unblinking in its concentration, all feathery and focused. The egret didn't spook when they drifted by but rather dipped its long black bill into the stream and came up with a mouthful of fingerlings. One little fish dropped free, spared from the bird's throbbing gullet. Rounding another bend, they entered a faster section of the river, and Atwater sculled them carefully around a big rock and along a bleached log where a turtle was sunning itself and probably had been for centuries. To the west, a vineyard ascended a hillside in tiered rows. The bodies of old cars and trucks formed a barrier at the base of the property, dumped behind a mesh of fence to keep the valuable soil in place.

Atwater quit paddling for a moment to wipe the sweat from his face. The heat was every bit as bad as he'd figured it would be. He dipped a bandanna in the river and wrapped it around his neck, another trick he'd learned in Troop 48. "It's amazing how much of that Boy Scout crap I still remember, Anna," he said, enjoying a trickle of water down his spine. "I was thinking about it in the barn last night while I was getting us ready."

"Be prepared, right?"

"That's right."

"So what else do you remember?" she asked.

"Well, you take that manual I gave you. I remember the first damn sentence in it: 'The canoe was handed down to us from the Indians.' "

"Bravo, Arthur. You really are the weirdest man. What I wouldn't give to have a peek inside your head."

"You'd be scared silly in there."

"Did you earn a merit badge for canoeing?"

He checked to see if she was poking fun at him, but she didn't appear to be. "Of course I did. I had the most badges of anybody in my troop. Rabbit raising, mammal study, wood carving, you name it."

"Any others?" Anna took off her shirt to get some more sun. She wasn't wearing a bra.

"Jesus," Atwater said, flattered by the display but unwilling to share it with anybody else. "Are you just going to ride along like that?"

"Yes, I am. Tell me some more stuff, Arthur. Make it up if you have to. Entertain me."

"Well, here's one that cracks me up." He was in fact feeling very merry and honored to be blessed with such a challenging companion. "A Scout's supposed to be helpful, right? So we had a whole menu of helpful things to do."

"Like what?"

" 'Pick up broken glass from the street,' " Atwater said, in an evangelical voice. " 'Move furniture for an old person. Make a scrapbook for a hospital.' "

"Please," Anna said, laughing along with him. "No more now."

" 'Clean trash off a vacant lot. Do errands for a sick person. Get a child's kite down from a tree.' I actually used to walk around Napa searching for kites to rescue!"

"I mean it, Arthur. Just quit it. I have to pee. Stop somewhere, will you?"

He nosed the canoe into a cove. Anna grabbed her shirt, stepped out, and walked rapidly toward a handy clump of bushes. Atwater shook his arms to freshen the flagging muscles and observed the flowing green river and the many oaks, laurels, and madronas, the whispering grasses and the sky above streaked with a lone cirrus cloud. He unwrapped a stick of spearmint gum, broke it in two, and commenced to chew it, his head tilted back to watch the cloud move, and he felt the wind stir and listened to the shiny leaves of a nearby poplar rustle and chime. Anna came out of the bushes after a while and sat in the bow again, clearly distressed and trying to hide it from him, not saying anything or venturing a look his way.

"It's nothing," she told him before he could ask. "I'm having some cramps."

"Do you want an aspirin? I've got some."

"No, really, Arthur. It's nothing. I'll be fine."

"You should put on your hat."

"Hats don't cure cramps." She was short with him, even irritated. "Can we go? I'll feel better in a minute."

He didn't argue. He just pushed them off again with his paddle. They drifted down a willow-choked channel that opened onto some tumbling water peaked with miniature whitecaps. The canoe bounced and teetered as some small but energetic waves smashed against its hull. The river whacked the aluminum and sprayed them with rainbow droplets of froth. Ahead, in a rocky gorge, the current turned even stronger, and they giggled like kids on a Ferris wheel when it tossed them to the brink of tipping over. Atwater had to employ all his merit badge skills to keep them afloat, oaring madly with quartering strokes to lessen the rise and fall of their bow and stern. He plowed into the trough of one wave straight on, and water roared up in a plume and drenched them. Anna shrieked in delight. When she turned to face him, he shrugged and quartered some more until they were out of the chop.

They passed under an old green trestle bridge. There was a campground near it pitched with mushrooming tents. They floated by a party of boys and girls, who were messing around in the water. The kids waved and showed off for them by executing fancy dives from a sandbar. One energetic boy swung toward them on a rope tied to an oak limb and cannonballed into the river, barely missing the canoe. They went around another bend and through a stretch that was almost becalmed. Anna took up the paddling, while Atwater knotted a swivel to his fishing line and attached a lure to it, a Rapala meant to imitate a wounded minnow, and cast it out behind them. He hooked the river bottom first and next a fat, ugly squawfish whose skull he rapped thuddingly against the stern thwart, leaving it to bob belly-up in the stream until an osprey swooped down to pluck it.

"Those are trash fish," he explained to Anna, heading off her objection. "They feed on steelhead fry."

"There must be a reason for it, no?"

"Only in the biology books."

Noon came and went. Atwater was beginning to reel under the heat of the sun, his brain nearly fried despite his protective baseball cap. He had no idea how far they had gone, although he guessed that they must be about halfway to town. He saw a shadowy side channel lined with some towering redwoods and veered into it. There were only a few trees, but the huge canopy of branches blocked enough light to lower the temperature. The redwoods were like a forest apart, an enchanted place, and that brought him some relief, but soon the canoe was in open water again and passing a vineyard where a farmer tended a pile of burning brush and then a cattle ranch where some Aberdeen Angus ambled about in a dry and stubbly pasture.

"When is lunchtime?" Atwater asked.

"Any time the captain's hungry."

"He's been hungry since breakfast."

She pointed to a clearing among some cottonwoods on the far shore. Filtered sunlight fell through the leaves to dapple the sand and gravel. Atwater beached the canoe and held out a hand to Anna, then lifted the picnic basket and set it down where she directed him to, on a flat bit of ground. She spread out a checkered tablecloth and arranged some plastic forks and knives on it and some cloth napkins rolled up in wooden rings. Every precise detail, Atwater reflected in awe. *Such a fortunate beneficiary am I.* Anna had the promised roast chicken neatly carved into quarters—he could smell the rosemary and garlic—along with a bowl of potato salad, sliced tomatoes from her garden, and a baguette from the patisserie.

He sat cross-legged in the dappled light and surveyed the banquet before him. "I'm a lucky fellow, Anna," he said.

"What would you like to drink? I've got two beers, two Cokes, and a bottle of Evian."

"I'll have a Coke, please."

He unscrewed the cap and swallowed mightily, quenching a thirst he had not been aware of until that very instant. He polished off a chicken breast and helped himself to seconds on the salads, his appetite as usual in full fury.

"We never had picnics like this in the Boy Scouts," he told her, with appreciation. "Our big meal was 'caveman steak.' The meat cooked right on the hot coals. No grill, no aluminum foil, no nothing. That was the toughest cow I ever ate, plus it was covered with soot."

"I'm spoiling you, I'm afraid."

Atwater stared at her hard. Anna is not herself, he thought. She's too quiet. She's not laughing at the jokes. He didn't like what he saw at all. Her face was pale, and she seemed distracted and shaky. "You're not eating anything," he said, chiding her. "You didn't touch your chicken."

"Am I being scolded?"

"I'm concerned about you."

"Don't be," Anna told him. "I'm just a little off today."

"You're all sweaty, too."

"It's the heat. Relax, Arthur. Why don't you put your head in my lap and take a nap?"

"You sure?"

"I'm sure. Do as I say."

He took a last sip of soda, settled next to her where she sat, and put his head in her lap. It was what he had wanted to do more than anything, really. He was surprised that she had known his secret desire and could so readily accommodate it, which was a talent of hers from the start. Anna understood him, and that was one reason why she was so precious to him. To be understood was a glorious thing, Atwater thought. He felt the softness of her thighs against his cheek, smelled the creamy sunscreen she'd applied, and wished he could find the right words to thank her as her cool fingers touched his forehead and ran through his hair to massage his scalp, ministering to him with a tenderness that he had always craved deep in his soul but had rarely encountered.

"Does that feel good?" Anna asked, smiling down at him.

"Better than I could ever say."

"Dear, dear Mr. Atwater."

He fell into a dozey sleep. In the torpor of the afternoon, he had hallucinatory dreams that blazed through him at great speed, one after another, and he hardly noticed when Anna gently nudged him off her lap and slipped the folded tablecloth beneath his head. She was not there when he woke some fifteen minutes later, but he could hear her in the bushes. He stretched and yawned and brushed some grass from his hair, feeling pleasantly restored. Yellow jackets were buzzing around the picnic basket, and he swatted at them with a napkin. Other canoes were on the river now, launched from the campground, and he watched them go by with their cargo of boisterous folks on holiday, young men stripped to the waist and young women in revealing bikinis, with wet-furred dogs on their prows.

He was loading up the canoe when Anna reappeared. She had sweated right through her shirt, he saw, and the top button of her shorts was undone. She seemed bewildered, blinded by the sun. Her legs were trembling so wildly that Atwater thought she might collapse.

"You need to get me to town as soon as possible," she told him evenly. "I need to see a doctor."

"What is it?" he asked, taking her arm to steady her, but she could not or would not say. Instead, she broke away from him and lay down in the bow of the canoe.

"I can't talk about it, Arthur. There isn't time. Let's go," Anna begged him. "Can we just go?"

He did as she asked. He had no other choice. The river looked different to him now, though, broader and more intimidating. It looked endless, really. He paddled as hard as he could in the sloggy current, stroke after stroke, and assured himself that everything would be all right. Anna was just suffering from some womanly complaint she couldn't properly explain to him. Soon there would be a town on the horizon, there would be answers and solutions, and they would go back in time to the clearing among the cottonwoods and be at peace together once more. Atwater told himself all that over and over again, but he didn't honestly believe it, not deep down, and when Anna asked him to bring her the bottled water in the picnic basket, he reeled at the sight of the reddish stain at her crotch and knew she must be hemmorhaging.

"Don't worry," she said to him, her face ashen. "It's not bad. It doesn't hurt."

He paddled on hopelessly, rounding yet another bend and shooting forward on a tide of white water that pitched him into a canyon strewn with deadfall, the wrack of winter storms. Trees had blown down from the granite cliffs and were lodged against boulders and knitted into barriers, piled up to form obstructions. Again there was the whack of waves against the aluminum hull. Spume showered over them and made it difficult for Atwater to see. He swerved to miss a redwood pinned between two rocks, only to collide with a big dead fir that knocked the canoe sideways and into a precipitous drop. He was in the center of some pluming haystacks and used his paddle as a brace to right himself, praying that the bow wouldn't go under. He saw Anna clinging tightly to the gunwales. The bow took a huge dip and seemed for a few seconds to be sinking, but it rose at the end of the drop, and they were out of the haystacks and into an eddying pool.

Atwater bailed with his bleach bottle. He threw buckets over the side, berating himself, the river, and the fates. *This is where your foolish love has led you. This is what you get. This is what you deserve.* Arm-weary, he knelt in the stern and kept paddling. Ahead the river was growing wider and ever more still, and he saw the town of Carson Valley in the distance on its pretty bluff. He had never seen it that way before, from that particular angle, had never in his life approached it in a spirit of welcome.

"We're almost there," he said to Anna, and she offered a weak smile, her shorts now richly stained with blood.

They were soon at the town beach. With the very dregs of his energy, Atwater hopped from the canoe and dragged it scraping onto the shore. Anna leaned on him getting out, asked for the tablecloth, and tied it around her waist. Shaken and vulnerable, she looked profoundly beautiful to him, stripped of every attitude. From a pay phone in the parking lot he called her father, and the old man arrived in less than five minutes, hastened by the urgency he must have heard in Atwater's voice.

"Anna?" Torelli asked, his dismay evident at the sight of his daughter. "What is it?"

"I need a doctor."

"What happened? Arthur, what the hell happened here? She's got blood on her shoes."

"Please, not now," Anna insisted. "Just get me to the hospital."

Torelli helped Atwater lift the canoe into the bed of his truck. They were in such a hurry that they didn't bother to secure it with any rope. They piled into the cab, with Anna seated between them, and the old man rushed over to Carson Valley General. There, Anna was ushered behind closed doors, where an intern examined her, after which an immediate summons went out for Ed Sawyer. Atwater was left to wait with Torelli, confined to a chair in a sterile, airless room that grated against his every sense. He sat hushed and uncomfortable for a few minutes until the old man spoke.

"Tell me what this is about, will you, Arthur?"

"I can't. She wouldn't say."

Torelli's voice cracked. "You must have some goddam idea."

"I asked her, Victor." Atwater was short with him. "I already told you, she wouldn't say."

"Some kind of female problem, is it?"

"It appears to be."

They sat for more than two hours together, taking turns to get up and pace, before Ed Sawyer finally joined them. He told them straight out that Anna had suffered a miscarriage, described the procedure he had performed, a simple D&C, and expressed his sympathy. She would recover quickly and would not have any ill effects from the surgery, he said, although they would keep her overnight, just as a precaution. She was exhausted and in shock from so much sun.

"You can go in if you like. Anna's conscious and alert. But don't stay too long. Don't tax her."

Atwater felt something in him spin and recoil. He couldn't bear to face her. "You go ahead, Victor," he said abruptly. "I'll come and get her tomorrow morning."

"She'll want to see you, you know."

"Tomorrow," he insisted.

"All right," the old man said with annoyance. "But it's a hell of a stunt to pull! Go on and get out of here."

Then Atwater was striding away from the hospital, his head aching with confusion. *This is where your foolish love has led you. This is what you deserve.* The image of Anna in her stained white shorts, standing before him on tottery legs with such pleading in her eyes, tore at his heart. He truly could not bear it. He could not rectify it. There was nothing he could do, nothing at all, so he walked along the river and over a bridge to the town square, where the only taxi that operated in Carson Valley was parked at a curb, its driver asleep at the wheel. He engaged the cabbie's services for a flat fare of fifteen dollars and rode in the backseat angry and saddened through familiar vineyard country to the darkness of the farm, returned again to his mortal condition, slipping into it with the utmost regret, once again alone.

15

S un, water, and blood—those were the images that swirled through Anna Torelli's mind while she lay in her hospital bed. The images blended at times into a single seamless element as bright and colorful as a psychedelic fragment, eerie, vibrant, and un-settling. All night she drifted down the river in that canoe, all night the horror of her trip stayed with her. She had been torn from the simple everyday world into a world of consequences, yanked abruptly out of her fantasies by a crashing dose of reality. She felt disconnected, at loose ends. Only Atwater, her partner in this sad episode, could bring her any solace. He would hold her, and they would talk it over and soothe each other. So Anna believed.

She waited for him in the morning, but he didn't come to her. The hours went by—eight, nine, ten o'clock—without any trace of him, and she became anxious and impatient, wanting desperately to be res-cued and restored to her proper place among the healthy ones. When she heard some footsteps outside her door at last, she sat up in antici-pation, but it was her father who knocked politely, clean-shaven as if for a special occasion and toting a small suitcase with some fresh clothes for her. He moved about in a slump-shouldered way, laboring under a conscript's unwilling sense of duty and muttering to himself while Anna got dressed. He took her by the elbow and guided her to his truck even though she had no serious pain, just a slight tenderness all over that was due as much to trauma as to her surgery.

"Where's Arthur?" she asked him directly.

"He had to run over to Napa on business. That's what I'm supposed to tell you." Torelli fiddled with his key chain. "Ah, hell, Anna, I
can't figure out what's up with him. He's as skittish as can be."

Her spirits sank. She should have known better than to expect Atwater to make it easy for her. His view of things was one-dimensional,
held in the purest possible contrast of black and white. He had a
man's hammering need for reasons and would demand the sort of
logical explanation that she could never give him, not in a million
years.

The old man drove through town at a cautious crawl, double-
checking himself at every stoplight and intersection. How odd, Anna
thought, that he should be so sensitive to her fragile state, especially
since she showed no outward signs of distress. All her scars were inter-
nal this time, located in the mass of conflicting feelings that were still
collecting around the miscarriage. It was an accident, of course,
merely the breakdown of a biological process that was beyond her
control, yet she had a child's desire to pretend that it had never happened whenever she remembered Atwater's anguished look and his
frantic paddling attempts to shepherd her to safety.

Her father sat in silence, his eyes fixed on the road.

"Don't be upset with me, please," Anna said contritely. "I'm
ashamed enough as it is. I made a mess, I know."

"It is that," he told her, with a sigh. "But you're not the first person
to get pregnant by mistake."

She stared out a window, a finger drawing patterns on the glass.
"Arthur must be angry with me. I don't blame him, I guess."

"I doubt he'll hold it against you," Torelli assured her. "He's a
grown man. It's not like you led him down the primrose path."

"That's true, I guess," she said, but then the doubts set in again.
"It came as a shock to him, though. I kept it a secret from him."

The old man glared at her. "Why would you do a thing like that?"

"To protect him. And because I was confused."

He slammed a palm against the dashboard. "Ah, for Chrissakes,
Anna! For Chrissakes!"

They arrived at the farm just before noon. Anna had only been
gone for a day, but it seemed much longer to her, a dream time, an

eternity. She heard the familiar chugging of a tractor and saw Atwater perched in his usual seat, the dust billowing up around him. She was sure he hadn't been anywhere near Napa. Instead, he was hoping to disappear into his work, to become one with the dust. That would be his form of denial, she thought, his method of defense. A pair of field hands, both new to her, were thinning a block of Cabernet Sauvignon near the house, and they took off their caps and made slight but formal bows when she passed them. Her father carried in the suitcase, packed now with her soiled clothes from the canoe trip, and set it on the porch. His judgmental expression had changed to a look of concern.

"Anything else I can do for you?" he asked. "You can stay with me if you'd rather."

"No, I'll be fine here. I can use some time to think."

"He won't hold it against you forever, Anna. You'll both get over it in time."

She smiled wanly when the old man hugged her. "Such an optimist you are," she said.

After he left, Anna sat in a kitchen chair. She had eaten a light breakfast at the hospital and had no appetite for lunch. Her picnic basket was on the floor by the stove, every item in it spotless—courtesy of Arthur, she gathered, and probably his unconscious way of underscoring the extent of her messiness—and she got up and stored it in a closet, sharply aware of her isolation. She had betrayed him, hadn't she? Anna felt that if he were to attack her with his probing questions right then, she'd be unable to handle it—she would shatter into pieces. The experience would be too intense, too draining, so she locked the front and back doors, withdrew to her bedroom, and slept solidly for several hours.

The walls had shaded to a dusky blue by the time she roused herself again. She went downstairs to pick at some cheese and bread and noticed that Atwater's Jeep wasn't parked in its accustomed spot. He had gone off somewhere without her, and his absence hurt her now. It was an insult, a deliberate affront, Anna thought, and in the vast loneliness of the old farmhouse, with night falling in black sheets, she finally began to weep, wandering aimlessly from room to room, switching on a lamp and turning it off, and staring blankly at the moonlit fields. She lay on the parlor couch with her face buried in a cushion and gave in to the tears and let them flow, an unquenchable tide that rose up from the core of her being as she wept for all the sorrows of the earth, for false hope and simple loss.

In the morning, she was much better, emptied of her grief. She showered in the hottest water she could stand, scrubbing and scrubbing, and put on some clean clothes. She was still upset with Arthur, still expecting him at any minute, still of two minds. Throughout the long afternoon, Anna kept hearing the scrape of his boots on the porch steps, and she would hurry to the door to embrace him, but there was never anyone outside except for the same pair of field hands who, as in a comic routine based on a repeated irony, bowed and took off their caps each time she appeared. Every now and then, she caught a glimpse of Atwater in the vineyard, ever in motion, a darting animal presence disappearing in the leafy green, and by that evening she was furious with him. If he wanted apartness, she would grant it to him. She wouldn't stoop to hunting him down.

There was no point in her staying on until the end of the month, Anna realized, no point to it at all anymore. On the spot, she decided to leave as soon as she could and managed to book a red-eye flight to JFK through Carson Valley Travel at a reasonable price. Her plane departed on Saturday, two days hence. She called Jane Weiss immediately to break the news and get some moral support and her brother to say good-bye. Roger was on his way to Tokyo himself in a couple of weeks, cheerful at the prospect of potential enlightenment. To avoid a mawkish airport scene with her father, Anna phoned around in search of a chauffeur, trying Betty Chambers first, who couldn't get free, and then Jack Farrell, her eternally devoted suitor, who agreed to do it in a split second.

She spent most of the next day packing. Late in the afternoon, she allowed herself a hike around the farm, laying claim to it through the naming of names—coast live oak and California buckeye, mesquite and greasewood dotting the far hills, a sharp-shinned hawk in sparkling blue-gray fettle on the branch of a madrona. The specifics of place were something she would take away with her, at any rate, something of value to be salvaged from this grand season of loss. As she strolled up the dirt road for the mail, with Daisy yipping along behind her, she was feeling remarkably calm until she saw Atwater in his Jeep, returning from town. She had been too busy to think much about him, but when he slowed down and offered a listless grin and a dull, defeated wave, she banged on a fender and forced him to stop.

"Arthur?" She was at his Jeep window. She saw no anger in him, only the pain in his eyes. "Talk to me, please?"

"I'm having a hard time with this, Anna," he said, his head lowered. "It's got me tied up in knots."

"Why didn't you come for me at the hospital? You haven't even called me."

"I came last night," he told her. "Your door was locked, and the lights were off. I figured to give it a few more days."

Anna felt guilty, but she pressed on. "The days are running out, Arthur," she said quietly. "I'm leaving on Saturday night."

He was devastated. That, too, she could see in his eyes, but all he said was, "I'm sorry to hear it."

"We have to talk before I go. It's not as though I committed a crime, is it? You do owe me that much."

"Nobody owes anybody anything," he said flatly. "You ought to know that by now."

"You do owe me," she insisted. "Tell me when."

"Tomorrow, then." Atwater glanced away. "In the evening after work. You'll find me in the barn."

Friday turned into Anna's day for farewells. She began with her father. He had expressed no concrete opinion about her sudden change of plans, only a series of grunts that indicated mild disapproval. From her garden she harvested a sack of vegetables for him, some cherry tomatoes, a half-dozen ears of white corn, and a handful of tiny green beans. The door to his house was wide open when she arrived, and she walked into the living room and through a sliding-glass door into the backyard, where the old man was curled up on the lawn in the shade of some hedges with a pair of grass clippers in his right hand, snoring loudly. Anna laughed out loud, but it didn't affect him. He just dozed on, the tyrant reduced in size and scale, as vulnerable as anybody now, mortal at last.

She inspected him closely as he slept, committing him to memory. He had on a ribbed singlet and some faded, ill-fitting madras Bermudas she could not have imagined him owning. When he sucked in a gulp of air, she got a good look at his teeth, all of them yellowed and a few of them chipped, except for his shiny gold-crowned molars. Tufts of springy hair sprouted generously from his ears. The hair on his chest was a downy white, while the hair under his arms was a blend of gray and some youthful strands of black. She studied the scab on his left wrist, his bare feet with their calloused toes and calcified toenails, and the wedding band trapped below his knobby arthritic knuckle, a ring he would wear to the grave. There they are, Anna thought, the loving particulars.

She watched the steady rise and fall of his rib cage until his eyes fluttered open.

"Anna?" he asked in a muddled way. "What the hell time is it?"

"Almost three."

With some effort, Torelli heaved himself to a sitting position. Anna heard the snapping complaint of his tendons. "I was out for almost an hour," he told her, scratching his head. "I don't sleep that solid at night."

"Here, brace yourself against me."

The old man struggled to his feet. "Did you hear that Fred Vescio's getting a new hip? That son of a bitch walks better than I do."

"Would you like a new hip?"

"I'd like a new everything. Come inside where it's cool."

Anna followed him into the house. It was his place now and no one else's, stale with his odors and cluttered with all the things he had ignored or forgotten, his mangy socks balled up beneath the couch, unopened envelopes from charitable organizations stacked on an end table, and a bowl of pennies yet to be rolled into wrappers and cashed at the bank. A current *Valley Herald* was spread over an arm of his recliner, its pages open to an article about a new Chinese herbalist on the square, and a few videos were piled next to a rash of clipped coupons, the old man's idle time measured out in the dimes and quarters that he would someday save on Hamburger Helper and Gino's Frozen Pizza.

He made some pink lemonade for them from a can of frozen concentrate, bending over an ice-cube tray in the kitchen sink. The improbable Bermudas slipped farther down his hips to expose the pleated elastic waistband of his underwear.

"Where did you get those shorts, anyway?" Anna asked him.

"At a garage sale down the block. You like 'em on me?"

"They're lovely."

"Guess how much they cost?"

"I give up."

He was beaming. "Two dollars."

They sat at a redwood picnic table on the patio to drink their lemonade. The riotous sounds of a weekend afternoon in the suburbs echoed around them, balls bouncing and bicycle bells tinkling.

"You remember that I'm taking off early tomorrow, don't you?" Anna asked him.

"Of course, I do," he said. "Your flight leaves a little before midnight. I better pick you up, oh, about eight-thirty."

"I've asked Jack Farrell to drive me down," Anna told him, holding her breath. "It's a long trip, and I didn't want to put you out."

She was startled by his reply. "Well, that's probably right," her father said. "I don't see so good at night anymore. Pretty soon, I'll be creeping around on the back roads like Pepper Harris does." He laughed. "I'll tell you what, Anna."

"What?"

"Don't get old if you can help it."

They played a cribbage match, two out of three games. Torelli won, collected $1.05, and once again displayed his uncanny knack for celebrating at his victim's expense. He walked Anna to the Taurus afterward. She threaded an arm through his as she had done on her wedding day, recalling his dignified bearing and how she had relied on him for support. She had floated around inside her billowy bridal gown, her body fragrant with perfume and aching to be touched. She remembered the crimson carpet down the aisle, the worn mahogany pews, and the women seated in them shedding what she had believed in her innocence to be tears of joy, although she knew better now.

"It's been wonderful having you here, Anna," the old man said, leaning against her car door. "You're not a grape grower yet, but you're on your way."

"I'll miss you terribly." Anna thought she might cry. She would not see him again for a while. She might never see him again, in fact. "I don't suppose I could coax you to New York for a vacation?"

"I don't suppose you could."

"Well, the house is here for me. I may surprise you yet and move back in."

"That would be a fine surprise, all right," he said. "What are you doing with that little dog of yours?"

"I was going to return it to Arthur."

"It might not hurt me to have that dog for company."

"Are you saying you want Daisy?"

"I wouldn't mind having her."

Anna was amused that destiny would play such a mean trick on the pup. She touched her father's hand. "I'll call you when I get home," she told him. "Thanks for everything."

"Oh, no," he said. "You got it backward. It goes the other way."

She drove out to the valley in a good mood, elated to have gotten through the visit without any conflict or stumbling. If she could reach a similar accord with Atwater, she might yet leave the farm on a small grace note. She wondered how to present herself to him as she rummaged through the few clothes she hadn't packed. In her bureau, she found the lingerie that she had gifted him with in the madness of her passion and inspected it as if it had fallen into the drawer from another planet. That was never me, she thought, not really. But maybe it was someone I was hoping to become, she thought again.

After deliberating, she chose to go to Arthur as she was, plainly, without any decoration. He was where he said he would be, waiting in the barn. He had done nothing to improve himself either. His hair was uncombed, and an oily streak was splotched across his cheek. Anna took in the strong, familiar smell of him and understood that he was a part of the farm and what she loved about it, and that her time to be with him was truly over.

"Will you walk with me?" she asked him.

He looked at her. Again the pain was in his eyes. "Where?"

"Anywhere. By the river?"

They started down the path along the edge of the vineyard. The dogs trailed after them, barking and chasing one another, but Atwater spun around and yelled at them so loudly and irritably that they turned tail and ran back to the trailer. Anna was at his side and fumbled for his hand, but he pulled it away from her as though her touch had a corruptive sting. He lengthened his stride and moved a few paces ahead of her, and she was upset again at how wrong everything had gone, but what had she expected? A handshake and a kiss? These affairs always ended badly for her.

A rank odor off the river colored the air, a stink of frogs and scummy algae, of ooze and mud that hung in the evening heat. Some mallards came winging along the water from the distant oxbow, dark shapes flying in determined splendor until they sensed a human presence and bolted higher into the sky. Anna sat on the big serpentine rock in a wash of fading light that was an electric blue. Atwater crouched a few feet away from her. She was aware of how coiled and tense he was. He didn't say anything to her at first. Instead, he picked up some pebbles and threw them into the river as a boy might do.

"Why did you keep it a secret from me, Anna?" he asked at last in a calm voice. "That's what I keep wrestling with."

"I'm not absolutely sure," she told him, forced into the sort of explaining she had dreaded, that men in their implacable devotion to logic seemed always to require. "What if I said I was enjoying myself? Would that sound strange?"

"Yes. Because it was at my expense."

"No, it wasn't at *your* expense." Anna was frustrated and had to resist an urge to scream at him. "Don't judge me for a minute, okay? It's easy to judge somebody else, and you're very good at it."

His face was blank. He let the remark pass. "Go on."

"I was enjoying the way I felt, enjoying the changes in my body. Enjoying the fantasy of having a child. Is that so awful? What happened was only an accident."

"Accident or not, it hurt," Atwater said, tossing another pebble. "I wouldn't hide something like that from you. I'd figure it was your business, too."

"Believe me, I wasn't trying to hide anything! It confused me at first, and I couldn't decide what to do. Then it got decided for me. A week, ten days, that isn't a long time, is it? Are you going to let one mistake spoil all the good between us?"

"I could have helped you decide, Anna. Did that ever occur to you?"

"Yes, it did. And what would you have said if I'd asked you?"

Atwater was staring at the river. The space between them was growing, becoming a gulf. "I would have told you to have the kid."

Anna was surprised. "Would you really?"

He nodded. "Sure. Because it might have kept you here with me a while longer."

"So it would have been a trap."

"That's right," Atwater agreed. "It would have been a trap."

This is the story we are agreeing to tell, Anna thought bitterly. This is the narrative we are evolving to account for the unaccountable. This will give us something to hold onto, it will allow us to continue. "Then maybe what happened was for the best."

"I'd say it was," he told her. "You're not cut out for this life, Anna. You don't belong on a farm in the middle of nowhere. Nothing between us was ever real."

"So it seems," she said halfheartedly. Again she reached for his hand, and again he pulled it away. "Will you always be angry with me?"

"It isn't anger. It's just disappointment. I knew better than to get involved with you. I knew it from the start."

"Do you know how much you've meant to me?" Anna asked him. "Have I made it clear how much I care?"

"Yes, you have. But it wasn't enough for me, was it? That's my fault. I take the blame for that." Atwater clambered to his feet. "There's no sense in any more talk, Anna. It only makes things worse. What's done is done. I should never have fallen in love with you. But I just couldn't help myself."

He had said the one thing that she hoped he wouldn't say. "I'm so sorry about everything," she said, looking away, the sadness everywhere now.

"Don't be sorry," he told her softly. "I do love you, Anna."

Atwater did something then that astonished her. He came to her where she sat and gathered her into an embrace that drew all the fire from her. All the strength, all the iron will that she had built up to survive the moment flowed out of her, and she held him tightly and had an intense longing to go back to that time and place when they were in such harmony, two lovers balanced on a dusky porch, birds about them, although she knew it could never be.

"I'll call you some time," she said, feeling his lips against her hair.

"Don't do that," he warned her harshly. "Don't call me unless you have something I might want to hear."

He left her where she stood, marching swiftly up the rise and never pausing for a backward glance. Anna waited almost until dark to walk up the hill herself and saw that his Jeep was gone again. She did the very last of her packing and drank a little wine, touring the old house room by room. How would it look to her on her next visit, and the one after that? Would her father still be alive? And where would At-water be? How much of him would she carry away with her? She felt a sudden and pressing need to add something essential to their conversation, so she took up a pen and paper and started writing, crossing out one word after another until she had cut through all her attitudes and poses to arrive at a single sentence that seemed just then to be all she could ask of him and all she had to say.

Promptly at nine o'clock, Jack Farrell pulled into the circular drive-way. He delivered himself to Anna on a waft of Old Spice cologne, his teeth pearly and polished and the new shirt he wore crosshatched with creases from its cardboard packaging. He humped her luggage down the porch stairs and stowed it in his trunk while Anna shut off the lights and locked up behind her. She was aching inside, lost and broken, fearful of the future, and tired, so tired. "I'll just be a second, Jack," she told Farrell, walking to the trailer as she had done so many times before. She could hear the dogs inside scratching and sniffing as she reached up and tacked her note to Atwater's door, unburdened of its simple, plangent message, *Forgive me, love.*

16

The first grapes to be splashed with a distinctive varietal color that summer were some nice Gray Rieslings on Dick Rhodes's farm. He told his wife about them at lunch, and she mentioned them to their teenage daughter, and the girl, who worked part-time at a winery, passed on the news to her boss, three visitors from Seattle, a UPS delivery man, and a tall, handsome boy that she had a crush on, the one in charge of landscaping. That same evening, a handful of curious growers arrived at Rhodes's place for a tour of inspection. They sniffed the reddish-tan berries, pinged them with their fingers, squeezed them, tasted them, and agreed that these particular grapes were indeed well on their way to ripeness and could be interpreted as either a good or a bad omen of the coming harvest, depending on your orientation. The precise date was August sixteenth.

"We'll be pulling the crop off early this year," said Charlie Grimes, a crabbed hand jabbing down the seat of his trousers to explore all the available nooks and crannies. "Did you see the moon last night? There hasn't been a moon like that since nineteen and fifty-nine."

"It isn't moonlight that brings up the sugar," Dick Rhodes replied, and his comment opened the floodgates of opinion. Soon the men were all talking at once, their voices strictly at cross purposes and none of them doing much listening.

"The linnets will be after those grapes for sure," whispered Grimes to Pepper Harris. "They favor Rieslings smartly."

Harris pushed away some leaves for a closer look at the fruit. "Feel this stem here, how woody it is," he said to Fred Vescio. "I had a Mexican boy one time, his grape knife split from its handle, and he took to biting off clusters with his teeth. That kid was some picker."

"My Riesling stunted on me," Vescio confided to the stranger next to him. "The flower thrips got 'em, so I replanted to Merlot, like Pepper here. Bugs won't eat that grape, and it don't get sick."

"German grapes I just don't trust," the stranger said to nobody in particular. He was Emory Carter, a retired engineer, who had a hobby vineyard and operated his ham radio at all hours to broadcast the Christian gospel to heathen foreigners across the water. "Those Gewürzs of mine all died on me, and no expert in California could tell me why."

"You figure it was a plot?" Arthur Atwater asked him.

"I'm not saying that. But it's a helluva mystery, don't you think?"

On a signal from his wife that his supper was ready, Dick Rhodes brought out a twelve-pack of cold beer to cut short the conversation. His thirsty brethren guzzled with gusto while offering their hosannas and benedictions, wiping the dirt from their faces, blowing their noses, and helping themselves to a second can for the ride home. Only Atwater abstained, choosing a 7-Up instead. He still felt too unmoored to risk anything stronger.

Atwater's mood these days was often blue. True, almost two months had gone by since Anna had left, but he still hadn't recuperated. He thought frequently about their meeting by the river and what he might have done differently to win her over. He had a painful memory of himself walking away from her and driving out to the coast to clear his head, a woeful and panicky flight during which he had taken the curves at a daredevil speed in spite of his Jeep's rattling camshaft and the knocking complaint of its engine. The two-lane blacktop he followed led him over the mountains, through a forest of pine and fir, along the Gualala River, and across the invisible San Andreas fault to Stewart's Point, which was not so much a town as a few sheep ranches grouped around a general store and a post office on a bluff above the ocean.

He had tried to lose himself there. He hiked through the coastal scrub in a raging fury, Heathcliff on the moors, absolutely direction-less, his collar turned up against a fierce Pacific wind as he tripped on bracken fern and tangled underbrush and talked to himself or to the impervious sea. The great suck and blast of the breakers below roared in his ears like some elemental form of laughter. He hiked to the squawking of gulls and the flapping of brown pelicans until thick wet sheets of fog obscured what little he could make out of the ground beneath his feet, at which point he retired to the shelter of his Jeep and sat vacant and empty through a starless night, ruined by love once more, by the sadness of love, the terror of love, even by the same childish desire for the world to be other than it *could* be that had foiled him all his life. He slept and woke and slept again, and then at sunrise ate a breakfast of hot coffee and packaged cherry pie at the general store before returning to the farm, certain that Anna would no longer be there.

His blundered affair had made him the object of considerable gossip in the valley, of course. There were many jokes formulated at his expense, generally revolving around his command of birth con-trol, and he received one ugly anonymous letter from a pro-lifer in-forming him that he would burn in hell through all eternity, but he already knew that. Most people in town were sympathetic, really, and offered their condolences, sometimes pulling him aside and telling him in a hushed voice about similarly awkward episodes in their own lives. They spoke of adulterous affairs, unrequited passions, acts of nonpareil stupidity, alcoholic adventures in gambling towns, liaisons with prostitutes, and bastard children hurried out of the county only seconds after the poor infants had emerged from the womb. Atwater soon grew tired of these confessions and wished he could put his hands over his ears like the hear-no-evil monkey. He was being in-ducted into a club he had no interest in joining. Loss, loss, and more loss—that was the text and subtext of every tale. When would it all stop, he asked himself, as if the answer wasn't already etched into his soul: *never.*

At first, he had expected Anna to call or write, even though he'd forbidden it, but the weeks kept spinning by without any word from her. That had discouraged him from contacting her, as well, and also caused him to abandon the fantasy that he would hold her again someday. Still, he kept her farewell note squirreled inside a book on his bedside table and reread it almost every night. Sometimes the message made him wish he could fly to New York and strangle her, while at others it touched him and raised all the emotions he was trying to suppress. He wondered if he had been too tough on her, if she would have responded to more kindness and less intensity, or if instead he had been *too* kind and had failed to give her the sort of rotten treatment that she craved. These matters were all relative. What concerned him finally was that she had fled, leaving him to master again the sad art of sleeping alone, more difficult than ever now when she came to torment him, and he remembered the feel of her soft, soft skin. In those sweet, gone moments like no others, he had rested, was complete.

The morning after his trip to Rhodes's farm, Atwater crouched on a rise to wait out a thunderstorm. Rain rarely fell in August, but when it did it could damage the crop by inducing bunch rot. Bruised-looking clouds blew in over the hills, and there was a trembling sound in the leaves. He chewed a stalk of dry rattlesnake grass and watched the sky, testing the wind direction with a finger. *Blow north, goddam it.* A north wind would knock a hole right through the storm and open a corridor for some hot weather to hasten the ripening process. On into the afternoon he waited, plotting strategies to deal with the eventualities and thinking back over all the things he could have done but didn't, involved in his traditional preharvest attempt to get the horse back in the barn. The harvest itself he imagined as a force of nature that began and ended of its own accord, a creature born of heat and light that would sweep through the valley as a tornado might, with only the slightest advance warning.

He saw Antonio Lopez coming toward him to announce the already known. "I got to go over to Hawk Wind, Arthur," Lopez said by rote, as he did each day after lunch. "They want me up there at two o'clock."

"This is the last of it," Atwater told him peevishly. "Did you give them your notice?"

"They don't have any notice up there. They just pay us in cash. People can stay or go. Hawk Wind doesn't give a shit."

"You be around here full-time on Monday. You understand, partner?"

"Sure." Lopez gazed at the threatening clouds. "You think it's going to rain?"

"I don't know, Antonio. Would I be sitting here if I knew?"

"Probably not."

Atwater frowned. "I almost sprayed the Zins with captan yesterday, but there wasn't a cloud in the sky. Did you listen to the weather report last night? 'We'll have a beautiful day tomorrow, temperatures in the eighties, time for everybody to go for it!' "

"You sound like a girl!" Lopez told him, laughing at the impersonation.

"Yeah, well. The weather report woman was a girl."

"You can't count on those weather reporters, Arthur! They're just actors."

"I thought you were going."

"I am. See you later, man."

The storm unraveled late that afternoon. The wind didn't shift, but it stopped blowing so hard, and the clouds lost their look of menace and were shot through with bright and provident columns of sunlight. Atwater, sore in the knees, smiled and repaired to his trailer.

He passed the evening paying bills. He was behind on every account, ten days here, a whole month there. He could not recall when he had last shopped for groceries. His shelves were bare except for two cans of plum tomatoes, a package of Golden Grain macaroni, and a tin of the anchovies his wife had liked and that he must have been carrying around with him since the demise of his marriage. He was behind, too, on his reports to Victor Torelli. He had promised to stop by once a week to discuss the state of the vineyard, even though Torelli ordinarily cut him off in five minutes or less, but he vowed to make amends the next evening and actually did, knocking on the old man's door right at twilight.

Torelli was in elevated spirits, enthroned in his recliner before his big Sony TV with a glass of wine at hand and Daisy on his lap. "You ever seen 'Wheel of Fortune'?" he asked, grabbing the pup by its ears and nuzzling her nose-to-nose. "I'll bet I solve the puzzle before you do. Is a dollar too rich for your blood?"

"No, I can handle that." Atwater dropped onto the couch, his mind elsewhere. He asked after a respectful time, as he did on each visit, "Hear anything from Anna lately, Victor?"

"Yes, sir. She phoned just the other night. She wanted to know how the grapes are going. She's doing fine."

"I'm glad of that," Atwater said, although he had secretly been enjoying a vision of Anna roaming the streets of Manhattan sobbing and tearing her hair out by the roots because she had been foolish enough to leave Carson Valley and the good, decent, honorable man who loved her. "She must be happy to be home."

"I wouldn't say that. Some women, they get so damn emotional! They make up their mind, they change it, and then they cry."

"She was crying?"

"Well, she wasn't crying. But she was upset about something. What was the puzzle again?"

"An object," Atwater told him. "You find it in the kitchen." He cleared his throat. "Did she ask about me?"

"I'd buy some vowels if I was that lady." The old man turned toward him, his cheeks aflame. "No, she didn't."

"I see."

"Arthur," Torelli said, "I hope you understand I don't hold it against you, what happened. I feel real bad about it for both of you. I'm so old, and I've seen so much goddam cruelty in my time, that sleeping together seems about as harmless a thing as two people can do."

"I guess so." Except for the affection involved, Atwater thought. Except for what attaches to the act.

"A human being isn't much different from a dog, really," Torelli went on. "Take this little mutt here. I'll demonstrate for you." He reached down, gripped the pup's tail, and yanked it hard. Daisy howled, dived off his lap to the floor, and flattened out with a whimper. "See that? We'd all rather be petted, wouldn't we?"

"Colander!" Atwater yelled.

The old man gave him a cockeyed look and passed over a dollar bill. "You must have cheated when I wasn't looking," he said.

Rawley Kimball showed up at the farm the next afternoon, his clipboard to the fore. Atwater had learned over the weeks not to take the criticism personally. He had deduced at last that Kimball's nature was carved in stone, at once nerdish, neurotic, and compulsive. Kimball was the sort of man who could only cope with the world in measured doses, who set out his clothes for the morning before he went to bed and accepted it as an article of faith that a sense of order could always be salvaged from the prevailing chaos. The only order Atwater had ever encountered was in a vineyard, and even there his grasp of it was slight.

They made their usual rounds. Kimball scribbled notes in a cramped hand such as schoolboys use to prevent laggard fellow students from copying their work. When they were done, he said, "I see some real progress, Arthur."

"We aim to please," Atwater told him.

"I have to admit, you were right about your Zinfandel. You might just get six tons to the acre."

Atwater nodded and steeled himself for the spinsterish faults that were about to be pointed out for his edification.

Kimball ground his teeth a bit, as if it hurt him to even bring up the perceived shortfall. "I'm still a trifle concerned about your Cabs, though," he said, drumming a pencil eraser on the sheets. "You're going to have to pull off those grapes right quick when the big heat comes, or else they'll raisin up on you."

"Yes, sir, I'll do just that."

"Those two rows of Chardonnay nearest the river? You've got a few spider mites. I'd send some boys through tomorrow and have them pick and shake."

"I'll be damned." Atwater pressed his knuckles to his lips. "Would you believe that was my exact plan?" He clapped Kimball on the back. "Rawley, I must be getting the hang of this!"

"There you go," Kimball said cheerfully. "That's the attitude!"

In the mail, there came some brochures that Atwater had requested from Carson Valley Travel, glossy pictorials of life as it was never lived by the inhabitants of the countries portrayed, the whole of existence reduced to an unblemished Sunday supplement. He sat with tea after supper to consider how and where he might squander his bonus money after the harvest. He was in serious need of a holiday and flirted with the idea of himself as a bohemian gadabout, graying and bearded but not yet stripped of his romantic appeal, with a carefully knotted red bandanna around his neck—jeez, Arthur! He thought Mexico might be the proper destination for such a weary desperado. A brochure called "The Mysteries of the Yucatán" appealed to him the most, rich in Mayan intrigue, with the ruins of a great civilization heaped about like so much trash. He recited the place-names to himself as an incantation, Mérida, Copán, Campeche, dreaming up a storm, until he got to Las Islas Mujeres and, reminded of Anna, threw the brochures on the floor.

Days went by. On the twenty-third of August, Atwater sampled a Zinfandel grape and nearly choked on the sour, astringent taste. He spat out the seeds and pulp and kicked some dirt over them, conducting a burial service for his brash optimism. He had known better, really. Grapes didn't become edible fruit in such dreary weather as he'd been dealt that afternoon, a second layer of fog piled onto the fog that had been there in the morning, with the landscape wintry and the temperature never reaching seventy degrees. The junkie robins and finches addicted to sugar were nowhere around either, being wiser than him and content to bide their time and bank their energies against a more certain payoff in the future.

He cleaned up on Friday and went to see a movie at the only theater in town. Santa Rosa showcased first-run releases, but the little valley cinema, a sixty-seater converted from a defunct Woolworth's, specialized in classics, foreign films with subtitles, and Hollywood blockbusters that had failed to bust any blocks. For a mere $2.50, Atwater availed himself of a double feature and sat all the way through the first film, *The Treasure of Sierra Madre*, consuming a family-size box of popcorn and trying to orient the mountains on-screen with the Mysteries of the Yucatán, calculating distances in his head and silently aping Bogart's dialogue, and halfway through the second, a Cary Grant comedy he had watched not long ago at home.

He strolled across the square afterward, past the fountain, the palm trees, and a Mexican couple on a bench. They were madly fondling each other until they sensed a *gringo* nearby, their embrace instantly dissolving to be replaced by an enigmatic smile and a musical "*Buenas noches, señor.*" Atwater stopped at The Rib Room and nursed a beer at the bar. The place was packed with upscale revelers who had money to burn—white-collar types, the very people Anna would be reveling with in Manhattan as she hunted for her new lover—and he felt uncomfortable and would have left if the bartender, a shag-haired blond in her late twenties, hadn't kept circling back to chat with him. Atwater was sure that she would give him her phone number if he asked for it, and she did, and though he knew he would probably never even call her, he took from this tiny triumph a belief that he was at least beginning to be healed.

17

Now in the waning hours of another Carson Valley afternoon, with the bells at St. Brigid's ringing five times live on tape, Victor Torelli continued the job of cleaning out the office he was finally vacating, packing away thirty years or so of largely worthless materials that he hoped to put in storage and never see again. The light falling across the town square had a melancholy foretaste of autumn in it, an edge of clarity that divided tree from tree and robin from robin, but Torelli barely noticed. He was too preoccupied with his archaeological dig, rooting about in a bottom drawer that had so far yielded a penknife and a mummified orange. The orange held a special fascination for him. It was covered with a grayish green mold that flecked off in noxious little clouds. Rooms own us, the old man thought, and not the other way around. Rooms, houses, the very air.

His few valuable possessions he had already carted away with Antonio Lopez's help, his TV and his VCR, his deer rifle, and the plaque he had once been awarded as "Merchant of the Year," coveting it even though he had never done any retail business and knew well enough that the Chamber of Commerce gave out such trophies on a revolving basis without any regard for merit. Those objects, each deemed useful, nostalgic, or salable, had been jammed into the spare bedroom on Quail Court. Torelli was down to the true detritus of his so-called professional life now, the items whose presence in his office seemed linked to an unfathomable practical joke, here a plastic doll's arm and there an entire slab of Easter Seals, hundreds of fake stamps not worth a goddam penny. Whatever we manage to save, he thought, we must save by accident.

He could not account for the crumbling roll of Tums in his other bottom drawer, a remedy he might in fact have benefited from after lunch that very day when his bowl of chili began riding too high, nor did he have a clue how a mousetrap and a fragment of incredibly hard cheddar cheese had come to rest beside it. Farther back, he found a marble, a jack of spades, and a grocery list in Claire's fine script, her perfectly formed Palmer-method letters still elegant to his eye. *Two pounds ground chuck, hamburger buns, toilet paper, cookies for the kids,* the ghosts were everywhere, circling him, and he had no place to hide.

Torelli stumbled up and sat in his chair. He felt bushed, and his pulse was racing. Only his three-drawer metal filing cabinet was left for him to empty. He had removed from it all but his most recent correspondence, the sum of which amounted to a last series of bills to be paid and three hokey birthday cards—he had turned eighty a week before—of the sub-Hallmark variety sent by prelapsarian business associates of his, who probably kept a list of such occasions somewhere and continued to extend greetings automatically to everyone on it, not bothering to check on whether the party in question was dead or alive. Torelli was delighted by the notion that he would still receive such cards when he was cold and in his grave. He scrawled some checks to dispatch the bills and settled back to read his single letter from the morning mail, a bulletin from Consolidated Vintners that encouraged him to think that the world might yet quit its confounded spinning.

Dear Victor,

It gives me a whole lot of pleasure to send you the enclosed. It will be the last report from your Consolidated Vintners field advisor Rawley Kimball that you will get prior to the all important time when our annual harvest begins.

I am sure you will agree with me when I say the report could not be better. With Rawley's expertise and advice, your vineyard is in better shape than ever. This report shows the kind of real progress we at CV always hope for. I am sure you can look forward to the prospect of good news when the harvest is over.

At CV, we are expecting a banner year this harvest. Everything has worked out just about as well as it could. The weather has been cooperative, and all we need now is some of our famous "Indian Summer" sunshine to bring up the sugar in our grapes. Every indicator we use to assist us in predicting how the crop will go tells us to expect the very best.

Let me add on a personal note how glad I am to have the Torelli holdings in our portfolio. I would also like to take this opportunity to express my sympathy over the recent tragedy involving your daughter. We went through something similar with our youngest. All I can say is, bad things sometimes happen to good people.

I look forward to celebrating with you after the grapes are in and the crush is over. Don't forget the treat will be on me. Maybe you'll agree to join me for one of our Rotary Club feeds at La Bella Italia.

Meanwhile, please go over our report and let me know if you have any questions. As ever, I and my staff are at your service.

Wishing you the best at harvest time,
Wade Saunders

WS:rw
Enclosed: CV report, CV T-shirt, CV baseball cap

18

The six wood frame cabins behind Roy's Market, each layered with decades of flaking paint and upgraded for the harvest season with a new brass numeral from Ace Hardware, stood in a semicircle around a huge, mossy live oak. No other vegetation grew anywhere nearby, except for grapevines. The cabins rented for $600 a month. They had linoleum floors recently swabbed with Pine Sol, bulbless light fixtures in both bedrooms, and tiny kitchenettes where a scarred Formica-topped table was pushed into a corner. Bathing and toilet facilities were communal, in a concrete-block wash-house out of which a trickle of foul-smelling water was always dribbling from a dented drainpipe. Only men were allowed to live in the camp, and they lived there only while they had fruit to pick, splitting up the cost among their bunkmates, eight or ten or a dozen ways.

Antonio Lopez had shared a harvest cabin during his first summer in the valley. He still recalled with true feeling the good times he had enjoyed, the constant ribbing and raillery and the empty cans of Budweiser stacked in pyramids, as well as the beguiling confidences that the lonely pickers traded on the long, hot nights when they sat up late listening to someone strum a guitar. They played card games and had penny pitching contests and little fiestas every payday, simple rewards for the painstaking labor that Lopez, having risen from the ranks, was currently denied. Now he was a family man, a salaried employee with responsibilities, and his carefree days were over. He had never actually missed them before, but he felt a stab of nostalgia when he stopped at Roy's after work one evening late in August to secure a place for his cousin Omar Perez who, wanted or not, would be arriving that Sunday.

He didn't bother to go into the market to ask about vacancies. The clerks never kept track of how the cabins were being divided up, and Roy himself intervened only if the rent wasn't paid on time or the frequent parties were too noisy. Anybody interested in a bunk had to wander like a supplicant from door to door, hoping to find a fellow picker sympathetic, desperate, or greedy enough to strike a bargain, so Lopez began walking and knocking. He had no success until he reached cabin four, where a teenager, stripped to his Jockey shorts and all alone, lay on a cot reading a *novela*.

"*Buenas tardes*," Lopez said in a gracious way, smiling to show that he meant no harm. He granted the youth a few seconds to comprehend the essential fact that he was older, more experienced, and deserving of respect. "How you doing today?"

"Okay."

"Where are your *amigos* at?"

"They coming. *Mañana*."

"From where, man?"

"Baja."

"*Podría poner otro hombre en la habitación?*" There appeared to be some space in the second bedroom, Lopez thought, peering around a corner. "You got a cot left in here?"

The youth scarcely paid attention. "*No soy el capitán*," he said, turning a page.

"Of course you're not the captain, you're too fucking stupid, aren't you?" Lopez asked, still smiling but speaking very rapidly in English to obscure his meaning and create an impression that he might be there in an official capacity. He hoped to provoke the fidgety unease that he had often experienced himself. "Isn't that right?"

"Yes." The youth nodded. "Okay, sir."

Satisfied that he had asserted his dominion, Lopez made a splashy show of touring the cabin. It was decorated after a fashion with the debris of its former tenants, who had pinned up everything from snapshots of themselves to the postcards that their relatives in Mexico had sent. The postcards were often displayed with the picture side to the wall, so that the benevolent wishes and fervent prayers written on them could be accessed as necessary. Above the sink was a penciled cardboard sign, NO PEEING HERE. A poster of a blond model in a Tecate T-shirt, her nipples straining against the flimsy fabric, was central to the ambience and had the vibrant quality of a much-adored icon at which countless pilgrims had worshipped on their knees.

Lopez did indeed find a cot at the back as yet unclaimed, its availability advertised by the absence of any shoes, bundled clothes, or food stored beneath it. It lacked sheets, but it had a thin blanket thrown over it and a stained and lumpy pillow. He tested the mattress by punching it and hurt his knuckles.

"*Tiene agua caliente aqui?*" he asked when he returned to the other room.

"*Sí.*"

"The toilets working?"

"*Sí.*"

He passed over a five-dollar bill. "*Esto es para usted,*" he said, explaining that the money was a small gratuity, even a *mordida,* to reserve the cot for his cousin, and that only an idiot who had never done any business in the United States would refuse it. "Five more for you next time. *La cama esta reservada. Diga el capitán.* No mistakes, okay?"

"Okay." The youth grinned stupidly and stuffed the bill into his underpants.

Sunday came before Lopez was ready for it. There were tattered clouds in a gray-blue sky. He escorted his wife and daughter to Mass as usual, nervous about his cousin's arrival and wishing that in a moment of weakness he had never bragged to the boy. To complicate matters, Elena was actually looking forward to meeting Omar, imagining him to be a welcome member of the family, a relative from the wilds of Jalisco. Her romantic view of things helped to sink Lopez further into gloom. Now that Elena wasn't working herself and had nothing to do except care for one easy baby, she was discouragingly upbeat about everything, he thought.

"Remember how you acted when you first got here? How excited you were?" she asked him on the drive home from lunch, trying to boost his spirits.

"Sure, I remember. But you didn't know me then."

"You told me about it, though. Your cousin looked out for you, right?"

"He looked out for me a little bit."

Elena rested a calming hand on his shoulder and rubbed him gently. "Don't take it so hard, Antonio," she told him. "This should be fun for you. You're an idol to him."

"I'm like his Elvis Presley?"

"That's right. And you're my Elvis, too."

He waited for the boy at the Greyhound station in Santa Rosa that afternoon. It was a small, plain, odorless room adjoining a car rental agency. Inside were a couple of video games, a burbling coffee machine, and some chairs in which a few people were sitting. They were mostly white and obviously poor, elderly retired folks who looked defeated, all the life energy sucked out of them, their skin horrible for Lopez to see, pale and wrinkled and brown with liver spots, their false teeth shining and clacking. He roamed about impatiently and tried to put the best possible face on his situation, recalling Omar's mother, a sister to his own late father. She was a kind woman who had fed him whenever he came to her door hungry, and if he concentrated on her it helped him to gain a sense of mission. He began to feel the nobility of somebody honoring a debt, yet he was worried that he wouldn't even recognize Omar, whose face was lost to him, submerged in a stream of time, a watery image he couldn't quite bring into focus.

The bus pulled up at two o'clock, right on schedule. There was a hiss of pnuematic air as the doors swung open. The driver preceded his passengers down the steps, lifted a panel to the luggage compartment, and started unloading some luggage and a few cardboard cartons bound with twine or fastened with strapping tape. Lopez watched the steady descent of stiff-limbed travelers and saw how each was met in turn, sister joined to brother, father to child, in the midst of joyous greetings, tender embraces, jokes, and tears. It troubled him that he felt no such emotions himself. He felt nothing really except aggravation—he could not seem to get beyond it. He kept watching until a boy who could not be other than his cousin emerged from the bus, a cocky, strutting kid who puffed on a cigarette and wore a cheap leather jacket dyed a bumblebee yellow, saddle-stitched on the collar and embroidered with his name *Omar* over a breast pocket.

Lopez moved toward him with foreboding. The boy jumped into the air at the sight of him and ducked past the hand he offered to bestow a clumsy *abrazo*. "*Yo soy Omar*," he said, his voice high-pitched and full of good humor. "*Hermano*, don't you know me?"

"*Cómo no?* From Guadalajara."

"*Eso es!*" The boy laughed uproariously, as if he were at a carnival, and gripped Antonio's biceps to look him over. "*Tu pareces differente, sabes?*"

"Different? How?"

"*El pelo!*" Omar cried in delight.

Lopez lifted his thick ponytail. "It wasn't like this before?"

"*No, no! Más corto!*" The boy ran his fingers through the ponytail, his admiration manifest. "*Muy guapo, Antonio.* You are very handsome in it."

"Yeah, well, we better get going."

Omar had just one bag, a woven *costela* in choleric Indian reds and blues that he carried slung over a shoulder. It bulged with clothes and gift-wrapped packages. He, too, was a handsome fellow, although there was something about him—an eagerness to please, a disingenuous quality—that put Lopez on the alert. In the car, Antonio had to listen as the boy related the tiresome tale of his border crossing as if it were a feat that only he had ever accomplished. Omar boasted about his own heroism and praised his own knack for survival by telling how he had snuck up the coast from San Diego to Oceanside and how he had landed a job at a nursery there for almost four dollars an hour. He had lived with some Mixtecs from Oaxaca, who taught him how to swipe flower bulbs, hide them on his person, and sell them to another nursery down the road, where the owner asked no questions.

"So you're a thief?" Lopez said to him. "*Un ladrón, eh?* That's really something to be proud of."

"No, *hermano*." The boy shook his head in fervent denial. "Only for this." He reached into his bag and produced an Alien Registration Receipt Card. It was not green but a rosy pink. Laminated in plastic, it bore a passport photo of one Omar Rosario Perez, along with his date of birth and the date on which he had supposedly migrated into the United States through the legal port of entry at San Ysidro. " 'I yam of good moral character,' " Omar said, with a smirk. "I have my *documentos*."

Lopez tapped the card against the dashboard, annoyed in spite of how resourceful his cousin had been. His instincts warned him against the boy. "It's fake, right?" he asked. "How much did it cost you? Or did you steal it, too?"

"No, no stealing." Omar seemed anxious and unsure of himself now. "I pay money for it. Forty-five dollar."

"But it's fake, right?" The boy shrugged and looked out the window. "Do you understand what a risk I'm taking here? I could go to prison for helping you."

"It can't happen that way, *hermano*."

"Put out that cigarette," Lopez ordered him. He saw that he had all the power and that he liked having it and would exercise it if he had to. "I don't allow any smoking in my vehicle, man, so you better get used to it."

"Sorry, *hermano*."

"And you can forget this 'brother' shit. You're not my brother, Omar. This isn't Oceanside up here, *hermano*," Antonio went on sarcastically. "We're not a bunch of Mixtecs in Santa Rosa. You keep walking around like you're some kind of king, and you'll take a fall. That jacket of yours?" He grabbed the lapel. "This is a jacket for fucking Mexicans, man. The border patrol would pick you out in a second."

"I take it off," Omar said, tugging at a sleeve.

"People in California, they don't dress like that."

"I take it off."

The boy was thoroughly chastised and obedient by the time they reached the Lopez house, but Elena soon cured him of that. She hugged him, pinched his cheeks, and fussed over him like he had just won the Big Spin, remarking on his resemblance to her husband, which caused Antonio to turn away in utter distress because there was, to his eye, no likeness at all. She pretended to be in awe of his journey and the imaginary bravery he continued to yammer about in ceaseless self-celebration, not the least bit shy. Elena's attitude toward Mexico was very unrealistic, Lopez thought, probably because she had never lived there, or been billeted in a single roach-infested room with a bunch of battling siblings, or had to survive on rice, beans, and tortillas. She had cooked a grand feast for the boy, in fact, but before she could steer them all to the table Omar rummaged in his bag and gave her one of the wrapped packages. It was a box of caramels with an old white lady's photo on the front.

"Oh, look, Antonio!" Elena showed off the box "Mrs. See's. It's my favorite kind."

"That's expensive candy," Antonio agreed, wanting the day to be over right then.

Omar had a package for Dolores, too, and the infant drooled, giggled, and fumbled with the wrapping paper for about an hour until she got a fist inside and extracted a fluffy toy duck by its throat. She pecked Omar on the nose, oblivious of his guile.

"Hey, she kiss me!" the boy said, giggling himself. "She kiss her cousin!" He squeezed the duck to make it squeak, and Dolores kicked her legs in her high chair, almost beside herself with joy.

Lopez ate slowly and contemptuously. His food tasted like poison. It was as if his daughter had never had a gift before, as if all the stuffed animals in her crib amounted to nothing. When Elena offered some chocolate cake for desert, he rejected his slice and watched in disgust as Omar tapped out a Marlboro and started squeezing the duck again and making silly faces. The boy tried to pour more coffee for him, but he covered his cup with a saucer and told Omar to hurry up and eat. They had to leave.

"Where we going, *hermano?*" the boy asked in dismay.

"To Carson Valley."

"Oh, it's so late, Antonio," Elena put in hastily, siding with Perez. "Why don't we let Omar sleep here tonight? He's probably tired from his trip."

"I am very, very, very tired, yes," Omar said. He pressed his palms together and rested his cheek on them, his eyes shut.

"You can take him out to the valley with you in the morning, can't you? Wouldn't that be easier? Just one trip instead of two? Antonio?"

Lopez did not reply. He was thinking, *You little bastard, you. Only once do you get away with this!*

So began an unending evening of duck squeezing, cigarette smoking, and inflated stories about old Guadalajara from which Antonio felt himself entirely excluded. Omar dogged Elena's every step and fondled every object in the house, especially the TV and the stereo, flattering her and fawning over her to such a sickening degree that

Lopez was certain that she would see through him. But she put up with his nonstop monologue and *oohe*d and *ahh*ed and even made him a cup of cocoa when at midnight he was ready to sleep at last and lay down on the couch.

Lopez couldn't wait for the morning to come. He was up and dressed at first light, pulling on the boy's hair and dragging him out of his cozy cocoon of blankets. Omar was shuffled into the car before he was fully awake, his plea for a glass of milk denied. Elena said good-bye to him with sentimental words that seemed infinite in their duration, but then they were finally on the road, and Antonio breathed a sigh of relief. He enjoyed the unhappy way that his cousin was slumped in his seat, figuring that the boy was probably depressed by the dawning realization that a ration of back-breaking work might reside at the core of his adventure. The valley was at the peak of its late-summer glory, green everywhere, with a trace of lemony sunlight slanting down through another set of tattered blue-gray clouds, and this, too, improved his mood. No other landscape held quite the same purchase on Lopez, no other place on earth guaranteed him such an exalted position among its stewards.

"You never saw this before," he bragged to the boy. "Not in Mexico you didn't."

"I never saw it," Omar replied in a dull voice.

"Take a good look, *amigo*. Because you're going to know it real well before you leave. Your nose is going to touch that ground a thousand times."

The man who was known as the captain was now installed at cabin four. Bearded and big-bellied, with a damaged left eye that was permanently bloodshot, he ruled his roost from the choicest corner of the front room, his cot right next to an open window and bedded with clean linens. His authority could be read in the half-quart cans of Bud and the sacks of pork cracklings on the windowsill, treasures in full view of every occupant but in no danger of being snatched. The captain resisted Antonio's attempts to strike a bargain, glaring at Omar as he might have at a worm, and denied that any transaction had oc-curred between Lopez and his *compañero*, the youth who, against the odds, still reclined on his cot in his Jockey shorts and continued his perusal of the identical *novela*.

"*Es un asunto mío!*" the captain shouted, banging a fist against his chest. It was his business, and nobody else's.

Lopez pushed Omar forward. "He's a good kid, honest, just a little green. I'll give you a hundred dollars through the harvest."

"Two hundred."

"*Escuchame, hombre.* I live here. *Conosces el rancho Torelli?* I run those crews over there."

"Big fucking deal," the captain said.

"One-fifty, final."

Grumbling, the captain scratched his hairy stomach, grunted with majestic weariness to indicate his boredom over the inability of the world to present him with anything remotely resembling a surprise, and accepted the one-fifty. He led Omar to the approved cot in back, shook a finger in the boy's face to apprise him of the NO PEEING HERE sign, and returned to his choice corner. When the youth who was reading mustered enough energy to raise himself on an elbow and hold out a beggarly hand for the payoff he unaccountably expected, Lopez slapped him away and said in a ferocious whisper, "*Chinga tu madre,* man. *Cien por ciento.*" One hundred percent.

The deal was done. Lopez wanted to get out to the Torelli farm right away, but Omar acted clingy and seemed concerned that he was being abandoned.

"When you come for me?" the boy asked, absurd in his yellow bumblebee jacket.

"Tomorrow, Omar," Lopez said with exasperation. "I already told you that three whole times. *Escucha, por favor!* Tomorrow or maybe the next day."

"I wait you tomorrow."

"There's no grapes to pick yet, Omar. They're not ripe. It could be tomorrow, or it could be next week. It could be into September. I told you that on the phone, didn't I?"

"*Sí, hermano.*"

"So why are you fucking with me? I didn't ask you to come here to work, did I?"

"You didn't ask me, no. But you invite me to your house."

For a moment, Lopez thought the boy was going to cry. He saw how frightened Omar was behind his mask of confidence, how babyish and innocent, and it moved him to a pity he did not care to feel. Life could be hard for the new pickers who had not yet learned the ropes—he recalled his own trials in that regard. Men such as the Captain were always taking advantage of the rookies, and there was really nothing anyone could do about it.

"It's going to be okay," he told the boy. "Come on. Let's go into Roy's."

Indeed, Omar was snuffling. With a muttered oath, Lopez threw an arm around him, led him into the market, and bought him some cupcakes, a six-pack of Coke, a toothbrush, some toothpaste, and his own roll of toilet paper. The boy paused at a spinner rack of magazines, an antique that had ceased to rotate long ago, and fondled an old copy of *Motor Trend,* so Antonio bought that for him, too, and added some chewing gum at the counter. A cardboard carton by the cash register was filled with grape knives in a point-of-sale display, each curved and glittering blade honed to a fine edge at the factory and sunk into a compact plastic handle meant to sit comfortably in the palm of a picker's hand.

"Try this, Omar," Lopez said. He gave the boy a knife and showed him how to grip it and make a swift cutting stroke to sever the stem of a grape cluster from its stem. "How does it feel?"

The boy's eyes were wide in wonder. "It's very good," he said. "I like it!"

While the tab was being settled, Omar juggled his knife in a private game, tossing it higher and higher toward the fly-blown rafters until it flipped once too often on its downward journey and revolved a half-turn too many. He snatched after it again, but he caught it blade first this time and yelped when it sliced into his fingers. His blood began dripping onto the plank floor.

"Antonio!" he said excitedly. *"Mira!"*

Lopez looked at the blood drops and frowned. This boy, he thought, will not be lucky.

19

Those same tattered clouds in a blue-gray sky, day after day. The weather refused to cooperate with the harvest, but that was a given of the season, something that the old-timers knew in their bones. It had turned them into habitual pessimists who spat and cussed and courted providence. Whatever had happened last year, the obstacles presented and sometimes surmounted, could be counted on never to occur again, not in a million years—it would be too easy. The only worthwhile thing a grower could do, the reasoning went, was to prepare for disappointment. Better to imagine a vineyard full of raisins than to anticipate a profit. Hopes were meant to be dashed, after all, and history was a record of losses. Nature survived, Dick Rhodes liked to say, by relying on its knuckleball.

Everywhere in Carson Valley yearning prevailed. There were veiled threats and strange incantations. Some hippie printers in town, dope smokers par excellence and purveyors of obscure poetry in fine letterpress editions, spent three sleepless nights studying Aztec mythology and subsequently distributed a broadside paean to the sun god, swearing that it would break the stalemate. Instead, a fog descended. It was thick, cold, and damp, born of unfavorable ocean vapors, and when it finally burned off in the late afternoon the clouds were still tattered and the sky was still blue-gray. August was about to slide into September without a single grape being picked. The stainless steel

tanks at wineries remained empty. Bored workers yelled into them for
fun, an ear to the echo of their voices.

The first would-be pickers were roaming the country roads, advance troops for the teeming army that would soon be arriving in
force. They walked or drove from farm to farm looking to hire on,
their rate of pay to be established up front against a pledge of good
behavior—no temper tantrums, disappearing acts, or romantic dis-
plays of petulance. Some of them belonged to a rootless and hard-
nosed migrant tribe that was always harvesting one crop or another in
California—almonds in Orland, onions in Vacaville, strawberries in
Watsonville, dates in Indio—while others were just in from Mexico
and behaved as harmlessly as choirboys. They guaranteed their potential employers such desirable qualities as speed, sobriety, and
simple diligence, then bedded down in bunkhouses, cabins, or under
bridges on the river to wait for the signal to begin.

That signal was slow to come. A remark of Fred Vescio's was
widely quoted to sum up the situation. "It's so goddam gray out there
today even a little baby couldn't get its ass sunburned." He made the
comment while drinking coffee in his kitchen and watching a dia-
pered grandchild whose name he had forgotten scramble across the
floor. Vescio was known to be severely frustrated. He had finished
every article in his monthly *Reader's Digest,* had swamped out his pump-
house, and had even gone so far as to trade in his old Red Wing boots
for a new pair, and he didn't have a notion what to do with himself
next. Other farmers, equally stymied, fell to improvising. Pepper Harris left on a gambling trip to South Lake Tahoe, assuming that the sun
would shine full strength to spite him while he was away, but he was
wrong. The sun paid him no mind at all, and he lost five hundred dollars at the blackjack tables and returned a chastened man.

Arthur Atwater surprised himself by staying calm. Nothing
seemed to faze him. Every chore on his short list was completed. The
hydraulic hoses on his harvest loader were in good condition, he had
changed the points and plugs in the flatbed truck he used for hauling
grapes, and had scrubbed the purple stains from the plastic tubs his
pickers would carry. His barn was as spotless as a barn *could* be. His
harvest bins were clean, too, and he had ordered two chemical toilets
to be delivered and set up in the fields. When a pernicious patch of

Johnson grass sprouted in a row of Cabernet Sauvignon, he plowed it under without any sense that he had been singled out for attack and also killed off some bindweed near it, pleased when the pretty flowers, morning glories in a classic trumpet shape, curled up and died.

He had also conducted his summit meeting with Antonio Lopez on the subject of a crew and had approved the starting lineup as proposed, including its newest member, a boy from Guadalajara in an outrageous yellow jacket.

"This is my cousin, Omar," Lopez had said during a solemn introduction.

"He ever picked before?"

"Oh, yeah. Back home he did. He picked all kinds of stuff."

"Can he talk?"

"Mostly in Spanish. But he's learning fast."

"He's got his documents, right?"

"Sure, he does. Show him, Omar."

The boy passed over his green card and grinned his silly grin. "I yam of good moral character," he said, tugging on an ear.

"He does stand-up comedy, too?" Atwater asked archly.

"He's a good kid, honest," Lopez told him. "He's just a little nervous."

In his log, Atwater wrote,

WEDNESDAY, SEPTEMBER 3RD. Still cool, big wind this afternoon to 20, maybe 25 mph. Ate a few grapes as sour as lemons. This time last year we were picking Chardonnay at Brix 23. Saw some gopher holes on Thunder Hill, must shoot some poison down them tomorrow.

THURSDAY, SEPTEMBER 4TH. Cool and foggy again. Took a nap after lunch out of boredom. Dogs bored, too. Everybody bored, probably. Rejected three guys this aft. who wanted to pick, sent them up to Hawk Wind to bust rocks instead.

His breakfast the next morning was the usual lackluster fare. He chewed on a gummy pastry, stared idly through dancing motes of dust at the view downriver to the oxbow of the Russian, and was struck by the sharpest possible sensation of Anna's absence, feeling all around him the empty space of love gone wrong. Purely physical, the sensation came over him infrequently and never lasted long, but it always hit him like a blow to the solar plexus, and he could not breathe right for a time. He could not think right. Nothing in his ex- perience compared to it, nothing had ever so unhinged him from the compass of his being. When he had separated from Laura, she had lived on in him as a dull incurable ache whose source he understood —it was disappointment, really, in the face of human frailty—but this was different, a type of possession, the hormonal equivalent of warp speed.

He still had received no word from Anna, of course, and nagged himself for continuing to be hopeful. Often he took himself to task for not extinguishing the tiny flickering torch he foolishly carried for her. As for his part, he had written her three letters and torn them all up, although one actually made it inside a stamped envelope before he shredded it. What it came down to, Atwater felt, was that he had no more to say to her than he had said when they were parting, nothing that would improve on or embellish his simple declaration. He was not the sort of man who could, possessed of a jolly mood, pick up the phone, give her a casual call, and have a chatty but subversive con- versation to find out what she was up to, and his intuition warned him that any contact in a more serious vein would only bring him more woe.

FRIDAY, SEPTEMBER 5TH. Sent a bunch of Guatemalans up to Hawk Wind, should be charging those guys a commission. Found two dead gophers, good! Grapes a little sweeter, but still not up to Brix 18 (my guess). Must test by instrument soon.

SATURDAY, SEPTEMBER 6TH. Omar here by himself at seven this a.m., walked over from Roy's and asked for five dollars until his first payday. He's a skunky little bastard. I took a break at lunch and wrote Anna again. I'll be glad when the picking starts and the thinking ends.

The following day, Atwater woke at dawn to perfect peace, with brilliant light flowing through the windows of his trailer. He marched naked to his deck, licked an index finger, and held it up to the elements—oh rapture, there was no wind! He smiled and gave his dogs a tender stroking. The sun crested a far ridge in minutes and sparked a chorus of insects into an electrified drone. The temperature hit eighty-five degrees by midmorning and almost a hundred by midafternoon, only to drop into the fifties once the hills were dark and the crickets had started their immemorial chirping. Such conditions were ideal. The heat increased the sugar content in every grape, and the cool nights allowed that sugar to blend with tannic, malic, and lactic acids to form a characteristic varietal flavor. It was a time of extremes in Carson Valley, of huge swings in every gradient, a time of magnitude and plenty.

Here at last was fabled Indian summer. Atwater thought of ghost stories, inner tubes, bicycle rides at twilight, and spitting watermelon seeds in distance contests. He remembered cutting school to catch frogs and how he and Junior Thompson would put them in jars topped with mesh and feed them fat and lazy end-of-the-season houseflies that they swatted to death with their homemade weapons, old newspapers rolled tightly and bound with rubber bands. He remembered swallowing a peach pit by accident and swallowing in turn an ancient lie about the peach tree that was growing in his stomach. The image had troubled him for fully a month before he let it go. These memories all spoke to what was left of the boy in him—not very much—and made him, however briefly, almost happy.

He went at the end of the week to his broad patch of riverside Chardonnay, the earliest of his grapes to mature. Toting a bucket, he picked a sample of fruit randomly from different rows and took it to the barn for testing. He was ultraserious, in his astrophysics mode. He stored his refractometer in a box on a high shelf, out of harm's way. It was a finicky, handheld instrument with a prism at its tip. He pressed the grapes with his fingers to extract some juice and transferred a smudge to the prism glass, then walked outside and exposed the prism to the light. That caused a shadow to fall across a Brix scale etched inside. The scale was used to estimate sugar content and translate it into a number. Atwater looked through the eyepiece and took a reading of 21.8 degrees Brix, just below the optimal range of 22 to 22.5 degrees that was stipulated in the CV contract.

Overjoyed, he cornered Antonio Lopez right away and instructed him to have the picking crew ready to go in the morning. He developed a major case of anxiety himself, poised on the cusp of a thousand potential mistakes. He worried that his alarm would not go off, for instance, and slept poorly through the night, but it worked fine and jolted him out of bed at five o'clock. The world beyond the trailer was still dark, although he could see a few rattletrap cars already parked on the dirt road. The cars had disgorged about fifteen pickers, and they were huddled together and bouncing up and down on their toes, blowing into their cupped palms against the chill, eager to begin.

After a quick cup of tea, Atwater approached his crew. It was important that he make a strong first impression. He noticed a couple of women and approved of their presence. He knew that they would be steady workers, much steadier than the men. A man at harvest time usually proved to be either a genius or a dud, or a genius one day and a dud the next, his emotional swings wide and unpredictable and tainted by the supposedly hysterical mood swings that he attributed in private to his wife or his girlfriend. A woman, at least in Atwater's opinion, tackled the job of picking with the same domestic patience she might bring to knitting, cooking, or ironing, in no particular hurry to get finished, careful about the fine points and glad for a chance to think her private thoughts.

Atwater stopped before the assembled company. Everyone was staring at him in silence. He felt their sharp scrutiny and the unspoken challenge in it. He composed himself as best he could, trying to look stern and unforgiving, the absolute embodiment of any picker's nightmare vision of an overly demanding boss. With a flick of his wrist, he had them all in line and took down the information that he was required by law to record.

"Name?" he asked the first man.

"Rudolfo Mendez." Mendez had a mustache and above it a splayed nose that could have been flattened by a stiff jab in a prize ring.

"You live here?"

"No, *señor.* In Durango. But I have Social Security."

Atwater took his card and jotted down the ID number. He did not look too closely at it. Mendez grabbed a plastic tub and jogged into the vineyard. The tub held a lug of grapes, or about thirty-five pounds, and he would be paid a dollar every time he filled it. Next came a hefty woman who carried a tin lunchbox with the Power Rangers on it.

"Serena Cedillo, *señor.* Social Security 243-62-7115."

Then came Tomaso, Alberto, and Roberto Hernandez. They lived near Lopez in Santa Rosa and sang out their numbers like an a cappella tune.

"Very nice, Hernandezes," Atwater told them with a smile.

"Thank you," Roberto said. "We didn't plan it out. It just comes natural to us like that." They grabbed their tubs and ran into the vineyard.

Next, Omar Perez presented himself with red eyes and a runny nose. "How are you today, boss?" he asked merrily. "I pick real good for you. I love to pick a grape!"

Atwater saw some bandages speckled with blood on his right hand, a hospital dressing. "What happened to you?"

"*No comprendo,*" the boy said, shrugging.

"Go pick, Omar."

So the harvest was underway. The pickers wrangled about seniority and who would get the choicest positions, those that were shady or flat or both. Whenever they had filled a tub, they dashed with it to the end of their row, sometimes balancing the load on a shoulder or on their heads, and dumped it into a steel harvest bin. Eloy Hidalgo, who was trustworthy and good at math, tallied the lug on a paysheet he kept. The pickers were pushing themselves too hard, Atwater thought, impatient after their long wait in the dark. They were uneasy, too, wanting to rely on the others on the crew but also guarding against the effect an enemy among them might have, someone who was slow, lazy, or lacking in dexterity. Often in their haste they bumped into one another and caused traffic jams and accidents—a collison, a tub dropped and spilled—that were impediments to the beneficial harmony they all hoped to achieve in the great green labyrinth in which they toiled.

Here at the fulcrum of the harvest, Antonio Lopez truly earned his keep. He was a respected crew boss, considerate, firm, and never less than fair. Observing him from afar, Atwater was again taken with his management skills. Antonio seemed to be everywhere at once, his eye on every picker. He showed one Hernandez a better way to cut through a cluster stem, passed a paper cup of water to another Hernandez who must have closed down a *cantina* the night before, and settled an argument between two geriatric pickers who were about to come to blows. His most careful attentions he saved for his struggling cousin. The boy appeared to be fighting against the tedium of dealing with so many tricky little grapes concealed beneath so many interfering leaves, and he was already sweating profusely and had thrown down his yellow jacket in frustration.

"Is Omar going to make it?" Atwater asked when Lopez jogged over.

"Yeah, he'll make it. He just wants everything to happen fast."

"That's how you used to be."

"Not anymore, man. I got too many responsibilities."

Atwater arched his back and luxuriated in the fragrant morning air. "Well, we're off to a fine start here, anyhow. I have an excellent feeling about this harvest."

Lopez looked at him in disbelief. "Pretend you never said that, Arthur. Take it back right now."

"Why?" Atwater said amiably. "You afraid I'll jinx us?"

"I'm serious, man." Lopez made a prayerful sign of the cross. "You never said it."

"Okay, I never said it."

Obstreperous shouts from the vineyard interrupted them. The pickers had filled a harvest bin to the top with fruit and were yelling for the boss to haul it away and empty it. When Atwater rode up on his tractor with a hydraulic loader hitched to it, he was met by a knot of grumbling men. They seemed to regard him as a cheat who had contrived to screw them for reasons they would never know. He even heard a picker call him *cabrón* behind his back, an insult commonly applied to employers, although seldom while they were around. He chose to ignore the slur rather than run the risk of alienating his crew and just gripped the bin with the loader—it worked like a forklift— ferried it to his truck, lifted it up, and dumped the fruit into one of two steel tanks called gondolas that were mounted on the flatbed. Each gondola held five-plus tons of grapes.

His rhythm for the day was established now. He would remove full bins, empty them, and replace them, a job that appeared very simple on the surface and yet had to be integrated into the more complicated rhythm of the entire harvest, not only on the Torelli farm but all through the valley. It was a matter of the parts meshing smoothly with the whole, of things fitting together in a dovetailed way that had more to do with instinct than with any conscious intent. Atwater's anxious flutter and his rusty touch with the hydraulic controls vanished as he worked on. Three more times before noon he made trips to the flatbed truck, and then four times after lunch, unloading more than eight tons of supremely sweet Chardonnay grapes bleeding juice and circled by squadrons of drunken bees.

Atwater swatted at the bees with a wrinkled old towel he kept in the cab for just that purpose and stepped up on a tire to raise himself to the level of his cargo. He inhaled the winey aroma, ate a few grapes for an energy boost, and saw from his lofty perch that Lopez was gazing up at him from down below.

"We got a problem, Arthur."

"Of course we have a problem." Atwater jumped down, his fingertips stained. He patted Lopez on the back. "This is the harvest. Have we ever had a harvest without problems?"

"It's those chemical toilets. The company, they didn't put in any toilet paper."

"Ah, for crying out loud! How could they forget a thing like that?"

"It's probably a mistake," Lopez told him.

"There's a couple extra rolls in my trailer. You can go on and get them." Atwater stopped and pondered. "What about my grapes here, Antonio? Are they riding right?"

"Real good. You got some room left, too."

"Yeah, I do. But I've been thinking I might make a trial run over to the CV outlet. See what the drill's like over there."

"A trial run, it couldn't hurt."

"You figure that's the best option?"

"What do you think?"

"I already told you what I think. Why in the hell don't you listen to me?"

"I did listen," Lopez complained. "You're all wound up, man. You better take a blood pressure pill or something. Else you might explode."

"I give up." Atwater climbed into the cab and slammed the door. "You're in charge while I'm gone, Antonio. Anything bad happens, and it's your fault."

"Why is it my fault?"

"Because I said so. *Hasta la vista!*"

Atwater drove off with a wave. These jaunts to town with a loaded truck were like a little holiday for him. They gave him a break from the monotony of the fields and refreshed him, at least when the harvest was going well. The tight focus of his individual concerns opened onto a comforting panorama of the valley under siege, and he felt less solitary in his obsessions and connected to a giant machine that was operating of its own accord. All along the road, he saw cars parked by vineyards and crews with tubs inching devotedly across the fields. He stopped at Roy's for a cold soda and more toilet paper and read with wry amusement a new sign by the register, TODAS MOCHILAS DEBEN DEJAR ENFRENTE. Drop those backpacks at the front counter, you Mexicans.

At the north end of town, he turned onto Black Oak Road and drove west for a few miles through some heavily wooded land. The road dropped down into a gulley and followed a streambed caked over with a whitish crust. The winery was an old stone building covered with ivy across a one-lane bridge. CV had bought it a couple of years ago to expand and modernize. Some old oak wine barrels had been sawed in half and used as planters, and they spilled over with sapphire blue lobelia, pansies, and violas in many different colors. There were no visitors around because the winery wasn't open to the public. It did no retail business and dealt strictly with growers under contract to CV, accepting loads of grapes from seven in the morning until nine at night, six days a week.

Atwater sounded his horn as a precaution and went over the bridge and around a bend to the main winery entrance, where four flatbed trucks, each mounted with gondolas and loaded with an early ripening varietal, not only Chardonnay but also some Gewürztraminer and some Gray Riesling, waited in line at the sugar shack. He set his emergency brake and got down from his cab. He didn't know the man ahead of him, who was red-faced from the sun and wore a painter's cap with polka dots on it. Some drivers were true growers like Atwater, while others were just employed for the harvest. Brothers, uncles, and friends were also pressed into service sometimes.

"You got some good-looking grapes there," he greeted the fellow. "Where you from?"

"Up Cloverdale way. The Zambrusco ranch. We're just about done pulling off our Gewürz. We've been at it for a week solid."

"Any red grapes ready yet?"

"No, they're a month or so away. Maybe three weeks if it stays this hot. Next we'll pull off our Chardonnay. Is that Chardonnay you're hauling?"

Atwater nodded. "This is my first run. We pulled these off this morning."

"Count your blessings," the man said, lifting his cap to scratch at his matted hair. "That's one less run you've got to make before you're finished."

The trucks moved forward, and Atwater returned to his cab. In another five minutes, he had inched his way up to an open-sided shanty on stilts. The floor of the sugar shack was not quite level and fell a few feet below the tip of his gondola. A tester stood there as on the deck of a ship and lowered a tubular, stainless-steel coring device to collect a sampling of the load. The cored fruit he tossed into a hopper that fed into a grape press. The press made a grinding noise, and Atwater listened intently to it and felt his nerves go jangly again as the juice trickled into a bucket, his year's labor concentrated in those few leaky drops. Here was the first in a series of tense and quietly dramatic moments he would have to endure until every vine was picked clean, a procedure cold, precise, scientific, and ultimately no more inviting to him than a triple bypass.

He watched as the tester dipped into the rendered juice and took a reading with a refractometer.

"Chardonnay?" the tester asked.

"Yes, sir. From over at the Torelli place."

"Twenty-two-point-three." The tester wrote the number on a slip and handed it down. "You hit it right on the nose, bud."

Atwater resisted an urge to cheer out loud. "I guess I wouldn't complain if it went like that every trip," he said, almost bashful.

"I don't guess you would. You'll earn you a little extra money on that load. That's about as close to perfect as it gets."

Atwater put the paper in a pocket and got back in his cab. The truck stuttered forward, and he braked to a stop on a scale and weighed in. Next, he parked by a crusher in the winery, where a worker with a hoist lifted one gondola and then the other to send his grapes showering down a chute. He started the motor again and weighed out. He made one more run to the winery that evening before the gates were locked and again logged in a top-notch score for his grapes. On the drive home, he felt a welcome fatigue all through his body and congratulated himself on not being able to think beyond the moment. He would sleep the dreamless sleep of the righteous tonight. Tomorrow would be a day much like this one, and that seemed to him a useful circumstance. He wanted nothing more from life just now than to be suspended in the hypnotic effort of the harvest.

20

⸺⚬⚬⚬⸺

The little bookstore Anna Torelli held a share in, a hole in the wall on the Upper West Side, was sandwiched between a relic candy store that still flew a Brooklyn Dodgers pennant over the cash register and a Korean greengrocer who stayed open until midnight. The shop consisted of four small, cramped, over-stocked rooms that caused first-time visitors to describe it as "quaint," "old-fashioned," and even "Dickensian." That wasn't the effect its owners had intended, but since they had gone into business with no retail experience at all, armed only with a love of books and litera-ture—the worst possible qualification, Jane would later quip—they settled for any compliments they could get. If a customer pressed them about the decor, they would claim to have borrowed it from a shop they'd stumbled on in the English countryside in Shropshire, on Housman's home turf.

To the good, their rent was very low by Manhattan standards. They also had a generous ten-year lease with an option to renew. Still, Anna had been convinced at the start that their doors would close in under a year, but they had flourished instead, largely due to the loyal patronage of a quirky market sector composed of yuppies, aesthetes, single women, and elderly gentlemen of character, all of whom were dedicated to boycotting the giant chains and franchises that threat-ened to ruin the atmosphere of the neighborhood. By happy accident,

Jane had pushed for them to deal in both new and used books, and when they learned how high the markup on their used stock could be, cycling toward the paranormal, they began scouring the city for modern literary classics that would appeal to collectors.

Anna in particular enjoyed this aspect of the game. There was a definite buccaneering thrill for her in unearthing a valuable novel tossed away in a discount bin at somebody else's store. Fine poetry could always be found at a bargain, too. She and Jane learned to purchase multiple copies of any promising first book and bank them against an author's potential fame in the future, they went to auctions and honed their bidding technique, and they earned a reputation for paying top dollar for private libraries. Some of their competitors made the mistake of trying to cherry pick, but Anna was willing to acquire ten Floyd Dells and eight Pearl Bucks to get the lone F. Scott Fitzgerald in the lot. Her most treasured first editions were displayed in a glass case up front, locked against thieves and surrounded by framed photos of such immortals as Joyce, Pound, and Hemingway, who, by virtue of their position, had the look of house security.

Anna was putting in long hours at the store, partly to repay Jane for all the favors and partly to keep herself occupied. Her first month or so at home had passed pleasantly enough as she inched back into her familiar routine, but her forward progress had stopped abruptly in August when she fell into a mild and lingering depression that she had yet to shake. She was bored and irritable and thought about Arthur Atwater far more often than she wanted to, still troubled by the horrible way their affair had ended. Given some distance from it, she could see how traumatic the miscarriage was for her and how much she had read into it, honoring it with a mystical significance. Atwater, too, had overreacted and lost his bearings, Anna felt. It was as if they'd both been waiting for a symbolic event to prove how wrong they were for each other and had relied on the same natural forces that had brought them together to tear them apart. Neither of them had been brave enough when the chips were down, she thought.

But at the same time Anna had become absolutely certain that the farm was not for her. She could never have adapted herself to the quirky rhythms of Atwater's life, to his intensity or his inflexibility. As for the daunting beauty of the valley, it had indeed helped her to heal, but she believed that her powerful response to it would eventually diminish. And she had no serious interest in growing wine grapes either—that was just another fantasy. When she and Roger inherited the vineyard, hopefully many years down the line, they would hire someone to manage it for them, an Atwater type. Arthur himself would surely be gone by then. It was inevitable that he would butt heads with her father and do his final disappearing act. How could she ever have imagined that she was in love with him? It seemed preposterous, and yet there were moments every day when he was so vividly present that she could feel him on her skin, when she ached for him, when he was the only possible one.

These visitations had a paralyzing effect on Anna. They kept her from going forward. Lately she'd been so desultory that her friends had taken to lecturing her on the importance of a fresh start. That was the best method for beating the blues, the quickest tactic for mending, and so on and so forth. She resisted their advice, of course, until she caught herself browsing in the store's self-help section and searching for answers in the collected works of Deepak Chopra, after which she agreed that some decisiveness on her part was definitely appropriate. What she needed at present was not another wild fling, though, but rather a bit of basic cheering up; so when Sam McNally phoned to chat, she accepted his invitation to lunch. Sam was nothing if not upbeat and couldn't last more than two minutes without making a joke or pointing out an absurdity.

They set a date for just after Labor Day. Anna left the store about noon to meet McNally across town, stopping at the front counter to check on Julie, her head clerk. Julie's eyeliner was smudged again, probably from the tears she was shedding for a Princeton boy who had wooed her all summer, and then had dropped her instantly when he went back to college for the fall term.

"How are you doing?" Anna asked her. "I can still cancel if I have to."

"I'll be fine." Julie applied a shredded tissue to her streaked cheeks. "If I don't get over him soon, I'm going on Zoloft, I swear."

September in Manhattan. The city was in the grip of muggy weather, broiling under an ugly brown chemical sky as impenetrable as a lid. All the tabloids at the corner kiosk guaranteed that the heat would continue through the weekend and shatter a record set during the La Guardia administration in the 1930s. Anna stood in the moil and fumes and tried to hail a cab. Since her return, she had felt like a stranger in New York, a hick out of synch with the flow, somebody who lacked the proper skills to survive. As if to validate that status, four vacant taxis sped right by her before a fifth finally stopped. The cabbie was singing along with some loud Nigerian dance music. He gave her a rainbow smile and assured her that the roads through Central Park were all open and would provide them with a shortcut to the East Side. The true odds were no better than fifty-fifty, but Anna was already running late.

There were, predictably, sawhorse blockades midway through the park. The cabbie began to gesticulate and explain, regaling her with a tale of profligate yesterdays when such roads were never closed, but Anna tuned out the static and let her head rest against the seatback. In spite of the heat, a few trees had already taken on a hint of autumn color, and she found herself recalling her first autumn in the city and how in weather that in memory remained forever crisp, cool, and clear, she and her new husband would take bike rides together, splurge on grand picnics in the Sheep Meadow, or drive up to the Cloisters to look at the old masterpieces all cracked and tarnished and then stroll along a bluff above the Hudson while the leaves blew about them and fell. She had seen herself as a perfect inheritor of the civilized world back then and never as just another small-town girl going through an urban rite of passage.

Anna remembered their first apartment on Sixty-ninth Street, a tiny, one-bedroom gem in a rent-controlled brownstone that a colleague of Bud's had handed down to them for a modest bribe. She remembered the thrill, terror, and ultimate disenchantment of actually living with the man she had married and adapting to his vagrant domestic habits—almost all bad, from neglecting to roll up the toothpaste tube to failing to lower the toilet seat. Every night over dinner, she had to listen while Bud reported on his adventures at his law firm, a bastion of public probity and backroom scandal. She would repress her own interests, scarcely aware that she had any, and repeat to herself how fortunate she was. Everyone else reinforced that perception—everyone except her father—as she shared in Bud's victories and pumped him up when he endured a rare defeat, never doubting any of her choices and yet doubting them all in secret, wishing that she had the nerve to leave him. Instead, she had built a wall around herself and forced him to make the move.

The restaurant on Lexington was new to her. It was a French-style bistro with splashes of Moroccan decor. She was almost thirty minutes late and would have been in a frenzy if Sam McNally were the type to get rattled, but he sat calmly at a corner table nursing a martini, the thinning hair on his head in subtle disarray and his eyes behind half-frame reading glasses scanning the sports page of the *Times*. He was a courtly, witty, generous man, a Georgian by birth, who could be counted on to spot her from across the room, rise to take both of her hands, and say with genuine warmth and affection, "Anna, it's so good to see you!"

She made the usual apologies—the traffic, a crazy cabbie, the humidity, and so on. "I've lost my survival skills," she said with a harried smile. "I might as well be from Peoria."

"A drink? Iced tea?"

"Iced tea would be lovely."

Anna had known McNally for about three years. He held the title of executive editor at a medium-size publishing house and could have been a vice president if he had any ambition, but Sam had come into some family money early on and enjoyed his creature comforts. She had met him not too long after her divorce when he went out of his way to escort a jittery, egomaniacal, and much-heralded author of his ("Our postmodern Proust," the ads had trumpeted, but Anna, trying to read the novel in question, felt as if she were being force-fed bricks) to her store to sign some books. Anna was embarrassed by the tiny size of the crowd, but McNally took her aside and charmed her out of it. He had a talent for making her feel good about herself, and they embarked on an on-again, off-again relationship that Sam would have liked to make more permanent. Twice they had reached that threshold, and Anna had split with him both times.

"You look wonderful," McNally said after a waiter had taken their orders. She had done herself up for their lunch, pulling back her hair in a bun held with an ivory comb and choosing a short but fashionable skirt that showed off her legs. "Your vacation must have agreed with you."

"It was hardly a vacation," Anna corrected him. "But some good things did come out of it."

"Some bad things, too?"

She nodded, her eyes averted. "Some bad things, too."

"I was sorry to hear about your mother, Anna. How's everybody else in your family doing?"

"Surprisingly well. My father's sick of being a farmer, so he hired somebody to manage his vineyard. He's staying in the house he rents in town. My brother Roger—have you ever known anyone who's always happy, Sam?"

"Only holy idiots."

"Well, maybe that's what Roger is. He has his problems, of course, but he gets over them in a flash."

"More power to him," McNally said.

"Anyway, he's in Tokyo with a massage therapist. They're delving into the mysteries."

McNally grinned. "That's a California story, for sure," he said. "Mind you, I'm not knocking it. One of the best weekends I ever spent was in a hot tub up in Topanga Canyon."

"So you've been baptized."

"That's right. I have been baptized."

Anna was staring at his hands. He had no calluses, bruises, or scratches. She sniffed lightly to see what she could smell of him, but there was nothing distinct, only a faint odor of cologne.

"Are you getting a cold?" McNally asked her solicitously.

"It's the air-conditioning." Anna patted his wrist. "Tell me every-thing, Sam. What's on your fall list? Is Alfred Fletcher ever going to finish his book?"

This was McNally's meat. He was a veteran of the midtown pub-lishing lunch and adept at its intrigues. "Fletcher has decided to jump ship," he said in a stage whisper. "He's going to sign with Simon and Schuster."

"But you earned him a million on his last novel!"

"It is Fletcher's opinion," McNally intoned, "or the opinion of his agent, that we cost him his reputation with the critics by wrestling him onto the best-seller lists. He used to be compared to Graham Greene. Now he's compared to Robert Ludlum."

"So now that he's rich, he wants to be poor again?"

"Something like that. He wants respect. He wants praise. He's a writer, Anna, so he's batshit. They're all batshit, every last one of them." McNally sipped his martini, enjoying himself. "It's about ideals, Fletcher says. Money doesn't enter it."

"Ah, I get it," Anna said. "They made him a better offer."

"How clever of you," McNally replied playfully. "I think you have a future in this business."

Anna had always responded to Sam's conviviality. He was funny, informed, droll, and nasty in just the right measure. Talk rolled off his honeyed tongue and kept her entertained throughout their lunch. She learned from him and fenced with him, parry and thrust, and once they fell into the beat of a conversation, they could go on for hours. It seemed to her at times that Manhattan was made up of words and voices such as theirs, concocted from monologues, dialogues, tropes, diatribes, rhetoric, and liberal doses of the sheerest hyperbole. The city could not have existed without a language to create it, whereas Carson Valley was as still, solid, and permanent as the moon.

"I have a proposal for you," McNally said to her over coffee. "Why don't you come out to my place on Long Island this weekend and get away from the godawful heat."

"Is that a threat or an invitation?"

"Both. Nothing would make me happier."

"Thank you, Sam," Anna said. "Let me think about it, okay?"

"Naturally. You can decide at the last minute, if you like."

"I may do that."

"I have plenty of bedrooms." McNally was pretending to be serious now, but it was his least plausible mode of discourse. "We can be perfect grown-ups about the whole thing."

"That would take some doing in your case."

"Ah, Anna," he conceded with a smile, throwing down his napkin. "You know me all too well."

Walking up Lexington to Fifty-ninth, Anna passed miles of men. Tall, attractive, well-dressed, vigorous, decrepit, crawling on all fours, carrying briefcases and folded newspapers (the *Post* had slapped a grainy black-and-white of Fiorello La Guardia in a bathing suit on its front page, and it was not a pretty sight), hatless and hairless, louche, depraved, deep into fantasies, their desires writ large—how she had rushed by them in the old days, ashamed to have provoked their admiring glances and hurrying home to preserve the great gift of herself for her husband! The image struck her as wholly comic now, with Anna Torelli cast as Virtue Embodied while she tried to outrun the very experiences that she had most coveted. She ducked the glances now, too, although for a different reason. Romance was for the young and foolish, she told herself. So was passion and its compliment, the unavoidable remorse. A mature woman ought to be grateful for (if not exactly ecstatic about) the rogue attentions of a Sam McNally.

Anna got back to the store about three and picked up her messages from Julie. The poor child was still downcast. Three nights a week, Julie studied fashion design at a junior college in Queens. She went in for black clothes and pierced body parts, but her favorite author was J.R.R. Tolkien. She could recite passages from *The Hobbit* verbatim.

"The Doubleday salesman is coming in next Tuesday, if that's convenient for you," she told Anna. "And some guy from Carson Valley called."

Anna snatched up the message slips, but she lost her excitement when she managed to decipher her clerk's backslanting scrawl, *Jack Farrell just wanted to say high!*

"He sounded like he might be a psycho." Julie paused to blow her nose. "I think I'm coming down with the flu, Anna. I threw up while you were gone."

Anna touched her forehead. "You don't feel hot. Could it be something you ate?"

"All I had was a Sprite for breakfast," Julie said defensively. "Can I ask you a personal question?"

"As long as it's not *too* personal."

"It isn't. It isn't to me, anyhow. How come every guy I really care about dumps on me? Is that normal?"

"No, it's not normal," Anna said, thinking *Normal is a useless concept, dear.* "You're just having some tough luck."

"I hope so because I'm fed up with it. It's like you're born with a certain amount of love from your parents and from God, right, and you start giving it away to guys you trust, and they dump on you, and before long you don't have that much love left."

"You'll have lots of love when the right man comes along," Anna told her, thinking *I am a million years old!*

"Yeah, well, I better meet him before I'm dead."

"You won't be dead for a long time, Julie."

"I'm not so sure. I get bad ideas in my head sometimes. Black ideas, you know?"

Anna sent the poor child home to nurse her broken heart and upset stomach. Broken hearts must be epidemic in the city, she thought, as numberless as the men and women who walked the streets. The two were doubtlessly related. Had she ever broken a heart herself? Probably Atwater's. The realization caused her some grief and led her where she didn't want to go, back into the sadness. But how did people cope with affairs of the heart? Anna couldn't think of any advice her mother had ever given her on the subject. They had never talked openly about either sex or love. Claire Torelli always fell back on pieties and platitudes, a farm woman to the core. Only once had she dared to visit her daughter in New York, in fact, wide-eyed and frightened by turns, tramping patiently through art galleries and botanical gardens before confiding that what she wanted more than anything was to see *Man of La Mancha* on Broadway. She owned the cast album and had a crush on Richard Kiley. There were mysteries beyond mysteries.

Ah, love! It was a plague, it was a bane, it was the pits. Anna had loved not only Bud Wright but also Eddie Santini, a track record best kept under wraps. It comforted her to note that the immortals whose pictures graced her bookstore walls hadn't fared any better. T. S. Eliot and F. Scott Fitzgerald had nutty wives, while the caped and piratical Ezra Pound was a virtual bigamist in his dalliance with Olga Rudge. Hemingway could not be seriously discussed in the context. Edmund Wilson fucked chambermaids, Dreiser masturbated daily, Faulkner chased skirt whether drunk or sober, and Jack Kerouac seemed to have no idea which end was up and became a Buddhist lover of the universe instead. So much for the men, but how about the women? Hardly a winner in the bunch. Virginia Woolf, George Sand, Willa Cather, Gertrude Stein—well, you couldn't knock Gertrude. She had been a devoted husband to Alice B. Toklas.

The pace accelerated at the store around five o'clock when

burned-out office workers began pouring through the door in search of a sanctuary and the solace of print. They bought books on stress management, beta carotene, the Zen of golf and tennis, and exceptional diets conceived in foreign lands, as well as thick books of nonfiction and slender volumes of verse. Alfred Fletcher's latest bestseller, *Storm Over Tehran*, new in paperback and soon to be a major motion picture, was selling briskly, Anna observed. Her night clerk, wholesome and dependable, his heart apparently intact, relieved her promptly at six, and Jane Weiss came in right after him toting a gym bag. Jane had recently taken up fitness with a vengeance.

"Quitting time," she said, fingering her watch. Her style was not unlike a drill sergeant's. "Time to pump some iron, girl. Chest-fly time. Time to firm it up."

"I can't face those machines tonight," Anna said wearily. "I've had it, Jane. I don't want to be a new woman anymore."

"Sure you do, honey. Even men want to be a new woman."

The city at twilight seemed softer, rounder, and more palatable to Anna, freed for a while from the ratchety grinding of the money wheel. It did not grate so forcefully against her nerves. Jane's health club was on the upper floor of a converted warehouse a few blocks away. They changed in the locker room to the slap of bouncing feet and the push and grunt of bodies being toned. Steam billowed from shower stalls, and the air was thick with hairspray and perfume.

Halfway through her usual exercises Anna stopped, too tired to continue, and collapsed on a mat with her back against a wall and her knees clutched to her chest. Through the big warehouse windows she could see a hazy indigo sky. Early evening was the hardest time of day for her, the time when Atwater came unavoidably to mind, and she would join him again on the porch of the old farmhouse and look downriver to the great oxbow of the Russian. She could hear the crickets, the frogs, and the sorrowful song of the sparrows. Lambent—that was the word for it. Everything was lambent. She imagined herself reaching out and running a finger over Arthur's lips, encouraging him to move closer. He was grinning that toothy grin. *Atwater*, she told him, *I have to forget you. I'm sorry. Go away.* But he refused to budge.

Jane treated her to a light supper at the club's cafe, and they strolled up Columbus Avenue afterward. Manhattan had given in to the mugginess and turned itself inside out, spilling private lives recklessly into public. They could have been in the tropics, in Rangoon or Sumatra. People wallowed in the sultriness and sat half-naked on stoops and fenders or roamed the streets in noisy packs sniffing out adventure. There were smells of marijuana, cooking grease, pizza, and cigarettes. Anna saw couples holding hands and fondling each other in alleys, lazily exploring while cats rubbed up against their legs. Laughter and music echoed from taverns, along with curses and woeful sighs as the perenially sagging Mets sank further into the cellar ooze of the National League East. Hips swayed and voices babbled. The night was a tongue lapping at things.

"This weather reminds me of New Orleans," Jane said, swinging her gym bag in a cadenced, girlish way. She was still riding an aerobic high, flushed with healthy color. "What we need are some gulf oysters and a couple of sailors."

Anna fell into stride with her. "I've never been to New Orleans," she said.

"Ever had a sailor?"

"Nope."

"Then you have two reasons to go," Jane told her. "It's a marvelous town, really. I got so steamy down there I didn't do anything but lie around in my hotel room, drink Pearl beer, and daydream about sex. All that natural lubrication. You'd like it, I bet."

"I like every place in the abstract," Anna said. "I'm just never very happy where I am."

Her friend gave her a questioning look. " 'Happy' is a lot to ask for at your age. Why don't you try 'contented'?"

"Are you contented?"

"Yes, I am, right now. But I may be a malcontent again in the morning."

"So you change from moment to moment."

"Precisely. We all do."

They passed a team of young rugby players still in uniform, who were streaking toward an Irish pub in a muddy, grass-stained throng. Pints of frothy Guinness were waiting for them, the glasses already lined up. Some helmeted cyclists zoomed by and almost collided with a homeless man plucking crushed hot dog buns from a trash can. The arc lights of the Korean greengrocer loomed ahead and cast an eerie, flying-saucer glow over the avenue.

"How was your lunch?" Jane asked as they strolled on.

"It was fun. Sam's an old shoe. We're comfortable together."

"Heard anything from the valley lately?" There was an edge to the comment.

"How strange that you should ask," Anna said, smiling to herself. "I had a call from Jack Farrell today. You remember him, don't you? He *is* the Chamber of Commerce."

"But nothing from Arthur?"

"No, and I don't expect anything. You know better than to ask that."

"Why don't you call him, then?"

"We've been over this ground before," Anna said testily. "He asked me not to, and he was right to protect himself. I've already caused him enough trouble. I won't meddle in his life anymore."

Again Jane gave her a look. "You're driving all your friends crazy with this stuff. I was out there, I met the man. I saw how you were with him."

"How was I?"

"I'd say you were contented." Anna saw how pleased Jane was to have scored a point. "You're still involved with him, whether or not you admit it. There's nothing settled between you two."

"*Every*thing is settled."

"Go on and be stubborn, if you like. But I don't see what you'd have to lose by picking up the phone. I used to think of you as my impulsive friend. My daring friend."

"I was. Look where it got me."

"So you'd rather suffer?" Jane asked.

"Time will pass. Someone new will come along."

"Is that what you want?"

"It's what will happen."

They parted in front of the greengrocer's. The family's eldest son was on duty, a moon-faced teen in a Metallica T-shirt. He bagged some plums and apples for Anna, careful not to disturb the lavish display. Earth's bounty was visible even here in a matrix of steel, glass, and concrete, she thought, in this pinprick of light flickering like a candle cupped in a hollow of formidable buildings. Pears, peaches, cantaloupes, and table grapes, too—it would be Indian summer on the farm, and the harvest would be underway. The surging sweep of it would carry the valley to its pinnacle of purpose—to ripeness, deliverance, and release—and Anna had a fervent momentary wish to be transported directly into the center of it, so she could ride out its furious energies.

Her apartment was five blocks up and three over. The central air-conditioning was on full blast and gave her a chill when she unlocked the door; she shut it off and threw open some windows to the animal roar of the city. Nights had been difficult for her since her return. She had never been truly lonely before, but she felt alone in a deep and painful way now. She had trouble sleeping as well, so she poured a glass of white wine, sat in her dark living room, and looked out at the twinkle and glow of Manhattan. Again the writers on her bookstore walls entered her thoughts, and she found herself mulling over how their lives had ended, Fitzgerald alone and dead of a heart attack, Hemingway alone with his shotgun, and Kerouac alone with a bottle of cheap port. Was it the absence of love, the failure of art, or merely the human condition? That was another of the unanswerable questions Anna had begun to pose to herself in the futile insomniac hours.

21

Autumn came to Carson Valley. The changes it brought were subtle at first and lost on the local farmers, who were still caught up in the grueling labor of the harvest. They failed to notice the Lombardy poplars turning yellow or the Big-leaf maples beginning to wither, flame, and die. They had no time to remark on the heartbreaking light, the supreme clarity of the air, or the noisy ducks and geese on the wing. Their work was waiting for them every morning, and it put them to sleep every night. They paid no attention to the rest of life and missed the equinox entirely, a luminous Thursday toward the end of September when a pair of pileated woodpeckers as big as crows attacked an old black walnut tree on the edge of town, tearing off the bark to feast on the insects beneath it.

The birds beat their great wings and put on a spectacular show, but only Victor Torelli stopped to watch. He parked on a shoulder of the road and stood for nearly an hour in the shade of an old water tower while bits of bark showered down. Trucks loaded with grapes rolled by him, and he could smell a musky odor of fermentation and waved whenever somebody honked. Harvests were behind him now, happily so, and he felt no need to hurry on. The woodpeckers in their blind intensity were beautiful to him, a gift. He listened to their hammering beaks and imagined the poor terrified bugs trying to escape and wondered if the bugs were really terrified or just surprised, or if they had any emotions at all.

It was late in the afternoon before he packed up his binoculars and left. There was a slight chill in the air as he passed through town, crossed the bridge by the hospital, and saw ahead the place he was looking for, George's Firewood, a fenced yard between a tire mart and a self-storage warehouse. The yard was crowded with cast-off refrigerators and washing machines as well as cordwood stacked in tiers. A bad-tempered German shepherd tethered to the fence barked viciously when Torelli pulled up, baring its fangs. The wood man himself sat on a folding chair inside a ratty shack and applied a pencil nub to a crossword puzzle. His cheeks were sunken, and he lacked a few important teeth and wore the oily coveralls of a mechanic.

"Yes, sir!" he bellowed, clearly glad to have a customer. "What can I do you for today?"

Torelli yanked a crumpled *Valley Herald* from his back pocket. There were holes in it where he had clipped out coupons and any significant news items. "I'm here about this advertised special of yours," he said, pointing to an ad that featured a badly reproduced drawing of a Bunyanesque logger. "This mixed cord of oak and madrona."

"Oh, that's the prettiest wood! Nice and dry."

"How long you been seasoning it for?"

"It must be a good six months or so," the wood man said, chewing on his pencil.

"Where'd you cut it at?"

"Well, now, that's a fair question, but I couldn't exactly say where."

"How could you forget a thing like that?" Torelli asked him bluntly. He never would have made such an error himself.

"Hell, mister, I got all kinds of wood in here," the wood man said in self-defense. "Some of it I cut, and some of it my partner cut. Some of it we brought down from Oregon. It all gets tossed in together."

The old man reacted with concern. He had never bought firewood from a dealer before and worried about getting cheated. Always he had cut his own wood and swore as his father had done before him that the wood a person cut for himself burned hotter, better, and in some crucial sense more truly. "Maybe I ought to think it over," he said. "There's no goddam rush."

"Thinking can be costly," the wood man told him with some urgency. "Our prices shoot right up in winter. That's why the special's so special."

"What'll it run me for a half cord?"

"I could let you have a half cord for, oh, seventy dollars. But if you're value-conscious, why not get some eucalyptus with a little fir mixed in? I'd sell you a whole cord of that for a hundred bucks."

"I don't burn soft woods," Torelli said with distaste.

"Make it ninety dollars, then. Or eighty-five."

"I don't burn eucalyptus. I'll take the oak and madrona, a half cord."

"Stove length or fireplace?"

"Fireplace."

The wood man put on some gloves, repaired to a chockablock pile, and started throwing eighteen-inch lengths into the old man's truck. The logs landed with a clatter, and the German shepherd yapped and howled. Torelli made as if to assist and picked up two stray pieces, but he stopped when his breath came short and instead leaned an elbow on the hood and let the last bit of sun warm his face.

"This looks like a decent business you've got here," he said by way of conversation.

"It keeps me out of trouble," the wood man told him.

"Are you George?"

"No, sir. George is my partner. You won't find him around when there's a truck to be loaded."

"He sounds like a smart one."

"He's no smarter than me," the wood man said. "But he put up the money to get us going. Plus he only has one arm."

"He ought to be hanging paper."

"Don't I know it. I'd quit on the son of a bitch, but I got a family to feed."

"Any children?" Torelli asked.

"Mmm-hmm. Too many of 'em. My wife's a breeder."

"I've got a son and a daughter myself."

The wood man glanced up at him. "You'd think by your age, you'd be shut of them."

Torelli smiled. "They don't just disappear."

"More's the goddam pity," the wood man said, bending to toss more wood. "Where do your kids live at?"

"My boy's visiting Japan. My girl's in New York." He had clipped out an article for Anna that very morning about the progress of the harvest, in fact. Across the top he had written *Thought this might interest you,* and when that seemed too flat, he had added an exclamation point. He had not yet decided how to sign it.

"The only place I ever visited was Grenada in a uniform," the wood man said sourly. "I've had better vacations."

"Well, at least you got yourself a good job."

"Wood's as honest as it gets."

Torelli listened to the clatter of the logs and the rumble of trucks in the distance. "I cut some wood around this valley in my time," he said in a nostalgic way, his eyes a bit filmy. "Up there on Pine Ridge."

"Pine's a soft wood," the wood man told him.

"We only took the oaks. Lot of oaks up there in those days."

"Lot of everything in those days."

"I won't argue with you about that."

The wood man finished up with the logs and brushed some shavings from his chest. "You have any interest in buying a washing machine, mister? A used one from Sears all refixed?"

"No, thank you."

"We got them on special this week, too."

"I'll stick with the firewood."

"What about a dog?" The wood man nodded at the German shepherd. "I'd sell you that dog over there in a minute."

"I'm all set for dogs right now," Torelli said, smiling.

"What if I pay you something to take the ugly bastard? How about that?"

"Sorry, no deal."

"I'll tell you what, mister," the wood man said, throaty with despair. "That dog is driving me right around the bend. If he keeps barking like that, he's going to wind up with a bullet in his head. So why don't you go on and take him?"

"It's hard to shoot a dog," the old man said.

The wood man came closer. His face was all scrunched up as he angled his head to peer into Torelli's eyes and read whatever miraculous message might be behind them. "You ever tried?"

"Yes, sir, I did."

"And you couldn't do it?"

"No, I couldn't."

"Maybe you're not as mean as I am," the wood man said.

Torelli handed over some cash. He drove out of the yard and across a river bridge and dropped in at The Bullshot for a quick drink. None of his friends were around, not Grimes or Vescio or Pepper Harris. They were still out in the fields or hauling their grapes to a winery, lined up and about to be judged, so he sat by himself enjoying the relative quiet of the tavern and the rough taste of the bourbon going down. He was happy about seeing the woodpeckers and also felt very tranquil and thought fleetingly about his many nagging aches and about death, too, and the words *laid to rest* and *rest in peace*. He released his grip on every living thing to let himself float freely in space. It was a good feeling, not at all scary, and one he'd never had before.

He thought about the bedraggled wood man and his one-armed partner and chuckled to himself as he recalled how he had gathered wood every spring of his youth, heading into the hills with his brothers as soon as the ground was dry. They carried a gasoline can, their only chain saw, and an ancient crosscut saw whose use often resulted in fistfights when one Torelli boy demonstrated his superior strength by pulling another Torelli boy off balance and smack into a trunk. They cut down oaks that were diseased and any tree that lightning had struck and blackened, and they uprooted stumps and chopped up any deadfall worth saving, drenched in sweat from the effort, each isolated in the muscular net of his being, proud and without a care.

The old man finished his drink and walked the streets. Halloween costumes were already displayed in a window at the Ben Franklin Store, gossamer fairy gowns, peaked hats for witches, and rocketeer costumes with fancy epaulets for little cadets traveling to the Milky Way. More familiar to him were the cardboard skeletons doing their jangly dance and some snaggle-toothed plastic pumpkins. He didn't see any children. They were all back in school again and bent to their homework at desks and tables down every block. He passed his former office on the square and saw that it still had not been rented. Shadows crept between the buildings, and mourning doves took up their fretful cooing in the crown of an ornamental palm.

He thought about his son and daughter as he walked on, both so far away from him now, and missed them with all his heart, especially Anna who had not yet found a comfortable way to be in the world and suffered because of it. He had gone through the same sort of tribulations when he was young, the same sort of arguing with the often brutal and unacceptable facts involved in being alive, all the cruelty and stupidity of existence, and such contentment as he had finally known had come to him much later on, when he had run out of the energy he needed to conduct his argument and had learned, besides, that nobody was listening.

Those goddam woodpeckers sure were beautiful, he said to himself.

Home the old man drove with his load of wood. It rattled around with every bump he hit and every curve in the road. Tomorrow or the next day or the day after that, he would hire a neighborhood kid to stack the logs on his patio. That would give him a good feeling, too— the nearness of fire, a glowing hearth at his command, a gob of spit in the face of winter. The wood was like a buck shot clean and butchered for its meat, or a steelhead gutted, filleted, and packed for the freezer. It pleased him enormously, and when he parked his truck in his driveway, he was compelled to admire it again before going inside. The madrona was slick and smooth to his touch, a reddish-brown in color, while the oak had thick bark and was bearded in places with webs of Spanish moss. How solid the wood felt to him, and yet in the hills he had seen wood crumble to powder. A man has nothing to lose and he loses it, Torelli thought, and that is just the beginning.

22

They were working in a row of riverside Chardonnay and moving as swiftly as they could from vine to vine, two pickers parting the dusty leaves with their skilled fingers, using their knives to cut through the short peduncles, and gently dropping one cluster of grapes after another into their stained plastic tubs. The grapes were a rich amber color and very sweet. Whenever a tub was full to overflowing, they ran with it to the end of the row and dumped it in a bin, making sure that Eloy Hidalgo tallied the lug. The work was hard but rewarding. Because the fruit on the Torelli farm was abundant and of superb quality, they put in ten- and sometimes twelve-hour days without objecting, thinking of themselves as rich men, fortunate men, even men of a certain choice destiny.

It was cool and damp in the shade by the river. The pickers could smell the funk of algae blooming and the foul and lingering scent of a skunk that had been maneuvering along the deer fence the night before. The two of them were almost invisible to the others on the crew, concealed in the lushness of the greenery, their presence registering only as a flutter of energy that rippled like a current through the vineyard and made it seem more alive than ever, a thing unto itself, an ocean or a cloud. They were gathered up into it and served it, whistling as they went along, humming melodies to themselves, and when they came to a slight rise that led them into a curved beam of sunlight, they stopped as if signaled, nodded at each other, and grinned.

"*Muy bonito, hombre,*" said Omar Perez, stretching and flexing his arms toward the sky.

"*Es verdad,*" the other man agreed. Skinny and pimply faced, he always wore a green watch cap and was known as *El Serrano* on account of it.

They began picking again. Omar was an expert now, but that wasn't the case at first. He had barely survived his apprenticeship. The job looked easy to him, but he couldn't keep up with the pace. He was too rough and mashed the grapes in his tub, his fingers cramped up on him, and his back and shoulders burned with pain in spite of the aspirins he took in heaping doses. He had been humiliated, in fact. He was about to quit and go back to the nursery in Oceanside, but after three days, or maybe four, he had experienced a transcendent moment when he lost all consciousness of his knife as a foreign object. It melted into his flesh and became a part of him, something he no longer had to worry about, and he treated it respectfully after that, padding the handle with masking tape to cushion the grip and tying it to his wrist with a string so that it dangled freely between cuts. At every opportunity he sharpened the serrated edge with a file.

The crew broke for lunch well before noon. They were hungry and fetched the sandwiches and drinks that they had stowed in their cars. Omar liked to buy his food from the wife of another picker, who showed up at the same time each day with burritos wrapped in foil, tamales still warm from the oven, and Cokes iced in a cooler. Today he bought some potato chips and a brownie from her, too, and walked over to the barn where his cousin and the boss Atwater sat in privileged sanctity at a card table piled with ledger books and papers, eating burritos themselves and passing a jar of jalapeño peppers and vinegary carrots between them.

"*Con permiso?*"

"Hello, Omar," Atwater said to him. "How's your moral character this morning, buddy?"

"Good, boss."

"Then we'll let you sit with us, won't we, Antonio?"

"He can sit with us," Antonio said slyly. "But he can't have any of our peppers."

"I doubt he even wants any. Do you, Omar?" Atwater held out the jar, and when the boy reached for it, he snatched it right back. "You see? I told you he didn't want any."

Omar feigned uninterest and sat cross-legged on the ground. He peeled away the aluminum foil on his burrito, bit into the flour tortilla, and pouched his cheek with rice, beans, and roast pork. He cast away some hated green peas before taking a second huge bite, listening carefully to the talk in English. He understood some words but not others and had to parse out the meaning. The boss Atwater was saying something about how if he had his own farm, how on that farm he would just taste the fruit and fuck all the scientific something, and Antonio was saying something about an old man by the name of Victor, and the boss was saying yes, the old man knew, he got reports by *teléfono*, all superior news so far and something about grapes both red and white.

"Now, can I have a pepper, please?" Omar's fingers were busy between his teeth.

"Yes, you can have a pepper, you no-good little bastard." Atwater passed over the jar. "You'll need it to keep your strength up. We start on the red grapes soon."

"I can pick any grape," the boy bragged. "I am a *campeón*."

"Yeah, well, wait till you try our Cabernet. I had a picker cry on me once, he got so pissed off."

Antonio made a circle the size of a BB shot with a thumb and an index finger. "Check this out, Omar. Those grapes are this small, man. You get in there, you never saw so many clusters on one plant. And they stink like weeds."

"Cabs are way tart, too," Atwater put in.

"You eat some Cabernet off the vine," Antonio advised the boy, "and your mouth will pucker up as tight as your asshole."

Omar pushed around the peas he'd thrown away, linking them in a circle. "I can pick any grape," he said again. "*Any* grape."

The crew labored until late in the afternoon, steady and determined. At quitting time, Omar had logged in thirty-eight lugs, an average day for him. Only three pickers had done better. He did not know how many clusters that represented. It could have been four, five, even seven thousand. It could have been a whole million. He had tried counting once, but the arithmetic was too tough for him, with the numbers cycling upward so fast that he couldn't keep track of them. The numbers interfered with the smooth flow of his body in action, so he had let them go. *Adios,* arithmetic.

He wrapped a handkerchief around his grape knife, put it in a pocket, and walked up the dirt road to the spot where all the cars were parked. His tired mates stood around gulping water from bottles, repaying and incurring debts, and arranging their rides home. There was always someone going Omar's way. The valley at twilight was thronged with pickers on wheels, heading into town or south toward Santa Rosa. They were all involved in a unique mass-transit system that had no fixed rules and turned instead on the sentimental attachments of clans and *pueblos*. Sometimes the boy had to shell out a small fare for the trip, but that happened only when he rode with a person who was not on his crew or not from Jalisco.

That evening, as ever, he got out at Roy's Market and went into the store to buy his dinner. He encountered the usual racket inside as men jostled in the aisles, joking around, trading gossip and insults, and crowing about the progress they had made in the fields, often exaggerating their claims and translating them into a vast and imaginary sum of money that would accrue to them, which was translated again into more bricks or concrete blocks for the houses that many of them were building, harvest by harvest, in Mexico. Omar browsed through the deli case and selected a day-old ham and cheese sandwich on a torpedo roll that was priced at a discount, some chocolate milk, and a bag of Fritos, and he felt honored and substantial when the lady clerk let him put his purchase on a tab to be paid at the end of the week.

The cabin was a bane to him now. Overcrowding had robbed him of what little privacy he had. So many men came and went that he never knew for sure who would be bunking next to him. The captain ruled with a tyrant's fist and even collected a few quarters from the *pobrecitos* who were forced to sleep in blankets on the floor. The space intended for six or eight people routinely housed fifteen or twenty. It was cramped and dirty and stank of the food stored under cots and the sweaty clothes that nobody had time to wash, except on Sunday.

Omar had feared that the conditions would attract *la migra*, but he had learned that *la migra* almost never sent any agents to Carson Valley while the grapes were being picked.

"*Buenas tardes!*" the captain greeted him jovially as he entered. "*El muchacho amarillo!*"

The men reclining on their cots all laughed. Every picker in the cabin had a nickname, whether or not he liked it, because the captain wanted it that way. Omar was among those who did not like it. He was called Yellow Boy because of his bumblebee jacket.

In the dark before dawn, he woke to a grumbling rustle of activity. Someone was pissing in the sink, someone blew his nose, someone tuned a radio to syncopated salsa music, and someone else groaned and coughed up sputum. The men put on the same soiled shirts and caked jeans that they had worn the day before and took turns marching to the washhouse. They boiled water for coffee on hot plates and ate a breakfast of whatever they had at hand, canned peanuts or licorice whips or cereal eaten dry, right from the box. Omar rode to the farm with *El Remolacho,* who had a beet-red face and was known casually as Remo, and a terribly filthy picker, *El Feo,* whose face was so wretched and ugly that a child who had looked at it by accident once had reportedly dropped dead. They sat in the bed of a Nissan truck driven by the ugly one's brother, huddling together in the chill morning breeze and watching as the light spread over the valley and the grapevines came into view all splotched with dots of color, the ambers, pink-tinged greens, red-browns, and blacks that they had come to know so well.

It was a Friday. They were picking Chardonnay again and finished with the very last rows around eleven o'clock. Omar was puzzled about what he would do with himself if there was no more work that afternoon. He milled about with the others until word filtered into their ranks that the weekly paychecks were being distributed. He walked to the barn with the beet-faced picker and joined a line at the card table, where the boss sat punching figures into an electronic calculator. Atwater looked harried and distracted, and he surprised everyone when he announced that they would not pick on Saturday or Sunday either because the Cabernet Sauvignon grapes needed a little more time on the vine.

"Here you go, Omar." The boy accepted his check—only a piece

of paper but of great value. "Put that in the vault with the rest of
your fortune."

The check was for almost two hundred dollars after taxes. Already
Omar had paid back his cousin and had banked more than five hundred dollars of his own. He tapped the paper against the palm of one
hand and mulled over what he might do with his unexpected free
time. He saw a leisurely gap between the white and red grapes that
was like the parting of a curtain or the opening of a door, and it suggested the possibility of a fiesta to him, a little celebration. He and
Antonio ought to drink many beers together as men did on such occasions, so he issued an invitation.

"I take you to La Perla Roja, Antonio," he said eagerly, beckoning
to his cousin. "Come with me there, yes?"

Lopez was refilling a gas can. "I got a million things to do here,
Omar. You go on without me."

"Ah, he's just scared of his wife," Atwater quipped. "She'll bust his
balls if he doesn't head straight home."

"At least I have a wife," Lopez shot back. "You don't even have a
girlfriend anymore."

"Maybe I don't want one."

"Everybody wants one, man. Everybody."

"Come with me, Antonio," Omar asked again, almost pleading.
"Don't you like me?"

"Why don't you go with the kid?" Atwater said. "A break would do
you some good. We all could use a break. I'm sick of you guys' faces."

Lopez set down the gas can and slapped at the bees that were still
swarming over the farm. "You want to go to La Perla?" he challenged
Omar. "Okay, I'll go with you. But just for *one* beer."

"*Vamos*," the boy said excitedly. "Yes, let's go!"

"And I'm not afraid of my wife either, Arthur."

"Of course you aren't," Atwater told him.

They left in Lopez's car and stopped first at the cabin so that
Omar could wash up and change his clothes. The boy was imbued
with a profound sense of well-being and felt warmly sheltered in his
cousin's presence, as if nothing could ever go wrong. Even the captain
seemed to hold Antonio in esteem and understood his prominence,
insisting that they all have a drink from his special bottle of Johnny

Walker. Omar belted down a swallow, gagged on it, and spit most of it out. Everyone laughed at him, but for once he didn't mind. He was a man among men, after all, and bound for a *fiesta*. He dabbed his underarms with stick deodorant, stuffed the tails of his only clean shirt, a powder-blue polyester, into his dress slacks, put on his yellow jacket despite the heat, and laboriously endorsed his check so that he could deposit it at Carson Valley Savings Bank, reserving sixty dollars in cash for the party.

La Perla Roja, directly across from the bank, was rippling with energy. Omar could feel the pulse of it as he and his cousin stood outside, a throbbing in the veins of the sidewalk as strong as the beating of blood. He peered through a dark window streaked with crimson neon, but he couldn't really see anything and became apprehensive. He was not old enough to drink legally and was about to mention it when Antonio led him through the door. The tavern fell silent, and everybody looked at them for a few seconds, but then the customers grunted, ignored them, and returned to their beer guzzling, card playing, and games of eight ball. All the anxieties Omar had harbored vanished in an instant, and he was as comfortable as he would have been at home in Guadalajara.

He and Antonio located a vacant table, but they couldn't have a proper conversation. The jukebox was screaming, so they just leaned back in their chairs and watched people pass through the room, letting the music pound at them. The music was full of joyous release like the songs of *mariachis,* and Omar snapped his fingers to the trumpets, horns, *guitarras,* and drums, relaxing and enjoying the raucous atmosphere. He wished that he had a woman to dance with, some beautiful blond as richly endowed as the Tecate girl on the poster in his cabin. After a while, he saw Remo come in and waved madly to him, and Remo joined them at the table and shouted about how fucking much his muscles hurt and how glad he was to be free of the vineyard, if only for a couple of days.

"*No me gusta mucho las uvas!*" he yelled. Omar smiled. Remo had stated the obvious—he didn't like those grapes!

"You got it easy, man!" Lopez shouted back, and Omar moved closer to him to hear. "When I was picking, we only made fifty cents a lug!"

"Es verdad?"

"It's true. Sometimes they even tried to stiff us. One guy over on Pine Ridge, the checks he gave us bounced. They were, like, rubber."

"Rubber?" Omar asked, unable to picture it. Why would anyone write a check on rubber? It would be like writing on a tire or a basketball.

"Yeah, rubber! But we took care of that guy. We snuck back there one night and poured sugar in the gas tank of his car." Antonio grinned smugly. "It didn't run too good after that."

"Bravo!" Remo congratulated him with a pat on his shoulder and called to a barmaid for another round of Budweisers. "You live here a long time, *amigo?"*

"He is a *veterano,"* Omar said with arrogance, as if by being related to Antonio he, too, had acquired an exalted status.

"I been here eight years, Remo," his cousin said. "But I'll never become an American, man."

"Por qué no?"

"I want my own *ejido,* where I can be the *jefe."*

Remo took this in and came up with a question. *"Hay ai una buena discoteca acqui?"*

Lopez chuckled, shook his head, and slapped the table to underscore his mirth. "A disco? In Carson Valley? No, we don't have a good disco here."

"Quisiera una muchacha," the beet-faced man said genially, unembarrassed by his ignorance. "I want some pussy tonight!"

Remo's exuberance captured the attention of two dissolute fellows, who were lounging by the jukebox. Omar looked up when one of them began speaking. "Go to Santa Rosa," the jukebox man told them, cupping his hands beneath his pectorals and leering. "They got topless dancers there. Stripteasers."

Omar jumped on the suggestion. *"Me gustaría ir alla, Antonio,"* he said, with enthusiasm. "Yes, take us to the pussy!"

"I know the club he means," Antonio warned them all. "It isn't cheap, *comprende?* A bottle of plain beer, it could cost you up to four dollars. You might have to pay a charge at the door, too."

Rabbity with ardor, Omar fanned his wad of cash. "I pay!" he shrieked. "Take us to there!"

"They might not like us," his cousin told him. "Some high-class places, they're hard to get into."

"I pay," Omar reiterated, showing off his wad of money again.

"Yeah, you can pay. But you'll still be a Mexican."

"Do you go there before?" the boy asked, his brow knitted. He wanted more than anything for Antonio to lead them to this place.

"Sure, I've been there. Those people at that club, I'm real friendly with them. Probably if I go with you I can get you in."

"Muchachas!" Remo yelled once more, gripping Omar's shoulder and squeezing it. "Tonight I fuck a California girl!"

They left La Perla Roja in a caravan. The two jukebox men drove an old Chevy, and the beet-faced picker rode a motorcycle. It was dark now, and Omar was feeling the effects of the beer. He could remember nothing about Santa Rosa except for the Greyhound station and observed vigilantly and in wonder as they passed several trailer parks, used-car lots, fast-food joints, and a motel where no one at all was staying and arrived finally at a big rectangular building with bright lights all around it. It had an illuminated sign on the roof, but he couldn't read it. He pointed to the sign and asked his cousin what it said.

"The Show Room," Antonio told him. "Because of what the girls show you."

"What do they show?"

"Their tits and everything."

They all parked in the lot and assembled as a group. Omar was fretful that they might fail to pass muster and be rejected. There was indeed a bouncer at the door, who was collecting a small cover charge. He was barechested under a leather vest, had a shaved head and an earring in the shape of a skull, and started whooping as soon as Lopez and the pickers advanced toward him.

"Be careful now," Antonio whispered to the others. The boy had a childish urge to hold his cousin's hand. He felt that if he did not get into the club it would be the worst thing that had ever happened to him—worse than dying, even. "Be cool now."

When they reached the door, the bouncer laughed right in their faces and rapped his knuckles on the beet-faced picker's head. "You plan to wear this all night?" he asked. "You look like a freakin' astronaut."

"*Ay!*" Remo fumbled with the chinstrap of his helmet. "I forget!"

They joined in the laughter then, greatly relieved, and poked at Remo's helmet with their fingers and punched it with their fists, while the bouncer accepted dollars from several hands, although not from Omar's. "Where's your ID?" he demanded of the boy. "I need to see a picture ID to let you in."

"ID?" Omar repeated.

"How old are you, kid?"

"He's twenty-three," Antonio said briskly.

"If he's twenty-three, he must have some kind of fucked-up disease." The bouncer glanced around. "Give me a ten, and I'll let you slide," he said to the boy out of the side of his mouth. "But I never saw you, kid, did I?"

"You never did see me ever," Omar agreed.

"That's right. I don't know how the hell you got in, do I? You snuck in, didn't you?"

Omar's head bobbed up and down. "I did sneak in."

The pickers entered a crowded fetid arena, where a blue spotlight fell on a small stage framed at the apron by red lightbulbs. There were chairs around the stage, some tables to the rear, and a few leatherette booths against the back wall. Omar stopped in his tracks, transfixed by the action. He simply could not move. A young woman with a frizzy permanent, naked except for a G-string, was coiling her willowy legs around a metal firepole to the deafening blast of the Rolling Stones. She looked like a snake to him, someone capable of killing a man with a squeeze of her thighs. He saw other women in bikinis, babydolls, and fishnet stockings circulating to serve cocktails, and if a man held up a bill, one of the waitresses would sit in his lap and wriggle up against him. This was actually taking place in front of Omar's eyes, a scenario beyond his wildest dreams. He was so frozen in place he might never have moved another inch if his cousin hadn't grabbed him angrily by his shirt collar and towed him to a table in the second row.

"That's no way to act in here!" he heard Antonio scream at him. "Act like you been here a lot, will you?"

Omar hung his head in shame. A round of Budweisers appeared on the table, and he paid for them out of guilt. There went another twenty of his dollars.

When the song ended, the frizzy blond started retrieving the clothes she had dropped on stage. Men were throwing bills at her, tossing them at her like baseballs, and she put a hand to her lips and blew them all kisses. The next dancer was so unique that she made Omar gape. His mouth just fell wide open. She was blubbery in the stomach and hips, with cascading rolls of fat, but she had mammoth breasts that she could shake and twirl and even suck. The tassels on her nipples spun mightily. Here was another feminine trick that Omar never would have imagined. He touched his own chest and jiggled his shoulders, trying to duplicate the feat. He felt no desire for the woman really, only an incredulity over her God-given talents. The other pickers at the table poked fun at her, though. One jukebox man snatched at his friend's crotch and held his hands two feet apart to show the huge size of the hard-on he'd supposedly found there.

The third dancer was much better-looking, a tall redhead whose nipples were pierced with rings, and as she wrapped her legs around the firepole and began humping it, Omar got seriously aroused for the first time, grew bolder, and encouraged her by yelling, "Yes, you are so pretty!" and "Go, baby, go!" He was ready to have a woman sit on him now, ready for an experience. When a waitress brought them more beer, he held up a five-dollar bill and waved it at her, but Remo, who was sitting across from him, did the same thing, except that his bill was worth ten dollars. The boy cursed himself. How could he be so stupid! The waitress chose Remo, of course. She was a spindly brunette balanced precariously on spike heels, and as she settled into the beet-faced picker's lap, Omar felt cheated and hurt. His brain woozy from drink, he was certain that he had fallen in love with the woman in an unnatural, magical, and utterly compelling way.

He watched with extreme jealously as she adjusted her bra straps and reconfigured her position. She was wearing a sheer nightgown, flimsy and blue, and she put her mouth to Remo's ear. What could she be whispering? Had she told Remo that he was handsome? That she liked his penis? Omar's heart sank as the beet-faced picker thrust his pelvis against her ass and gyrated as if he were fucking her. The boy saw Remo run his fingers along the woman's arms and brush them over her panties and down between her legs. She shimmied and ground against him, and Omar wanted to cry out. He saw Remo slip an exploratory finger under the panties and try to touch her *chocha,* and he was not at all unhappy when the woman went *loca* and shoved Remo away, leaping up from his lap and slapping him across the face.

"I asked you not to do that, didn't I?" She reminded Omar of a scolding nun. "Didn't I ask you not to do that? I told you to keep your hands away from there!"

"*Yo no he hecho nada,*" Remo demurred, looking to his fellows for support. He hadn't done anything wrong, had he?

Omar felt no sympathy for him. You are a dog, Remo, he thought. I hate you. You dog.

"He can't even speak English, can he?" the woman asked, pinching Remo's earlobe and twisting it until his face was an even brighter red. "You're a dirty man. That's what you are." She tugged at her bra straps again. "You don't belong in here, any of you. You're all dirty, dirty, dirty!"

They made no argument when the bouncer ordered them to leave. They all hung their heads as they straggled into the parking lot, but the altercation somehow changed its meaning for Omar once he was outside. What else had they expected? The Show Room was not La Perla Roja, after all. The entire episode seemed funny to the boy now, and he teased the beet-faced picker about his wandering fingers and asked if he could sniff them. Remo gave him a push and then a hug. Yes, Omar thought, these are my brothers, dear to me every one, and in his beery, emotional condition, he felt honored to be counted among the hardworking men of the vineyards on their journey through the transfigured night.

A jukebox man suggested that they continue their *fiesta* at another club nearby where there was live music.

"Not me, man," Antonio said, shaking his head. Omar was helping to support him, an arm around his waist. "I'm too old for this shit. It's almost midnight. I'm going to eat, and then I'm going home to bed."

Remo put his arms around both of them. He was swaying. "*Menudo, amigos,*" he said, donning his helmet. "*El mejor.* You follow me."

Off Remo roared on his motorcycle. Omar watched the darting flight of his taillight through the Toyota's windshield, feeling a tender wave of affection for Antonio and admiring his strong features in profile. Here was the person who had made everything possible for him. Omar had never really lived before, he had never tasted the sweetness of life until Antonio had offered him some guidance. He owed his cousin an enormous debt that he couldn't ever repay. He looked out at some wealthy residences fenced and dark, and then he and Antonio were speeding downhill toward a dense strip of businesses along the freeway. The boy was awed in the moment by the extent of what he didn't know about Santa Rosa or the big world beyond his *pueblo*. He almost collapsed under the thunderous weight of what he did not know, in fact, and it came to him disturbingly, as in an unwanted prophecy, that the harvest would not go on forever. The grapes would all be picked someday. He pictured the vines withered, worthless, and drifted with snow, although he did not truly believe that snow would fall, and saw himself alone and without a purpose.

"I stay here," he said, in a stubborn voice.

"Yeah, whatever," his cousin told him.

"Yes, I stay!" Omar poked at his chest, at his heart, and there were tears in his eyes. "I stay here in Carson Valley!"

Remo had led them to another *cantina*, a popular spot that was rocking at all hours. The bar was three deep with rowdy men and women, and the balls on four pool tables were clacking in rhythm. A layer of cigarette smoke hovered near the ceiling, and smoke curled around the hunched forms of customers slurping soups and stews and plying their bowls with warm corn tortillas. At the front counter, Omar ordered *menudo* all around and spiced his own with chopped onions and liberal sprinklings of oregano, cilantro, and hot sauce. He drank even more beer and felt the blaring music throb in his veins, and in his ecstasy he was pulled to his feet and started dancing, twirling in giddy uncontrollable circles, his arms outstretched, his head thrown back, and his eyes closed. He was the only dancer in the *cantina*, the only one possessed, and he clapped and stomped on the floor, aware that everybody was watching him, beautiful in his soul.

"Hey, Omar!" Antonio shouted to him. "Sit down, man!"

But Omar couldn't stop himself. He imagined that he was one of the dancers at The Show Room and with cloying fingers unbuttoned the top buttons of his shirt to reveal a muscular, hairless chest.

"*Maricón*," someone hissed.

Omar pretended not to hear the person and danced on, spinning about and unbuttoning more buttons, still beautiful in his soul.

Again came the single word, a single hiss, harsher now. *"Maricón!"*

Omar stopped twirling. He was giving something to the people, surrendering his soul to the music, to its poetry, and he had been gravely insulted. He stared hotly at his accuser, who returned his stare in a mocking way.

"Fairy boy," the man said with a smirk. "Cocksucker."

"Déjeme en paz," Omar told him. He wanted to be left in peace. What was wrong with this terrible man?

The man was slovenly and very drunk, and he had eyes the color of gravy and greasy black hair that hung in strands over his forehead. He seemed to be spoiling for a fight and toyed with the zipper of his trousers, taunting Omar. In a panic, the boy turned away and saw that his cousin was rising from a chair as he might have in a dream to defend him.

"Please, Ernesto," he heard Antonio say. "Leave him alone. He's just a kid. He doesn't mean any harm."

"Hey, you remember me!" the terrible man said, giggling now. "That's very good. Yes, I am Ernesto Morales! You fire me from your farm, you remember that, too, Lopez?"

"I didn't fire you, Ernesto. The boss fired you. You fucked up, man."

"But you didn't help me, did you, *amigo?*"

"I tried to help. I warned you it might happen."

"You didn't help me for shit, asshole." Morales spat into an empty bowl. "No work for me anymore." He smiled and thrust a thumb toward his mouth. "Now I drink, yes?"

"I buy you one Budweiser," Omar offered, fumbling with the last of his cash. His shirt flew away from him to expose more of his chest. "Please?"

"Maricón!" Morales was dismissive. "Why you fuck me over with your grape money?"

"Está bien," Omar said with resignation. The situation was hopeless.

"Is that little boy your special boyfriend?" Morales was addressing Antonio again. Omar watched as the terrible man stumbled up from his table and produced a hunting knife from a sheath on his belt. "I don't like no *maricón* in here."

"*Serense*, Morales!" His cousin had drawn a line. "I'm asking you real nice, man. Put it away."

Omar stepped back in horror as Morales lurched forward and almost fell down. He saw Remo try to grab him from behind, but Morales swung around with surprising deftness and slashed furiously at the air. Then Antonio had him firmly by the wrist and was smashing that wrist against his own knee, but Morales wrestled free, snarled, and sank his teeth into Lopez's forearm. They broke apart for a few seconds, and the boy saw blood bubbling up from his cousin's wound. Morales snatched a beer bottle and slugged at it while he stared in a dumbfounded way at the broken wrist that now hung limp and useless before him. The extent of his injury seemed to dawn on him then, and he howled indignantly and rushed toward Omar, who backed away. Still Morales pursued him with his blade, slashing and slashing.

23

A sea breeze blew through the woods behind Sam McNally's house in East Hampton and ruffled a windsock above the deck off the living room, where Anna Torelli reclined in a chaise lounge. She was still in her bathing suit after a midmorning swim and was smoking a cigarette borrowed from a pack her host had left out. Anna wasn't ordinarily a smoker, but the tobacco tasted strong and very good on her freshened palate. The ocean had affected her senses that way since earliest childhood, washing the farm dust from her throat. Her father hated to be torn from his routines, but once or twice every summer the family ganged up on him and forced him into a trip out to the coast, to Salmon Creek or Shell Beach. The water was really too cold for swimming, but Anna had enjoyed the wading and always came away with a feeling of having been cleansed and revitalized.

A rolling lawn ran downhill to a road that separated McNally's property from a potato field. The field had recently been cut to stubble, and flocks of grackles and lark buntings were dipping into it to for the chaff. Sam had bought his two-plus acres many years ago when the real estate prices were still fairly reasonable on that part of the island and had built his house in stages. That gave the place an informal, homey, handmade quality Anna liked. Big windows in every room delivered cascades of marine light at almost any hour of the day. The house was ideal for entertaining, with a galley kitchen that opened onto a living and dining area, where a long country pine table held sway. The floors were plank, and sliding glass doors led to three separate decks. The four bedrooms, two up and two down, were stacked with books and decorated with the nautical prints and folk art that McNally had collected in his travels.

Anna had chosen to spend the previous night, the Friday of their arrival, in McNally's bedroom. She hadn't planned to sleep with him, but they drank a little wine after they got in on the jitney, and when he kissed her it seemed silly to refuse. Sam was a skillful, familiar, and attentive lover, so the interlude was agreeable enough, but it was also spectacularly without impact for her. Only later did she understand that she had probably been trying to find that out. Her failure to become truly aroused and lose herself in the act told her that she was outside rather than inside it, observing from a distance. There were no sparks, no animal sense of release. A simple disagreement with Arthur had engaged her at a deeper level. He was most definitely the third person in the bed.

Go away, Atwater, she told him again. *I will forget you, goddam it!*

Anna had almost dropped into a slumber when McNally appeared on the deck with a chilled Bloody Mary in each hand. He was barefooted and chewing on a piece of celery.

"I'm not going to move from this spot," she told him with an easy smile. "Not ever. I feel wonderful, Sam."

McNally flopped into the chaise lounge next to hers. He wore a bathing suit and a T-shirt that bunched up over his modest belly. He was trim but lacking in muscle tone. The only exercise he ever got was on the golf course. "That was a fine swim, wasn't it?"

"I enjoyed every stroke of it."

"Has anybody ever told you that your legs are a little bowed?"

"Don't be ridiculous." Anna was slightly offended and also surprised at the extent of her vanity. "They are not."

"Yes, they are. I never noticed it before. It's sort of alluring."

"Alluring? I don't think it's alluring at all," Anna told him. "Next you'll be saying my breasts are sagging."

"Your breasts are not sagging. Take my word for it."

She let her head rest on his shoulder. "You're such a nice guy, Sam. We have a good time together, don't we?"

"Yes, we do."

Weekends with McNally always involved a whirlwind of social activity. He played in a middle-aged, coed softball game every Saturday afternoon and talked Anna into starting in right field for his team, where she misjudged two fly balls but compensated by going three for four at the plate—which, as she pointed out, said everything about the caliber of the competition. Then they were off to town in the car Sam kept on the island, buying up seafood and some fresh vegetables over in Amagansett for the dinner party he had put together in her honor. Anna was envious of the ease with which he moved from village to village and shop to shop, friendly with the fishmonger and the tomato lady and taking delight in every transaction. Sam was comfortable with the simple givens of life, or so it appeared on the surface. He insisted on giving her his grand tour of the East End, showing her the famous cemetery in Springs where so many dead painters and writers were buried and driving through Sag Harbor to see the street where Steinbeck had lived.

Clouds began forming over the water around five o'clock. The birds in the potato field were whipped into a frenzy, beating their wings in anticipation of a thunderstorm. Anna watched them while she was scrubbing some littleneck clams at the kitchen sink. McNally stood next to her rinsing some lettuce. She could smell a charge in the air, a whiff of electricity.

"You know what I'd like right now, Sam?" she told him. "A nap."

"Go on and have one. There isn't a whole lot left to do here. I can handle it by myself."

"All right. I will." She kissed him lightly. "You're spoiling me."

"That's the idea."

Anna dried her hands on a towel and walked past the master bedroom to some stairs leading to the second floor. She was conscious of testing McNally this time, drawing a boundary to see whether or not he would cross it. She went into a bedroom, sat on the bed, and waited. Sam didn't come to her. That was what she had hoped for— some respect for her privacy, no overt claims of intimacy or privilege on his part. He had passed the test, and yet Anna felt curiously disappointed. Bowed legs, sagging breasts—her powers of attraction must be diminishing! No, that wasn't it. It was McNally's fault, wasn't it? He lacked the necessary passion. He was too much the proper gentleman, and she had married a proper gentlemen, etcetera, and all this cogitation, Anna knew, would get her nowhere. She was appalled at her own self-involvement and the number of hours that she had lately been squandering on what she now thought of as her predicament.

In the mail that week, she had received a clipping from the *Valley Herald* from her father, an article about the harvest. It was written in the paper's usual reportorial style, gushy and full of grammatical errors, but it had a powerful impact on her, anyway. The old man had never in all his years sent her so much as a postcard, and when she read the sentences he had scrawled across the margin in his trembly hand, *Thought this might interest you! Bought some nice firewood today, Love, Your Dad,* it had moved her almost to tears. Victor Torelli was aging, aging, and soon he would be gone. Whenever Anna talked with him on the phone, his voice sounded less and less forceful, fading in and out, with no trace of rancor, a disembodied and even ghostly thing, and she could hear in his faltering words a growing acceptance of the silence that would ultimately capture him. It was not so much the fact that he would die someday that upset her, but rather that there was so much unfinished business between them. In her heedless and ambitious youth, she had never allowed for this moment. She had not included death in her master plan.

She lay down and covered herself with an afghan. The first drops of rain fell faintly on the roof, but in minutes the windows were drumming under a colossal downpour. The bedroom seemed to swell with earthy fragrances, with odors of grass and loam. Anna dozed for a while and woke and turned onto her side, a cheek resting on her folded hands. She felt comfortably sealed inside the rain, even protected by it, beyond the meshing gears of time, and she dozed again and slept hard and well. It was McNally who finally brought her back to life by tugging on her toes. She saw that the sky was rosy now and stitched with seams of blue.

"You had a good nap." He looked at her with fondness. "You've been out for a couple of hours."

Anna lazily held up her arms to him. "Come here, Sam. Be with me for a minute."

"I'm your man," McNally said, joining her on the bed.

"I didn't have a single dream. Isn't that strange?"

"That's a good sign. It means you're a righteous person."

"I like being with you like this, Sam. I'm far away from all my problems."

"Don't go too far on me, Anna," he said. "I wouldn't want to lose sight of you."

Their dinner guests began arriving around seven-thirty, two couples who were old friends of McNally's and a stout young man with very long hair that swept over his shoulders. He worked as an editorial assistant to Sam and introduced himself simply as Malcolm. Anna fixed him a gin and tonic and led him to the backyard deck. It was warm enough to eat outside, so she and Sam had spread a tablecloth over a picnic table and lit some citronella candles to keep away the bugs. Malcolm seemed uncomfortable in polite company and stuck a finger under his shirt collar to probe his neck.

Anna tried to put him at ease. "So you work with Sam, do you?"

"Yeah, I do the hatchet stuff." Malcolm had a quality of free-floating moroseness. "I get to tell people when their books are going out of print. Sometimes Sam lets me read a manuscript he isn't interested in."

"Do you enjoy it?"

"One job's the same as another to me."

"You don't sound like a go-getter," she teased him. "Actually, you sound a lot like Sam."

"That's true," Malcolm said with sincerity. "I don't have any ambition. But I better find some, or my girlfriend's going to dump me. She doesn't think I make enough money."

"What do you think?" Anna asked him.

Malcolm grinned in a way that showed how unnatural it was for him. "If it was up to me, I'd be on unemployment."

"You must be devoted to her."

"I am. I'm in love with her big time."

"How lucky for you. And for her."

He shrugged. "Her parents despise me, though. Celeste is Chinese."

Anna paused to take this in. She thought of her clerk, Julie, and was tempted to set up an introduction. A match made in heaven, she thought. "Have you two been together very long?"

"Yeah, almost five months. We'd be married if I didn't have such a crummy job." He quickly corrected himself. "I mean, *I* don't think it's crummy, but her parents do. It's like she has to be with a doctor or a lawyer or somebody like that."

"So what will you do?"

"I applied to med school."

"You must really care about her," Anna said. "I hope she appreciates it."

"She's too young, probably. She's, like, five years younger than me." Malcolm downed his drink in a single gulp. "Is that too much of an age difference?"

"No, I don't think so."

"It better not be. Have you ever been married?"

"I was once," Anna said.

"Was it fun?"

She laughed. "It can be fun, yes."

"But it can also be a pain in the ass, right?"

"That's right, Malcolm."

McNally spared her any further interrogation by summoning everyone to the dinner table. The guests were a convivial bunch, talkative and witty. Sam served the clams as a starter and next a fish stew and a salad of mixed greens, circling the table to keep the wine glasses filled. Anna found herself relaxing into an entertaining evening of the sort that could be repeated infinitely through a lifetime. Yet it also seemed to her that she had met the guests before and often knew what they would say before they opened their mouths—except, of course, for Malcolm. Again, she was bothered by a lack of impact. *Why isn't this enough?* Another in her plague of unanswerable questions.

"Anna's family has been in the wine business for almost a century." Sam touched her bare shoulder with his fingertips on his rounds. "Out in California."

"In the Napa Valley?" someone asked.

"No, in a much smaller valley over in Sonoma County," Anna told him. "We're just grape growers, not vintners. The harvest is going on right now."

"So you're the farmer's daughter?"

"There's no denying it."

"I could live on a farm," McNally said, and everybody looked at him as though he were out of his mind. "No, really, I could. I'd go for all that peace and quiet. I'd smoke pot and study my navel."

Anna challenged him. "Come on, Sam! You can't exist without a phone and a fax machine. You've never done any manual labor in your life!"

"Sure, I have. Who do you think built the deck you're sitting on?"

"I'll bet a carpenter built it."

"Well, you're partly right," McNally conceded, pretending to be downcast. "A carpenter and I built it."

They had coffee and dessert inside. The guests lingered and chatted and didn't leave until after midnight. There were dishes to be cleared after that, and when everything was stacked on a kitchen sideboard, it made such an intimidating mess that Sam refused to deal with it until the next morning. Instead, he opened a bottle of Sauterne and poured a couple of glasses. McNally had always hated for an evening to end. He was the original boy who didn't want to go to bed.

"None for me, thanks." Anna watched as he dumped her Sauterne into his glass. "I couldn't eat or drink another thing."

"Suit yourself. I'm going to put on some music."

"It's late, Sam. I'm ready to turn in. I've done enough playing for one day."

McNally flopped down next to her on the couch. "I'm worried about you, Anna. You used to be such a wild girl."

"Why do people keep telling me how I used to be?" she asked him, honestly curious.

He didn't reply. "Did you get a kick out of my assistant?"

Anna smiled and let McNally take her hand. "Poor Malcolm. He wanted to know if marriage was fun."

"And what did you say?"

"That's privileged information. Then at the table he said that love must be different when you're older."

"He's wrong about that." McNally rested his glass on an arm of the couch. "If you come closer, I'll prove it to you."

"Love, not fucking, Sam. Besides, what do you know about love?"

McNally's voice rose in mock outrage. "Oh, I know plenty! I got my heart broken just today."

Anna stared at him. He didn't seem to be kidding. "I believe you're telling the truth."

"Totally. And you're the one who broke it."

"Am I? How is that?"

"You called me a 'nice guy!'" McNally snorted with contempt. "That's the worst thing any woman can say to a man. Check it out in the movies. Check it out in books. A nice guy always loses the girl. Nice guys *do* finish last."

"I didn't mean it that way. You know better than that."

"It doesn't matter how you meant it! It still hurt my feelings." He had a belt of Sauterne, invested in his role as an injured party. "*Malcolm* is a nice guy, for crying out loud."

Anna tried to lure him away from the subject. "You're making this up, aren't you?"

"Of course not." McNally brooded. "Nice guys don't make things up."

"You see?" Anna laughed. "You can't help yourself. Everything turns into a joke with you sooner or later."

"What if I told you I loved you? Does that sound like a joke? What would you say to that?"

"I'd say you've had a lot to drink tonight."

"I'll tell you the same thing in the morning," McNally said loudly, filled with bravado. "I'll say it stone cold sober. I'll say it a month from now. I'll say it in, oh, 1998."

Anna was concerned about how worked up he was getting. "Sam," she said gently, "can we drop it for now, please?"

But McNally wouldn't quit. "This isn't a joke, Anna. I value love too much to debase it."

"Come to bed." She tried to pull him up from the couch. "You're not making any sense."

"Do you value love?" Sam demanded. "Well, answer me! It's not such a hard question, is it?"

Anna felt unfairly confronted. "I think I do."

"You'd better." McNally stumbled to his feet. "Because you still have a chance at it."

"And you don't?"

"No way. I'm too old. I'll be fifty in three years. Men my age are done for. We're burned out. We've had it."

"There's always hope, Sam."

McNally scoffed at her. "Are you really naive enough to believe that?"

She considered it. "Yes, I guess I am."

"There isn't always hope, Anna," he told her harshly. "Not when it comes to love."

He was calmer in a little while, apologetic for making a scene. Anna stayed the night with him again, but she was awake through most of it. His words had affected her like a body blow, and she saw with utter clarity that she would never be able to think her way into the future. It was a question of leaping, of risking a dive off a high cliff with no guarantee of safety. What did the old Italians say? *Forza! Corragio!* Strength and courage. There must be different levels and kinds of pain, Anna felt, but the worst must come to those who refuse to take a plunge. Enough! She listened to McNally's heavy breathing, as far away from him as she possibly could be, and watched the distant stars framed in the skylight above his bed.

24

O n Sunday, Arthur Atwater was at peace, thankful for some time off from work. He had no precise memory of his last such break. It seemed as historical to him as the Peloponnesian War he had once studied in school. Over a rare unhurried breakfast, he caught up on his mail and browsed through the accumulated catalogs, deciding he would reward himself with a new down vest when the crush was over. He clipped his neglected toe- and fingernails, showered, and put on some clean underwear, then dusted the dogs with flea powder before brewing a second pot of tea. His log was before him on the table, and when he thumbed through his entries for the year, he was impressed by the sheer bulk of them. Here was a literal record of his efforts, testimony to the fact that he had done his job, or at least had tried to.

SUNDAY, OCT. 6TH. White grapes all in now, with top dollar due on the Chardonnay. Cloudy and cool this a.m., a light breeze from the north. We start picking Cabs tomorrow, tested out at 23.1 yesterday. Zins almost ready, will come up fast if it gets warm, could be trouble. Some pretty color in the leaves. Fall, I guess. I missed it.

He had no plans for his day off except to relax, but his thoughts kept revolving around the harvest and all those red grapes about to pop. After a while, he copied some figures onto a legal tablet and drove into town to deliver another of his progress reports to Victor Torelli, but the old man refused to even acknowledge him this trip, being hypnotically devoted to a '49ers football game. His recliner was pushed up close to a fireplace that was throwing out enough BTUs to melt paint. Atwater left him to a mean household temperature of about eighty-five degrees and stopped at Charlie Grimes's farm on his way home to borrow a back-up fanbelt for his tractor. He found Charlie and a local winemaker sampling some grape juice, green and frothy and fresh from a press. The winemaker passed the beaker under his nose.

"Go on and taste it," Grimes commanded him. "It won't kill you, Arthur."

Atwater took a sip and swirled it in his mouth. "Chardonnay," he said, smacking his lips. "Very nice. The flavor's real strong. Apples, definitely. Maybe a touch of citrus."

"Those grapes were goddam perfect. If you want a thirty-dollar bottle of wine, come back here in three years."

"I'll mark it down on my calendar."

"You had better. Because we'll be sold out in an eyeblink." Grimes pressed a knuckle to a nostril and blew some snot toward a pumice of grape skins on the floor. "You pull off any blacks yet?" he asked, subjecting his other nostril to the same unblocking.

"Not yet. Tomorrow we start. I'm itchy about it, to tell you the truth."

"How they looking?"

"The Cabs are just right. The Zins need some more heat."

"I don't envy you, no sir," Grimes said, clucking his tongue. "I had a year like that in nineteen and eighty-three. Every goddam black grape was ready all at once. They was pelting me like hailstones."

"They come at you hard and fast, don't they?"

"The co-op I belonged to then, those people were backed up for hours. One fellow, he had a hammock strung under his flatbed so he could take naps. I about expired myself."

"But you lived to tell the tale."

"Some would have it."

They proceeded to a toolshed where Grimes stored a truly monumental selection of spare parts. Atwater watched him rudely tossing aside spark plugs and oil filters to unearth a litter of fanbelts. They moved off into the light and walked past the barn. It was inordinately white and loomed over the property like a hole in the sky that needed to be filled.

"You going to leave your barn that way?" Atwater asked.

"No, I'll do something with it sooner or later," Grimes told him. "But I'm not about to rush myself. Creative ideas, they don't come easy."

"You're a true artist, Charlie."

Grimes showed unusual humility. "It's been said before."

Atwater motored around his own vineyard that afternoon and tasted some Zinfandel grapes from different rows. One from the inside of a cluster and one from the outside, one from the cane and one from the head. He chewed, spat, and ticked off the seconds to gauge how long the flavor held, how richly it was concentrated—four, seven, even ten seconds. It would be a fine vintage, he thought, and would produce big red wines of a decisive varietal character. He lay down to rest on a hilltop after that, sampling what it felt like to be lazy, his hands cupped behind his head and his imagination streaking toward Anna in faraway New York as it often did at such undefended moments. He saw her striding down a broad boulevard and cutting a swath through the crowd, like a bright flame. He loved how she burned. He smiled to himself and understood to his astonishment that he must have forgiven her. It was possible he'd forgiven himself, too. There was a new clarity in the air, and he allowed himself to think he'd been right not to extinguish that tiny flicker of hope.

"Oh bullshit, Atwater," he shouted to an audience of grapes and crows, disgusted with himself. "Bullshit, bullshit, bullshit!" Besides, he'd been busy in bed with that bartender from The Rib Room.

Early the next morning, in the gnawing dark, he dressed and listened for the familiar sounds of his crew arriving, the coughing and the joking, but the vineyard was unnaturally quiet. He listened more intently and heard a muted drone and then nothing more. The pickers must be waiting to be told when and where to begin on the red grapes, he figured, so he shot through the door without a bite to eat and hustled toward some human shapes who were still in the process of emerging from the fading night. They were glancing nervously about, as if to locate in the shadows a presence to give them an assurance they seemed to require.

Atwater saw the reason why. Antonio Lopez was missing. *"Donde está Antonio?"* he asked them.

His question was met with shrugs and downcast eyes.

"Dígame la verdad," he repeated. *"Donde está Antonio?"*

"Not here, *señor!"* somebody piped up.

"Desaparecido," another voice added. Lopez had disappeared, and nobody knew his whereabouts.

There was no time for further discussion. Every lost second would be tallied on the negative side of the ledger, Atwater knew. He led the crew to the ripest block of Cabernet Sauvignon, distributed the hosed-down plastic tubs, and got everybody started. He noticed then that Omar Perez was also missing, as were all three Hernandezes. He was short a total of five pickers, and that meant he would harvest far fewer lugs on the day. An average of about thirty lugs per picker, so one hundred and fifty times thirty-five pounds a lug—the rough calculation came to about five thousand pounds of grapes. All those grapes would remain on the vine, fruit that was very nearly at its peak and under a threat of raisining if Atwater didn't correct the shortfall in manpower as quickly as he could.

The pickers sensed that something had gone haywire. Deprived of their routine, they were acting contrary. They dawdled, cut corners, and competed among themselves instead of helping one another. Without Lopez to supervise them and set a pace, they were in rebellion.

"What's going on here?" Atwater asked Rudolfo Mendez, who seemed not to be moving at all. *"Que pasa?"*

Mendez pointed solemnly. He had a row that curved uphill and didn't want to do any climbing.

"Well, shit, go pick over there, then," Atwater told him, shoving him toward level ground.

But Mendez wouldn't budge. He nodded malignly at the picker in the row next to him. *"Me esta sigiuendo,"* he griped.

"I won't let him follow you. Just go!"

Atwater broke for his trailer and phoned Lopez at home. He got no answer, only a dull, distant, uninterrupted ringing. He returned to the vineyard in a fury and caught Serena Cedillo hastily dumping her full tub into a harvest bin and dashing off before he could speak to her. Hoisting himself above the rim of the bin, he saw why. It was filled with grapes that were mashed, split, and leaking juice. The juice would oxidize and cause some fermentation, so he leaned over and plucked away the damaged clusters. He tossed out the imperfect ones, too, those with shot, puckered, or shriveled berries that should have been left on the vine. The pickers were grabbing anything at all without regard to quality.

Atwater whistled loudly to call a halt. The crew gathered to face him, dragging their heels. They were cantankerous and wouldn't look at him when he held up a flawed cluster and ordered them not to pick such grapes. It was useless, he thought. They were beyond caring and would continue to do as they pleased.

"*Ándale!*" he yelled with fake enthusiasm, clapping his hands. "*Ándale! Ándale!*"

He left the farm to search for some replacements. He scoured Carson Valley Road, but the men who'd been loitering in strategic positions just yesterday had hired on somewhere or had merely given up and gone home to Mexico. Ordinarily, idlers were as thick as flies in front of Roy's Market, but Atwater didn't see a single person there. He tried all the cabins as well, banging on every door, and failed to rouse anybody, except for a surly fellow who sat by himself near a window in cabin four, playing solitaire and sipping from a bottle of Johnny Walker.

"I've got work," Atwater told him, as if that were the best news the fellow could ever hear. "I need a picker."

"I am no interest in picking."

"I'll go to a dollar and a half a lug for the right man."

"*Qué lástima!* I am the captain, *señor.*"

Atwater made for the farm again, having exhausted his prospects for the moment. He consoled himself with thoughts of all the things that might have gone wrong for Antonio Lopez, the many minor impediments that could have forced him to be late, an emergency involving his car or his daughter or even his stomach that would surely be fixed by now. So vehemently did he pursue this fantasy that he expected Lopez's old Toyota to be parked in its usual spot, but he was mistaken. The rebellion in his vineyard had become more entrenched, in fact. Two men had put down their tubs and stopped picking altogether, crouching in the shade as if to set a desultory example for the other crew members to follow. They had not so much quit their jobs as gone out on strike, Atwater surmised, since they were still on the property and so were still open to negotiation.

"Yes?" He addressed them as graciously as he could under the circumstances. *"Hay algun problema?"*

"Me he torcido la muñeca," the first picker replied. His wrist was sprained.

"Me duele todo el cuerpo," said the second picker. His entire body hurt.

They had more grievances, too. Atwater knelt next to them and heard them out, his expression one of utmost concern. These new red grapes were much smaller than the old white grapes and were concealed more intricately and deviously in trickier foliage, the pickers claimed. Even if a man pushed himself to the limit, he still could not earn as much money as he had earned on the old white grapes. That was nature's fault, of course, and not the boss's, both pickers agreed, but it was still unjust and unacceptable. At other vineyards, the boss used a blower to remove the leaves in advance and make the picking easier. The whole crew was discouraged, in pain, sick at heart.

"Yo comprendo," Atwater told them, drawing circles in the dirt with a twig. He explained that he felt pity for the pickers—how could he not, being a laborer himself?—but the *patrón* had to make a profit for the farm to survive. He couldn't afford any special equipment to blow away the leaves. The *patrón* was a person of high honor and integrity, though, and he wouldn't want his crew to suffer unduly, so five dollars would be added to everyone's pay at the end of the day.

"Five dollars?"

"Every day?"

Atwater confirmed it. The grinning pickers congratulated one another by shaking hands. They were cured miraculously and simultaneously of their ailments and trotted into the vineyard to spread the word.

The raise in pay greased the wheels of commerce. The harvest machine and all its component parts clicked back into gear and began to run at optimum speed once more, with each important movement falling as if by divine intervention into its appropriate groove. There was a smoothness to the flow again, and Atwater permitted himself a moment of pride, congratulating himself for being a genius bilingual mediator who had saved his crop from certain failure. In the mesh of shadow and light, he could hear a distinct hum that was the hallmark of a harvest going well.

He hauled his first load of red grapes, eight-plus tons, to the winery late that afternoon and had to wait for more than an hour in a line of trucks that extended beyond the horizon, but he was grateful enough just to be there. The fields were dark on his return. He spent his evening on the phone talking to neighboring growers and asking for some help. Again and again he tried to reach Antonio Lopez, without any success. The silence nagged at him, but he was too tired to go hunting for his foreman in the wilds of Santa Rosa. Something very bad must have happened, he had to admit.

Morning brought with it a promise of deliverance. Atwater woke with a surge of unanticipated energy, his spirits refreshed by a good night's sleep. The weather was warmer, and the world looked gentler around the edges, rosier and more accommodating, robbed of its menace. He wished that he had a football to throw in homage to the glories of autumn. With his right arm, he performed a quarterback's feint and pretended to release an arching spiral toward the sky. He saw that a few pickers were already at work, while others drank coffee and prepared themselves. He counted heads and was delighted to find that he had not lost anyone. Some new men were present, too. On loan from Charlie Grimes was a stocky old veteran he knew simply as Manuel, and Dick Rhodes had sent him a pair of young brothers just in from Oregon, where they had harvested apples and pears in the orchards around Medford.

The brothers had never picked any grapes before, so Atwater conducted a tutorial. They were fast learners, skillful with their knives and eager to satisfy. Manuel, on the other hand, needed no instruction at all. He was an imperturbable master of his craft and could be trusted to keep the crew on its best behavior. Atwater assigned him the task of maintaining order and walked over to run a test on a block of hillside Zinfandel. His refractometer showed him in empirical terms what he had suspected. The warming trend was affecting the sugar level in the grapes. It was rising rapidly. Soon he would be swimming in ripe fruit, tons of it, so he decided to rig a trailer behind the flatbed truck for double hauling, outfitting it with four gondolas instead of two. That way he'd make just one trip to the winery daily instead of two or three and wouldn't waste his precious time waiting in line.

The pickers worked straight through the noon hour, fueling themselves with snacks eaten on the fly. The fruit was coming off nicely now, still smoothly, and they refused to break the rhythm for fear that they could never capture it again. Their efforts were all of a piece, braided together toward a common goal. They were inside the harvest machine and looked unstoppable, Atwater thought. Sweat poured from them and streaked their faces, and grime and dust coated their arms. The men had stripped down to T-shirts that were stained and spotted with purple blotches, while the women wore broad-brimmed straw hats and had knotted kerchiefs and bandannas around their necks to protect themselves from the brutal sun.

Atwater stayed apart. He was busy on his tractor and emptied one bin after another into his gondolas. The rig was capacious and would hold upward of twenty tons of grapes. Around three o'clock, with every muscle in his body stretched to its elastic limits, he took a breather, drove to Roy's, and brought back some cases of cold beer and soda to invigorate the crew. He packed the cans in two buckets, layered them with cracked ice, and toted them from row to row, saying, "Here you go, here's something to kill that taste of dust, here you go, have yourself a cold drink."

"We are a winning team!" Manuel hoisted a can and toasted the other pickers with an impromptu cheer. "Teamwork!"

"*Eso es!*"

Atwater pressed a frigid Coke to his forehead like a compress and smiled. "You're a goddam wonderful team, if you ask me," he told them all. "You saved my bacon."

"Wonderful team."

"We save the bacon!" There was merriment all around.

Back to work the pickers went, pushing themselves, enduring. The sun dropped toward the far hills, and the valley floor was rich with a last incandescent torrent of light so powerful that it added a patina of burnished color to everybody's skin. Every tinge of red in the soil, every lateritic particle, grew bright. Atwater watched his crew slow to a crawl. They were in a trance and stared out as though at a fiery hearth. When Serena Cedillo took off her straw hat, shook out her hair, and combed the tangles from it with rough strokes, the light caught in each auburn strand and rippled about her in an aura. The sun kept dropping until it became an orange disc balanced atop some pines and firs on a distant ridge, and then it was abruptly gone, guttered out, and shadows fell across the vineyard. The thump of buckets went on, but the lively racket of voices began to die down.

The brothers from Oregon were the first to call it quits. Stoical to the core, they showed off the raw and bloody blisters on their hands, but they vowed to return in the morning anyway and were praised for their manly attitude, their simple courage. Others followed them shortly, shouting farewells, stowing away their grape knives, and collecting the sweaters and jackets that they had cast aside or hung on grape stakes in the heat of the day. As they walked doggedly from the vineyard, they had the thoroughly depleted look of athletes at the close of a grueling contest, Atwater thought, winners who had barely snatched a victory from the jaws of defeat.

It was a little past six o'clock when he started for the CV outlet to deliver his monster load of grapes. The drive would take him about twenty minutes. He flipped on his headlights in the gathering dusk. The gondolas rumbled noisily behind his truck and swayed with the weight of his cargo, filled up nearly to the brim. He didn't know for sure how many tons of fruit he was hauling—seventeen, eighteen, it could have been a full twenty tons. It was a solid payload, at any rate, and it gave him a good feeling in his gut and a sense of money in the bank. He looked out at the dry brown hills and the fields now fading from view and saw everywhere the same comradely scene of dispatch as more and more picking crews unraveled to go their separate ways. The spiraling dust, the arms raised in salute, the figures solitary and committed, all were beautiful to him.

He passed over a creek where a trace of water still trickled and moss slicked about. He was whistling and unaware of it. When he reached the CV outlet, he was shocked to see how many trucks were lined up ahead of him—not only trucks but also many tractors pulling gondolas. It was worse than the previous day by far. The line stretched back across the bridge for hundreds of yards. By craning his neck, Atwater could just make out the lit platform of the sugar shack. He was so far away from the winery proper that he couldn't hear the purr of the crusher or the whine of the transfer pumps that moved the grape juice from tank to tank. All down the line, drivers had climbed from their cabs to wait on the road. In the foul and heavy exhaust fumes from their idling engines, they smoked and talked softly and aimlessly as they passed around a box of doughnuts.

Atwater joined them. "What's the trouble?" he asked.

"Trouble?" he was told. "Trouble is, every red grape in Carson Valley decided to get ripe at the same goddam time."

"Ah, shit, that's just an excuse," another driver said angrily. "They could kick it along a lot faster if they wanted to. I came out with a load this morning and got through in under an hour."

"Everybody's tired," said a third driver. "CV, they weren't prepared for this. They need a whole lot more help. Some of the boys inside, they're about to fall over on their faces."

"Have a doughnut here, pal." Atwater chose a honey glazed from a box and ate it greedily in a couple of bites. "Go on, have another one. There's no reason to starve yourself to death just because you're desperate, is there?"

The line of trucks inched forward. The drivers watched to see if the advance would merit a return to their cabs, but the fleet had only traveled a few feet. So they stayed where they were and chatted and flung about accusations and alibis until the next jump forward opened the space between vehicles a little wider and created an illusion of progress. Atwater climbed up with the rest, shifted into first gear, and drove on for about five yards until he had to stop again. He got down after that and walked past the men on the road as if in a delirium and started counting the trucks ahead of him, but he was soon discouraged. The exercise was pointless. The number of trucks didn't matter. The line, however long it was, would move or not move of its own accord, at a rate of speed over which he had no control. His hopes and desires were immaterial. He resigned himself to waiting.

Whenever a truck that was emptied of its load went by the line on its way out, the liberated driver would honk or give a wave of solidarity, but it happened in time that a truck still piled with grapes passed by the men and disappeared without any fanfare. Atwater stuck his head out the window and listened to the drivers relay news of spoiled and rejected fruit.

"Bunch rot," he heard it said, and "They tried to downgrade him," and "He wouldn't swallow it," and "He told 'em where to shove it."

"What's he going to do now?" Atwater shouted above the rattling trucks.

"Damned if I know. There's nobody else around who's even open. He might as well shovel those grapes into a creekbed."

In about two more hours, Atwater was in clear sight of the sugar shack at last. Six trucks were still in front of him, while three stragglers lagged behind him. He watched a tester on the platform of the shack plunge a corer into a load of grapes to take a reading. The tester was so fatigued and trudged about so sluggishly that he might have been drugged. Atwater felt stiff and ornery himself, severely put upon, and he closed his eyes and slept for a few minutes. When he woke and looked at the shack again, the platform was vacant and the light inside it had gone out. He saw Wade Saunders hustling down a ladder and some workers swinging shut the big wrought-iron gates in front of the winery. He couldn't believe it—he was being locked out. He threw open his door and ran toward Saunders in his heavy work boots, tripping over a sprung lace and shouting, "Wade! Hey, Wade! Hold on!" until Saunders yielded to his cry and spun around on his heels.

Hands on his hips, Atwater leaned forward to catch his breath. "Wade?" he asked. "Where are you going?"

"Home," Saunders told him sharply. "I've been roasting in that shack like a stuck pig since before noon. This heat is the damnedest thing."

"My grapes," Atwater said, still gasping. "Who's going to log me in?"

"You'll have to come back tomorrow, Arthur."

"But I've been waiting almost four hours out here!"

"Well, I'm sorry about that." Saunders cupped a hand around his lighter and fired up a cigarette. "But you can't fault me, can you? Do you know what time it is?"

"I don't have a watch. Past ten?"

"Pretty near. And I'm supposed to shut those gates at nine. You fellows all know that. It's spelled out in your contract, and it's up on that sign right over there."

Atwater felt ambushed. "But I got here way before nine!"

"You saw how busy we were yesterday," Saunders reminded him. "You should have built that into your calculations. To turn up at the last minute, well . . ."

"The last minute! I just told you, Wade, I've been waiting four hours!" Atwater shrieked. He was almost beside himself, and yet he knew there was some truth to Saunders's accusation. He could have played it safe and brought in smaller loads, but he had chosen to roll the dice and gamble it all on one big double haul. "How dare you say that to me!"

"All right, I stand corrected. But you only see your side of things, Arthur. This situation, it happens once in a lifetime. It took CV by complete surprise!"

Atwater pointed to his cargo. "Those are the best grapes in Carson Valley. I remember how bad you wanted them."

"I won't deny it, but I have to draw the line somewhere, don't I?" Saunders asked. "Else there won't ever be an end to it. Look!"

Another truck had pulled up to the winery, piloted by a driver even more ill-fated and behind schedule than the others who were still waiting.

"Cut me some slack, Wade," Atwater begged. "Do me just this one favor, and I'll never ask you for another."

"I couldn't cut you any slack even if I wanted to," Saunders replied, his voice raspy. "I've done all the favors I can get away with for one day. You see those workers by the gates? They're on time and a half. It's costing me money just to talk to you."

"Only ten of us are left. At most, it'd take you another half hour."

"I wish I could help you, Arthur, but I can't. The winery's closed, and that's all she wrote."

Atwater grabbed Saunders by the arm. "My grapes will turn overnight in this heat, Wade."

Saunders yanked his arm back. "And you want to hang the blame on me." He chuckled and shook his head at the irony. "Isn't that the shits?"

"I'm not blaming anybody."

"The hell you aren't. Every goddam one of you fellows makes me out to be the scapegoat. Since when am I responsible for your errors in judgment, Arthur? Since when is that? The fact is, you weren't paying attention. Hundreds of trucks have run through here today without a problem. It's *your* goddam fault, brother, not mine."

"The winery's never been this crowded."

"I guess I get blamed for that, too. Okay. I accept it. Go right ahead and hang it on me."

"Come on, Wade." Atwater hated himself for groveling. "Just this once. Just ten more trucks."

"There'll be eleven by the time I open again."

Atwater swallowed hard. "Have it your way, then," he said, seeing that it was a lost cause. "But do you have to be such a prick about it?"

"Excuse me?"

"You enjoy turning us away. You're being a prick about it."

"Is that what I am?" Saunders looked outraged. "A prick? When I already stayed open an hour past closing time to help out a couple dozen growers? I can't save everybody in the world! The only people who think Wade Saunders is a prick are the ten assholes left in line."

The other drivers got wind of the conversation. They climbed down and came at Saunders with pleas of their own.

"Well, it may look simple to you," Saunders told them slowly, as if they were dullards. "But it isn't. This involves more than a few truck-loads of fruit. It involves a whole corporation. I have a boss of my own I have to answer to." He sighed. "I don't make the rules, friends, I only follow them. If it was strictly up to me, I'd open those gates in a second."

"No, you wouldn't." Atwater stared at the ground. "Because you're a prick."

"Pardon me, gentlemen, but I've had about enough of this," Saunders said as he brushed past them. "It's been a long day, and I am going home."

The drivers made no move to block him. They stood there in a stunned pack and railed about the harshness of their treatment, but their hands were tied. They had no means of appeal, so they returned to their trucks, swung them around, and drove away, everybody except Atwater, who was unable to summon the energy to leave. He dozed some more in his cab and woke again in the middle of the night. The moon was low in the sky, and he got out and felt how hot the air still was. He stood on a tire and reached up into the gondola to taste a grape. As he expected, the skin was puckered, and it was way too sweet. The same thing was true of every other grape he tasted. All his work, all his striving, had come down to this—a roll of the dice and boom! Snake eyes.

A first streak of dawn light showed on the horizon. Soon workers who'd been tossed unceremoniously from their beds after a few hours of sleep began arriving at the winery again, unlocking the big gates and hosing down the concrete floors, padding around in rubber boots as they racked yesterday's juice and measured the juice already in their tanks to calibrate its relative acidity and the level of its residual sugar.

At seven o'clock, Atwater pulled up to the sugar shack and lifted his battered and dejected face to Rawley Kimball, who had his clipboard in his good hand and was scribbling away on it.

"Hey there, Arthur!" Kimball yelled to him in a chipper way. "Ain't you the early bird!"

"It's because I was the goddam late bird yesterday," Atwater said, convinced now that the fault was at least half his. "That prick Wade Saunders closed me out."

"Oh, I am sorry to hear that." Kimball sounded honestly concerned.

"Not nearly as sorry as I am, Rawley."

A tester stepped to the platform and went through the usual routine. Atwater awaited a verdict that he already knew in advance. He watched the tester run the sample through a grape press and catch the juice in a bucket before sinking a refractometer into it.

"Cabernet?" the tester asked.

"That's right."

The tester left the platform, and Kimball came back out after a little while. Atwater ignored the Brix number scribbled on the slip of paper Kimball gave him.

"Those grapes turned on you in the night," Kimball told him. "What you've got there now is damaged goods."

"I'm aware of that," Atwater said.

"I don't like to downgrade you, Arthur, but I have to. Your grapes aren't good for much, except maybe our low-end jug wines. That's B-grade fruit."

"I'll go dump the load inside."

"Listen," Kimball said to him with some urgency. "I feel real bad about this. I know how hard you worked."

"Thank you, Rawley."

"It's unfair, and I know it. But it happens to a few growers every year. It's part of the game. Sometimes it's just your turn to go through it. I still feel real bad for you, though."

Atwater smiled. "Did you say 'unfair'?"

"I did."

"That's what I thought you said."

He stuffed the paper into a pocket and got back in his cab. The truck stuttered forward, and he weighed in, dumped his grapes, and weighed out. The difference was about eighteen tons. According to the CV contract, B-grade fruit went for $100 less per ton than A-grade fruit, so that represented an $1,800 loss for Victor Torelli right there, to which Atwater would have to add the extra money he was paying his pickers, another $75 dollars or so a day for about three more weeks—he figured his mistake had cost the old man five grand, or somewhere near it. Torelli would not be pleased. Again, Atwater had let him down.

The crew was already picking at the farm when he drove up, and he spoke to Manuel and put him formally in charge, while he, Atwater, the boss, ran some errands—that was how he phrased it, anyhow. Then he took off in his Jeep without changing his funky clothes and bought a torpedo sandwich, some potato chips, and a six-pack of beer at Roy's. He had polished off all but one of the beers way before noon and began to entertain a sudden and highly irrational notion that happiness in this life might yet be his. He was about a hundred miles from Carson Valley at the time and traveling steadily north. In Laytonville, he stopped at a loggers' bar for a shot of whiskey and drank three shots instead, thinking that he ought to check into a motel and get some sleep, but in fact his forehead was soon resting on the mahogany bar, and he slept like that into the early afternoon.

25

The knocking came while Antonio Lopez was resting in bed in a dark and cloistered room, where the blinds had been drawn now for three straight days. He ignored the sound as he had ignored the occasional ringing of his telephone. He was relieved when the knocking stopped, but it began again right away, more insistently and with a loud knuckle-rapping quality that suggested authority, so he swung his legs free of the sheets and rose gingerly and unsteadily to his feet. He had difficulty breathing and sucked in air through his clenched teeth. A messy bandage of gauze and tape was plastered to his rib cage just above his liver, and he moved forward in a hunched and defensive posture to protect the wound beneath it from even the most delicate contact.

He grabbed a shirt from a doorknob and padded down the hallway in his underwear. His house was abnormally quiet, stripped of the forces that gave it life. It seemed as foreboding to Antonio as the still and somehow deathly church his mother used to drag him to for penance whenever he had committed a mortal sin as a boy. He felt weak in both flesh and spirit, in fact. During his recent stay in the hospital, he had suffered through a terrifying dream about losing his daughter to a band of marauding angels who had flown down from a mosaic heaven to steal her away. The angels had clasped Dolores to them and shielded her with their wings, and though Lopez had screamed and pointed to them as they escaped into the sky, no one would help him. A policeman in the same dream told him that he had gotten exactly what he deserved.

Without unlatching the chain lock, he opened the door a crack and peered out with a squinty eye. There stood Arthur Atwater looking shaggy, forlorn, and beat-up. He had an ugly scab on his forehead and appeared to have been in some kind of accident.

"Are you going to let me in?" Atwater asked him. "Or are you just going to stare at me?"

"You can come in."

"Thank you so much. And good morning to you."

Lopez was baffled by this visit. He led Atwater into the living room, where the blinds were also drawn, and shoved some crayons and coloring books off a chair and sat down. The TV was playing soundlessly. He could smell the whiskey on his guest, as well as a sour and repellent staleness that was unlike the potent but acceptable odor a man developed in the fields.

Atwater crossed one leg over another, as if to begin a friendly chat. His hair was plastered to his head and had tiny things in it, bits of fluff and even part of a leaf. "I don't feel as bad as I look," he said cordially.

"That's good," Lopez told him. "Because you look awful, Arthur."

"You don't look so hot yourself."

"I was asleep."

"Asleep?"

"Yeah, asleep. For three days so far."

They gazed in silence at the TV for a time. Then Atwater started in again. "You're a tough guy to get ahold of, Mr. Rip Van Winkle," he said, not quite so cordial now. "You ever think about investing in an answering machine?"

"No way, man. They cost a lot of money," Lopez said. "What do I need one of those for?"

"So that people can leave you a message. Then you wouldn't miss out on anything important."

"Like what?"

"Like a call from your boss."

It dawned on Lopez what Atwater was getting at, and he was startled. "Didn't Elena call you?" he asked. "I told her at the hospital she should let you know what happened."

"Well, she didn't. And I was short five pickers."

"It could be that she did call, and you weren't there?"

"No, she would have left me a message," Atwater said curtly. "On my answering machine."

Lopez hung his head in shame. "There was some trouble, Arthur."

"What kind of trouble?"

"You remember my cousin?" The boy's face floated up from the land of ghosts to be present in the room. "He got us into a really bad fight."

"Ah, shit," Atwater said with disgust. "Don't you know any better than that?"

"I do know better. But still it can happen."

Lopez described for Atwater how the crew members had gone to La Perla Roja to celebrate and how he had joined them on a foray to Santa Rosa against his better judgment. He told about the topless dancers at The Show Room and how the horny beet-faced picker got them kicked out for feeling up a girl and how after their embarrassing expulsion they went to eat *menudo* at a big *cantina* off the freeway and bumped into Ernesto Morales, who insulted Omar and pulled a hunting knife on him without the slightest provocation. None of the pickers wanted a fight, he said, but Morales kept taunting the boy in public and persisted in calling him dirty names, so it became a matter of family honor into which he, Antonio Lopez, was forced to intercede. He told how the knife flew at him and demonstrated how he had blocked its thrust, pushed Morales away, and grabbed him by the throat, only to feel the blade thud against his chest anyway and slip between two of his ribs. Blood was everywhere, he said, and he had fainted then.

"Here's where he got me." Lopez lifted his shirt and daintily touched his bandage. "Sixteen stitches. He almost cut my liver in half."

"Where's Morales now?" Atwater asked.

"He's in the county jail. He might never get out. They charged him with attempted murder."

"What about Omar?"

Lopez looked at the floor. "Omar, he was lucky."

"What's that supposed to mean?"

"He ran away, Arthur. He got away free and clear before the police even came. Probably he's back in Mexico by now with all his saved-up money."

"And he was the one who started the fight?"

"He didn't start it. But if he wasn't with us, there wouldn't have been any fight."

They were quiet again. Lopez turned moody and a little sad and got up to shut off the TV. He wondered if Elena would come home to him that night, or if she would continue to remain with her parents as she had been doing. He thought that she must be missing him by now and would at least agree to talk with him on the phone, and if that occurred it would only be a short distance from their conversation to complete forgiveness. He could see resolution before him like a path.

"I always knew Morales was a bad apple," Atwater sighed. "I doubt he ever had a pleasant day in his whole life."

"How's the harvest going?" Lopez asked him hesitantly, fearing the worst.

"We got killed."

"It's my fault, Arthur." Lopez hung his head again. "I should have been there."

"Yeah, you should have been there," Atwater agreed. "But it's not your fault. It's mine."

"It's mine, too," Lopez insisted.

Atwater grinned at him. "All right, Antonio. I'll give you your share of the blame. How much do you want?"

"Half?"

"No, that's way too much. Maybe ten percent. Will you settle for that?"

"Sure," Lopez told him. "Whatever you say is fair."

"Fair doesn't enter into it."

Lopez was quiet for a moment, then said, "Tell me how it went."

"That prick Wade Saunders screwed me," Atwater said. "I hauled a double load of grapes over to the winery Tuesday evening, and they were backed up over the bridge and shut me out."

"No! Saunders didn't do that!"

"He sure as hell did. He shut out eighteen tons of ripe Cabernet.

CV downgraded the whole goddam load. Victor will be delighted, I'm sure."

"Wade Saunders should be the one to get stabbed," Lopez said.

"It doesn't seem to work that way."

"Son of a bitch!" He punched his palm. "What are you going to do about it?"

"There isn't much I *can* do about," Atwater told him. "I tried running away. I got as far as Laytonville and fell asleep in a bar." He touched his scab and laughed. "I banged the shit out of my head."

"You came back, though, Arthur. That's a good thing."

"I guess it is. I got back in time to deliver a small load late yesterday."

"It *is* a good thing," Lopez repeated with an enthusiasm he didn't entirely feel.

"Well, I don't have it in me to disappear on Victor again. I'll just have to face the music this time around. At least I didn't wake up with a tattooed lady."

"There you go," Lopez said encouragingly. "That's another good thing. In the future, everything will be fine."

"I sincerely doubt it."

"You got any pickers left out there?"

"I got a patched-together crew working on our Zins. Charlie Grimes sent me old Manuel. He's a helluva picker."

"I never picked with him," Lopez said.

"You ought to try it some time. Old Manuel, he can pick. He even ran the loader and filled the gondolas while I was gone."

"What about your bonus, Arthur?"

"There isn't going to be one."

"Not for me, either?"

"Nope. Sorry, *amigo.*"

"Son of a bitch!" Lopez punched his palm again. "And all because of Ernesto Morales!"

"Only that skunky little Omar came out ahead this year," Atwater said.

"*Todos nuestros esfueztos no han servido para nada.*"

"What's that mean?"

"All our work? It went down the drain."

"I won't argue with that."

"You want a beer, Arthur?" Lopez asked.

Atwater gave him a funny look. "I don't think a beer is particularly called for. Do you have any soda? I have to get back to the farm pretty quick."

They went to the kitchen, but they didn't talk much anymore, not to any real purpose. It seemed to Lopez that Atwater had emptied himself of all the important stuff and had nothing further to relate. His own melancholy was growing broader, deeper, and more treacherous. He truly did feel responsible for the grapes that had turned, and more than ten percent. He was guilty, too, about an idea that he had been considering since his stabbing and accused himself in private of being a traitor, even though he hadn't yet committed treason and wasn't at all convinced that he ever would.

On his way out, Atwater stopped at the door and asked, "Did they say how long you have to take it easy?"

"They pull the stitches out soon," Lopez said. "But I still got to rest."

"Does it hurt much?"

"It's hard for my breathing. And when I cough."

"What if you laugh?"

"I haven't laughed yet."

"Elena's taking good care of you, I hope?"

"Yeah, she's a real good nurse."

"Well, come on back to the vineyard when you're ready," Atwater told him. "I can always find something simple for you to do."

"I don't know, Arthur," Lopez said, his eyes on the ceiling. "I been thinking maybe I might change my job."

"And go to work for somebody else?"

"No, not in grapes, man."

"What kind of work?"

"I been thinking about roofing. They pay good money."

"Ah, that's a dirty business," Atwater said dismissively. "It's for the monkeys. You don't want to be a monkey, do you? Frying your butt up on tar beach?"

"I'm not saying I made up my mind for sure yet," Lopez said, and that wasn't a lie. "First, I need to be more healed."

"Don't do anything without talking to me. Because I'd hate to lose a good hand like you."

"You won't lose me." *But maybe you might,* Lopez thought.

He crept back to his sickbed when Atwater had gone. He was very tired now and took some Tylenol with codeine and soon was floating on a cloud. He looked around the bedroom and noticed Omar's yellow jacket draped over a chair. The boy had left it behind at the *cantina* in his haste to escape. It appeared to be glowing in the dark, and Lopez hated the sight of it. It was as if the jacket were meant to torment him, as if it had been brushed with something of the boy's soul, dusted with his pollen, so he got up, rolled it into a ball, and threw it into a closet. Then he stepped on it for good measure. He lay down after that and struggled to stay awake, imagining that he was high up on a roof somewhere and restored to his rightful place among the fortunate ones, those who were blessed with good luck.

26

When the harvest ended that autumn, Victor Torelli shocked his friends by actually turning over his books to an accountant. Instead of setting himself up as usual at a folding card table with a green plastic visor and a manual adding machine as obsolete as the carbon paper he sometimes used for making copies, he engaged the services of Lloyd Chambers, Betty's husband. Like any accountant worth his salt, Chambers was a fastidious and devious type, and through some careful manipulation of the numbers and strategic deployment of various loopholes in the agricultural tax laws, he established that the farm would earn a decent profit for the year and owe no money to the government. These findings he packaged in a cardboard binder embossed with his initials and sent them to his client, along with a bill for $750.

Torelli was so happy with the results that he paid the bill on receipt, no questions asked. He wrote a second check at the same time, drafting it with exquisite care in his spidery hand, and then stuffed it into an envelope and left home for an appointment with his vineyard manager. They were to meet at The Country Kitchen at three o'clock, but the old man had misread his watch and got there thirty minutes early. He took a booth at the back to wait. A waitress brought him some coffee, and he heaped it with cream and sugar and watched the dim light of fading afternoon play upon the knotty pine walls. The days were shorter now, more crisp and clear, and the winds from the west were stronger and colder and kept the cloud chamber alive with shifting shapes. Soon the winter rains would start. Torelli welcomed the prospect of a big storm. He had his goddam firewood.

The restaurant reeked of pie. The old man stared with undivided attention at a glass case on the lunch counter where some delicious-looking specimens were cooling—apple, of course, but also blueberry, cherry, rhubarb, and peach. The pies were all missing a wedge or two, and when he saw a waitress take out a gorgeous fluffy lemon meringue job and serve a portion, he gave up on being polite and waiting for his guest and asked for a slice of cherry pie à la mode. He attacked it with a fork and spoon and swore that he had never tasted anything so good in his entire life. There was a time when pleasure had seemed magnificent and even unattainable to him, something he would have to search for in the great forest of the world, but the years had cured him of such ideas. Here he sat at The Country Kitchen with every ounce of desire in his body concentrated on the next mouthful of cherries.

Torelli polished off the pie with a few more bites and called for a second helping. Pie was what he wanted, and pie was what he would have. He watched the vanilla ice cream melt and pool up beautifully in the crannies of the crust, off-white against the rich red syrup and fruit, and got so absorbed in the abstract swirl of colors that he didn't register the fact of Atwater's arrival. He became aware quite suddenly that someone was standing by his booth and felt as if he'd been caught in a revealing act that was not entirely wholesome. In public, he had proved himself to be a pie-eating fool. He rubbed at his lips with a napkin, amazed that he could be sitting there with so much food smeared across his face. How little there was to care about at this stage of the game, the old man thought. A single teenage pimple used to make him feel like Frankenstein.

"Arthur," he said with a nod. He worked his tongue over his teeth and gums to police up any stray morsels. "Sit down, why don't you? Care for a piece of pie?"

"Just coffee, thanks."

They huddled over the accountant's report and shuffled papers between them. Atwater pored over the columns of numbers and looked doubtful. He seemed not to want to accept Chambers's brilliantly manipulated conclusions.

"We didn't come out too bad after all, did we?" Torelli asked, coaching him. "All things considered?"

Atwater threw down the report, causing the pages to flutter. "Lloyd did a good job. I'll give him credit for that. He makes it look nice and tidy, but we both know what really happened."

"Read the bottom line, Arthur. It says we came out ahead. We made a profit."

"We should have done much better."

"You can always do better." He wants to hang onto his sense of failure, Torelli thought. Why should that be? "Every farmer knows that. Nobody gets all the weeds."

"You don't have to go easy on me," Atwater complained. "I let you down again, and I'm sorry."

"Some things can't be helped," the old man told him. "What would you like me to do about it? Punish you because you gambled and lost? Every grower has to gamble. Don't you get enough punishment as it is?"

"I cost you a lot of money, Victor. You can't just write it off."

"You earned me a lot of money, too. Look how the Chardonnay did! So quit your pissing and moaning." He took out the envelope he'd brought and slid it across the table. "Go on and open it." He watched Atwater fumble with the check inside, one for five thousand dollars. He felt unexpectedly splendid about the transaction, recalling all the times he'd been small and mean and tight with his money and all the things he had denied his wife, his children, and even himself for no reason that he could currently imagine, dolls, dresses, furniture, and baseball gloves. Why not be generous when you have the opportunity? There you go, Victor, he told himself. Congratulations. That's the goddam spirit!

"What's this for?" Atwater asked him, clearly flustered.

"It's your bonus."

Atwater made a prissy face, returned the check to the envelope, and slid it back. "No way. I won't accept something I didn't earn. I'm not a charity case yet."

"I say you did earn it." The old man sat smugly, his arms folded. "And I'm the boss."

"Listen, this is silly, Victor," Atwater protested. "You're treating me like a child."

"Let me tell you a little story." Torell's brain was in a whirl as he invented an object lesson on the spot. "Suppose you wear out a pair of work boots. What do you do with them? You put 'em out with the garbage. They're not worth a goddam thing to you anymore. Hell, you're glad to get rid of them, in fact! Well, who should come along the next morning but a fellow that's barefoot."

"Why is he barefoot?"

"He just is, Arthur. I never told this story before."

"I see," Atwater said with the hint of a smile.

"Anyway, this barefooted fellow, he spies those boots, and it's like he's found a treasure! He won't be barefooted anymore! Do you get my point?"

"Not really."

"It all depends on how you look at things." The old man pushed the envelope across the table. "If you think you failed, then you did. But I think you succeeded. So you deserve your bonus."

"I respectfully decline."

"Arthur, you are a very stubborn person. I believe I'll have one more piece of pie."

Torelli summoned the waitress and chose a wedge of blueberry this time around. He ate ravenously and obliviously and lifted his eyes from his plate only when Atwater spoke again.

"It's not that I don't appreciate it," Atwater was saying in an earnest way. "I do. I really do."

"Take the goddam check," Torelli urged him. "Go on a vacation. Have some fun while you still can."

"All right, I give up. I'm not going to fight you about it forever." Atwater picked up the envelope and stuffed it into a pocket. "Thank you, Victor. I'll split it with Antonio."

"Whatever you want. It's your money now. Is he coming back to work?"

"No, he's got his mind set on being a roofer. I can't talk him out of it."

"People will do what they're going to do."

"That's the truth, I guess."

Torelli narrowed his eyes, examined Atwater in all his dimensions, and saw how young he was and how much he still had to learn. "Well, at least this harvest taught you something, Arthur," he said.

"I don't know what on earth that might be," Atwater replied.

"A Rotarian'll screw you just as quick as anybody else," the old man told him, digging into the last of his pie.

27

The Vescios threw a big hoedown in honor of their pickers when the grapes were in every year. It always took place toward the end of November, right before Thanksgiving. All the crew members were invited, plus their families and sixty or seventy of Fred's intimates, semi-intimates, and nodding acquaintances. On the morning of the grand event, Vescio's men dug a pit near the main house on the property and lined it with some dry oak and grape cuttings. Then they lit a fire, and when the pit was white-hot with ashes, they brought out a spitted calf and fixed it to an old iron rotisserie. The calf was a thing of beauty, marinated in red wine and virgin olive oil, studded with garlic, and rubbed with a mixture of herbs, and it would cook slowly for hours until a crust had formed and the meat was fork-tender and falling off the bone.

The guests started arriving around five o'clock. They were in a festive mood. A complimentary harvest edition of the *Valley Herald* had landed on most doorsteps that day, and its evaluation of the crop was wildly optimistic and held in much higher regard than it probably should have been, given the paper's long history of boosterism. Of the dozen growers interviewed, only one had expressed any doubts about quality, but his wife had just left him for an Episcopal minister over in another county, so his opinion was roundly discounted. The other growers were full of praise. They conspired to put forth a theory whereby the late-maturing red grapes were bound to have an exceptional concentration of flavors, making for a vintage that would cellar well and be awarded blue ribbons even in foreign countries, including France.

There were folding tables set up not far from the barbecue pit, each covered with a dime-store tablecloth and laden with food. The beef was served on three large ceramic platters that were hand-painted in intense yellows and blues and decorated with crowing roosters. Bowls of pinto beans, rice flecked with peas and tomato pulp, green salad, coleslaw, potato salad, *nopales,* and several kinds of salsa ranging from mild to infernal were set out in an order that led logically to baskets of corn and flour tortillas. A few guests had never rolled their own taco or burrito, so Vescio was called upon to demonstrate and rose to the occasion. He wore a Mexican wedding shirt of incalculable age and a pair of *huaraches,* while on his head was a sombrero purchased years ago in Tijuana, with the legend VIVA ZAPATA! stitched across its crown.

"There's nothing to it," he told Irwin Poplinger, sidling along the buffet. "This isn't some candy-ass deal like using chopsticks. To a Mexican, a tortilla is the same as his fingers. You put whatever's your pleasure on one and wrap it up real tight."

"You make it look so easy."

"Easy as pulling teeth, Doc."

Arthur Atwater attended the party in his new down vest. He had finished picking his crop about a week before—on November sixteenth, to be exact—when he pulled off the last grapes from his thriving block of hillside Zinfandel. The Zins had come in first rate, almost six tons to the acre, and there were no more ugly incidents at the CV outlet. Wade Saunders had even offered something like an apology, and Atwater had pretended to accept it, although he really wanted to drag Saunders around a corner and give him a stout pummeling. Still, he was mostly satisfied with how things had turned out. If the harvest had not been all he had hoped for, neither had it gone completely sour. He would have other years and other chances. His bonus check he had split in half and sent the other share to Antonio, who was very glad to get it now that Elena was pregnant again. He planned to spend his own money on a trip to Oaxaca in the spring, between budbreak and bloom, and he would explore the much-lauded Mysteries of the Yucatán.

The Vescios had hired a mariachi band from Santa Rosa to provide some atmosphere. The five musicians showed up at twilight, each in a bolero jacket, frilly pink shirt, and tight black trousers. They set up near a makeshift dance floor outside the barn and played such rousing standards as "Cucurrucucu Paloma," and "Guadalajara," as well as a plaintive version of "Si Estás Dormida" that had many of the pickers and their wives in tears. Atwater allowed himself a small whiskey for the sake of boldness and danced twice with a pretty blond he hadn't ever seen before. She worked in the office at Hawk Wind, laughed easily, and invited him to tour the winery with her some time when he felt like it. He thought he would feel like it quite soon. He was in the market for a new girlfriend, in fact, having concluded his brief fling with the bartender, who drove him from her bed early in the game by talking about commitment.

Atwater released the blond reluctantly to another fellow and sat on the steps of the house to bask in the music. He felt so grateful and ordinary that he didn't protest when Jack Farrell lowered his bulk to the step below him, with his elbows splayed back for additional support and his gut flopping.

"I don't have a single gripe in the world," Farrell said sweetly. "Isn't this the nicest night?"

"Yes, it is," Atwater agreed.

"Who was that woman you were dancing with, Arthur?"

"Just nobody, Jack."

"She work up at Hawk Wind, does she?"

"I wouldn't know."

"Anyhow, you'd be better off with her than you would have been with Anna. She never returned any of my phone calls. Can you believe it?"

"If I try real hard, I can," Atwater said. His obsession with Anna had dimmed during the toil of the harvest, but he knew that it was likely to come back. He knew it very well.

Farrell stroked his belly. "Well, I guess it wasn't meant to be between me and her. That's how it goes with romance sometimes. Shakespeare, he wrote about it in the olden days."

"So you were Romeo, and Anna was Juliet?"

"I think that's fair enough to say."

"It's funny," Atwater said pointedly. "I never pictured you two that way."

"How did your grapes come out, Arthur? Didn't I hear you had some problems?"

"No problems, Jack. We did real fine."

"Victor, he was happy?"

"About as happy as he gets."

"He doesn't look so good," Farrell said with concern. "Maybe it's the change in the weather. My tennis elbow hurt like a son of a bitch last night."

"I never knew you were a tennis player."

"I'm not. But I've still got the elbow. You figure old Fred is going to let loose a piglet tonight?"

"Yes, I do," Atwater said. "I'm absolutely certain of it."

"He must have a screw loose somewhere."

Atwater didn't stay around for the piglet routine. He left early, before ten o'clock. The harvest might be over, but he still had work to do. The vineyard looked desolate now with the vines all tattered and ruined, as if a gale-force wind had blown through it. Every leaf was dry and crinkly to the touch, and every dying filament burned with color. He walked among declensions of flame red, among pale yellows and fulminate golds. There were small, worthless bunches of grapes hanging from some canes, a second crop never to be picked, fodder for the birds, and also a few raisiny clusters that the crew had correctly passed up. The soil had turned to hardpan, so he took to his tractor and tore it apart with a harrow, opening its pores to the winter rains. He spread fertilizer as necessary and spent hours packing away the special harvest gear, his hands in rubber gloves as he scrubbed out the plastic tubs, with soap bubbles floating all about him.

Already November was almost over. Atwater found that scarcely credible and thoroughly unacceptable. Time that once had been his friend was becoming his enemy—fleeting time, time as quicksilver, every bearded cliché was coming home to roost. Often he thought about a crotchety aunt of his, who was always going on about the general speeding up of things as the aging process slowed her down. She got as splintery as a chicken bone, wrapped herself in black shawls, and nattered around with a cane. She even bought herself an

hourglass and kept it on her dining room table, next to the salt and
pepper. Atwater himself felt old. He felt he knew too much about too
little. He felt lonely in the broad and tranquil sweep of the fields as
well, and it was almost like a blessing when he admitted to himself
that he was overextended and needed another pair of hands, so he
put out the word on the valley tom-tom and hired a half brother to
the vaunted Manuel. The youth's name was Salazar Gallego, and his
reputation for being honest and dependable was high.

Atwater enjoyed the company of his new field hand. Gallego was
shy, quiet, and very serious. His manners were impeccable, and he
didn't sing any melancholy songs. Together they began the tedious but
essential job of clearing away the diseased Chardonnay vines by the
river. The rootstock was more than thirty years old, gnarled and historical. It could tell us stories, Atwater thought, if we only knew how
to listen. He and Salazar used spades and pitchforks to dig up the ancient trunks and roots and replaced them with Ganzin Number One.
The Ganzin came in bundles of fifty. Each seedling was about a foot
long and an inch thick. Delicate greenery sprouted from the seedlings
and attracted gophers, rabbits, and deer, so they had to slide an empty
milk carton down each grape stake to form a protective barrier. The
work was not difficult, but it demanded care and patience. They were
kept busy, pressed close to the earth.

It happened one afternoon that Atwater looked up while they were
crawling around and saw an unfamiliar car approaching on the dirt
road. He got to his feet, ran a hand through his hair, and tried to
figure out who it might be. While he waited, he occupied himself by
counting the number of rows still to be replanted and musing on
other chores yet to be done before the rainy season began. Dust
swirled up from the road and made it hard to see, but when the car
came closer, he could make out the driver's face and saw that it was
Anna. That didn't seem possible to him, but it *was* her, undeniably,
and he knew in an instant of revelation that he had been expecting
her all along, although he couldn't have predicted when or how or in
what shape or form. He had imagined just such a scene in his dreami-
est moments, but now that she was really here he was not the least bit
certain what to do.

She parked not far from the row where they were working and
walked toward him with her confident stride. Her simple cotton shirt,

those long legs in jeans, that rich bounty of hair he had so often lost himself in—Atwater had not forgotten a single thing. A part of him wanted to turn from her and hike away in the opposite direction, fording the river, climbing into the hills and over the Coast Range, and continuing on to the ocean and thence to China, but instead he moved forward with the faltering step of a man stunned by a blow to the temple. Every aspect of him was divided. He had a half smile on his face, he had half a mind to run her off the property, and he was half ready to take her into his arms.

What he said was, "Hello, stranger."

Anna stopped a few feet from him. He recognized that she, too, was nervous and a little frightened. "Hello yourself," she said.

He said next, cursing himself for it, "We're planting the new rootstock. You remember that Ganzin Number One you found for us? It's what we're using."

"The harvest is over?" She sounded disappointed.

"We finished about a week ago."

"I'm sorry I missed it. I hoped I might get here for the last of it."

"Salazar!" Atwater cried, motioning to Gallego. "This is Anna Torelli! *La hija de Victor!* Come say hello!"

Gallego wiped his hands on his jeans, rubbing and rubbing, and did Atwater's bidding. "Welcome, *señora,*" he said, elegant in his bearing.

"He's a damn good worker," Atwater told her as Gallego turned his attentions back to planting. "Antonio, he decided to become a roofer."

Anna was walking toward him again, closing the gap between them, and making his throat go dry. "Will you hold me, please?" she asked, her face turned up to him, imploring.

He could not have done otherwise. He held her tightly and brushed his lips against her hair. He thought that he would feel a surge of joy, but instead he felt an odd but not disagreeable emotion that combined sorrow, loss, and resignation, as if he were embracing those very qualities and not the woman he had loved and probably still did love, although that love was more complicated to him now, not so pure or easy to pin down.

"Did you think about me?" Anna asked quietly.

"Yes, I did."

"I wrote you a hundred letters in my head. I must have picked up the phone to call you fifty times." She was suddenly fretful. "This is a mistake, isn't it, Arthur? I shouldn't have come. I should have left well enough alone."

"I don't know," he said honestly.

"You won't be angry with me, will you? Promise?"

He stroked her shoulders. "I won't be angry."

"I couldn't bear it anymore. I couldn't bear to have it end that way between us. I tried hard to forget you, but I couldn't. And I missed you so. Are you upset with me? You look upset."

"I'm just sort of surprised," he told her.

She drew back from him. "I tried to think things through and make a rational decision, but it didn't help. I kept going around in circles."

"Those circles are real familiar to me," Atwater conceded.

"A couple of weeks ago, I woke up in absolute despair and bought a plane ticket. I didn't think I'd really use it, but here I am."

"Here you are."

"I want the pain on my own terms."

He failed to understand. "All right," he said anyway.

Anna seemed to need something more from him, some reassurance. "Do you still care about me?" she asked in a small voice.

"It goes beyond that." There was an awkward pause. He thought for a second or two, and said, "Are you hungry?"

"Hungry?"

"Yes. Would you like something to eat?"

"Oh, my!" Anna laughed in delight. "I really *am* here."

Atwater wouldn't ride up to the house with her. He was too filthy, his clothes were too shoddy. He felt apart from her, as though she had dropped in on him from a parallel universe. He gave the rental car a wide berth and trudged along behind it. His feelings were in a boil, hot and soupy, spilling over. There was a key to the door under the mat, and he bent to fetch it and stepped aside so that Anna could enter before him. She gasped at the mustiness and went straight to the kitchen, where the counters were again peppered with mouse turds and the stove gave off a stink of gas. She was equally distressed when she looked out at her ruined garden and saw the cornstalks brown and crippled, the cantaloupes split, rotting, and drawing flies, the green tomatoes never to ripen, and the bean runners coiled up and strangling themselves.

Atwater tried to cheer her up. "Your melons came in nice and sweet, Anna. I ate them right through October."

"That's something, at least."

He opened the fridge and found a jar of peanut butter that had not gone bad, spread it on a few Saltines from a sealed box in the cupboard, and felt as he set the plate in front of her that it was the single most ridiculous gesture he had ever made.

"This is stupid," he said, tired of his lifelong ineptness at such moments. "I've got plenty of food up at my place."

Anna grabbed his hand. She stung him with her eyes, and he fell into her once more. "It doesn't matter, Arthur. Sit down with me, will you? I just want to be close to you. Tell me everything that's happened. Tell me about the harvest."

Here was a narrative that Atwater had rehearsed late at night as he lay sleepless in the churning hours, a tale of treachery and even villainy that had served him as an emblem for all the miseries attendant to the human condition, but he found that he could not relate it to Anna with any degree of conviction. The moral of it had evaporated on him as his life had slipped back into a common groove, tracking along again with billions of other lives, invisible and without impact, so he only alluded to the trouble that he'd had with his pickers and failed to summon the outrage he needed to paint Wade Saunders as a monster. He omitted his crazy run to Laytonville altogether. Time had pulled another trick on him, it seemed. It had stolen his ability to complain.

The light in the kitchen had grown dim. "It's getting dark so soon, isn't it?" Anna said with a shiver. "Winter will be here before you know it."

Atwater woke to his whereabouts and eyed the clock. "Jesus! I forgot all about Salazar. I'd better go deal with him. He's probably standing around out there with nothing to do."

"But you'll come back when you're finished?" She sounded anxious.

"I'll come back. Yes, ma'am."

"Good." Anna smiled at him. "I'm going to build us a fire."

They made love at twilight on some couch cushions arranged before the fireplace. Atwater shook with desire at first and fumbled with Anna's clothes, but he relaxed when she rolled over on top of him. Her eyes were shut, her lips were wet and parted, and there was such evident release in her expression, such utter abandon, that he could see right into her. Consciously or not, she had dropped all her defenses to show him a face that was remarkably innocent, the face that must have been hers as a child, before anything had ever hurt her —blissful, unlined, without any edges. He saw how much she trusted him, although he might never hear it from her in words. The fire was reflected in a gallery of windowpanes, and he watched it flicker and spoke her name twice, petting her and believing that she might never get enough, but she did at last and sank toward him as he came, her body against him all down the length of his own body, the full weight of it upon him and welcome, welcome.

Now she was ravenous, of course. Atwater had to dress and dash down to the trailer, where his neglected dogs accused him with baleful whimpers, as if he were about to abandon them again. He threw some cheese, some bread, and a couple of apples into a paper sack and returned to the house in a sublime state of wonder. Anna had put the room back together while he was gone and sat on the couch in her shirt. The fire was roaring, and she was smiling at him in a way that was better than nourishment. They had a little picnic and chatted, and he had to bite his tongue to keep from asking, *Why did you really come back here? What's this all about, Anna? Can I count on you to stay?* Wrong questions, every last one.

Instead he said, "How is New York?"

"Awful." Anna helped herself to more cheese. "Well, maybe not awful. But very strange."

"In what way?"

"I couldn't fit back into my life. It was like some other person had taken over for me."

"It's those body snatchers again," Atwater joked, high on the miracle before him.

"No, I don't think so, Arthur," she said. "I doubt that aliens were involved."

"They can be tricky, Anna."

"I'm sure they can. But this was something different. Everything felt weird and wrong to me, and I got so bored. Even the bookstore doesn't seem to mean that much to me anymore."

"Does Victor know you're here?"

Anna shook her head. "Not yet. I'm going to surprise him for Thanksgiving. At least that was my excuse for buying the ticket. I missed him, too."

"You're full of surprises, aren't you?"

"I suppose I am." She was quiet for a moment, then plunged ahead. "There's something I have to tell you, Arthur, and you're not going to like it. But I made up my mind on the plane. There can't be any secrets between us anymore. Fair enough?"

"Fair enough."

"Another reason New York was so strange," Anna said in a halting way, "was because I took up with an old lover of mine. It's over now."

"You did what?" he asked mildly, thinking she had a punch line to deliver, a follow-up that would put things back in the proper perspective.

"I got involved with an old lover of mine. He should be the ideal man for me, but he isn't."

Atwater saw that she was serious and swallowed hard. "Well, that's very nice to know. Thank you for sharing it with me, Anna."

"If you'd had an experience like that," Anna said, "I'd want to hear about it. Secrets always explode. Look what happened to us. I'd prefer to know if I were you."

"But you're not me, are you?" he protested. His voice rose an octave. "Because if you *were* me, you wouldn't have gone to bed with him."

"Haven't you been seeing anyone?"

It took him less than a split second to decide that his companion from The Rib Room would go unmentioned. "No, I've been *pining*," he said with a vengeance.

Anna, unmoved, stood her ground. "I'm sorry, Arthur. I knew you wouldn't like it. But it was necessary for me. I had some things to learn."

"What a fine way to get a lesson!" Atwater was on his feet, his mind ablaze with horrible carnal images. "I'll bet he gave you a good grade, too, didn't he?"

"We approach things differently."

"I'll say we do!"

"I thought you'd want me to be honest."

He sat on the couch again. His brain ached. "My head is made of wood," he said, cradling it in his hands.

"I beg your pardon?"

"My goddam head is made of wood."

Anna put an arm over his shoulders to console him. "What *do* you want from me, Arthur? A pledge of undying love?"

He looked at her. "Yes."

"I can't give that to you. I nearly ruined my life with pledges."

"I understand."

She eyed him with suspicion. "Do you really?"

"Yes, I do. But I don't like it, not one bit."

Anna ran a hand along his thigh. "Will you come upstairs and make love to me one more time before we sleep?"

"Not just now," Atwater said evenly, although he was about to self-destruct and fly apart into bits. "I've got to see to my dogs first."

He left without another word, liberated Prince and Rosie from his trailer, and let them run free. They were glad for the exercise, spirited in their play. They caught the scent of a deer on the other side of the vineyard fence and chased it downhill for a hundred yards until it vanished into the willows and cottonwoods by the river, a good-size buck with prominent antlers. Atwater had enough light to see it clearly and admire its leaping, muscular flight. He whistled for the dogs after a while and jogged home with them, his breath visible in the cool autumn air. In his kitchen, he filled their bowls with food and water and listened to their lapping pleasure, thinking he would sleep in his own bed that night because to sleep elsewhere would only lead to further complications.

He did actually go into his bedroom, but he kept his clothes on and stood staring at the lights up in the big house as he had done so often in the past. He let it sink into his wooden head that Anna had truly come back to Carson Valley and largely because of him. He had missed her so terribly, and yet he hadn't confessed it to her, not even once. All the imaginary and loving dialogues he'd had with her during her absence had added up to one long silence! *Oh, Arthur, will you never get it right?* He, too, had lessons to learn. Atwater heard old Victor Torelli's railing admonitions ringing in his ears and wondered exactly who he meant to punish. There was no love without risk, of course. He knew that and had known it all along, and he was swept up from his quandary and dismay and delivered to Anna on a surge of emotion as powerful as wings.

She was already upstairs, asleep in her bed. Atwater undressed and slipped in next to her.

"Is it you, Arthur?" she asked in a drowsy whisper.

"Yes, it is."

"Dear Mr. Atwater." She reached behind her to touch him. "Will you stay with me all night and keep me warm?"

"I will."

He drew close to her and felt with utter gratitude her body next to his. Thankfully he embraced her, an arm around her waist. If life could never be made right, he thought, it could at least be made rounder and richer for a time, almost whole.

28

The year turned in Carson Valley, its muted passage marked in the usual way by the starling flocks out to glean the last of the vineyard chaff. The birds were as black as grains of pepper against the sky and moved about in huge wheeling arcs that brought forth an audible crack of cartilage from a multitude of wings. Angry field hands shouted and threw stones at them whenever they settled among the rows, but the starlings were scarcely bothered. So many farms did they have at their disposal that their response amounted to little more than a shrug in the face of folly. They just pecked and scratched and waited for a signal that no human being had ever heard, and then rose together in a pack with their wings cracking and flew off again, as if to taunt all those still earthbound, left below.

It proved to be a rough winter for grape growers. Storm after storm crested the coastal mountains and often made the ground too soggy to be tilled with heavy machinery. Thirty-one inches of rain poured down in January, followed by another twenty-seven inches in February, and the pruning crews fell far behind. A few old foot-bridges washed out, and some streams were in a constant state of flooding. Only the local fishermen had any praise for the weather. So many steelhead were spawning in the river that even the dullest, laziest, least-motivated anglers caught one to enter in the Ace Hardware over it presently. The crick in his arthritic knee improved, too, and soon he could walk all the way from his house to the town square, where his elderly brethren were often resting on benches, their aged heads sinking toward their rheumy chests. They looked to him like sepia-toned photographs now, apparitions from the past, and he would stop to knock on wood—a tree, a sign, a wall, it didn't matter—to insure his own continued good health. It was a riddle to him how suffering got parceled out, why one man endures and another doesn't. I'll die for sure, he told himself, but not just yet.

In a month or so, he had developed a strict training regimen. He walked two miles after breakfast and another two miles in the late afternoon. His toes became blistered from the extra effort, and when he checked his shoes, he saw that he had practically worn away the soles. At a sporting goods store in Santa Rosa—Ed's had been sold at last and was now a Radio Shack—the old man shopped for some proper footwear. He had not been aware that sneakers of such intrepid design existed, every pair tailored for a specific game, pastime, or aerobics routine, and all endorsed by famous athletes and manufactured in artsy, futuristic styles that enhanced the very concept of feet. With the help of a young clerk who quizzed him closely about his activities, he chose a spanking-new white pair of Reeboks and winced as he paid for them with three twenty-dollar bills.

The Reeboks seemed to lift Torelli into the air. He floated along on pillowy cushions, his arches fully supported for the first time in his life. He walked with his own peculiar grace, often thinking about Michael Jordan and wondering what quirk of tendon, ligament, or bone permitted a person to soar to such improbable heights, up there among the clouds. He had known only one black man well, a dapper fellow named Frank Hawley, who had driven a truck for a dairy back when dairies were still plentiful in the valley and then had quit his job and disappeared. Although Hawley was tall and lanky and a star pitcher on La Bella Italia's softball team, he had never demonstrated any superior jumping ability and needed a folding stepladder to haul the aluminum milk jugs down from his flatbed.

There came a day in early March when the old man woke to a curious but satisfying sense of possibility. The rain-washed streets outside his house looked fresh and clean, and he could smell a good

derby. The early front-runner was a sophomore on the varsity basketball team, who had the prize money sewed up until his best friend revealed that he'd actually bought his trophy fish, an eighteen pounder,
from a Yurok gillnetter up north.

The boy's trickery led to quite a scandal, as well as a concerned
editorial in the *Valley Herald* titled "What's Wrong With Our Youth
Today?" Victor Torelli read it with amusement in his hospital bed at
Carson Valley General. He didn't know or care what was wrong with
our youth today and honestly believed that they were no different
than ever. Famine, pestilence, bloodshed, lust, despair, crop failure,
and teens who committed petty crimes in imitation of their greedy
elders could not be said to surprise. The right question to ask, the old
man felt, was "Does One Rotten Apple Really Spoil the Barrel?" The
world had been going to hell in a handbasket since the very moment
of creation, he thought, and if the speed appeared to be picking up,
that was probably because of TV, special effects, or some other type
of filter thrust between what people truly perceived and what they
hoped or expected to be true.

Torelli had entered the new year in declining health. He had lost
two molars to softening gums around Christmas and later suffered a
couple of blackouts that scared him enough to consult a cardiologist,
who informed him that he was an ideal candidate for a pacemaker.
He resisted the idea, of course, and argued that technology couldn't
be trusted, but his friends and family finally won him over, and he
submitted to the surgery. The pacemaker turned out to be utter
magic. The old man could barely credit the positive changes it made
in his poor circulation and fluttery heartbeat. How could a chip so
tiny have such a profoundly beneficial effect on an organism as big
as he was? The only mark on his entire body was a minuscule four-
inch scar above a pectoral muscle that he gladly showed off even to
strangers without being asked. He was a goddam miracle of modern
medicine, all right, and never once did he complain about having his
vital organs hooked up to a computer somewhere in the galaxy.

After his release from the hospital, Torelli began walking for exercise. He was tentative at first, measuring out his steps with care and
pausing frequently so as not to overexert himself. It spooked him to
have no tightness in his chest and no shortness of breath, but he got

grassy scent that signified a warming trend. He ate his regular bowl of grape-nuts, laced up his sneakers, whistled for his dog, and hit the sidewalk, treading cautiously around some bloated earthworms and a banana slug dazzled by the sun and dozing in his driveway. At the end of Quail Court, he made a sharp right turn instead of his customary left and headed north, away from town. It gave him a small but definite thrill to be breaking a habit that he had formed for no particular reason. He passed two real estate offices, a Chinese restaurant, and a mill yard stacked with lumber and plywood, and went on for a mile or so until he reached Carson Valley Road.

He thought he would walk out and have a peek at the farm. He hadn't seen it since the holidays. His decision pleased him and discharged another little thrill into his system. He knew exactly how far he had to go, if the odometer in his truck could be trusted—8.2 miles. That would be a challenge, but he felt up to it. The day was just perfect for a hike, too—balmy, springlike, and dappled with sunlight. The first vineyard Torelli went by was almost ready to pop, shimmery with delicate green shoots that were only a couple of weeks away from bursting into bud. He listened to Daisy's happy panting and leaned down to pluck a sticker from her fur, passing cows and pasture fences and the notorious spot where a giant redwood had once crashed down and crushed an automobile.

Torelli had never been much of a singer, but he started singing after he'd gone about three miles. It was as if all the extra oxygen pumping into his lungs had demanded a release. He sang "O, Susannah," "My Darlin' Clementine," and "The Impossible Dream," a song Claire had played so often on the hi-fi that he had learned to hate it, along with the actor who performed it on Broadway. He crooned through a few more unlikely tunes until Charlie Grimes's spread appeared on the horizon. He simply couldn't resist a visit and the chance to brag about himself. Sweat poured off him as he unlatched a gate that led to a dirt road much like his own. His face was already raw and sunburned, and he wished that he had dodged his vanity and worn a hat. He walked about a hundred yards and rounded a corner, and there was Grimes by his pure white barn in a stomping fluster, hanging onto the reins of a horse he hadn't owned before and trying desperately to lead it somewhere.

"Old Charlie Grimes!" Torelli yelled.

Grimes stared at him bug-eyed, as if he were a phantom. "I didn't hear you pull up, Victor. Where'd you park at?"

"I didn't park anywhere. I walked out."

"The hell you say."

Torelli pointed to his Reeboks. "I'm a walking fool, Charlie."

"You're some kind of fool, anyhow," Grimes allowed.

"Is that a horse you've got there?"

"Yes, sir." He stroked the animal's flank. "And she's a nice little horse, too."

The mare was a chestnut of indeterminate age, with a white blaze on her forehead. The old man used his knuckles to rub her gently, while Daisy sniffed around her legs. "She have a name?"

"Diablo Fury, she's called. She's an honest-to-god Thoroughbred. She ran over at the county fair last summer."

"Did she win?"

"No, but she finished."

Torelli did some counting. "She's got all her legs, anyway. How'd you get her?"

Grimes scratched his butt and grunted. "Willie Tyler, his niece is marrying some fancy dan of a chiropractor, so Willie come by and asked me to make him a price on five cases of sparkling wine for the reception. I made him a price, and Willie asked me if I'd be interested in trading for a horse instead. Seems his niece used to stable this here mare in town, but she won't be riding anymore on account of moving away, so I took the mare and now I don't know *what* the hell I'm going to do with her."

"Diablo Fury."

"There you go. Diablo Fury."

They sat in the shade of Grimes's veranda for a while, drinking Cokes and chatting. It was past noon, and the sun had climbed high up in the sky.

"Looks like budbreak's about to come on," Torelli said, chugging at his soda to soothe his parched throat.

"I give it ten days," said Grimes. "You figure Atwater'll get home in time?"

"He had better."

"He still down there in Mexico with Anna, is he?"

"Yes, sir. They've got a couple more days of vacation left. They're way down there in the Yucatán, where those Mayans used to live. I got a postcard from 'em in the mail yesterday."

"Was the picture pretty?" Grimes asked eagerly, sitting forward.

"Goddam beautiful, Charlie. It showed the Gulf of Mexico and a whole bunch of pink flamingos."

"Did it make you want to go there?"

"It did."

Grimes farted a few times and scratched himself some more. "Then it must be a pretty picture, all right. You figure those two will ever get married?"

Torelli debated the question privately. "I wouldn't put my money on it," he said.

"How come?"

"Well, I asked Anna the same thing once, and all she said was that her life was in transition."

"That's a helluva answer," Grimes grumbled. "Why would any-body talk like that?

"Probably it's from those books she reads," Torelli said, although he wasn't really certain. "She still hasn't sold her half of the store yet, plus she's living mostly down in that apartment she rented in San Francisco."

Grimes reacted strongly to the information. "You let Atwater stay in your house by himself?"

"Anna's with him some of the time. She's there about every week-end. In the summer, she'll be there more, she says."

"I can't make hide nor hair of the situation," Grimes confessed with some frustration. "Either you love somebody or you don't. This in-between business, I don't hold with it at all."

"There're different kinds of love," Torelli told him. "There isn't but just the one kind."

"Do you believe it to be so?"

"I do."

Grimes spat. "Goddam that Lucy Carpenter."

Together they walked up to the gate. Grimes loaned his friend a baseball cap and pressed a bag of M&Ms on him for a quick energy boost. With a grin and a salute, Torelli departed. He was a bit worn out and had stiffened up during his rest, but he felt some limberness return by the time he reached the main road. He passed the boundary of Grimes's property and walked along the fenced perimeter of the next vineyard in line, where clumps of yellow mustard flowers had sprouted in profusion. The stumpy rootstock looked naked in the midst of so much raging vegetation. He could see the knobs, scars, and whorls on each trunk, a record of sorts carved into the wood. Sparrows were kicking about in the pruned canes, searching for seeds and busting them open with their beaks.

Torelli didn't know who owned this particular vineyard anymore. That troubled him and caused him to recite in defense the names of all the families whose farms he still *could* identify, not only such intimates as the Vescios and Dick Rhodes but also those valley clans that were like foreigners to him, the Van Dusens, say, or the Schmidts. He marched forward along the curve of his remembering and covered another mile before he ran out of people to count. He paused then to eat the M&Ms and politely rejected two friendly drivers who slowed down to offer him a ride. Ahead lay the Poplingers' estate, and he passed it at a steady clip and noticed a golf ball tucked into the roadside weeds. It spoke to him of mysteries. If the weeds could hide a golf ball, they must be hiding other things, too, so he rooted through every straggly patch after that and was rewarded with a marble, a plastic soldier, and the bladeless handle of a grape knife while he covered another mile.

It was late in the afternoon before the hills that framed his own home place came into view. Torelli shifted into high gear and walked toward his farm in a spirit of exhilarating triumph. His legs ached now, and he had a knotted muscle in one thigh, but he ignored the minor discomforts and crossed a bridge that spanned Wappo Creek, watching a torrent of muddy water pulse down to the river through some drenched willows. Then he swung to the right as if yanked in that direction by a magnet and started along the old dirt road that would lead him to his destination. He had been traveling it for as long as he could recall, from before the time when his grandfather had bulldozed and graded it to accommodate cars, back when the only paved streets anywhere around were the four that converged on a single stoplight in the center of town.

The oaks, madronas, and bay laurels opened onto the vineyard. The sun was dipping behind the hills, and deep shadows fell across the farm to pool up in inky swales that stood out against the emerald-green grass of the meadow. Torelli could feel the sweat drying on his skin as he took in the scene before him. There as ever stood the great house that had sheltered his family, its windows dark for now and its rooms emptied of voices and curiously without consequence. He had expected to be moved by the sight of it, but the house was nothing to him, really, just bricks and nails and boards. What mattered in the end were the blood ties, he thought—the press of flesh and the human community. Three field hands were busy hoeing in a block of Chardonnay, and he didn't recognize any of them except as echoes of all the other men who had worked for him, their collective labors somehow of a piece.

"Gallego around?" he shouted, and one fellow raised an arm and gestured toward the bunkhouse trailer.

The old man headed for it. He was very tired now and a little chilly, his feet swollen and cramped despite the nurturing Reeboks. He hammered on the trailer door until Salazar Gallego unlocked it. Gallego wore no shirt and had apparently been treating the upper half of his body to a scrubbing at the kitchen sink.

"Salazar," Torelli said with a courtly bow.

Gallego seemed puzzled about how his boss could have material-ized on his doorstep without making a stitch of noise. "Hello, *señor*."

"Could I trouble you for a drink of water?"

"Please." Gallego stepped aside. "Come in, Victor."

Torelli found himself in a living room that was even more thread-bare and sparsely furnished than it had been during the tenure of its previous occupant. When Gallego handed him a glass of ice-cold water, he sipped it daintily so as not to shock his system and thought about Atwater and his daughter down there in Mexico. What a thing that was! Celestun was the village pictured on the postcard, and Anna wrote about how they had eaten shrimp fresh from the gulf and how an *hombre* in a skiff had poled them out to get a good close look at the flamingos, hundreds of birds in shades that ranged from pale coral to bright red. The old man imagined Anna stretched out on a beach towel on the whitest sand and wished only that Arthur would love her as hard as he could for as long as he could, and that she would do the same. He wished for their hearts to hold in the bad times. He wished them peace.

You're full of goddam wishes today, aren't you? he asked himself.

"Salazar, I need a favor." Torelli had some difficulty getting to his feet, so stiff had he become. "I got it into my head to walk out here, but I never thought about getting back. Did Arthur leave you his keys?"

"Yes, Victor."

"Could you drive me and Daisy into town?"

Gallego was an immensely cautious driver. He clutched the wheel tightly, kept his eyes straight ahead, and didn't dare to speak. The valley was dark now but for the firefly blinking of farmhouses set back from the road.

"You got a girlfriend, Salazar?" Torelli asked him.

Gallego grinned from ear to ear. "*Sí, señor*," he said. "In Mazatlán."

"What's her name?"

"Gloria."

"She send you letters, does she?"

"Sometimes."

"You send her letters back?"

"Sometimes."

Torelli was so exhausted when he arrived home that he didn't even bother with supper. He drank some more water and a single can of beer, soaked his feet in a tub of hot water, stripped off his clothes, fell into bed, and slept straight through until morning. He expected to be sore from his hike, but he felt refreshed instead and decided to violate his health and fitness program by cooking up the kind of country breakfast his mother used to serve at the farmhouse, eggs basted in butter, rashers of bacon, slabs of ham, and hash brown potatoes. *Lot of everything in those days!* He doused it all in Tabasco sauce and washed it down with a pot of coffee as thick as molasses, then laced up his Reeboks and went for his usual morning constitutional.

It was a Sunday. The town was very still and sleepy. The only sounds Torelli heard were the cooing of doves in the ornamental palm trees and the taped bells ringing over at St. Brigid's, where a Mass was going on. He continued on down to the river and heard something else there, the yapping bark of a German shepherd tethered behind the chain-link fence at George's Firewood. He was glad that the dog had been spared. There were real dog shooters around— the old man knew it for certain—but he didn't number himself among them and didn't honestly believe that the wood man was a dog shooter, either. The poor wood man was just down on his luck and saddled with too many goddam kids and a one-armed partner. Things would change for him as they changed for everybody sooner or later, Torelli thought, tacking another wish onto his list, this one for a world where every dog would be redeemed.

He walked from the river uphill to the cemetery at St. Brigid's and stood among the headstones of his beloved dead, while the many tangled lives that made up a place called Carson Valley reposed in the hollow below him. There were invisible connections in the air, sights seen but not acknowledged, ghosts in the forest, and spirits in the deep. The old man felt comfortable where he was and grateful for the many gifts that had been given to him in his long years on earth, although he missed terribly what had been taken away, all the inevitable losses. Father, mother, brothers, one sister, such treasured friends as Thomas Atwater, his three hundred pounds no more sturdy than a thistle at the last—they were buried in the ground. Torelli stopped at Claire's grave and spoke her name out loud. Soon he would be following her. All would follow soon.

ACKNOWLEDGMENTS

Although I lived for years in vineyard country, I had only a passing acquaintance with the fine points of growing wine grapes and furthered my education by consulting various helpful sources during the writing of this book. The classic text is still *General Viticulture* by A. J. Winkler (University of California Press), but I also found some useful information in Joy Sterling's *A Cultivated Life* (Villard) and Jack W. Florence, Sr.'s *A Noble Heritage,* published by the author. Of particular importance was *A Vineyard Year* (Chronicle Books) by Joseph Novitski, an elegantly written, grower's-eye view of farming wine grapes that captures the joys and sorrows of the fields and also suggested to me that Arthur Atwater ought to keep a vineyard log. The book of Japanese poetry alluded to is *Only Companion* (Shambhala Centaur Editions), carefully translated by Sam Hamill.

I would like to thank the Marin Arts Council for its support, and I owe a special thanks as well to Ed and Donna Seghesio of Seghesio Winery in Healdsburg, who fed me a wonderful lunch, graciously spent an afternoon answering my questions, and sent me home with a complimentary bottle of their superb 1994 Old Vine Zinfandel. We should all be so lucky. Such errors as remain are mine, of course, though I should add that in a couple of instances I altered the facts slightly for the purposes of fiction.

ABOUT THE AUTHOR

BILL BARICH is the author of *Laughing in the Hills, Big Dreams, Travelling Light,* and *Hard to Be Good.* He is the recipient of a Guggenheim Fellowship in fiction and his work has been included in *Best American Short Stories.* He lives in the San Francisco area.

Barich, Bill.

Carson Valley.

$24.50

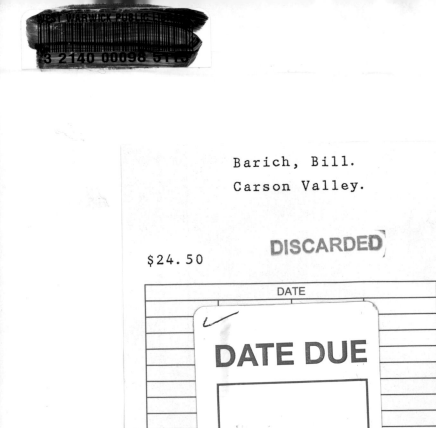

DATE

DATE DUE

03-97

001283   6034131